MUCKRAKERS & MINOTAURS

TERRA HAVEN CHRONICLES BOOK 3

REBECCA CHASTAIN

Copyright © 2021 by Rebecca Chastain
Excerpt from *Magic of the Gargoyles* copyright © by Rebecca Chastain
Cover design by Yocla Designs
Author photograph by Cody Watson

www.rebeccachastain.com

Mind Your Muse Books
P.O. Box 374
Rocklin, CA 95677
ISBN: 978-1-7344939-5-5

ALSO BY REBECCA CHASTAIN

NOVELS OF TERRA HAVEN

TERRA HAVEN CHRONICLES

Deadlines & Dryads (prequel)

Leads & Lynxes

Headlines & Hydras

Muckrakers & Minotaurs

GARGOYLE GUARDIAN CHRONICLES

Magic of the Gargoyles

Curse of the Gargoyles

Secret of the Gargoyles

Lured (newsletter exclusive)

THE MADISON FOX ADVENTURES

A Fistful of Evil

A Fistful of Fire

A Fistful of Flirtation (newsletter exclusive)

A Fistful of Frost

Madison Fox Novella Box Set

STAND ALONE

Tiny Glitches

Sign up for Rebecca's VIP List to receive newsletter-exclusive content.

ACKNOWLEDGMENTS

This book is in your hands because of a lot of hard work—mine (this book took a lot out of me!), but also because I had help along the way, and my gratitude is infinite.

Both Kylie and the plot of this novel are enriched thanks to the feedback of my glorious beta readers. Thank you, Renea Kania, Seana Waldon, Wim Sweerman, Sarah Gibson, Jillian Cori Lippert, Rebecca Moore, and Scott Ferguson for your insightful comments. For the final polish, thanks go to my wonderful copyeditor, Crystal Watanabe, and proofreader, Cheryl Murphy Lowrance.

The book is complete (and isn't still a muddled mess on my hard drive) thanks in part to my husband, Cody. I jumped into this series with a very limited idea of how I was going to resolve it. This was fun when writing the early books, but when it came time to wrap up the story arcs, it was stressful. Cody endured a great deal of whining, frustration, and nonlinear babbling in the name of helping me. Thanks for being so patient with me, Cody—and for coming up with the minotaurs' business name.

But mostly, Kylie and Quinn's adventures exist because you said you wanted more gargoyle-filled novels. Thank you! If you want even more adventures in this world, please leave a review and let me know.

Constructive Elements

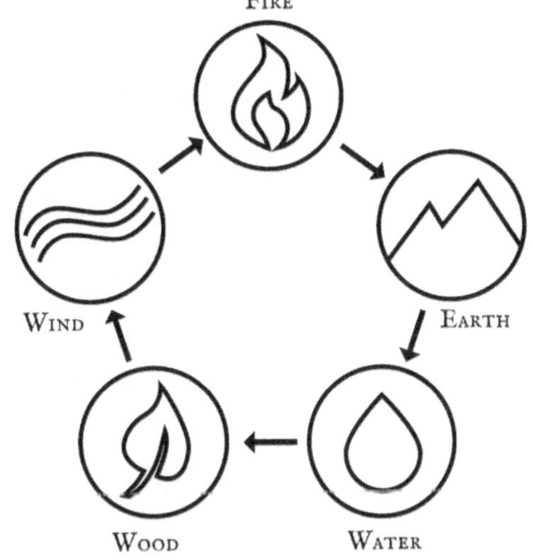

Destructive Elements

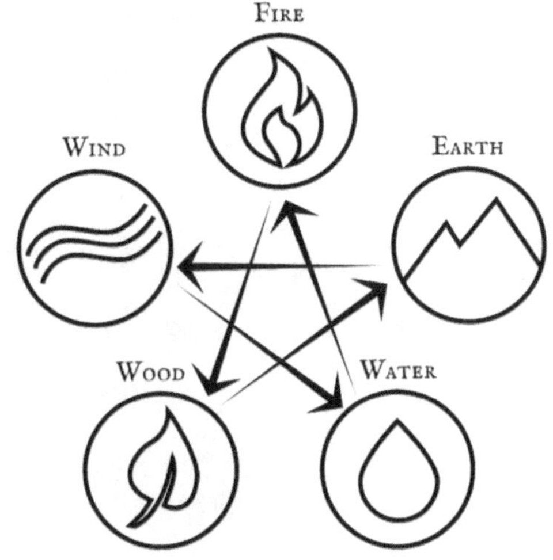

1

My heart hammered against my rib cage, desperation clogging my throat. *Not Airstrong. Please, don't let it be Airstrong burning.* In the still summer air, the column of black smoke billowed high into the sky, easily visible half the city away. The echo of the explosion still rang in my ears.

"Hang on," Grant ordered.

I tightened my grip on his belt. Squeezed cross-legged behind Grant on his personal flying carpet, I leaned into the turn as he took the corner fast enough to raise a spiral of dust from the cobblestones eight feet below. Ocher clapboard and a dizzying rush of reflective windows flashed past inches from my shoulder, whipping my hair into my face. I blinked stinging tears from my eyes and searched the horizon.

Grant barked orders into message spheres while dodging low-flying air carts and pedestrians on slower carpets. The elements cupped to his mouth prevented me from hearing his words, but I recognized the magical signatures of his squad embedded in each spell. In seconds, four disparate messages blasted into the air, arcing toward their intended recipients.

A slash of orange burst through the smoke tower, soaring on hawk-size wings. From this distance, I couldn't pick out the individual black bands on the bird's amber feathers, but its fiery marigold chest—and its proximity to the burning building—was enough to confirm my worst fears. The explosion was no accident; someone had planted a phoenix egg in the warehouse district and allowed it to hatch.

The carpet jumped, then dipped, and only my white-knuckled grip on Grant kept me from flying off the narrow surface. By the time I stabilized myself, the phoenix had caught an updraft. In seconds, it was little more than a speck against the magenta sunset.

I reached for the elements, feeling for Quinn. No boost amplified my magic. The gargoyle was still out of range. Whereas Grant and I were constrained by the limited levitation of the carpet, forced to zigzag through the streets of Terra Haven, Quinn had flown straight over the rooftops.

I silently willed speed to Quinn's flight. The people at the explosion site—the *hatching* site—needed his elemental boost.

The people. The generic term bounced around my head, a pointless attempt at distancing myself from my fear. Mom was *the people.* Mom had been at Airstrong today, managing her shipping company's operations. Mom would need Quinn's special magic. If she wasn't . . .

I refused to finish the thought, instead resuming my silent prayer. *Please don't let it be Airstrong.*

Somehow, Grant muscled more speed from the carpet's propulsion spell once we cleared the busy downtown district, pushing us to a reckless speed. Emerald Station raced past, the busy train terminal swarming with confusion and defensive spells. More than one person pointed to the sky, either at the smoke or the phoenix. The deadly bird's hatching would monopolize the front page of every newspaper tomorrow. Despite our mad dash to the scene, I wouldn't get the scoop, but I didn't care. The story could go to some other journalist—one not currently suspended—so long as Mom was safe. *Please let her be safe.*

We careened into the warehouse district, and relief chased the familiar gut-flipping sensation of a gargoyle's enhancement amplifying my elemental strength. Quinn was close. I drew on his boost, gathering twice as much magic as I'd previously held, prepared to offer aid in whatever form was needed. I no longer had to crane my head to see the column of smoke. It billowed far too close for my earlier prayers to be answered, funneling through a massive water-and-earth ward visible over the rooftops—a spell designed to contain fire. Then we banked around the final corner, and the last of my hopes died.

Airstrong burned.

A cavernous hole had been torn through the corner of the brick warehouse, from the first floor to the roof four stories above it. Chunks of wood and brick from the collapsed upper levels filled the bulk of the cavity at street level. Thick, acrid smoke streamed out the top of the jagged opening and poured through gaping holes where windows had once been.

The carpet shot sideways, the curved horn of a wild-eyed ox tearing through the air inches from my knee. The beast thundered past close enough for me to count the flecks of sweat on its flank, the flap of its torn harness strap whipping against the underside of our carpet. Panicked, the ox veered down the nearest alley, but not before clipping the corner of the brick building, shaking it on its foundation.

Grant slowed, and I jerked my gaze back to Airstrong. The pulverized wooden sidewalk and dozen-foot radius of decimated cobblestones defined the blast crater, but the damage extended much farther. Overturned carts, broken crates, and shattered glass lay strewn along the street in front of the ravaged building. Terrified hippogryphs and horses churned debris underfoot and threatened to trample the frantic riders and drivers attempting to soothe them.

Three buildings down from Airstrong, a trio of men in blacksmith leathers freed a centaur trapped beneath a mangled air sled. Injured and dazed people sat or lay sprawled among the havoc, healers already darting among them. Spells saturated the air, cooling, mending, containing, protecting—and speeding down side streets and over rooftops to carry messages to people beyond the disaster. I clung to Grant's waist, my gaze bouncing from one bloodied face to the next, my heart in my throat.

Where was Mom?

The oblong ward encasing the warehouse narrowed through the alleys on either side and bulged into the street, preventing the fire from spreading to nearby businesses. The fluidity of the spell's shape and the ever-shifting magic swirling within it radiated a herd harmony unattainable by ordinary humans. I scanned the ward's perimeter. A smattering of statuesque figures were posted at even increments along the spell. Each was over six feet tall, female, and as voluptuous as she was large boned. Each also possessed a tan-and-black bovine head. A frisson of hope cut through my panic. Minotaur magic cradled Airstrong. If the minotaurs had reacted fast enough, Mom might be all right.

Grant jerked the carpet to a halt, dropping the levitation

spell fast enough to click my teeth together. When he leapt to his feet, my fingers spasmed, cramping into a fist. Spinning, he planted a hand on my shoulder when I tried to rise.

"Wait here and be careful."

He jogged off before I could respond, calling out to city guards already on the scene. They readily relinquished control of the disaster site to him. As captain of the city's Federal Pentagon Defense squad, Grant Monaghan outranked everyone in the vicinity. He also possessed years of experience in the FPD working high-risk situations with volatile magic and deadly creatures. I hadn't had a chance to ask, but I doubted this was his first run-in with a phoenix. It obviously wasn't his first time running post-catastrophe cleanup. He quickly began constructing order in the chaos. If I hadn't been so worried, I would have been impressed.

Quinn dropped from the rooftop behind me, a flash of the late-evening sun reflecting off his citrine lion body catching my eye. Snapping open powerful wings, he slowed his descent, landing with a clatter of quartz paws on cobblestones. His wings kicked up debris and swirled smoke into my eyes, but I didn't care. Leaping off the carpet, I rushed to him.

"Have you found Mom?"

Quinn shook his head. "I'm boosting her, though, so she's close. In that direction." He pointed toward Airstrong just as a heavy crash inside loosed a cascade of broken bricks from the front wall. Someone on the street screamed. Fresh smoke gushed out of the roof and high windows.

My heart squeezed tight. A handful of people milled about between us and the warehouse, but Mom was tall, pale, and blond, like me. If she had been among them, I would have spotted her.

I crossed my fingers and spun together a tracking spell

with more speed than finesse. Maybe Mom was behind the warehouse, standing safely on the loading dock. To be certain, I tossed a second tracker high into the air. Both golden arrows dove straight into the burning building, disappearing for a breathless count of four seconds before returning through a smoke-choked window. I caught them in a trembling net of air.

Oh mercy. She was inside.

Alive, or my spell wouldn't have found her magical signature, but something was preventing her from escaping the warehouse on her own. I searched the street for Grant, but he had vanished. I couldn't delay.

Hang on, Mom. I'm coming. "Quinn, you should stay—"

"I go where you go," he declared.

I shot him a tight smile. "Thank you."

Banishing the extra tracker, I anchored the remaining arrow to me, then darted around a spilled bin of used horseshoes and scrap metal, Quinn on my heels. Broken glass and jagged hunks of wood forced me to slow when I wanted to sprint, and I almost fell when my foot slipped in a murky puddle leaking from toppled casks. Quinn caught me, and together we pushed through the ward. For one step, the spell bathed me in an elemental waterfall, cool and cleansing, the acrid odors of charred stone and campfire smoke washed away. Then heat battered me. I gasped, expelling clean oxygen from my lungs and swallowing a mouthful of ash.

"Child, no!"

The nearest minotaur lunged for me, and I dodged her long reach. "I'm going in. Mom's inside."

Her brown eyes widened when they snagged on the tracker quivering at my side, and her ears stiffened. "We missed one," she shouted to the minotaur on her right. "Someone's inside!"

The cry was taken up along the line of minotaurs, and their magic shifted, spiraling cool tendrils around me. I gratefully gathered their magic inside mine, forming a pocket of breathable air around myself and Quinn. Then I plunged into the wreckage.

The minotaurs' magic preceded us across the tattered threshold, pushing aside the smoke. A long, narrow room stretched the width of the warehouse. Yesterday, it had been a peaceful lobby with an assortment of comfortable furniture, large windows to let in light, and an employee's desk on the far right, where prospective clients claimed and booked shipments. Along the back wall, a sturdy door had guarded the warehouse, separating the lobby from the bustle and dangers of an active shipping yard.

Today, it was unrecognizable. A shadowy mound of rubble loomed on the left, all that remained of the front corner of the building. Thick wooden beams protruded from the floor at disorienting angles, flames licking along their ragged breaks despite the fire-retardant spells coating them. Broken bricks and grit were spewed across the lobby's encaustic tiles clear to the desk on the opposite side. Molten puddles of phoenix egg residue dotted the floors and walls, providing eerie, flickering lighting. I squinted against the gloom, hunting for the door to the warehouse. It was missing, along with half the wall and the no-trespassing ward that had previously defended the opening.

I flinched away from the splintered front doorway, the heat of the battered frame singeing my elbow through my thin cotton shirt. The tracker blazed bright in the dim interior, its tip pointing toward the remaining section of the back wall. *Thank goodness.* A bank of offices marched along the opposite side of the wall, accessible only from the warehouse. Beyond the offices stretched the open floor of the warehouse, stocked with shipments awaiting transport or pickup. Anything from textiles to fireworks to cockatrices could be stored inside the warehouse on a given day.

"Stay close," I told Quinn.

He pressed to my side, the coolness of his rock shoulder seeping through my jeans. We shoved our way under a crooked board and stumbled over a pile of plaster and wood that had once been the second floor. The material cracked and popped beneath Quinn's weight. I scurried forward, and Quinn leapt free before the wreckage collapsed. Dust and ash billowed into the air.

Swiping sweat from my brow, I formed a glowball and floated it ahead of us, forging a convoluted path through the detritus. The arrow gradually rotated, pointing first to our right, then behind us, but crumpled shipping crates blocked a direct route, forcing us deeper into the warehouse. The minotaurs' magic weakened the farther we traveled. When it faded completely, ash choked my shield and heat beat against my skin. Darkness pressed in on me, my light unable to penetrate more than a foot or two of smoke, turning the cavernous warehouse into a claustrophobic nightmare. My breath hitched, my pulse thundering in my ears. The groans and pops of burning boards became the rumble of rock above my head, threatening to collapse and bury me.

This isn't Lunacy Labyrinth, I reminded myself. *I don't have tons of rock above my head.*

Just one partially collapsed roof, more than heavy enough to crush Quinn and me both.

Not helpful, I told myself.

A spray of sparks rained from the ceiling, illuminating ghostly shapes in the destruction as they fell. The first two offices were unrecognizable, pulverized under the weight of the collapsed floors above them. My heart migrated up my throat, worry strangling me. The tracker pointed toward Mom's office at the end of the line. In the darkness, I couldn't make out if it was still whole. It had been farthest from the blast, but the ceiling might have—

A loud crack split the air above us. Short pops like bones snapping echoed through the building, then the warehouse released a pained growl.

"Watch out!" Quinn shoved me to the ground. I slammed to my knees, then to my stomach under the weight of Quinn's paw. Hunkering low, he straddled me, his wings forming a quartz cocoon even as I hardened a ward above us. Something heavy hit my shield and shattered it. Magic backlashed, whipping pain through my brain, and I sucked in an ash-clogged breath. Coughing, I scrambled for the elements. When I shoved a ward against the weight above us, it didn't budge. Cycling the elements, I attempted to purify the air, but it was too late. All the clean oxygen had dispersed.

"Are you all right?" Quinn asked, dipping his head to touch his cool nose to my cheek.

"I think so," I wheezed. Knitting a mask of water and air, I fitted it over my mouth and refined it until I could breathe through it. Then I replicated it for Quinn. It helped, but my lungs still burned, and I couldn't suppress my coughs. "You?"

Quinn flexed his wings, bumping up against solid surfaces on both sides. Carefully, he retracted them. Embers tumbled down on either side of him, following the arc of my ward. When nothing heavier followed, I shimmied out from under Quinn, groaning as pain spiked through my abraded forearms and bruised knees. A wooden beam as thick as my body canted against the demolished crate beside us, one end smoldering red hot. Even more charred and burning timber was piled behind Quinn, where it had slid off his wings. A dim light wavered above us, and the haze of smoke parted long enough to catch a glimpse of crepuscular sky through the fresh hole in the ceiling. The minotaurs' fire-smothering spell swelled to fill the opening, quelling the rooftop flames.

A curse whispered through the air, the voice as familiar as my own.

"Mom!" Fresh coughing wracked my body. "Hang on, we're coming for you."

In the thinning smoke, my glowball illuminated a clear path between pallets. Scrambling over a pile of goods I barely noticed, I sprinted for Mom's office.

The door frame stood, but the wall beside it had crumbled, blocking the entrance.

"Mom?"

"Kylie?" Her bewildered response sounded like a prayer.

"I see her," Quinn said. He stood with his front paws on the office's window frame, his face pressed to the miraculously intact pane of glass. "Or what I think is her foot."

I swiped soot from the window with my palm and peered into the office.

The right wall had caved into Mom's office, the busted plaster buried under a pair of heavy bookcases. A cascade of paper and part of the ceiling mounded around the collapse, and beneath all that stretched one of Mom's legs. A weak ward encased her sprawled limb and disappeared beneath the rubble, the thin elemental barrier the only safeguard preventing Mom from being crushed to death.

"We need in," I said.

Quinn punched a paw through the glass. I shot a

balance of all five elements through the ragged hole. Mom caught it, combining her magic with mine. The moment the link stabilized, I assumed command of Mom's ward, strengthening it with earth and wood, taking on the weight of the wall. My knees sagged, and I grabbed Quinn for balance. It felt as if I supported the whole building. Mom's magic quivered with exhaustion inside our link.

"I'm coming in," I said.

"No, you're not," Grant's deep voice rumbled from behind me.

I levitated, a short scream escaping my lips before I clamped them shut. Gratitude followed close in its wake. The minotaurs must have told him I was inside.

"My mom, she's trapped and needs help," I said, spinning to face Grant. I smacked into the broad chest of an even larger man. Marciano, the wood elemental of Grant's squad, leaned over me, his trunk-like arms bracketing me. Thick hands closed around my waist, and he lifted me, setting me beside him and blocking my view.

"We know."

"Link up," Grant ordered.

I gladly accepted the balance of elements he and Marciano offered me, quickly reinforcing the ward around Mom with their added magic. Grant waited until I was finished to assume control.

Marciano's large hand on my shoulder held me in place while Grant ran a rod of wood element around the window frame, breaking the remaining glass and collecting it into a ball. He set the shards aside, then vaulted into the room. His broad shoulders brushed the edges of the frame, and the wood groaned, but the wall held. Marciano wormed through after him. Leaning back out the window, Marciano pointed at me, then Quinn, then at my feet.

"Don't move."

I rushed to the window, and Quinn stood up on his hind legs to look inside. Grant spun a complex net of air along the undersides of the collapse, supporting the debris with precise magic. In one coordinated heave, he lifted the mass. Magic tugged from me through the link. Alone, even with Quinn's enhancement, I never would have been able to perform a similar feat of elemental strength.

Marciano swooped under the levitated heap and scooped Mom up in his arms. As seamlessly as if they had choreographed the extraction, Marciano pivoted to face the window, and Grant eased the wall to the floor. I scrambled back to give Marciano room to climb out of the office—a maneuver he managed gracefully only by floating Mom ahead of him. As soon as Marciano cleared the window frame, he cradled Mom against his chest again, holding her as if she weighed no more than a child. Grant exited on his heels. Behind him, the office creaked, the broken wall shifting and settling.

Blood stained the thigh of Mom's pants, and she was unnaturally pale beneath the fine powder of plaster coating her. Despite her obvious pain, she reached a hand out for me, and I clutched it, relief singing in my veins.

"Move out," Grant barked.

Marciano took the lead, and Quinn and I followed with Grant close behind me. Through the link, I sensed Marciano create an elemental filtration mask for Mom. Then Grant resumed control and stamped out flames along our path and throughout the warehouse. I no longer felt Mom's signature inside the link and realized Grant had delicately disentangled her to reduce the strain on her already taxed body. I glanced back to thank him, but his expression stole my words. In the dim light, the hard line of Grant's square jaw and the firm slash of his mouth was pure FPD captain. So was his vigilant scrutiny of our smoke-choked route. He looked competent and powerful, with a glint of anger simmering in his brown eyes.

A flush of heat that had nothing to do with our surroundings shot through me.

Inappropriate, I told myself. Mom was injured. Her most profitable warehouse and a major shipping hub of her business was burning around us. Someone had intentionally planted a phoenix egg on the premises.

But the relief of rescuing Mom combined with the heady sensation of Grant's electric magical signature wrapped around mine in the link entitled me to intensified emotions. Or so I told myself.

Piles of abandoned crates, saddlebags, and loose packages littered the loading platform behind the warehouse. I stumbled through them on Marciano's heels, coughing as I sucked in clean air. Five minotaurs held the fire-dampening ward on this side of the building, and as we emerged, they sent an *all-clear* message down their line.

Marciano didn't slow. Eyes watering, I jogged after him along the narrow alley between Airstrong and the adjacent building. The minotaurs' magic slid cool across my skin as we stepped into the street. Only then did Grant let our link dissolve.

Most of the building's flames had been extinguished, but lavalike puddles of the phoenix egg still smoldered among the broken cobblestones and glimmered inside the lobby. Water-laced air funnels pulled a thinning stream of smoke out of the warehouse, where it disappeared against the dusky sky. Soot coated the exterior of Airstrong, blackening the blue winged-A logo painted above the nonexistent door. The upended carts, piles of ruined goods, and shards of shattered glass still obstructed the street, but the animals and most of the humans had dispersed or relocated farther down the street.

Marciano carried Mom toward a thin dark-skinned woman waiting at the edge of the destruction, and she rushed to meet us. An ash-dusted emblem on the woman's top designated her a trained healer, as did her brisk demeanor. Her assessing gaze scanned each of us in turn, then returned to Mom.

"Hold her still," she instructed before sweeping a net of elements over her chosen patient. Mom's lips tightened, and her fingers crumpled the fabric of Marciano's shirt as the healer's complex magic dove into her bleeding thigh. I covered Mom's hand with my own.

"Fractures aren't my specialty," the healer said after several minutes of delicate spell work. "I've set the bone and closed the wound, but you'll need to rest and keep your weight off the leg or visit the healer hall soon."

Mom nodded. Pain no longer etched harsh lines in her face, but her eyelids drooped with fatigue. Rapid healing took a toll on the body, and she was already drained from holding up the wall. I gave her hand another squeeze and released her.

Apparently satisfied, the healer shifted her attention to me. A delicate elemental touch feathered across my skin. "You've been healed recently."

It wasn't a question, but I answered anyway. "Last night."

"With your permission," the healer said.

Again, it wasn't a question, but I nodded anyway.

A soothing blend of water and air alleviated the burning in my lungs and soothed my scratched esophagus, the magic so delicate I barely felt it. However, the cobblestones swam in my vision, the expedited healing leaving me surprisingly light-headed.

The healer gripped my shoulder, frowning into my eyes. "What were you seen for last night?"

"Complications with a few spells," I hedged.

"She was caught in three banned spells during an investigation," Grant said.

Mom gasped, and I gave her a tight smile. My message to her early this morning had carefully skirted that detail, only informing her I was healthy and home after having located the illegal spells stolen from one of Airstrong's shipments. I had planned to share the full details in person.

"Kylie Grayson?" the healer asked. Her fingers settled on my temples. "I didn't recognize you under all this grime."

A flush heated my cheeks. Was she one of the multitude of medics who paraded through my room last night while I was healed? Hopefully the fact that she remembered my name didn't mean I had achieved any level of fame among the healers. I never wanted to be treated like a medical curiosity again.

"We don't want to push your body too much. Let's keep this to a minimum, because you're better off healing naturally."

I nodded. She cleansed the scrapes on my forearms, then mended only the deepest abrasions with a gentle spell that tingled. When she finished, I laid a discreet hand on Quinn's offered shoulder, bracing myself until the black dots disappeared from my vision.

"Anyone else?" the healer asked, glancing over my shoulder at Grant. When he shook his head, she scurried off to assist others.

"Set me down, please," Mom said. "This is becoming embarrassing."

Marciano shared a look with Grant, then lowered Mom to her feet. She swayed, eyes closed, one hand on Marciano's arm.

"Charlotte? Do you need to sit?" he asked.

Breathing deep, Mom lifted her chin, rolled her shoulders back, and opened her sky-blue eyes. "Did everyone get out?" she asked.

"You were the last," Marciano said.

"Tyler? He was in the lobby when the explosion . . ."

"It was a phoenix hatching," I said.

Beneath the grime, Mom's face paled. I nodded tightly in response to the unspoken question in her eyes. I knew.

My hand lifted to my breastbone, to the pouch containing a peach-pit-size seed. It was a gift from an ever-lasting tree in response to my question: Where can I find the story of a lifetime? Following its clues would lead me to the answer.

I had envisioned a noble quest, at the end of which I would pen a grand story that would benefit thousands of people who religiously read the *Terra Haven Chronicle*. Instead, the seed had pointed me toward firebirds stolen from an Airstrong shipment, then to illegal spells pilfered from this same warehouse. Along the way, my parents' business had been dragged through the mud, I had been suspended from the paper, and I hadn't gotten to write a single relevant article.

Just when I thought things couldn't get worse, my seed evolved to resemble a phoenix egg. Which was how I came to learn early this morning that the FPD and Mom had been keeping a secret: along with the banned spells and firebirds, the thief had made off with a clutch of phoenix eggs from an FPD shipment in Airstrong's warehouse.

With Mom already under suspicion, my first concern

had been to clear her name. If she was found guilty of trafficking in deadly phoenixes, she would hang.

But I hadn't considered how the thief intended to use the phoenix eggs. I hadn't thought about the destruction the eggs could wreck on Terra Haven.

I had never dreamed the thief would use the eggs to attack Airstrong.

"It was so sudden," Mom said, shaking her head. "I was heading to the floor to check on a shipment from Pinkham's, and then there was the loudest bang, like a train had collided with the building. The wall collapsed so fast. My shield was pure instinct, but I wasn't quick enough . . ." Her hands gripped mine. "How did you know to come? Or that I was inside?"

"I saw the fireball from my place." From the roof, to be specific, where I had been enjoying a late-afternoon picnic with Grant. Quinn had been half asleep, and I had been snuggled up to Grant, savoring his teasing kisses, when the explosion echoed across the city. I peeked at Grant through my eyelashes. All traces of the man who flirted with me earlier were locked beneath his captain's mask. "We came as fast as we could."

"Thank you," she whispered. She spread her gratitude between Grant and Marciano, then opened her arms to me.

I walked into the hug, squeezing her tight.

"Are you all right?" she asked.

"I'm fine. I'm more concerned about you."

Worry clouded her eyes when we parted.

"Really, I'm fine," I repeated.

She pressed her lips together, cutting off whatever she might have said, and knelt to hug Quinn instead. He returned the embrace, gently cupping Mom in his stone wings. When she straightened, she pivoted to face Airstrong, and I realized she had been avoiding looking at the building. Anguish flashed in her gaze, then she shuttered it. Turning away, she squared her shoulders and said to Grant, "Captain, I need to see my people, then I need to talk to the investigator."

"O'Hara is there," Marciano said, pointing toward a cluster of grimy people seated against a wall down the street. A thin man crouched next to them, a notebook in hand and a recording sphere and glowball floating next to his head. The golden light glinted off his short-cropped gray hair and silver goatee. Like Grant and Marciano, FPD Investigator Hugh O'Hara radiated an air of readiness, as if he expected another attack at any moment.

"He better not be interrogating my people," Mom said. "They've been through enough today." Hands fisted at her sides, she took off at her usual brisk pace. However, her first step stuttered and her nostrils flared in suppressed pain. Grinding her teeth, she continued at half her original speed, her steps soft.

I tried to follow, but Grant's hand on my bicep pulled me up short. His everlasting seed peeked beyond the cuff of his uniform. Unlike my seed, which hadn't altered its shape, his had reformed into a sturdy bracelet, locking itself around his wrist. The five matching discs of interlinking black-and-white teardrops could have passed for stone, and any upscale jeweler would have been proud to claim their craftsmanship. Grant hadn't shared his theories about the seed's current form. He'd been equally evasive regarding his question for the tree—and curiosity ate at me to find out.

"I told you to stay with the carpet," Grant said, yanking me mentally back to the moment.

Frowning, I pulled against his grip. He didn't release me. He wasn't hurting me, just holding me.

"My mom—"

"One message, and I would have gotten her." A dark emotion I couldn't pinpoint smoldering in Grant's eyes.

Marciano mumbled something about finding Winnigan and his other squadmates. I barely noticed his departure, my glare locked on Grant.

"I didn't know how much time Mom had, and—" I tried to articulate the terror I had felt, but Grant didn't give me a chance.

"You're a civilian without an ounce of training. You put yourself in unnecessary danger—"

"My *mom* was trapped inside a burning building," I said too loud.

"And I was right here," Grant growled. "What if something had happened to you?"

I took a deep breath, realizing fear drove his anger. "Like you said, you were right here."

Grant shook his head, and I had no trouble reading his irritation. "Kylie, I can't—"

"Captain?" Marciano called. He stood next to two women, one petite and redheaded, the other muscular with short sandy-blond hair: Winnigan and Seradon, the water and earth elementals of Grant's squad. Winnigan spoke with the nearest minotaur, adding her magic to theirs with practiced ease. Around Seradon's feet, a handful of spells disintegrated sharp blades of glass to sand, but her keen brown eyes monitored our argument.

"Coming," Grant said. Frustration stamped his features when he turned back to me. Releasing my arm, he said, "Stay here, out of the way, and let me work without worrying about you."

Feeling as if he had slapped me, I stood rooted in place as he strode away.

2

Yanking my glare from Grant's backside, I searched for Mom. I had made the right choice in rushing to her rescue, and I would do it again in a heartbeat. When Grant had a chance to cool down, he would see it too.

"Come on," I said to Quinn, spotting Mom kneeling next to her employees, O'Hara at her shoulder. "I want to make sure Mom doesn't need help."

"Grant said to stay here."

"I know, but he's being overprotective and irrational. Besides, we're not going far." I forced myself to take a step toward Mom, my feet oddly reluctant. Quinn fell in with me, quiet except for the crunch of broken glass beneath his quartz paws.

Twilight deepened the shadows inside the surrounding buildings, but glowballs suspended around the street lit the cleanup efforts. Under Grant's orders, the minotaurs disbanded their ward and retreated to sit in front of the building next to Airstrong. A healer materialized among them, soothing burns and mending scratches with assistance from the uninjured minotaurs. O'Hara's team slipped into Airstrong, the three men and one woman taking different routes, their magic crawling, gliding, and scraping over every surface, hunting for clues. The egg hadn't appeared out of thin air; someone had dropped it on Airstrong's doorstep.

The FPD's strategy of keeping the phoenix egg thefts quiet was about to backfire catastrophically. Again.

Airstrong's reputation—already eroded by the previous thefts—would be the first casualty. No one would want to ship their goods with a company that couldn't guarantee safe delivery, especially not a company under suspicion of illegal activity. At this rate, Mom and Dad would be out of business before the end of the month.

And if O'Hara decided Mom was involved in the theft of the phoenix eggs, she would be imprisoned before nightfall.

Shivering, I picked up my pace. Seradon jogged past me, worry in her gaze when it swept over me. I tried to smile reassuringly, but my lips were too stiff. Marcus Velasquez, the fire elemental of Grant's squad, trailed her, his expression grim. Broad-shouldered, muscled, and tall, Velasquez could pass for Grant's younger brother, though they weren't related.

"Why am I not surprised to find you here?" he asked.

I shook my head, biting off a tart retort. Velasquez hadn't been shy in expressing his belief that I brought destruction and mayhem wherever I went. I wasn't about to argue with him about causation versus correlation. Not here. Not that I had a solid argument to stand on either. My life had imploded over the last several weeks. I had survived more close calls than I wanted to remember, most thanks to Grant and his squad. Velasquez saw me as a danger to those around me, specifically to my best friend,

Mika, who he had recently started dating. Sadly, I didn't completely disagree.

"A little help?" Seradon said. She swept a pile of debris toward the side of the road, using a net of air to contain the cloud of ash it raised. Velasquez shot me a final, suspicious scowl before catching up with her.

Shoulders slumping, I trudged to Mom's side.

". . . is different," Investigator O'Hara said to Mom. His gaze flicked to me, then Quinn at my side, before returning to Mom. "Can you think of anyone who wants to hurt you or Airstrong?"

"Not since you asked me yesterday." Mom's cool tone bordered on rude. "The thief has done plenty to harm Airstrong, but I never dreamed they wanted to physically hurt me or my employees."

"Did you notice anything different today?" O'Hara maintained a small recording sphere at his side, capturing the entire conversation. It was standard investigation protocol, but I wondered if he hoped to catch Mom in a lie. Despite everything I had done to assist his investigation, he still hadn't eliminated Mom from his list of suspects. "Maybe something small? Anyone leaving early or missing today's shift?"

Mom shook her head. "Everyone was accounted for. Nothing was abnormal today, at least not for this time of year. With the fair just a few days away, we're holding more inventory than normal—or rather, we're holding more than we were last week. We're not at capacity like we were in past years."

She said the last part quieter, a reluctant admission of the loss of business she and Dad had experienced. Lines of fatigue underscored her eyes, lines that hadn't been there a month ago. Three consecutive thefts from Airstrong, each worse than the last, had taken a toll on her as much as it had her business. Though she radiated authority and righteous anger as she talked to O'Hara, she appeared smaller than before. Thinner. I wished Dad were here for her to lean on, but he had been relegated to the East Coast, separated per FPD orders until the investigation concluded.

A phantom heat burned between my shoulder blades. I glanced around. Across the street, Grant stood with his arms folded, radiating disapproval. I tipped up my chin, silently letting him know he didn't intimidate me. A muscle in his jaw bounced. Uncrossing his arms, he stalked across the street, heading straight for me. My eyes widened, my heart rate kicking up in a rush of apprehension, even though I hadn't done anything wrong. I jerked to face O'Hara.

"Do you still need my people, or can I send them home?" Mom asked.

O'Hara took in the unnerved Airstrong employees clustered nearby. "I've gotten their statements. They can go. But not you."

"Of course." Mom broke the news to her employees, hugging each of them before they departed.

Tyler, the warehouse's receptionist, lingered. "I swear, I didn't see anyone. The lobby was quiet all afternoon. How could I have missed a *phoenix* egg?" His muscular hands flexed in distress. "This is my fault—"

"No," Mom interrupted. "This is the work of someone mentally deranged. We'll catch them too. But for now, go home. Give your wife a hug. We'll get this sorted, and it will look better in the morning."

Tyler sighed and nodded, and Mom continued to reassure him even as she ushered him toward the end of the street.

I recalled the destruction inside the warehouse, all the

water and smoke damage, the collapsed section of the roof, the obliterated offices. Mom's words might have reassured Tyler, but I knew better. Daylight wasn't going to improve the situation.

"What are you doing here?" O'Hara snipped.

I glanced around for a newcomer, then realized the investigator's question had been directed at me.

"Helping my mom."

"You were here when the phoenix hatched?"

"No. I saw it from my apartment."

"You were there?" O'Hara directed his question to my left, where Grant had stopped.

"Yes."

"It was your decision to bring the girl?"

Grant nodded.

"You shouldn't have," O'Hara said. "You're letting your emotions cloud your judgment."

"Yes, sir." Grant's voice was as emotionless as his expression.

"Do you really think Grant could have stopped me?" I demanded, irritated at being talked about as if I weren't standing two feet away. "Do you think *anything* could have stopped me from getting to my mom after I saw that explosion?"

O'Hara's gaze flicked down to my feet and back up to my eyes, as if he were tallying all the ways he could have restrained me.

"And just to be clear," I added, doing my best not to shout at the man I hoped would clear Mom of all wrong-doing, "I'm not *the girl*. My name is Harriet Kylie Grayson, and what happens at Airstrong is my business." A part of me couldn't believe I was claiming the name I hated and pretending I hadn't given up the family business years ago, but O'Hara needed to be reminded of who he was talking to.

"Monaghan, a word." Dismissing me, O'Hara strode toward the center of the street. Grant fell in beside him, and a soundproof ward sprang up around both men.

My jaw clenched, and I jumped when a gentle hand patted my back.

"I've felt the same way many times," Mom said, studying the two FPD men through slitted eyes. With a frustrated huff, she turned her attention to Quinn. Instantly, a smile lightened her face. "You were wonderful, Quinn. I felt the moment you arrived. You gave me the strength I desperately needed. I'm honored you shared your boost with me."

I smiled at Quinn too, his trust and loyalty filling me with pride. He had been my companion for less than a year, and I still marveled that he chose to accompany me. Most gargoyles gravitated toward full-spectrum families in a symbiotic relationship, the gargoyles gaining health and strength from enhancing large amounts of balanced elements, and the humans enjoying boosted levels of magic. Before Quinn, I had rarely experienced the honor of a gargoyle's enhancement. I understood the touch of wonder that filled Mom's voice. I felt the same every time Quinn leapt in to help me.

"I'll always enhance you, Charlotte Mom," Quinn said solemnly.

Mom laughed at Quinn's name for her, and the light sound mended the jagged rips fear had cut through my chest. The Airstrong warehouse might collapse, the business might dissolve, but Mom was safe and whole. It wasn't perfect, but it was far from the worst thing that could have happened today.

Quinn lifted a paw, patting the four-inch disc resting

against his chest. Though it glimmered a bright metallic green, and delicate copper filaments twisted across the surface, the pendant was actually Quinn's everlasting seed. A leather thong fit through an off-center hole in the seed's surface, an addition that made it possible for Quinn to wear his seed at all times.

"Did it change?"

I knelt for a better look. Quinn's seed had evolved twice so far, both times after he saved my life—which made sense, considering his question to the everlasting tree had been how best he could help me. Preventing me from dying ranked right at the top of that list.

"I don't think so." I flipped his seed. A mirror surface on the opposite side reflected my soot-smeared face back at me. "No, it's the same."

Quinn nodded, his expression pensive.

A flash popped brightly against the ruined facade of the warehouse. A second, then third photograph sent dots of light dancing in my vision as the camera turned toward us. Quinn growled. I slapped an opaque ward up between the three of us and the reporter, then pivoted to identify the culprit.

Acid churned in my gut. My nemesis Nathan Aspell, senior journalist for the *Terra Haven Chronicle*, sauntered down the street. He had castigated my parents and their company in this morning's paper, managing to insinuate their guilt and complicity in the theft of the recovered banned spells despite having witnessed—and reported on —the arrest of Persephone Kwan for those same crimes.

Of all the reporters Dahlia could have sent, why him? It should have been me covering this story. I had the inside scoop. I had been first on the scene. Most important, I wouldn't twist facts to suit an irrational grudge.

But the editor in chief had forbidden me from writing this story—the one my everlasting seed pointed me toward again and again—because Dahlia didn't believe I could be unbiased. Her point had become moot the moment she suspended me.

My nails gouged my palms, a familiar bitterness leaving a foul taste in my mouth.

Mom peeked around my ward, then cursed, short and sharp. Luther Wetherill bore down on us, his pounding boot steps echoing against the empty business fronts. Middle aged and pale, with curly brown hair going gray and a neat beard disguising the softening of his jaw, he could have passed for pleasant if he tried. He had spent a lifetime not trying. Despite the summer heat, Wetherill wore gray pinstriped wool slacks and a matching vest, the long-sleeve honey-colored silk shirt underneath it buttoned to his throat. An extravagant cooling spell woven through the luxurious fabric announced Wetherill's wealth to any passersby, in case they miraculously overlooked his entitled demeanor.

I hadn't expected to encounter Wetherill again so soon. I should have expected him, though. Nathan was so deep in Wetherill's pocket, I was surprised he could breathe without inhaling lint. Ever since the firebirds had been stolen from Airstrong, Wetherill had used the senior journalist as his mouthpiece to denigrate Mom and Airstrong. As the owner of Capstone Transportation, Airstrong's main competitor, Wetherill had the most to gain from Airstrong's downfall— and he never wasted an opportunity to smear Mom in public. Or me.

"The guards shouldn't have let him through," I groused, eyeing the lookie-loos being contained by a handful of city guards at the far end of the street. If they hadn't let Wetherill pass, Nathan wouldn't have slithered through on his coattails.

"Luther probably threatened their jobs if they didn't." Mom checked on O'Hara's location and winced. The investigator had halted his conversation with Grant to track Wetherill's progress. "The last thing this situation needs is Luther spewing his poisonous opinions."

"About that," I began, double-checking that Wetherill wasn't yet in hearing range. "He pushed hard to frame me for the theft of the banned spells." Spells his now-ex-fiancée, Persephone, had tucked away on her private island —at least those she hadn't saved for personal use. Wetherill's insistence of my guilt even in the face of overwhelming contrary evidence had raised my suspicions. Combined with his insider knowledge of the shipping industry, which would have made it possible for him to ferret out the contents of private FPD shipments—like those that carried illegal spells and phoenix eggs—as well as his personal benefit in Airstrong's downfall, Wetherill had become my number-one suspect. His actions matched those of a person carefully orchestrating Airstrong's demise, including using his pet reporter to push public opinion in his favor.

I just had to figure out how to prove it.

But before I could explain all this to Mom, Wetherill's voice rang out loud enough to carry to both ends of the block.

"Charlotte Grayson, your recklessness is criminal!"

Reluctantly, I disbanded my ward. Wetherill slammed to a stop far too close.

"A phoenix egg?" He leaned into Mom's personal space, raising an arm to point at the still-smoking shell of Airstrong's warehouse. His gray eyes glared into Mom's, and he didn't lower his voice from its theatrical volume. "Are you and your staff trying to kill us all? I thought you were certified for transporting phoenix eggs. What is the FPD going to do about this?" He whirled to include Investigator O'Hara and Grant in the last of his diatribe.

"Thank you for your concern, Luther," Mom said, her voice deceptively mild. She dropped a soundproof ward around us, incorporating Grant and O'Hara inside the circle. Unfortunately, her ward also included Nathan, who had sidled up to Wetherill's elbow. He snapped a picture in Mom's face and floated a recording sphere above our heads. Mom pretended he didn't exist. I wished I could do the same.

"There. Now you won't need to yell to be heard," she said, as if that had been the reason for Wetherill's shouts, not the audiences clustered at either end of the block.

A flush crept up Wetherill's neck at being outmaneuvered. He regrouped fast. "Your incompetence is deplorable, Charlotte. It's no wonder the people of our city are in hysterics and demanding Airstrong be closed."

Mom raised a cool eyebrow. "I see only one person in hysterics."

Wetherill's nostrils flared, and his jaw worked beneath his short beard. "First you lost the firebirds, then you allowed illegal, *deadly* spells to walk off your premises—spells you assured the FPD you could handle discreetly. Now you've bungled yet another FPD shipment, this time of a phoenix egg? Luckily, only your property was damaged. There's no telling who or what might be hurt next time. What if it's her?" He shoved a blunt finger in my face. "Or maybe you don't care. You've proven willing to toss your daughter into all manner of deadly situations to save yourself. You're as unfit a parent as you are a business owner."

Cold fury twisted Mom's expression, but Grant spoke first.

"Wetherill, you need to calm down and step away from Kylie."

"Captain Monaghan, ever ready to jump to your girlfriend's defense." Wetherill sneered, but he dropped his hand. He was still close enough to punch, and I wished I dared. "Will you extend that same protection to her mother? O'Hara, how long are you going to let Charlotte Grayson terrorize this city before you arrest her?"

"I'll make arrests as I see fit, Luther," O'Hara said mildly.

"What do you have to say for yourself, Charlotte?" Nathan asked.

I bristled at his casual address of my mom—as if he were her friend rather than the slimeball who had lambasted her in print every day for the last week.

"I'm grateful no one was seriously injured today and thankful for how quickly not only the local healers responded, but especially how fast the Femmes of the Furnace minotaurs rushed to our aid. The people of Terra Haven are a courageous lot."

Nathan shoved his thick-rimmed glasses up his nose in annoyance. Clearly he had expected Mom to fall into his trap and take a defensive stance. He had proven himself adept at twisting her words in previous articles, but she hadn't given him anything to manipulate this time. Which was likely why he hadn't jotted down a single note.

"And the other eggs?" he pressed. "What do you have to say about them?"

Mom's eyes cut to O'Hara. My stomach plummeted. Nathan knew? How? I had only learned about the missing clutch because Grant told me.

"What other eggs?" the investigator asked.

Glee lit Nathan's eyes. "Charlotte didn't tell you how many phoenix eggs she lost?"

"I'm wondering who told you."

"I'm a reporter." Nathan shot O'Hara a defiant glare, though it appeared aimed at the investigator's chin. "I won't reveal my source. People need to know they can trust me."

I might have mustered up grudging respect for Nathan's ethics if I didn't suspect his source stood at his side. Wetherill made a weak attempt to appear surprised at Nathan's announcement, but his acting skills needed work.

"And how many eggs did this source tell you were taken?" O'Hara asked, his tone bland but his gaze sharp.

"Five. That's correct, is it not?"

O'Hara ignored his fishing, but Nathan hadn't risen through the ranks at the *Terra Haven Chronicle* without solid instincts. He hadn't expected the investigator to answer his question and was already spitting out the next before O'Hara could turn away.

"Did this egg hatch on its own or was it forced? Security at Airstrong is notoriously lax, especially on the inside, but someone must have seen something."

It took all my willpower to keep my mouth shut, but defending Mom would only play into Nathan's hand. Quinn bumped his muzzle against my thigh, and I unclenched my fist to rest my palm on his neck. Stroking the glassy ripples of his mane helped clear the fury clouding my thoughts.

Phoenix eggs hatched one of two ways: naturally, when the bird was ready to emerge, or by force. The volatility of the eggs made them perfect weapons of war, as previous generations had discovered. Phoenixes' deadly nature, and the prevalence of their eggs being used for nefarious purposes by outlaws, was the reason the FPD captured wild phoenixes and relocated them to protected government lands.

The brick, wood, and glass radiating outward from the warehouse proved the egg had hatched *inside* the lobby. Tyler would have remembered someone chucking an egg into the lobby. Which meant the egg had hatched naturally. So how had Tyler and everyone else at Airstrong overlooked a foot-tall, glowing-hot egg sitting in the lobby?

"Whoever is hiding these eggs"—Nathan's eyes cut to Mom, and my fingers curled into Quinn's citrine mane—"knows to keep them separate. Otherwise today's hatching would have ignited the other eggs in a chain reaction. Have you checked the rest of the warehouse?"

"A better question," I said, unable to hold my tongue any longer, "is why would whoever stole the eggs from Airstrong bring one back? What would his motive be?" I focused my question on O'Hara, willing him to see the obvious. Only one person here benefited from today's explosion.

O'Hara's cool gaze landed on Wetherill.

Wetherill's chest puffed with indignation, and he jabbed a thumb at Mom. "*She* could have left an egg to hatch here to make herself appear innocent."

O'Hara's speculative gaze swung toward Mom, and I wanted to scream. Mom only shook her head, a sad smile adding to the hollows beneath her eyes.

"My boy Nathan brought up a good point," Wetherill pressed. "What are you going to do about the remaining four eggs? How do you expect the citizens of Terra Haven to lead normal, productive lives with the threat of *four phoenix eggs* hanging over our heads? This is unacceptable. The panic will be crippling! I won't stand for—"

"We'll all have to do our best to prevent panic for a few

days." Grant's dry tone cut through Wetherill's escalating theatrics.

"One way or the other, this will be resolved within the next week. Two, tops," O'Hara said.

"How can you be so sure?" I asked.

"Every egg in a clutch matures at approximately the same rate. This one hatched first, and its birth appears to have been natural, not forced. The others can't be far behind."

My heart sank. One egg had nearly leveled a building. Four more could cause untold damage and deaths—catastrophes Mom would pay for with her reputation, her freedom, and possibly her life . . . unless I could prove her innocence.

3

___

Wetherill gave a theatrical shudder. "I won't rest easy until those eggs are found. No one will." Pulling himself together with a deep breath, he pressed a hand to his chest and vowed to O'Hara, "But I assure you, Investigator, that my warehouses are safe from thieves and warded against assault. You can trust Capstone with any future FPD shipments. Just ask my clients. They know when they ship with Capstone Transportation, their items will arrive on time, in the same condition they were packaged."

This time, Nathan jotted notes.

"As I told you before, Luther, I do not decide who the Federal Pentagon Defense contracts with for shipping," O'Hara said. Stepping forward, he clapped the shorter man on the shoulder and turned him. "Thank you for your concern. Right now, I have an investigation to conduct."

"Yes, of course. Keep me informed about your progress," Wetherill said with the dictatorial pompousness only a full spectrum could emote.

Being born with elemental powers that outstripped ninety-five percent of the population's hadn't automatically fashioned Wetherill into a terrible person—believing in his own superiority did. His wealth and standing in high society hadn't helped. When he couldn't get his way with raw magic, he always had money or social capital to fall back on.

None of which made an impression on O'Hara, to Wetherill's obvious annoyance.

"If I have any future questions for you, I'll let you know," O'Hara said, dismissing him.

Wetherill's eyes narrowed, and he shot a final barb at Grant. "If your involvement with the Grayson girl interferes with your ability to do your job, I'll be the first to see you reassigned, Captain."

Grant held Wetherill's gaze until the lesser man spun away. Wetherill thrust a hand out as if to slap aside Mom's soundproof ward, but she dropped it before he could fracture her magic. Fatigue rounded Mom's shoulders, but her furious gaze never wavered from Wetherill's back. A subtle jerk of Grant's chin, and Seradon pivoted from where she had been pulverizing a mound of glass shards to follow soundlessly on Wetherill's heels. Wetherill shot her an irritated glower, but he saved his dramaturgy until he reached his audience. Once on the other side of the city guards' street-wide ward, he stopped to regale the curious onlookers with his version of the events, fielding questions from journalists who had been held at bay by the guards. Phrases like *irresponsible shipping practices* and *no regard for public safety* filtered back to us.

My molars ground together. O'Hara made no attempt to prevent Wetherill's rumormongering or even counter it by answering questions himself. How hard would it have been for him to send one of his squad to set the record straight? I was tempted to stomp down there and do it myself, but getting into a shouting match with Wetherill would only give credence to the lies he spewed.

I expected Wetherill's sycophant to trail out on his heels, but Nathan cozied up to the investigator.

"When will you allow Persephone Kwan to tell us her side of the story?" he asked.

"Us?" O'Hara asked.

"Terra Haven. The city is waiting to hear from her."

"The city will have to attend her trial, then. As I told your benefactor, I have an investigation, and you need to—"

"I have one more question about Harry," Nathan interrupted. "I mean Harriet— I mean Kylie."

My lip twitched with a sneer I couldn't fully suppress. Ever since learning my full name—and outing me to the world as Harriet Kylie Grayson, Airstrong heiress—Nathan had taken every opportunity to rub in my face not only my forsaken first name but also the nickname I despised.

"Is it true Ms. Kwan has been asking to speak with her?" Nathan asked.

The investigator's eyes cut to me. "Yes."

"With me? Why?" I demanded.

"She claims the two of you have a lot to discuss," O'Hara said. "About your mother."

My eyebrows floated toward my hairline. What did that mean? Did she . . . ? My heart hammered hard against my chest with a spurt of hope. Did she want to confess?

We had caught Persephone with the spells stolen from Airstrong yesterday, but how she had pulled off the heist remained a mystery. The only theory that made sense was for her to have an accomplice, one who knew the industry, knew which unmarked crates would contain disguised, dangerous spells, and knew the ins and outs of a warehouse. Someone like Luther Wetherill, shipping magnate and Persephone's ex-fiancé.

As far as I could tell, though, O'Hara's investigation remained focused on Mom—as if Mom would attempt to swindle the government and endanger her most profitable contract, Airstrong's reputation, her liberty, and her life in one fell swoop, all out of some hypothetical attempt to make a quick profit selling the spells and phoenix eggs on the black market. The most damning evidence O'Hara had was misguided correlation: Mom had been in Terra Haven during each of the thefts, which only proved someone else knew her schedule.

If I'd had something, anything, to take to O'Hara to back my suspicions, I would have. But all I had was conjecture and instinct, and neither held weight with the investigator. Especially not when he saw me as an extension of my mom and a potential suspect too.

"I should speak to Persephone," I said, my mind spinning. My hope for a confession was a long shot. I knew it logically, even if the possibility made my pulse race.

"No," Grant said.

I frowned at him. "Persephone might know something."

"And you think she'll tell you? The woman she tried to murder?"

"It's worth a shot."

"No, it's not."

A flush crept up my neck, anger chasing humiliation. Nathan smirked. So help me, if he piped up now, I would ram his camera—

"The captain is right," Mom said. "From what I've heard,

Persephone isn't herself anymore. How long did she wear the beguiling beads? If she wasn't insane before she put them on, she is now."

Like all mind-manipulation spells, the beguiling beads had been banned for being even more toxic to the spell caster than the victim. By the time she was arrested and her connection to the beguiling beads severed, a madwoman had peered out of Persephone's eyes. A day in jail might have restored her sanity, or she might be trapped in self-inflicted psychosis for the rest of her life. However, I couldn't turn my back on the chance that she might let slip a clue or confession that would prove Mom's innocence or prevent another hazardous hatching from harming anyone else.

"Has she mentioned the phoenix eggs at all?" I asked O'Hara. In my periphery, Nathan leaned closer. I hated asking the investigator for information in front of Nathan, but it couldn't be helped. The next egg could hatch any minute. I couldn't wait for a chance at a private conversation with O'Hara.

"I don't comment on ongoing investigations," O'Hara said.

In other words, if Persephone had mentioned the phoenix eggs, the investigator wouldn't be standing here. The eggs were too dangerous to ignore a single lead on their whereabouts, no matter the source.

"If she wants to talk to me, then maybe she'll tell me something she hasn't told you." I focused on O'Hara, attempting to block out Grant's thunderous expression. The investigator outranked Grant. It was his permission I needed. "Let me talk with Persephone. If there's the tiniest chance she'll tell me something—who her accomplice is or where the remaining eggs are—I need to try. Tonight. Before this happens again."

"Me too. I go where Kylie goes," Quinn said.

O'Hara studied me, then Quinn. "Fine."

Grant cursed under his breath. I bit down on my triumphant smile.

"Wait here." O'Hara shot Grant an unreadable look, then strode toward the decimated warehouse.

Nathan trotted after him, shouting his question loud enough to carry back to us. "How much longer will you allow Airstrong to continue to operate and endanger the public?"

"Velasquez," O'Hara said. "See that Mr. Aspell is reunited with his peers." The investigator tossed a low-slung barrier between Nathan and the sidewalk, halting the reporter in his tracks.

"Are you worried that the captain's affair with Harriet Grayson will interfere with the investigation?" Nathan shouted.

Nathan whipped his camera up, snapping a picture of the investigator's retreating back. The flash popped, momentarily blinding me. O'Hara disappeared inside without comment.

When I blinked my vision clear, Velasquez towered in front of Nathan. The journalist shrank back. Over six feet tall and stacked with muscle, Velasquez made Nathan look like an adolescent. Fierce blue eyes glared down at Nathan, and when Nathan started to bring his camera back up, a single growled *"Don't"* from Velasquez halted him in place.

With obnoxious deliberateness, Nathan stowed his camera, then strode to the end of the street. He walked with his chin high and his steps unrushed, but he didn't attempt to question the imposing fire elemental or veer off course. Good riddance, if too late. Nathan already had his quotes and his slant on tonight's events. Tomorrow's paper would include more damaging speculation against Mom and Airstrong. It wouldn't stop until we found the rest of the phoenix eggs either. And if the others hurt or killed someone . . .

Mom's cool fingers pressed to my arm, drawing my attention. "Talking to Persephone in her current condition might not be a good idea."

"Mom, I—"

"Let me finish." She tucked a strand of hair behind my ear, her eyes intent on mine. "I understand why you're doing it, and I hope you learn something useful. This . . ." She trailed off, her gaze sliding over the destruction of her warehouse. A pallor of anxiety clung to her cheeks that not even the warm glow of the elemental lights illuminating the street could dispel. "We cannot let this happen again. But be careful with Persephone."

"I will."

Charlotte crouched to Quinn's eye level. "You'll be careful too?"

"Yes, Charlotte Mom."

"Good. And thank you again for your help today. Your boost saved lives, including mine."

I stepped into Mom's arms for a hug when she straightened, holding her tighter and longer than normal. If I had been a minute later, if the egg had hatched one room closer...

"I'll come see you tomorrow," I promised.

"See that you do." Squaring her shoulders, Mom turned to Grant. "Captain, thank you for your assistance today."

Grant gave her a stiff nod.

"Excuse me. I have one more group to thank." Her walk a ginger echo of her usual forceful stride, Mom beelined for the soot-covered minotaurs. Dried blood blackened the leg of her pale pants, and ash and dirt smeared every other inch of her, but none of it detracted from her regal bearing.

I waited until she was out of hearing range before pivoting to Grant. He had the nerve to give me his stoic captain's mask, as if I couldn't see through to the fury beneath it.

"If you were trying to undermine me in front of O'Hara, mission accomplished," I snapped.

"Persephone's insane," Grant growled. "She hates you. She just wants another chance to torment you."

I crossed my arms. "It's a lead and all we have to go on."

"All we have?" Grant reached for me but stopped himself. The seed bracelet peeking beyond the sleeve of his uniform must have irritated him, because he gave it a harsh twist and shoved it out of sight. Blowing out a breath, he locked his eyes on mine. "This isn't a lead. This is manipulation, plain and simple. The lies that woman spews—"

"I'm a journalist. I interview people for a living. Parsing truth from lies is my job." I got the words out without my voice quavering. Point for me. Grant was as suspicious of Wetherill as I was. I didn't have to tell him why I wanted a private conversation with Persephone, and his lack of faith hurt.

Grant shoved his fingers through his hair, giving the short strands a tug. "I'm going to be busy here for several more hours."

I shrugged. "That's fine."

"If you wait until morning, I can go with you."

"I don't need you to—"

"What about Zipporah?"

My stomach bottomed out. I had forgotten about the harpy.

"She nearly killed you the last time she found you," Grant said.

Zipporah nearly killed me *every* time she showed up, though the last time had been the worst. I owed her. I had made a foolish bargain out of desperation, promising the harpy a debt equal to my own life. Every payment she had demanded since that horrible, stupid day had been impossible to deliver. When Zipporah learned of my latest failure to procure the illegal spells she had demanded . . . I shuddered. I might not survive her wrath.

I glanced at the sky. The lingering blush of the setting sun had faded, and stars pricked the ebony expanse. The odds of the harpy hunting me down at night were slim. Unfortunately, the possibility of another phoenix egg hatching were not.

"I can't wait."

"Damn it, yes, you can." Grant bent forward, forcing me to crick my neck to maintain eye contact without backing up. "You're smart, Kylie. Really intelligent. Take some time to think this through."

"How long? Until I agree with you?" The subtle tightening of his eyes told me I hit the mark. I shook my head. "Did it ever occur to you that I'm doing everything I can to save my mom? That I would do whatever it takes to recover those eggs before anyone else gets hurt? Why is it all right for you to take action, but not me? I thought we were past this."

"So did I."

"What's that supposed to mean?"

"You're not trained. You're not part of this investigation. Splinters, Kylie, you're not even a reporter right now."

My breath caught. Throwing my suspension from the

Chronicle in my face was a low blow. When Grant reached for me, I backed up, bumping my calves against Quinn.

"Kylie," he said, gravel in his voice.

"I'm also not useless." I spun on my heel and walked away before Grant could see the sheen of tears building in my eyes.

4

Lava rock crunched underfoot, threatening to twist my ankles with each step. If I were barefoot, the sharp stones would have lacerated my feet. They weren't much kinder on my boots, scuffing chalky red scratches into the sturdy suede. Quinn minced at my side, his quartz paws grinding and squeaking against the rocks.

"Does it hurt?" I asked.

"Only my hearing," he said, flattening his offended ears tight to his skull.

"If you had come during normal hours, the walkway would have been clear," Nolan Parisot, the jail's night warden, said over his shoulder. The wiry man stomped a winding path across the expanse of abrasive rocks toward the squat brick building twenty feet away, continuing to mutter under his breath.

Terra Haven's jail scowled at the world through high slitted windows crosshatched with black iron. Marooned in the sea of lava rocks, isolated from the surrounding buildings by a spiked fence, the jail didn't concern itself with aesthetics. Its sole purpose was containment. A net of spells overlaid the air, nipping against my skin, and concentrated elements seethed beneath the rocks.

I squinted as a glowball half the size of Quinn swept across the sky above us, locked on an orbital flight path around the jail. The next glowball floated past seconds later, then the next. The lights circled halfway between the building and the perimeter, ensuring sun-bright illumination of every square inch of the grounds all night long. My shadow swept across my feet, right to left, again and again, giving the illusion that the ground was sliding beneath my feet. I stumbled, catching myself against Quinn's shoulder.

"Don't look down."

I jerked in surprise at the woman's voice behind me. I had grown so accustomed to Anderson's silence that I had almost forgotten her presence.

O'Hara had assigned his fire elemental as my escort and witness during my conversation with Persephone. I had expected Anderson to interrogate me once we were alone, but the stocky woman had maintained her silence during the long walk to the jail. My half-hearted attempts to engage her in conversation—even to learn her first name—had gone unacknowledged and unanswered.

Her reticence suited my mood. I spent the bulk of our walk chewing my way through a particularly tough day-old sandwich from the only vendor open on our route and contemplating how to have a conversation with a woman who had tried to kill me twenty-four hours ago. My anxious thoughts did nothing to aid my digestion, but at least the food restored energy I needed after being healed.

"Good advice," I said, smiling over my shoulder at Anderson.

Her brown eyes touched on me, then flicked away, studying our surroundings. Did they train warriors on how to maintain an emotionless facade at the FPD academy? If so, Anderson had achieved master-level status. She might even be able to give Grant a pointer or two.

The next glowball swept across the barren yard, highlighting silver threaded through the three tight braids confining Anderson's honey-brown hair. Perhaps she merely had more experience than Grant. Anderson had to be at least my mom's age, and from the look of the muscles in her arms and neck, she had spent every day of her four decades engaged in strenuous physical activity.

Hot needles stung my left arm. I jumped sideways into Quinn with a hiss of pain. Magic flared in a fiery cyclone where my foot had just been, tracing a hidden pentagram beneath the lava rock. Prickles of pain shimmied down my forearm to my fingers. I shook my hand, but the torment intensified.

Water and earth magic whipped from Nolan, slapping my left side.

"Hey!" I protested before realizing the pain had abated.

"That's why I said to follow *exactly* where I step," the warden groused. He twisted elements together too fast to follow, then layered them over the blazing cyclone. The jail's offensive magic shrank and disappeared beneath the lava rock. "Civilians." Nolan shot a commiserative glance over my shoulder, but when Anderson didn't reciprocate his exasperation, giving him the same uninterested stare she gave me, he spun on a heel and flounced toward the jail, muttering under his breath.

I hid a smile. At least it wasn't me Anderson didn't like. Or *just* me.

Apologizing to Quinn for knocking into him, I locked my gaze on Nolan's blue jacket and zigzagged along behind him. He had avoided the logical, direct route from the outer gate to the jail door, and now I understood why: traps.

When Nolan reached the jail's iron door, he pressed a hand to the smooth surface. A raw collection of the five elements pulsed from his hand into the metal. The door popped open several inches with a soft sigh. The warden gripped the edge and pulled it the rest of the way open. A shimmer of magic coated the doorway, feeding into the walls on either side. The filaments of the spell were too delicate for me to decipher, but I recognized the general pattern of a sophisticated structural ward.

"Brace yourselves," Nolan said without bothering to turn around as he led the way into the sterile lobby.

I held my breath as I stepped across the threshold. Elements scoured my body from chest to back, fire and earth gritting across my skin. The building's magic snagged on Grant's badge clipped to the inside of my waistband, and a vise of earth locked around my hips.

With his magical signature embedded in the silver star, Grant could track the badge even if miles separated us. It was an insurance policy: If Zipporah abducted me again, Grant could find me. He could have placed a tracking spell on me, but the harpy might notice active magic and destroy it. She didn't know to look for the badge, and since it had saved my life in the past, I agreed to keep it on my person at all times.

Trapped in the jail's ward, I wished Grant had taken time to imbue something less personal with his magical signature. If I was caught with his badge, not only would Grant be reprimanded, but I could also be arrested for impersonating an FPD warrior.

Just when I was certain the ward would sound an alarm, it eased its hold. With indifferent intimacy, the foreign magic resumed its investigation, tugging at the simplistic knots of air woven into my hair to keep it in a neat ponytail, then biting down on the lingering traces of healing magic knitted into my forearms and lungs. I gritted my teeth, resisting the urge to snap out at the ward with my own magic. Doing so would only trigger the defensive spells layered within it. Finally, it released me, and I staggered into the jail's lobby, blinking to adjust to the dim interior lighting.

Nolan squinted at my hip, but he didn't ask the question I could read in his eyes. If the ward had sensed dangerous magic, it wouldn't have allowed me to enter. Any other spells in my possession were none of anyone else's business.

Quinn stalked into the jail without a problem, though his back dipped away from the ward's intrusive touch. He shook himself once he was clear, his long golden wings flaring to fill the small room. Anderson entered without a hitch. She carried obvious weapons—twin copper pipes strapped in an X formation across her back and a blade at her waist—and wore the standard-issue, spell-laden FPD uniform, but the jail's magic didn't register her as a threat. It must have been an FPD perk. That, or she was simply better at disguising her reaction to discomfiting magic.

The door closed itself, and the warden engaged a bar that anchored the door to the brick walls. Pressure built in my ears as the jail's spells resettled, and I flexed my jaw to release the tension on my eardrums.

"This way."

Nolan marched past a battered desk. A single hallway fed in a straight line to the rear of the jail. Brick walls rose to the ceiling on either side of us, but deeper inside, thick bars of holding cells encased in null wards defined the passage-way. Nolan stopped just beyond the mouth of the hallway in front of a petite woman with ebony hair scraped back in a no-nonsense bun.

"Your guests," Nolan said by way of introductions.

"Thank you, Warden Parisot," she said. I received a brief examination, and Anderson got a squint, but the woman didn't seem to know what to make of Quinn.

Grunting in acknowledgment, Nolan stalked off to check the cells.

An elemental recording sphere snapped into existence. "I am Protectorate Celine Northley. I was told you have questions for prisoner Kwan. I will supervise your conversation. Anything said or done in my presence will be reported to the assigned judge and used at trial. As a protectorate, I do not represent Kwan, the jail, or you. I represent justice, and it is my duty to ensure all parties obey the law and the prisoner is treated fairly until a jury of her peers decides her fate. Is this understood?"

"I, Vanessa Anderson, so understand and agree."

I clamped my mouth shut against the urge to tease Anderson for being so verbose. The setting, the jail's magic, and my impending confrontation with Persephone had all set my nerves on edge, but neither woman looked as if they would appreciate a moment of levity. When I realized Celine and Anderson were both waiting on me, I rushed to say, "I, Kylie, I mean Harriet Grayson, so understand and agree."

The protectorate frowned when I fumbled my own name. After a second, she turned to Quinn.

"I, Quinn, so understand and agree."

"Quinn is a gargoyle," Celine said, presumably for the benefit of the recording sphere and whatever judge might listen to its contents in the future. "The room is small. We won't be able to fit everyone." Her curious gaze returned to Quinn. "We'll need you to remain in the hall."

I bit the inside of my cheek, wanting to volunteer Anderson to wait outside instead.

Quinn took in my expression. "I'll be right here."

I rubbed my damp palms on my pants and nodded. In the aftermath of the phoenix's explosive hatching, confronting Persephone had been the logical next step. But the closer I got to standing face-to-face with a madwoman, the more anxiety knotted my stomach.

Persephone is the key, I reminded myself. She could expose Wetherill for the conniving bastard he was and confirm his involvement in the thefts. Once he was in custody, Grant and O'Hara could get the location of the remaining phoenix eggs from him.

Celine used a small key to unlock the door behind her, but she didn't immediately open it. "Prisoner Kwan is mentally unstable and easily distressed. For everyone's safety, please keep your distance."

I nodded, giving my palms another surreptitious swipe down my pants legs.

The protectorate opened the door and stepped into the room.

"Luther?" Persephone's plaintive query warbled into the hall. "Is that you, my love?"

An unexpected twinge of sympathy made me grimace. Luther Wetherill might have forgiven his fiancée's use of a potent mental-manipulation spell, but I suspected any shred of loyalty that may have existed in his withered heart had vanished the moment he learned the Kwan family was bankrupt. Like so many full-spectrum marriages, theirs had been a political arrangement, at least for Wetherill. But Persephone seemed to harbor genuine feelings for the loathsome man, which should have been my first clue she was unbalanced.

"He's not coming," Celine said gently.

"Luther? Luther!" Persephone's voice rose to a shriek.

Steeling myself, I stepped into the interrogation chamber. Four iron-caged lanterns lit the cramped interior, providing uniform illumination within the whitewashed brick walls. A plank of wood affixed to one wall served as a bench. The rest of the room was barren. Persephone sat on the bench. She wore drab brown prisoner's pants and a matching tunic that hung from her slender frame. Faded black slippers encased her feet, thin enough to be socks and guaranteed to tear if she attempted to traverse the harsh lava rock outside the jail's walls. Null cuffs confined her hands in front of her body, and a short, iron chain ran from the cuffs to the wall. She probably had enough slack to stand, but she didn't appear to have the strength. Gone was the elegant woman who had hosted this year's high-society summer solstice. A haggard shell of a woman slumped in her place.

Persephone blinked at me. Her long brown hair frizzed around her face, and purple smudges underscored her haunted eyes. In a day, she had aged a decade.

Recognition finally sparked, and she lunged toward me. I didn't flinch—barely.

"You!" Persephone's hands contorted into claws. The straps of the null cuffs bit into her wrists. Celine pressed a hand to Persephone's shoulder, gently pushing her back to the bench.

Muscles stiff with tension, I strode forward until I was directly across from Persephone. Less than eight feet separated us, and I fought not to press against the wall. The protectorate remained next to Persephone, her hands loose at her sides and her recording sphere floating near the center of the ceiling. Anderson filed in last, remaining by the door. Quinn sat in the doorway, and I took strength from his quiet presence.

"You should be dead, Harriet Grayson." Persephone spat, or tried to. The moisture dribbled down her chin. "You should be dead. Dead, dead, dead, dead, dead." She tipped her head, using the shoulder of her tunic to swipe the spit from her chin. Her lips continued to move, her eyes unfocused.

"I was told you wanted to speak with me."

"No, you stupid child." Persephone's head jerked up, her eyes seething with anger when they focused on me. "Why would I want to speak to you? You stole from me. You stole everything. You ruined it all." Her spine snapped straight, her expression morphing from hatred to condescension. "Kylie, that's what you like to be called, right, dear? Unlock these handcuffs. Unlock them *now*. You and I need to have a private talk."

"I can't do that."

"You *must*. I command you!" She tipped her head back and screamed until she ran out of air.

I shuffled in place, wanting to clamp my hands over my ears but unwilling to give Persephone a reaction. Perhaps that was the wrong strategy, though. I had envisioned pressuring her into a confession through logic and wit, but would either work on an insane mind? Maybe I would have better luck cajoling the truth out of her.

Slowly, I crouched, lowering myself below Persephone's eye line. I hated the vulnerability of the position. "Shh, it's all right, Persephone. You're all right," I soothed. "This is all a terrible mix-up. Help me figure it out. Help me understand what I ruined."

Persephone's head lolled forward. The hatred bled from

her eyes, and her face slackened. "Charlotte? I knew you would come."

I sucked in a breath. It wasn't the first time Persephone had mistaken me for Mom. I waited for her to see her mistake, but she continued to stare at me with something uncomfortably close to adoration.

"You didn't ruin anything, Charlotte. You helped me." A tear rolled down Persephone's cheek. "You were there for me when no one else was. Until you turned on me." This time, Persephone sounded resigned instead of angry.

"You're my friend. I wanted to help," I said. My stomach twisted at my dishonesty, but playing along with Persephone's delusion could save lives. It had to be my imagination that added judgmental weight to Anderson's impassive expression.

"It was only right that you did too," Persephone said tartly. "After all, I'm a Kwan. My family was one of the first full-spectrum families in Terra Haven."

"But you're having financial problems," I prompted.

She tilted her head, staring down her nose at me. "Some."

"Persephone." I tried to capture Mom's skill of turning a name into an admonishment.

Persephone's expression turned mulish. "Every family's finances goes through an occasional downturn."

"That's why you wanted the banned spells."

"You said they were worth a fortune. That they could get me out of debt. You said Luther would never find out."

I frowned, searching Persephone's eyes. Was she playing me? Was her insanity a ruse? "I don't understand. Are you sure it wasn't Luther who brought you the spells?"

"He would do no such thing! *You* gave them to me." Persephone jabbed a finger at me, snapping the cuffs tight around her wrists. "You *insisted* I take them. It was your idea that I sell them."

"Do you mean Charlotte Grayson or Kylie?" Anderson asked.

Persephone's head whipped toward the FPD warrior; then she recoiled, her gaze spinning around the room as if she were seeing it for the first time. Her hands dropped to her lap, her fingers fidgeting with the coarse fabric of her pants.

"Charlotte gave them to me," she said softly. Then more insistently, "It was Charlotte Grayson. She did this to me. She was jealous. That's why she set me up. She wanted her daughter to look good. A hero. It was all a publicity stunt." Persephone glared at me through her eyelashes. "You owe me, Harriet. Tell these women what you did. You know it should be Charlotte here instead of me. Tell them!"

I pushed to my feet, trying not to show how shaken I was by Persephone's conviction. "My mom had no part in this."

"Liar! She betrayed me."

I peeked at Anderson and the protectorate, wondering if they were buying into Persephone's madness. Neither woman's face gave me a clue as to what they were thinking.

"Charlotte used me. She wanted to turn you into a hero. She never cared about me. I should have killed you when I had the chance." Persephone said the last part with regret, and my guilt at leading her along evaporated.

"If anyone used you, it was Wetherill. He—"

"Luther had nothing to do with this. He wouldn't."

Her conviction sent an unwanted niggle of uncertainty through me. Was Grant right? Was she manipulating me? Or was she telling the truth? Irritated with my self-doubt, I changed tactics. "Someone helped you, and it wasn't my mom. Who are you protecting, Persephone?"

"Luther."

My breath hitched. Had she just implicated Wetherill as her co-conspirator? Before I could speak, Persephone barreled on.

"From you. I'm protecting Luther from your wicked designs." The madwoman bared her teeth at me. "I know you want him for yourself. You ruined me because you want to marry Luther. But you can't. He would never debase himself with a partial spectrum like you." When she laughed, it came out breathy and wild. "You thought you could save your precious Airstrong by marrying Luther." She laughed harder. "You're going to die poor and pitiful. How do you like that, Charlotte? You'll never be better than me. Never."

My stomach sank. Grant was right. Persephone had nothing but hatred and lies for me. Wielding a mental-manipulation spell had fried her mind. She could no longer distinguish between reality and her own made-up stories. I wouldn't be getting anything useful out of her. Worse, Persephone's continued insistence of Mom's guilt despite her own fragile mental state would feed O'Hara's suspicions.

"Persephone, what can you tell us about the phoenix eggs?" I asked when she got herself under control.

"Don't touch them." She cackled. "Don't cook with them." She laughed harder. "What do you call someone who tames phoenixes? Dead." She thrummed her heels against the floor with mirth.

I sagged against the wall. For a second, I thought she was going to give us something useful, but she was simply amusing herself with children's jokes.

"They're the only bird that likes to sail. They're born with a—"

Boom!

The explosion shook the concrete foundation. I spun toward the door, bracing a hand against the wall. Quinn stood, wings flared, facing the direction of the sound, and Anderson peered out into the hall, a copper rod gripped in her fist. Persephone collapsed in breathless laughter.

"Was that a—" A second explosion cut off my question, shaking the brick walls. Was someone throwing phoenix eggs at the jail? That made even less sense than using one to attack Airstrong.

"Watch out!" Celine shouted.

Anderson sprang clear of the doorway seconds before the heavy panel slammed shut—locking Quinn out and us in. The elements vanished.

My pulse spiked, my breath going shallow. The room shrank around us. Scrambling for magic, I lunged for the door. "Quinn!"

Anderson brought me up short with a hand to my solar plexus. She tried the handle. It turned, but even when she braced a foot against the wall and tugged, the door didn't budge. We were sealed inside this tiny box.

I sagged against the wall, bracing a palm against the cool bricks. Black dots danced in my vision, panic pounding through my veins. No amount of mental clawing enabled me to touch the elements. We were trapped in a null field.

Anderson gave up on the door and whirled to face Celine. "Explain."

The protectorate stared in the direction of the last explosion, as if she could see through the brick wall. "The outer ward has been breached. It triggered the internal safety measures. We're on lockdown."

Sweat broke out along my scalp. I focused on taking slow, even breaths. This wasn't Lunacy Labyrinth. I wasn't trapped. The ceiling wouldn't cave in on us.

"The jail's defensive measures include imprisoning the staff?" Anderson demanded.

"Any chamber holding a prisoner is automatically placed in a null field. It's not a perfect system, but such safety measures are necessary." Celine appeared unruffled by Anderson's glare. "Especially when dealing with mentally imbalanced prisoners."

Everyone turned to Persephone. She had caught the mood of the room and was no longer laughing. Twisting her fingers into the hem of her tunic, she finished her interrupted sentence with a whisper, "Born with a boom."

"Kylie!" Quinn shouted, his voice muffled through the heavy wooden panel.

"Quinn!"

"Are you all right?" we both shouted at the same time.

"Hush," Anderson ordered. Keeping an eye on Persephone, she tilted her face toward the door and shouted, "Quinn, can you open the door?"

"It's sealed with the elements, and—*ouch*. They're electric."

I flinched, but a gesture from Anderson kept me quiet.

"The seal will only respond to staff," Celine said.

"Quinn, where is Warden Parisot?"

"On the roof. Someone's attacking us. A lot of people. I'm boosting Nolan, but I think they're stronger." Quinn's voice trembled.

"Fetch him," Anderson ordered.

"No!" I pushed past Anderson to tug on the door handle. "It could be dangerous."

"I'm no help to Parisot in here." Anderson gently but firmly pushed me aside. "Quinn, go now. Hurry."

I strained to hear Quinn's retreating footsteps. Half of me wanted to call him back; the other half urged him faster.

The jail was under siege, and I was trapped in an oversized coffin without magic. Air scraped into my lungs, harsh and thin. Throwing myself into battle alongside Anderson and the warden sounded like the better plan, especially if it meant I could protect Quinn.

"Who's the target?" Anderson asked. She prowled the cramped room, touching the walls and standing on the bench to reach the ceiling. If she was looking for a way out or a section not covered by the null field, she didn't find it.

Celine shifted out of her way. "We have a handful of outlaws in our cells. It could be any of them."

Including Persephone? I tried to picture Wetherill lobbing phoenix eggs at the jail, and my brain stuttered over the ludicrous image. If he was going to free his ex-fiancée from jail, he was more likely to bribe a judge than launch an assault. This had to be about a different criminal. If I hadn't been trapped in an elementless tomb, I might have been excited by the prospect of getting the scoop on a front-page story.

You're suspended, my traitorous brain reminded me. Oddly, the familiar bitterness soothed the edge off my panic.

I pressed my ear to the door. Nothing. Dropping to my hands and knees, I peered through the slender gap at the threshold. A steady glow of elemental light shone through the crack, but I couldn't make out anything else.

A boom reverberated through the jail walls, much closer than the earlier explosions. I ducked instinctively, curling against the door. The next explosion followed fast on its heels, even closer. The third vibrated the brick walls, grinding loose mortar into a fine dust.

"They've reached the jail," Anderson said. If she was nervous, it couldn't be heard in her tone.

I pressed my face to the floor again. Where was Quinn? What was taking him so long?

"It doesn't matter," Celine said. "The cells are reinforced with a dozen spells each. No one can break them, not even a platoon of full spectrums."

"Not even if they capture a warden?"

Celine's lips pinched. "It takes more than a single person to open a cell during lockdown."

"That's good to hear." Anderson ran a hand over her head, checking the braids holding her hair in place, then methodically stretched her arms and legs.

Persephone lunged to her feet only to be brought short by the chains anchored to the wall. "I want to go home. Now. Take me out of here. Release me!" Her voice elevated to a shriek.

"Sit down," Celine ordered. When Persephone didn't comply, the protectorate pressed a hand to Persephone's shoulder, forcing her back to the bench.

The next explosion drowned out Persephone's softer pleas. Ears throbbing, I rose to a crouch, my back pressed to the door. That explosion had been the closest yet.

"They're working this way, looking for a weakness," Anderson said with enviable composure. "Are they going to find it?"

Celine's grim look was answer enough. "Only the cells have extra reinforcements."

"But not this room?" I asked.

She shook her head. Any other response she might have given was lost beneath a deafening crash just beyond the chamber's walls. Dust rained from the brick ceiling, and the lamplight bounced in the same erratic tempo as my heart. I strained for the elements, searching and re-searching the barren room for any means of defending myself.

"Everyone, get into the corner," Anderson ordered, pointing to the wall beside the door. "Protectorate, put the prisoner in the back. Hurry."

Celine hesitated for a fraction of a second, then yanked a key out of her pocket. "Hands," she ordered Persephone.

"Yes, take these off. I can help." Persephone held her hands up to Celine.

Instead of unlocking the null cuffs, the protectorate pressed Persephone's hands to the bench, then placed a knee on top of them. Persephone tried to tug them free, and Celine exerted just enough pressure to still her. Unlocking the chain from the wall, the protectorate reattached it to her own belt, tethering Persephone to herself.

"What are you doing, woman? Free me. That's an order." When her most haughty tone didn't work, Persephone tried whining. "I don't want to die. Let me help. I have powerful magic. I'll save you."

Celine ignored her. With steely strength I hadn't expected from her petite frame, Celine maneuvered Persephone into the corner, then crouched in front of her.

"You too, Grayson," Anderson ordered, pointing to the space next to the woman who had tried to kill me.

When I didn't jump to comply, she manhandled me into position, pushing me down into a crouch with her. My shoulder mashed against Persephone's, her hair tangling with mine. I tensed, waiting for Persephone to strike, if not with her bound hands or feet, then with her teeth. Instead, she peered at me through lashes damp with tears.

"Don't let me die, Charlotte," she whispered.

"Keep your heads down and covered," Anderson instructed. "When they breach the wall, they'll puncture the null field. Be prepared to defend yourself."

Celine tucked Persephone's head to her chest, then

curled her body around the handcuffed woman like a shield. Anderson dropped one knee to the floor and covered her head with her hands, positioning herself between me and the outer wall. I ducked my head.

Our harsh breathing and Persephone's whimpers filled the silence.

Footsteps clattered in the inner hallway, quartz striking concrete in a growing crescendo. I lifted my head slightly, hope blossoming in my chest. Quinn was coming.

"Kylie! The warden can't—"

The room imploded.

5

T he concussion slammed me into the wall. Pain and sound battered my equilibrium, but the null field fractured. I surged for the elements, seizing every drop I could hold. Flames roared into the brick chamber, and I slammed a sheet of water in front of us. The fireball hit my shield and extinguished. The collision of magic rang in my head, spiking agony behind my eyeballs, and the elements slid from my grasp.

Panicked, I clawed for magic. It tore through my head, setting my brain on fire. Gritting my teeth, I maintained my grip on the elements and braced for the next attack.

My eyes watered and my ears rang. I couldn't get a full breath of air. The room jumped in my vision, shapes shrouded in thick shadows. Celine lay sprawled on the floor, her legs akimbo in front of her and half buried by broken brick and the fractured bench. Persephone cowered behind her, head buried in the corner. Celine's fist wrapped around the chain binding Persephone to her. Blood coated the protectorate's palms and smeared her chest and face. A splinter of wood as thick as my forearm protruded from her thigh.

Something heavy shoved down on my hip, then released me. I pushed up from my crouch, only to fall on my butt when the room spun in my vision. The wall vibrated against my spine. Shattered brick bit into my palms as I braced myself through a coughing fit that ignited a pulsing pain at the base of my skull. Dust hung heavily in the room, so thick I couldn't see the far wall, only a nebulous glow outlining the ragged opening torn through it.

A hand clamped down on my wrist. I jerked, swallowing a scream. Anderson slouched against the wall on my left. Blood soaked half her face, forming a gruesome slurry with the dust that covered her from scalp to boots. I reached for her, but she squeezed my wrist again, her blood-slick palm twisting grit painfully against my flesh. Her gaze bounced from my left eye to my right, assessing. I read her lips more than heard her words.

"Can you stand?"

I nodded shakily, not sure if I was telling the truth.

"Check the door."

"Celine needs help." My voice was hollow inside my eardrums, and I couldn't tell how loud I was speaking.

"I see. Secure the door."

Anderson took a deep breath, coughed, then winced and reached for her head. She didn't quite touch the cut buried in her hairline. Instead, she sagged into the wall, using it to push to herself feet. Once standing, she swayed in place, eyes closed. Blood dripped from her left pinkie.

Dread burrowed into my gut. Anderson looked as if she would topple over from a strong wind. With the protectorate incapacitated, we were easy pickings for whoever lurked beyond the dust.

"Grayson." Anderson sounded as if she spoke into a pillow. Sharp pain pricked my scalp when she fisted my hair, forcing me to look her in the eye. "Stay with me. Check the door."

I nodded, wincing when the move pulled my hair. When Anderson released me, several strands stuck to her bloody hand and were yanked out. I attempted to take a deep breath to calm my fluttering heart, but dust scratched the back of my throat, setting off another coughing fit. Tugging my sleeve over my nose, I flashed back to being trapped in Lunacy Labyrinth. My head swam. The wall shuddered against my back, sprinkling dirt down my collar.

Door. This room has a door. The thought spurred me to my knees. I pivoted, distantly aware of lacerating pain in my knees. Grasping the door handle, I twisted and pulled. Numbness filled my head, stealing my magic. The door might as well as have been fused to the brick; not even hanging my weight off the handle budged it.

"Kylie!" Quinn's voice pierced the ringing in my ears. The wall shuddered again. "Ky-LIE!"

"Quinn!" The shout burst from me a second before I considered the stupidity of announcing my presence with our attackers lurking just outside. Not having been trapped inside the brick box when it imploded, they likely could still hear just fine.

"Kylie! What's happening?"

I pressed my mouth to the door's seam, attempting to speak softer. "Can you open the door?"

"It's still warded. Why can't I feel you?"

"Null field," I whispered, sinking back on my heels. Despite the breach, the magic-negating spell remained embedded in the interior wall. My ability to grasp the elements should have meant Quinn's boost could reach me, but the jail's defenses were thwarting him. Or he couldn't snake his boost through the jail and around the outside to connect with me via the gap in the exterior wall.

Pain pulsed in my temples, and I decided I would have to puzzle it out later. All that mattered was I couldn't penetrate the field on this side, and Quinn couldn't break the ward on his side. Six inches of brick and magic separated us, but it might as well have been a mountain.

"Persephone Kwan," boomed a strange man's voice, "we've come for you."

Persephone lifted her head, blinking wet eyes. I froze, horror sizzling down my spine. Anderson, Celine, and I had just been promoted from people in the wrong place at the wrong time to targets.

"Get Nolan. Hurry," I whispered to Quinn. Then I shoved away from the wall and grabbed the elements, fumbling them in my fear. What was going to come through that opening?

Anderson jabbed my side to get my attention. She pointed to the outer wall, which was still shrouded in a suspended cloud of dirt, then at herself and me, indicating we should fan out to either side.

Heart thumping, I nodded. Anderson wouldn't have been assigned to the ranks of an FPD investigator's squad unless she was exceptional, which put her among the most elite warriors in the nation. If I had to be pinned down by unknown enemies with anyone, I would have preferred Grant, but Anderson made a good second choice. Following her instructions was the best way to make it out of this nightmare alive.

Together we crept across the room, half blinded by the dust. My lungs burned for a full breath of clean oxygen, the scratch of a cough clawing the back of my throat. Broken bricks twisted beneath my feet, stealing my balance. I winced with each clatter and scrape. Over the buzz humming in my ears, I could make out the scuffle of footsteps on the lava rocks in the yard, as well as indeterminate shouts. Crashes and electric crackles reverberated in the yard. The battle raged on, with either the jail's wards or Nolan defending the facility. Hopefully both.

Light flared outside, highlighting the ragged hole blown through the brick wall. Footsteps crunched closer, and I stilled. Across the room, Anderson did the same, crouching as if preparing to launch herself over the mound of rubble. I gave the room one more hopeless sweep, silently cursing its lack of furniture to hide behind. We weren't getting out of here without a fight.

"We've got an in!" someone shouted. A siphon settled over the hole, drawing the dust from the room, stealing our camouflage.

My pulse thundered in my ears. The elements trembled in my grip as I prepared a ward. I waited for Anderson to give a signal, not wanting to give us away too soon. Steps pounded closer, loose lava rock pinging off the side of the jail. Damn it, where was the warden to break us out of this death trap?

Anderson dropped an illusion over me, hiding me. I shot her a desperate look, grateful for the cover but feeling no less helpless. She didn't try to disguise herself, and I couldn't make myself turn my back on the opening to check to see if she'd disguised Celine and Persephone too.

A ball of flame descended along the outside of the wall, its movements slow and controlled. I adjusted my mental spell to include more water, trying not to fixate on the power behind the seething globe. Heat flared inside the room, drying the sweat on my neck and face. Puffs of flames escaped the fireball, licking the air before dissipating.

"Can we get inside?" someone asked, the voice high enough that I couldn't determine if it was a man or woman.

A head poked around the edge of the wall. Backlit by the flames, I could only make out the outline—slender shoulders encased in an orange top, spindly arms, round face, and a wild topknot of black hair. Anderson shot a null net at the figure, but he cursed and ducked out of sight. Anderson's spell slapped the wall and dissipated.

"There's a fed inside," Topknot shouted. His fireball zipped into the air. It must have exploded out of sight, because light flashed across the opening, then dimmed.

"What's a fed doing here?" hissed a scared-sounding boy.

"I hate those Pentagon bastards."

"Who is it? The captain? That bastard owes us."

"It's a woman," Topknot said. He had moved away from the opening, but not far.

"Doesn't matter, Donny. Kill her," a gravelly voice commanded. He was the first to sound old enough to drink.

"You heard Apollo. Kill her," the scared boy urged.

A flurry of crashes and thumps sprayed across the rocky yard, eliciting a string of curses and shouts from the men outside. Anderson mouthed the words I had been thinking: *Fire Eaters.*

These men—and boys—had all the hallmarks of the Fire Eater gang: young, violent, and exclusively fire elementals. The city guards and FPD had been attempting to eradicate the band of youthful criminal for years, but they kept recruiting new members from the disenchanted population in the impoverished district known colloquially as the blight. Having lived on the fringe of the blight for the last couple of years, I was familiar with the antics of Fire Eaters as well as their rival gangs. Typically, they confined their battles to their own territory, though. Why would they be across town, attacking the heavily fortified jail in an attempt to free Persephone? It made no sense.

Unless *they* were Persephone's accomplices in the thefts, but that made even less sense than their current attack. How would she, a high-society full spectrum, have made an alliance with the savage mono-elemental gang? Even if she had, Fire Eaters weren't known for their subtlety. They had even less of a chance than Persephone of sneaking into Airstrong undetected and back out with banned spells and phoenix eggs—though they were far more likely to be fascinated rather than terrified of phoenix eggs.

"Why won't that bastard die already?" Apollo demanded. Air whistled with elemental weapons, but his guttural voice carried over it. "Varun, Lafe, get to the roof already. Take out that warden. Where is Obie?"

"Obie's dead," came the responding cry, a crack breaking the boy's voice.

Apollo cursed, and heavy footsteps sprinted away from us. His orders came back on a fading shout. "Donny, Melvin, kill the fed and bring me Kwan. We're getting paid."

Anderson used their distraction to scramble over the pile of rubble to one side of the opening, pressing her back to the remaining section of the outer wall. Her breathing appeared strained, and she wobbled in place despite the wall at her back. The spell disguising me wavered.

A spear of fire shot through the opening, imploding against the wall where Anderson had been standing moments earlier. Another volley of flames followed, scorching a black mark into the brick. Persephone's alarmed cry was cut short, as if someone had silenced her. I flattened myself to the opposite wall, turning my face away from the scalding heat and keeping the opening in my sight. My fingers brushed the edge of Anderson's illusion, and the spell cracked.

Anderson glanced at me, and I shook my head. I couldn't hide. No matter how well trained and extraordinary Anderson was, she had suffered a grievous head wound. I could see how much effort it cost her just to remain on her feet. She needed my help.

"Reinforcements should be on their way." Celine's rasped comment made me jump. The breathy quality of her voice harmonized with the stream of flames, and I chanced a glance in her direction. Her tan complexion was pale beneath a smudged layer of dirt, the bright golden beam casting gaunt shadows around her pain-bright eyes. A band of cloth cinched her upper thigh above the splinter of wood embedded in her leg. Blood oozed from the wound, but not as heavily as before. Anderson must have helped triage her wound while I was distracted by the nullified door.

"Defense only, Grayson," Anderson whispered. "Save your strength."

The flames subsided, but heat radiated from the charred wall. Sweat soaked my grimy eyebrows and dripped off my chin. I swiped it aside with the back of my hand and prepared a water-based ward. A muffled argument ensued outside, then Topknot—Donny—peeked through the opening.

Anderson was ready with a bolt of lightning. The call for her murder must have altered her objective from capturing the assailants to incapacitating them. Donny flung himself to the ground, and the lightning fizzled against the brick. Anderson blinked rapidly. Her aim had been more than two feet off. How badly was she concussed?

A scattered shot of fiery arrows blasted through the opening. I yanked a water-and-ice shield in front of myself, Celine, and Persephone. Pain pounded through my skull with each deflected arrow, and my magic thinned under the assault. Anderson flattened against the outer wall, relying on it for protection while shooting her own blazing knives out the ragged opening. Someone outside screamed, and the onslaught ceased while curses rent the air.

I bent in half, bracing my hands against my knees as I tried to catch my breath. Sweat dripped from my nose, partly from exertion, partly from the heat radiating from the brick walls. My ward trembled, and I let it collapse.

Anderson peeked into the yard, fired off several short bursts of knife-sharp ice, then launched a wad of magic into the sky. I caught the shape of a message spell embedded in something larger before the magic disappeared from sight.

"Catch that!" Donny yelled.

Fire speared into the sky after Anderson's magic, and she used that distraction to fling null nets out of the opening. The complex spells fluctuated and stretched, the intricate weaves unraveling midair. Anderson flattened herself to the wall, her lips pinched with pain. Fresh blood oozed from her temple.

Quinn, now would be a really good time for you to show up with the warden, I pleaded silently.

"Hey! Where are you going?" Donny shouted.

"We gotta leave," a young boy whined. "That was a call for reinforcements. We're screwed if we stay."

"That bitch burned me. We're not going anywhere until she pays."

"No way. I don't wanna die. We gotta—"

"Link. Now, Melvin, or so help me . . ."

"But I—" The dull thump of a fist meeting flesh cut off Melvin's protest.

"We're done playing around," Donny yelled at us. "We're gonna roast you alive."

"Wait!" Anderson's voice rang with authority. "Persephone Kwan is in here. You could kill her."

"She's in there?"

"I don't care," Donny said over Melvin's exclamation.

"Apollo said—"

"I don't care what Apollo says."

"What about the money?"

"Link," Anderson whispered while they were distracted. "Hurry, Grayson."

I thrust an even balance of the elements at Anderson, and she absorbed it into her magic. The flavor of her magical signature flowed back through the bond, steady and warm like a banked fire on the shore of a serene forest lake. A weaker bundle of magic joined the link, disrupting the calm exuding from Anderson with the sensation of a choking bundle of frosted vines burrowed in rocky soil. Protectorate Celine.

I cataloged both women's magical signatures even as Anderson constructed a shield across the blast opening. The tug of the elements through me hurt like an overused muscle. If I survived, I promised myself a full day of recuperation—as soon as I tracked down the missing phoenix eggs.

"Send the Kwan woman out," Donny ordered.

"I don't want to die," Persephone whimpered. "Let me out. Let me out now. I want out *now*."

I shared a glance with Anderson. She didn't attempt another attack, and now that I could feel the shaky quality of her magic, I marveled that she had been able to cobble together the earlier spells. Instead, she muffled Persephone's escalating screeches and turned her own head so her voice projected into the yard.

"Melvin is right, Donny; I called for reinforcements. But if you leave now, you might avoid being arrested."

"Liar!" Donny shouted. He and Melvin scrambled across the lava rock, retreating. "You're gonna die, fed scum."

A fireball sprang into existence with a roar of consumed air. The flames built, flooding the yard with light. Donny stood out in the open, a spindly figure with rage contorting his teenage face. Loose strands of his long hair fluttered in the wind gusting off the fireball. A smaller boy in ragged clothes slumped at his side, one hand holding a swollen eye, the other braced on the ground as Donny siphoned magic through him. The fireball grew, rolling into a tight knot of white-hot heat three feet across.

Anderson thrust control of the link to me. "Strengthen the ward and hold it. No matter what."

I fumbled with the combined magic of the other women. They both felt fragile within the link, especially Celine. Anderson's ward faltered, the spell hiccupping as I took control.

"Brace yourself," Anderson warned.

Donny flung the fireball with frightening strength. Heat flooded the room, then the fireball struck the ward. I screamed as pain flared across my brain, burning through my synapses even as the fireball ate through the ward. Desperate, I yanked magic from Celine and Anderson to strengthen the spell. Celine moaned. Undeterred, Donny fed more magic into his spell, and the fireball swelled to fill the opening.

I raised a hand to protect my face from the heat, shielding my eyes from the blinding light. Molten air scorched my throat and smoldered in my lungs. I poured water into the ward as fast as it evaporated, but the fireball raged on unaffected. Terror tasted metallic on my tongue. Holding the passive spell took every ounce of my energy and everything I could draw from Anderson and Celine. I didn't have the strength to fight back.

Anderson flinched away from the outer wall, her uniform smoking. The bricks glowed like embers, and I prayed they would hold and not crumble beneath the searing flame.

"It's too hot. I can't breathe. I'm dying," Persephone moaned, voicing my thoughts. If Donny didn't relent soon, we would bake in this brick oven. I licked dry lips, tasting blood.

Anderson grabbed a brick and flung it into the yard. It sailed through my ward, which wasn't designed to keep anything from exiting, but I couldn't tell where it landed. The roar of flames filled the chamber, and the light covered the hole in the wall, disguising everything beyond it. Anderson grabbed another brick fragment and heaved it, then another. She wasn't giving up. People were coming for us—powerful, full-spectrum FPD warriors. We only had to hold on a bit longer.

A clangor emanated from the hallway, loud enough to be heard over the flames. My heart sank. Had Fire Eaters breached the jail's ward in a different location? From the heavy pounding and scraping, a full-blown battle waged in the hallway. Something slammed into the wall, and the door rattled in its frame. Quinn roared. My stomach knotted as I pictured Fire Eaters attacking my friend.

My ward faltered, and flames burst through, licking along the ceiling. Persephone screamed. I jerked more magic through the link and resealed the opening. The bond faltered, the influx of magic thinning. Frantically, I searched for the reason, spotting Celine slumped on her side, unconscious. I dug deeper into my own well, ignoring the agony that pulsed with it. I couldn't fail us.

The racket in the hallway changed, becoming rhythmic. *Crack. Crack. Crack.* Someone was trying to break through. If it had been the warden, he would have opened the door with his magic.

"Gather up," Anderson panted between brick tosses.

Shading my eyes, I stumbled toward the protectorate. Persephone yanked at the chain securing her handcuffs to Celine's waist, rocking the unconscious woman. The jagged chunk of wood wobbled sickeningly where it protruded from the protectorate's thigh, and fresh blood slicked the cloth around the wound, trickling into a puddle on the floor.

"Stop that," I ordered.

Persephone ignored me, tugging harder. I stomped a foot down on the chain, jerking Persephone off balance and forcing her hands to the floor. Celine lolled against the wall, her chin tipped toward her chest. How long did it take O'Hara to mobilize his team? Shouldn't they have been here by now?

Quashing a wave of despair, I pushed Persephone back into the corner.

"Why are you doing this, Charlotte?" she whimpered.

"For your safety." I grunted at the effort to remain upright when Persephone clutched my leg. Her fingers dug like claws into my jeans. The fireball shoved itself another inch into the opening, my ward bowing beneath the pressure. I shuffled into a wider stance, trying to shield both women with my body. Anderson half walked, half stumbled to the wall next to Celine's feet and drew her knife.

"When they breach the inner wall, drop the ward over

us. Let them roast their own," Anderson said. "Focus on protecting us."

My stomach roiled, but I nodded.

Breathless, we stared at the inner wall. The bricks trembled, cracks snaking through the mortar. Any second now, Fire Eaters would burst through from the other side. I pulled harder on the elements. I didn't have the energy to sustain the ward on the outer wall as I built a protective layer around us. I would have a fraction of a second to transition the magic from one ward to the next. If I got it wrong, we would all die a horrible, agonizing death.

The first brick fell. The next punch scattered pulverized brick all the way to our feet. I caught a glimpse of gold on the other side. My stomach squeezed into my heart. On the next deafening hit, Quinn burst through the wall. Fragmented bricks ricocheted off the walls, pelting my bare arms and face. I hardly felt them. Quinn's front feet landed inside the room, his belly catching on the remaining wall. Electricity bit at his flanks.

He had broken down a solid wall by hammering through an electric ward. For me.

Quinn hopped all the way through the hole. The room shrank around him, and when he threw his head back and unleashed a roar, the furious cry vibrated my rib cage. Magic burst through me, his boost feeding Anderson and me simultaneously and tripling the elements I held.

I spun toward the fireball and shoved it. Hard.

The deadly sphere shot across the jail yard. Someone yelled in surprise, then the fireball exploded. Cool air rushed into the opening, and I gulped it down. Quinn surged across the room, headed for the dark jail yard, but I stopped him with a shout. I didn't know what danger lurked outside, and I didn't want him rushing into a battle he couldn't win.

"Give me the link," Anderson ordered, her voice a hoarse rasp. I scrutinized her as she reclaimed control of our combined magic, reassured when she didn't stagger under the increased power. With enviable skill, she launched a glowball into the yard even as she swirled a chilly ice-and-air spell through the room. Bricks crackled and mortar creaked, fracture lines webbing along the walls as they cooled.

"Watch the prisoner." Anderson limped to the opening, peeked out, then climbed into the yard. She paused with her hand on the wall, pulsing magic into the jail. The building's ward responded, stretching around her hand. Staggering to the opposite side of the busted wall, she dragged the spell with her. When she planted her hand on the jail's wall again, the spell sealed itself across the opening.

Even linked, I couldn't tell how she had done it.

Anderson's footsteps faded into the night, but I tracked her through the link. One null net formed and anchored faster than I could follow. The next null net slammed into place with a muffled male curse.

I lifted trembling fingers to brush hair out of my face. The world moved in slow motion, my brain still hyped for the next attack, but my body was too tired to do more than stand in one place.

Celine tipped, falling against my leg. I staggered under her weight, bracing a hand on Quinn's wing to stay upright. Persephone wriggled behind her, jostling the injured woman. I propped Celine against the wall, then whirled to stomp on the chain binding Persephone to Celine. "Hold still."

Persephone lifted her arms. The chain remained flat on

the floor. Shoving against the wall, Persephone stood. The null cuff dangled from one wrist, useless. Persephone's eyes burned with hatred hotter than any Fire Eater's attack.

"This is for destroying my life," she spat. Charged elements whipped through the chamber. The hair on the back of my neck stood on end as the air grew brittle. My breath caught. The last time I experienced this sensation, I had been battling thunderbirds. Then, it had been pouring rain, but there was no mistaking the biting feeling of electricity filling the air, one spark from igniting into lightning.

My fist shot out, connecting with Persephone's jaw before the thought crystallized in my brain. Her head snapped to the side, and a lightning bolt shot into the ceiling. The boom rocked the room, vibrating my head like a struck gong. Brick crumbled, bombarding my scalp. Quinn's wing braced my butt when I collapsed. With a shove, he propelled me to my feet. I lunged for the dangling cuff on Persephone's wrist, but I miscalculated which of the three cuffs in my vision was the real one. My hand wrapped around air. Persephone screamed, her magic gathering again. On my second swipe, I caught the cuff and yanked with all my strength. Persephone fell. I dropped on top of her, grabbed her free hand, and snapped the cuff into place, severing her connection to the elements.

A shriek tore from Persephone's throat, raw with pain and fury. The cuff key she had pilfered from Celine's unconscious body clattered to the floor. Persephone lunged for it, but Quinn stomped on the key and shoved it out of reach. Her screams devolved into curses, then into sobs.

I scooted clear of Persephone and dropped my pounding head into my palms.

6

For the second time that night, I stood on the sidelines while FPD warriors restored order in the aftermath of violence. O'Hara and his team stormed the jail minutes after Quinn burst into our room. Coordinating with the sheriff and a small army of protectorates and deputies summoned by Nolan, the investigator brought a swift end to the Fire Eaters' attack. Healers swarmed in the moment the fighting stopped. Once Celine had been stabilized and transported to the nearest healer hall and Persephone had been carted back to her cell, an elderly healer knelt before me amid the broken, blackened bricks.

"You again?" he asked.

I blinked at him, recognizing his magical signature though not his face. He had been one of the primary healers to patch me up last night after the banned spells had battered my mind and body. I tried to cobble together an appropriate statement of gratitude or even to recall his name, but my mind remained blank.

"I thought you were a journalist," he said.

"I am," I croaked.

"You should find a safer profession." Tendrils of his magic whispered across my skull, sinking deeper. Distant pain twinged through my brain, and he hummed with satisfaction. "Remarkable. No, don't take that as praise. I believe you were told to rest for at least a week. You're lucky you haven't done permanent damage to yourself . . ." He trailed off, his gaze unfocused as his magic flitted across my injuries. Tsking, he reinforced the residual spell laced through my lungs, cleansing them for the second time that night, this time as much from dust as smoke. My eardrums received delicate healing that hissed and popped but took away the pain and ringing. Everything else hurt as he delved sterilizing magic into lacerations on my knees, then a smattering of shallower cuts on my hands, arms, and cheeks, though he didn't heal the wounds. He also did nothing for the bruising pain of my knuckles where they had crunched against Persephone's jaw or the sunburn-like sensitivity of my face from the blazing heat of the fireball.

When the healer sat back, the room spun, and I braced a hand on the ground beside my hip to stay upright. For a second, I couldn't tell if I was going to pass out or vomit. Thankfully, both sensations passed as I concentrated on taking deep breaths. When I opened my eyes, the healer was watching me closely. I gave him a wan smile.

"Thank you. Again." I could no longer hear my own pulse echoing hollowly in my ears and could no longer feel each beat throb against the inside of my skull. It was enough. The rest of the injuries I could live with.

"Can you do anything for gargoyles?" I asked. Scratches etched Quinn's stomach, and a deep gouge cut into the bend of his wing, but it was his front paws that worried me. Thin fractures crisscrossed his pads and toes, half hidden beneath the rough abrasions and nicks marring his citrine flesh. He hadn't said anything, but it had to be excruciating.

"Unfortunately, no," the man said. "Though I've heard rumor of a gargoyle healer on the other side of the city."

"Mika Stillwater. We're familiar with her. Quinn, can you walk?"

"It's not that bad. Did Persephone say—"

"She said nothing." Anger made my voice harsh, and I brushed my fingers across his forehead in silent apology. I wasn't mad at Quinn; I was furious with myself. I had learned nothing—not one new detail about how Persephone had obtained the stolen spells or if she knew about the missing phoenix eggs. My whole body ached. My synapses and spirit were battered. Worse, Quinn had gotten hurt. Again.

All for nothing.

Just as Grant had predicted.

I pushed to my feet, using the wall for support.

"Your body has been through a great deal of trauma," the healer said, rising easily, one hand splayed between us as if he expected to have to catch me. "Too much healing isn't good for you, and we've already pushed your body to the limit. Perhaps this is for the best. Maybe if you have some reminders of your mortality, you'll take it easy."

I straightened my spine. If I showed weakness, he would haul me off to a healer hall, and Quinn would insist on coming with me rather than returning home to Mika. Cobbling together the last shreds of my energy, I plodded into the hall. Weariness weighted each step, but I managed to traverse the hallway to the lobby without stumbling. Quinn squeezed close to my side, padding gingerly.

"Grayson, hold up," Anderson called from deeper in the jail.

Biting back a sigh, I pivoted to face her. She closed the distance between us with a brisk stride, her clear-eyed gaze scanning me. The blood had been cleaned from the side of her face, the wound at her temple closed to a faint pink line of new skin. Aside from the grime coating her uniform and hair, the FPD warrior looked as if she had spent the evening relaxing, not in a harrowing battle. Perversely, her vigor amplified my fatigue. O'Hara jogged up the jail's corridor behind her. The wiry investigator swept me and Quinn in the same assessing glance, then he focused on the healer.

"Your skills are needed in the back," O'Hara said.

With one final squint in my direction and an admonishment to rest, the healer rushed off. O'Hara waited until he was out of earshot before asking, "Who knew you were coming here tonight?"

"You were there when I made the decision," I said, not bothering to hide my annoyance. "So you and your squad, Grant and his squad, and of course, Nathan Aspell, Luther Wetherill's favorite reporter."

"And your mom," O'Hara said.

"And Mom. Good memory." I was too tired to filter my words, but at least exhaustion robbed my voice of my intended sarcastic tone. "Were you able to capture the Fire Eaters? Did they tell you who paid them to break Persephone out?"

"We're looking into it."

I gritted my teeth. "Persephone is broke. If she promised them payment, it was a bluff. It's more likely whoever her accomplice is made the payment."

"Is that what Persephone told you?"

"No, it's common sense. I may not have your investigator training, but I have a brain. I know how to parse together motive and means, and how to do research." Quinn pressed his nose into my hip, likely to remind me to watch my tongue. Instead, it reminded me that every second we stood around was another second he suffered. I crossed my arms. "Anderson can tell you anything she said. Can you lend—"

"She can't speak to what was said when she wasn't in the room."

I shot Anderson a confused glance.

"After I ducked out," she said, jerking a thumb in the direction of the last location of the Fire Eaters.

I refrained from rolling my eyes. Only an FPD warrior would call leaping into a fray against powerful pyromaniacs *ducking out*. "Right. Let's see. Persephone expressed her wishes for my death, described some inventive ways I could do harm to myself, and then sobbed. It wasn't exactly coherent or illuminating."

O'Hara's dark gaze flicked from my eyes to my mouth and back, searching for a lie. "And before that, did you learn anything?"

"Only that this was a complete waste of time." Bitterness clipped my words. "Quinn needs a healer. Can you get someone from your team take us home?"

O'Hara studied me a moment longer before shaking his head. "I can't spare anyone. You'll have to contact your own ride." He pivoted on a heel and started to walk away, then turned back to face me. "See that you wait outside the jail's perimeter. This is an active crime scene. Anderson will see you out."

I stared, slack-jawed, at his retreating back until Anderson motioned toward the door. Clicking my teeth closed, I trudged ahead of her toward the exit.

The jail's sturdy door swung open with surprisingly little effort. I squinted into the day-bright yard. The circling glow-balls had been replaced with twice as many stationary lights. A cleared path of concrete arrowed from the jail to the gate, the crushed lava rock pushed aside, the traps deactivated along the route. I shielded my eyes with my hand, and Quinn and I stepped into the yard. Anderson followed on our heels, closing the door behind her.

My gaze snagged on a black outline marring the jail wall. After a few steps, the crude shape of a flying phoenix became discernible—the Fire Eaters' tag, sketched in charcoal. I had forgotten they considered phoenixes their mascot. Coincidence? Or did they take part in the theft of the eggs? Maybe a good night's sleep would help me figure it out.

Halfway to the gate, Anderson stepped in front of me, and I stumbled to a halt. She pulled a small packet from her pocket and placed it in my hand. "I thought Monaghan exaggerated your capabilities in his reports, but I was wrong."

I glanced at the packet. It was a Quick Boost, a specially formulated powder for enhancing elemental and physical endurance—or in my case, delaying my collapse.

"Thank you." I might have fooled the healer, but Anderson had felt how much energy I expended through our link.

The jerk of Anderson's chin could have been a nod or a gesture toward the gate. "I think you can make it the rest of the way on your own."

It wasn't until she strode away that I realized the taciturn woman had given me a compliment.

Now I really wanted to know what Grant had said about me in his reports.

A brackish odor wafted from the packet when I ripped it open, and my mouth twisted reflexively in disgust. Nevertheless, I gratefully tipped the contents into my mouth. I gagged, swallowed convulsively twice, and scraped my tongue on the roof of my mouth. Quick Boosts had all the flavor appeal of licking the underside of a bunyip, but by the time the urge to vomit subsided, energy edged back my fatigue.

Quinn and I continued our plod to the perimeter gate, heads swiveling to take in the destruction of the yard. Small craters and divots disrupted the layer of lava rocks, exposing blackened dirt. One long channel ran from the front wall and out of sight behind the jail, as if something— or someone—large had been dragged across the yard. A jagged pillar of glass spiked from the ground on our left, a patchwork of bloody handprints dotting its surface. Icicles dripped from the edge of the roof, the puddle beneath them a slurry of ash and pulverized lava rocks. Two small wards crackled on the right, the first empty, the far one containing a small, limp figure in trademark Fire Eater orange. I didn't look at it too closely; I didn't want to know if the boy was dead. This had been a battle, and the Fire Eaters had attempted to kill us to reach Persephone, but they were still children or hardly older. Their deaths served no one.

Turning away, I surreptitiously searched for Grant. I kept expecting him to barrel around a corner or shove through the gate, ready with a lecture for me about caution and safety. Even if he hadn't been with O'Hara when the investigator received Anderson's call for help, Grant couldn't have overlooked the attack. He was the city's FPD captain; it was his job to be the first on the scene for any large-scale acts of magical violence. Which meant something more pressing occupied him and his squad.

The thought did nothing to ease the tightness in my chest.

"How did all these people get here so fast?" Quinn asked, drawing my attention forward.

Beyond the jail's perimeter wall and behind a shiny new soundproof ward that hadn't existed when we entered, reporters milled in a camera-wielding mass.

"Loud and flashy things tend to attract journalists." I shot Quinn a wry look, and his canines peeked out in a quick smile. If Dahlia hadn't suspended me from the *Terra Haven Chronicle*—and if I hadn't been trapped inside the jail —we would have been among the crush clamoring outside the gate for a good picture and a solid quote.

My steps slowed. No one had exited the jail yet to address the journalists' questions. We would be the first. We would be the ones everyone pressed for a quote. We would be the ones they snapped pictures of.

I bit my bottom lip, weighing our options. O'Hara had been insistent that we leave the jail grounds, and a glance over my shoulder confirmed Anderson was watching from just outside the jail door to make sure we complied with the investigator's order. I didn't have the luxury of waiting for the sheriff to give a statement and attempting sneak out without anyone noticing us. I also couldn't send a message to Grant from inside the jail; a net of elements capped the grounds, preventing any spells from passing through.

I sighed, relinquishing the faint hope that the shocking nature of a gang-fueled attack on the jail would cause this story to eclipse the phoenix hatching at Airstrong. The moment I stepped through the jail's gate, I would be outed in yet another Airstrong heiress scandal. My presence would inevitably tie the jailbreak to the phoenix hatching. The papers would rake Mom and Airstrong through the muck even harder.

Quinn glanced over his shoulder at me, wincing when

he twisted a paw. "Should we wait?" he asked, obviously thinking along the same lines.

"We can't." And not just because Anderson was starting to scowl. Quinn needed healing. "Do you think you can fly out from here?"

Quinn eyed the spell-laden air and shook his head.

"All right. Once we're through the gate, get to a clear spot and take off. I'll meet you at home. There's no reason for you to wait."

"I should stay with you."

"No, you should get to Mika. I promise to wait for Grant. But I don't know how long it's going to take him." Or why he wasn't already present.

I stamped down hard on the squiggle of anxiety worming in my gut. Soon enough, Grant would be here, pointing out that he had been right and this had been a fool's errand. I'd happily listen to his admonition while he whisked me home to my warm bed. But I wouldn't be able to sleep until Quinn was healed.

"Plus," I added, seeing Quinn wasn't convinced, "the reporters aren't going to let me through easily." As much as I loved my profession, it had a darker side. The waiting journalists were hungry for a story, and they would press me until they got something they could use for their articles. Especially those reporting for the gossip rags and less-reputable papers, which lately had become fixated on publishing ludicrous, chimerical stories about me. "You can sneak around and—"

"I'm not leaving your side."

Despite Quinn's mulish expression, fear clouded his eyes. It occurred to me this wasn't about the reporters; it was about feeling safe. It must have been terrifying for Quinn, trapped inside the jail, not knowing what was happening to me. Right now, he needed the reassurance of my presence at his side, even if it meant delaying his own healing. I swallowed my protest and nodded instead. "You're right. We're a team. We'll elbow through them together."

I tugged the gate open. Flashes popped in my face. A surge of journalists pressed forward, mouths moving in questions I couldn't yet hear from the quiet side of the soundproof ward. Bracing myself, I crossed the gate's threshold. The thick spell clung to my skin, and I stumbled as I cleared its resistance. Dozens of voices shouted my name. Quinn shoved through the magic field with none of his usual grace, knocking against my leg and whipping his tail out for balance. The citrine tip clanged against the gate's metal frame, the high note cutting through the journalists' cacophony. For a suspended second, everyone was silent, then questions bombarded us.

"Harriet, how did you know Fire Eaters would strike the jail tonight?"

"Was this an assassination attempt on Persephone Kwan?"

"Are you protecting Kwan?"

I shoved forward a step, blinded by a kaleidoscope of flashes and disoriented by the swirling recording spheres eager to pounce on my words. Quinn glued himself to my side, tail tucked tight to his hindquarters and wings clamped to his sides. I tried to peer over the reporters' heads to plot our escape route, but I couldn't see beyond the people in front of me.

"Did you summon the Fire Eaters?"

"Is it true you're scared that Kwan will tell the world you orchestrated the Airstrong thefts?"

"I thought Captain Monaghan was your boyfriend. So where is he, Harriet?"

Give me some space, and I'll find out. Recording a message while being verbally bombarded by this mob would be next to impossible. It would have to wait until we were clear. With that in mind, I kept my head down and inched another step forward, pressing uncomfortably close to the stranger in front of me. That didn't seem to faze him. He shoved a recording sphere between us and bellowed his question.

"What happened in Dead Man's Swamp?"

"Harriet! I heard you wrestled a thunderbird. Can you tell us more?" the woman beside him blurted out.

"Harriet, whose idea was it to go to the swamp, yours or the captain's?"

"Harriet, did you—"

"My name is Kylie." A dozen spheres snapped around me as if magnetized to my mumbled words.

"You look terrible, Kylie," a man near my elbow said with cheerful enthusiasm. "What happened in there?"

I gave him a flat look. He was probably right. My shirt and pants were stained with dried blood and covered in ash, some of it from the jail, some from Airstrong. Grit coated my scalp, and more ground between my toes deep inside my boots. My hair hung in a snarl around my hot face, which I suspected was bright red from being partially cooked. Dirt powdered my tongue when I licked my lips, and it was caked beneath my fingernails. I was cut, bruised, and battered. If I were a man, he would have said I looked heroic. Instead, he insulted me and thought my vanity would insist I defend myself.

I hoped Quinn memorized his face and put him on his never-enhance list.

"You've had a rough couple of days. It might help to tell your side of the story," he cajoled.

The reporters held their collective breaths, waiting for my response.

"Perhaps one on one," he pushed.

"Our press room is only three blocks away," offered a female journalist from *The Terra Havener*, the *Chronicle's* main competition.

"It's been a long night," I said. "I just want to go home." I attempted to squeeze through a gap between two people, but they pressed together tighter.

"How did your secret meeting with Persephone Kwan go?" a familiar male voice called out from the back of the crowd.

My stomach sank. Of course Nathan was here. It wasn't enough that he had slithered past the guards to get exclusive access to Airstrong's destruction. Now he had a second chance to denigrate me and my family in the press. What an exciting, red-letter night for Nathan.

"I know you and Persephone are old friends. Didn't you visit her estate often as a child? She must trust you," he continued. "Did this covert meeting have anything to do with the phoenix egg hatching at Airstrong? Did you two discuss the remaining missing phoenix eggs allegedly stolen from Airstrong?"

His words ran like lightning through the reporters. They might have known about the egg that hatched hours earlier, but judging by their shocked expressions and the feverish light sparking in their eyes, they hadn't known multiple phoenix eggs had been stolen from Airstrong.

I clamped my lips shut. Anything I said would be turned against me. The gossip rags would twist my words to fit whatever dramatized narrative they invented, and the rest were little better, Nathan included. *Especially* Nathan. He had mastered the art of cherry-picking quotes to undermine the public's trust in my parents and their business, all while writing for the most respected paper in Terra Haven.

"How many eggs were stolen from Airstrong?" shouted the first journalist to recover after Nathan's announcement.

"Did you find any phoenix eggs in Dead Man's Swamp?"

"If the eggs were stolen, why did one hatch at Airstrong's warehouse tonight?"

Finally someone had a good question, though sadly it was the last. Increasingly absurd queries continued to batter me: Did Persephone have the eggs in prison with her? Were my parents breeding phoenixes so they could overthrow the government? Was this all a spat over Persephone's fiancé? With her out of the picture, would I try to "snag" Wetherill? Was I a secret member of the Fire Eaters? Were my parents?

I tucked my head and barreled several steps in the general direction of the street, doing my best to give nothing away in my expression. The questions about Wetherill were almost my undoing; I managed not to sneer, but I did shudder in revulsion.

"What is your reaction to your boyfriend arresting your mother?"

My head whipped up. Nathan's brown eyes brightened with delight when he saw his words hit home. Sensing my vulnerability, the rest of the reporters quieted.

Nudging his recording sphere closer, Nathan spoke louder, "Captain Grant Monaghan arrested Charlotte Grayson tonight in connection with Airstrong's string of alleged thefts, including the disappearance of four banned spells and a clutch of phoenix eggs Airstrong was contracted to ship in secrecy. What is your reaction, Harry?"

Grant wouldn't. Only . . .

Nathan's smug expression wasn't a bluff.

My stomach caved. A ringing swelled in my ears, though not loud enough to drown out Nathan's taunts.

"You didn't know, did you, Harry? Monaghan put Charlotte Grayson in null cuffs himself. I guess you'll have to read about it in tomorrow's paper. But what does this mean for your relationship?" Saccharine sympathy dripped from his voice, but his eyes never lost their triumphant gleam. He had fed his salacious information to the hungry journalists. It didn't matter what I said now: every paper would carry the news tomorrow. He may have given away his exclusive edge, but in doing so, Nathan had poisoned every newspaper in the city in one fell swoop. His smug smile said he considered it a fair trade.

Flashes popped in my face, catching my shock before I could mask it. The journalists resumed their verbal barrage, but their words washed over me.

I trusted Grant. He wouldn't arrest Mom for a crime she didn't commit. He had seen my everlasting seed. He had been with me every step of its evolution. He believed Mom was a victim, not a criminal. Or he had when I last saw him.

What had happened after I left Airstrong?

I needed to see Grant. Now.

7

"Excuse me, let us through," I said, attempting to be polite while forcing my words through gritted teeth. If anything, the reporters pressed closer, heedlessly jostling me and Quinn. A tiny whimper escaped Quinn's throat. Someone's knee knocked into his wing, and he moaned.

Enough. Seizing the elements, I slammed a ward of solid air around the two of us, clipping the hands, elbows, knees, and toes of the bullies surrounding us. A second surge of magic smacked the reporters back half a step, giving us breathing room. It was rude bordering on illegal. The same anti-violence laws that prohibited people from punching others—even smarmy offal like Nathan—applied to manhandling people with the elements. The journalists jumped back with startled shouts and dramatized cries of pain. I ignored them just as I ignored the dull pain thumping behind my eyes from holding too much magic too soon.

Kneeling, I spoke softly to Quinn. "Are you all right?"

"I think my wing is sprained." His words hissed between

clenched teeth. A trickle of golden sand sifted from the gouge in his wing, and citrine powder shimmered along the knees and thighs of nearby reporters. How many times had they shoved themselves into Quinn's wounds without even noticing?

Rage overflowed into my magic. I slapped a tint into the ward, filtering it so we could see out but no one—and no one's camera—could see in. A soundproof layer sprang into being, then I reshaped the circular ward into a wedge and drove it into the mob.

The reporters fell aside, mouths contorted with shouts I couldn't hear. Tomorrow's press would be especially vindictive, and I couldn't care less. No one present had been planning to write in support of my parents or me, and I was through being polite for the sake of my reputation. If these journalists didn't enjoy being knocked around, maybe they would think twice about doing it to someone else in the future.

My gaze snagged on Nathan's smug smile as he jotted notes in his journal, and impotent anger churned like acid in my stomach.

Quinn's pain ate at me, and I scrapped my plan of waiting near the jail wall. We needed to get somewhere quieter to contact Grant.

Our escape was hampered by Quinn's wincing steps, and despite my opaque ward, journalists hounded us for several blocks until we managed to fool them by ducking into the well of a cheese shop's doorway and crouching under an illusion. When they finally roamed away, I disbanded the complex spell and crafted elemental boots for Quinn. I had never created a spell quite like it before, but after my fourth attempt, I successfully wrapped Quinn's front paws in spongy cushions of air.

"It's squishy between my toes," Quinn said, taking exaggerated steps, his head bent nearly between his knees to examine his feet.

"Does it hurt?"

"It tickles." He grinned at me, pacing back and forth without wincing once. He still held his wing stiffly at his side, but his stride was twice as fast as before. "This feels so much better. Thank you."

"You're welcome."

"Are you sure it's not too much?"

I dropped my hand from my forehead, where I had been unconsciously massaging the pain throbbing at my temples. The Quick Boost had helped replenish my reserves, but it would take a full night's sleep and real food before I felt like myself.

"With your boost, it's easy," I said, giving Quinn a fond pet. His citrine mane was cool from the night air, his golden tones muted in the lamplight. I would endure a great deal more pain than a thumping headache if it meant he didn't have to suffer. I hated that I couldn't heal Quinn myself. As far as I knew, no one else in Terra Haven had Mika's skill with healing gargoyles. She had tried to teach me "basic" spells, but even those had been wildly too complex for me to master.

"Though I'm going to look into a flying carpet big enough for the two of us," I said, mentally grimacing. Anticipating Quinn being grievously injured *again* was depressing, but at the rate we were both getting hurt, having reliable transportation seemed prudent. One not dependent on our own bodies *or* on another person.

"I'll be able to fly again in no time," Quinn assured me.

"It would still be nice to have a way to fly together." I checked street signs to get my bearings.

A pair of rodents rummaged in the alley trash across the street, taking turns to glare us with small, beady eyes. The whoosh of a flying carpet zipping down a cross street disturbed the air, and a large airship circled in the distance, the moon's silvery light reflecting off its long balloon. A few streets over, a Pegasus Express fleet banked to land atop the post office, and the susurrus of the equines' wings echoed through the tall buildings. Good. I knew where we were.

"There's a bus stop this way."

"What about the harpy? Shouldn't we wait for Grant?" Quinn asked.

A fist of distress squeezed my heart, the thought of Grant setting off a cascade of doubts. What had he been thinking when he arrested Mom? What had changed his mind?

What had caused him to lose faith in me?

I rubbed my aching breastbone and focused on the problem in front of us.

"Returning to the jail isn't an option, and we're no safer here than on the move. Since we don't know how long Grant will be"—how long did it take to arrest an innocent woman?—"we can at least head home so you can be healed." I couldn't stomach the thought of twiddling my thumbs while Quinn suffered.

"We should still contact him," Quinn said, falling in stride beside me.

"I'm on it." Yanking the elements into a message sphere, I raised it to my lips. I meant to sound calm and collected, but my frayed emotions got the best of me. "How could you, Grant? How could you arrest Mom? I demand—"

"Maybe not *demand*," Quinn said. "And we only have Nathan's word."

"He wasn't lying. He wouldn't, not in front of all those journalists."

"Not even to make them chase the wrong story?"

My lips parted, but nothing came out.

"It would make all the other papers look bad if they reported false information," Quinn added.

I stared at him in shock. "Wow. That's devious." He waggled his round ears at me questioningly, and I ran through the various ways such a bald lie could play out. Finally, I shook my head. "You didn't see Nathan's face. It was true. He was too happy to be the one to tell me."

"I don't like him. He's mean to you and has a way of making everything sound bad."

"True. All right, let's try this." I disbanded the previous message sphere and built a new one tuned to Grant's magical signature. "Grant, I need you to—"

Magic slammed into the back of my knees, knocking me to the cobblestones. I caught myself with braced hands, the impact jolting pain to my elbows. The same blow swept Quinn's legs out from under him and slid him several feet past me. I slammed a ward down around the two of us even as I scrambled closer to Quinn, tightening the magic around us. Pain lanced through my skull, easily ignored in my panic.

Quinn shoved to his feet, one wing flared, the other clamped to his side. Remaining crouched, I spun in a tight circle, looking for our assailant. The answer came on a wave of eye-watering putrescence.

Zipporah dove past our heads, briefly underlit by a tall streetlamp. A hybrid of woman and bird, the harpy possessed a wingspan to rival a hippogryph's and the predatory instincts of a wyvern, but her cunning was pure human. The low light lent a ghoulish cast to her human features, elongating her sharp nose and flattening her harsh mouth. Featherless skin swept down her neck and across her chest like a bib of flesh, leaving her flaccid human breasts exposed. Blue-tinted rainbows ran through the oily sheen of her wing feathers, but the bulk of her nether region was coated in feces, offal, and other unidentifiable filth. Flapping hard, the harpy banked too late, her agility hampered by sharply shorn primary feathers on her right wing. That had been Grant's doing. She was no match for his magic. Me, she batted around according to her whims.

Ice churned in my gut, and I layered the inside of my ward with blades of air set to explode outward. Zipporah had caught us on a deserted street, far from a guard station. If any residents were nearby, they likely wouldn't intervene, though they might send for the guards. Judging by past interactions, I didn't have that kind of time.

"Get ready to run," I mouthed to Quinn.

Miraculously, I still held my message sphere. Tugging it to my lips, I whispered, "Track me," then wadded the elements tight and lifted my ward high enough for it to shoot across the road and out of sight.

Zipporah's talons screeched against the cobblestones. Tucking her tail, she slid to a halt amid a flurry of dislodged, dried excrement and feathers. Hopping on enormous eagle feet, she circled to face us, her breasts slapping obscenely against her leathery chest.

"Harriet Kylie Grayson." She hissed my name like a curse as she stalked closer.

I tested the elements, reinforcing my ward and the elemental blades beneath it. Even with Quinn's enhancement, it wouldn't be enough to keep us safe. Zipporah had proven she could overpower the two of us. But I wasn't planning to stick around to fight; we just needed enough time to escape.

"We made a deal," Zipporah said. Her yellow raptor eyes

gleamed in the lamplight, unblinking and uncanny in her human face. "It was a simple deal. I let you live so long as you bring me what I asked for." She tipped forward, her beak-like nose inches from my ward. The harpy and I were almost the same height, but her girth made her appear larger. So did her talons, which splayed long enough to encircle me—and were sharp enough skewer me.

"I couldn't—" My words caught on a gag as the foul rot of a trash heap baking in the summer sun hit my senses. Coughing, I tried to form an argument she would accept, but nothing came to mind. She had demanded I bring her the banned spells stolen from Airstrong. Even if I had been willing to place the deadly magic in the harpy's possession, I couldn't have. Investigator O'Hara and FPD specialists had confiscated the spells and disappeared with them. But Zipporah wasn't likely to be sympathetic to my reasoning.

"I've been extremely lenient with you," she continued in that same creepy tone.

Lenient? The last time we spoke, she tried to murder me —and nearly succeeded.

"I appreciate—"

"But my benevolence stretches only so far." A razor's edge was pillowy compared to her smile. "You owe me, and you will pay. Since I can't trust you to keep your word when you're out of my sight, you're coming home with me."

Terror spurted through me, loosening my limbs. If Zipporah hauled me back to her nest, I wouldn't survive. I suspected I could thank the sleepy neighborhood for her subdued demeanor. Here, people might wake and intervene. But once she had me isolated, she could unleash the anger simmering behind her eyes, and not even Grant would be swift enough to save me.

"Give me another task," I pleaded, knowing it wouldn't work but hoping to buy time.

"Drop the ward," Zipporah ordered. She didn't wait for me to comply. With a vicious slice of raw earth, she hacked at my barrier.

I sprang backward, expecting the strike to crush my magic. Instead, the blow reverberated like a struck gong inside my skull, and my ward held. Zipporah squawked her astonishment, half unfurling her wings. A fresh miasma of wet feces engulfed me, and I clamped my gaping mouth shut. How had that worked? Was Zipporah's magic weakened?

Not counting on my luck to hold against a second assault, I backpedaled to the edge of my barrier, careful not to breach it from the inside. Quinn slunk backward with me, his belly low to the ground. Keeping my hand tucked close to my side, I pointed at the nearby side street. Quinn nodded subtly.

"You're going to wish you had come willingly," Zipporah hissed, hurling a spear of solidified air thicker than my torso at the two of us.

"Run!" I dropped my ward and sprinted for the side street. My magical knives exploded in a rough semicircle. Most flew into empty air before dissipating, but a cluster bombarded Zipporah's feathered stomach. Her enraged cry was lost beneath the crash of her spear detonating against the cobblestones where Quinn and I had been standing seconds earlier. Chunks of rock pelted my legs, spurring me to greater speed.

I grabbed a lamppost at the intersection, using it to slingshot myself down the side street. Fire ignited in my palm, hot and sharp. I glanced down, expecting an attack, only to find my palm scraped from my earlier fall. Quinn loped at my side, head canted to stare behind us. He could easily outpace me, but he stuck loyally to my side.

"She's coming," he warned.

I hazarded a glance over my shoulder. Zipporah sprang into the air, slowed by her mismatched wings. Nothing impeded her magic, though. An air net spiked with wooden elemental splinters soared after us, closing fast. I pumped my legs, dodging up to the sidewalk. Quinn sprang to the opposite side of the street, but the net chased me. At the last second, I lashed out with earth and fire.

The net disintegrated.

Black spots danced in my vision, and I slammed into a knee-high freestanding A-frame sign in front of a pharmacy. The lightweight advertisement hit the wooden walkway with the bang of a firework. If the neighbors hadn't been woken by Zipporah blasting apart the street, they were awake now.

I dashed back into the street, lungs on fire. Quinn leapt over a potted shrub, landing with a clatter of quartz on cobblestones. His face scrunched in agony, but he didn't slow.

Mentally cursing, I hastily reformed his air boots. Attaching them to Quinn's moving feet taxed my limited concentration, and for several awkward strides, he ran lopsided with only one paw coated in air before I glommed a magical boot to his second injured paw. His front footsteps fell silent, but their cadence beat a dull rhythm inside my skull.

"Left," I barked, and Quinn dove into an alley hardly wide enough for his frame. I struggled to keep up, my legs burning in fatigue. I couldn't outrun a harpy on my most energized day, and today had been anything but restful. We needed a place to hole up where Zipporah couldn't reach us.

If we were closer, I would have sprinted home. My land-lady had wrapped our house in more defensive spells than a bank vault. Zipporah didn't stand a chance of cracking through them all to get me. But even if I could dodge or deflect the harpy's attacks, my legs would give out long before we reached the front porch. The air bus was out too. No driver would stop, let alone let me aboard, with an enraged harpy on my tail.

Zipporah disappeared behind the nearest building, but the heavy flap of her wings promised she would be back.

"Which way?" Quinn asked between gasped breaths.

I caught sight of a familiar haberdashery. "Right. Library." It was the closest building with protective wards, though I wasn't certain they would obstruct Zipporah. If I'd possessed more stamina, I would have aimed for the guard house five blocks farther away.

Without breaking his stride, Quinn sprang off the wall and catapulted himself into the street. I shoved after him, barely noticing the slap of pain against my palm. This street was narrower than the previous thoroughfare but equally as vacant. Where was a patrolling guard unit when I needed it?

I couldn't hear anything above the rasp of my own breaths and my thudding steps. Craning my head, I searched the skies for the harpy. The stars blurred in my vision, and a streetlamp blinded me.

"Duck!" Quinn shouted.

I dove into a bruising roll. Zipporah's talons clawed the air above me. She shrieked her disappointment, scrambling to regain altitude with her asymmetrical wings. Even as she blundered into an awning and gouged the side of a brick building to right herself, she hurled a wicked whirlwind of barbed air at me. Vaulting to my feet, I half jumped, half fell out of the whirlwind's path, flinging a buffer of earth between my heels and the hazardous magic. The whirlwind hit my elemental shield and shattered it, spiking pain deep inside my brain. Quinn stabilized me with his uninjured wing.

"Should I distort her magic?" he asked.

Quinn had once explained the way his boost worked. It involved folding raw elements—which I couldn't picture no matter how hard I tried—and purifying the magic before linking with whomever he wanted to enhance. As far as I knew, he was the only gargoyle to ever intentionally warp the elements, and the result had been dramatic. When he had forged a distorted link with Zipporah, her magic had failed in catastrophic and violent ways. It had also left Quinn woozy and given him a migraine.

"It's too risky," I panted. "Someone could get hurt." Even if Quinn was willing to risk his health, warped magic reacted unpredictably. If Quinn distorted the harpy's magic, her next attack would be as likely to backfire on Zipporah as it would decimate the block.

Zipporah flapped in a circle, throwing punches of solidified air. We shoved into a run. A blow hit the cobblestones behind me with a muted smack, and pulverized rock ricocheted against the nearby storefront. I shoved more speed into my rubbery legs. If one of those elemental punches hit me, it would break my bones.

Quinn and I zigzagged across the street and barged into a small park. Bushes tore at my clothes when I mistimed a jump. Quinn bounded off a wooden bench, fumbling the landing when the bench collapsed beneath his weight. Zipporah strafed the trees, pelting us with sharp knives of air. Pain sliced across my shoulder and down my bicep. I domed a ward above us, but my magic disintegrated after only three hits.

We burst out the other side of the park and careened through a disorienting series of alleys. Sweat stung my eyes, blurring the streets, but Quinn ran confidently. Trusting him to navigate, I deflected an anvil of air before it could flatten us, then shattered a wall of elemental thorns Zipporah lashed across our path. Agony split my skull, driving spikes of pain deeper with each step. When the library courtyard opened before us, I would have sobbed if I had the extra breath.

Moonlight bathed the daunting expanse of open cobblestones. No cover or protection existed between us and the library's three-story portico. Cackling, Zipporah soared above us.

"You're mine now, little morsel," she shouted.

Praying she was wrong, I pounded across the courtyard, Quinn galloping at my side. A second boost of magic swelled inside me. Bernette, the library's resident gargoyle, must have spotted us. Hope sparked. Maybe we would survive.

A gale of elementally driven wind slammed into me, knocking me sideways. I cut through Zipporah's magic with a machete of earth, only to scramble a ward into place to deflect an elemental cudgel from the opposite direction. A hearty blow hammered my shoulders, nearly sending me sprawling. The next assault knocked me into Quinn.

She was playing with me.

Any of those attacks could have flattened me—if Zipporah had wanted to. But the harpy thought she had us cornered, and she was having her fun. This was only a preview too. If she dragged me to her nest, my every waking moment would be torture.

I latched onto Quinn's uninjured wing. Then, pulling on every last ounce of magic offered by both gargoyles, I glommed a thick ward so tight around Quinn and myself that it hummed against my skin. Any bigger, and I wouldn't be able to hold it together. Zipporah's attacks continued to pummel us, but my dense spell deflected them.

"Go!"

Quinn surged into a sprint. I flew beside him, my feet barely touching the ground.

Magic hammered my ward. The elements trembled in my grip, and only my white-knuckled grip on Quinn kept me upright. Zipporah dropped out of her lazy orbit, spearing toward us with shocking speed for such a large creature.

We're not going to make it. The library was too far, and she was too fast.

The harpy's wings flared, her deadly talons lashing out. Quinn sprang into the air, yanking me with him. His feet punctured my ward from the inside, blasting a backlash of broken elements through my skull. My vision blackened, then my body struck something solid. Quinn was torn from my grip, and I skidded out of control.

Panic blazed through my body. Expecting Zipporah's talons to seize me in their crushing grip, I scrambled to my hands and knees. The elements sifted through my grasp. Quinn's boost was still there, and Bernette's too, but my mental muscles were too fatigued to make any use of it. I almost hung my head in defeat, but self-preservation pulled my gaze up.

Zipporah battered her wings against the air between two tall pillars, her talons scraping uselessly against the library's shield. Gnashing her sharp teeth, she unleashed a string of curses, each more colorful—and less physically feasible— than the last.

I sagged to my hip, taking my weight off my abraded

palms and knees. Quinn limped into place between me and the harpy, then flopped on his stomach, sides heaving. Zipporah's stench coated each breath I gasped, but I didn't care. We were alive. We were safe. The shield prevented the harpy's malicious magic from harming us. I had never loved the library more. If we needed to, we could wait here until the morning librarians arrived, and they would call in the guard to scare Zipporah away. Or, if I recovered sooner, I could send my own message to the nearest guard station.

"You're going to die for this, Harriet Kylie Grayson," Zipporah thundered.

"I was always going to die for it," I said, picturing her suffocating me in her feces-ridden nest or disemboweling me in a fit of rage—or the slow, agonizing death of sepsis.

"Yes, but you've made me look bad. For that, you're going to die screaming in agony, begging for your life." Her pitiless eyes flared in the library's lanterns. A sharp pentagram of air and earth spun from Zipporah to scratch along the ward, seeking out a weak point. "I've found humans to be especially sensitive to having their eyes gouged—"

A bolt of fire shot across the shadowy courtyard, searing a white bar across my vision. Zipporah cursed and slapped the attack aside with a mallet of air and water. Five more flaming spears followed in rapid succession, the flashes of light illuminating a formidable figure speeding our way atop a flying carpet.

Grant.

Zipporah sprang into the air, kicking off from a pillar to launch herself higher. Her half-shorn wing couldn't lift her fast enough, and flames singed her tail feathers. I clamped my elbow over my nose as the acrid scent of burnt feathers and excrement drowned me. Quinn gagged.

A flurry of fire chased Zipporah higher. The harpy

unleashed a torrent of feces, extinguishing the flames and distracting Grant as she flew over the nearest rooftop. Holding a shield above himself, Grant sped across the remaining distance separating us, his gaze on the sky. The harpy's awkward form reappeared in the east, silhouetted against the moon. I fancied I saw tendrils of smoke wafting from her tail, but it could have been my imagination. She didn't look like she was coming back.

For now.

I slumped against Quinn, replaying Zipporah's final words. She had agreed with me that she always planned to kill me, and I didn't think she was talking only about tonight's abduction attempt. Her first two missions had been death sentences. I had survived on luck and teamwork with my amazing gargoyle friend and Grant. But if I *had* managed to bring Zipporah either demanded prize, it wouldn't have been enough for the vindictive harpy. She demanded a debt worthy of my life; the only way she would consider the debt paid in full would be when my life had been forfeited.

I was a walking dead woman.

8

Grant leapt to the ground, abandoning his floating carpet in the courtyard, and bounded up the library steps—steps I had no memory of traversing. Quinn's final leap must have carried us both over them. A glowball shot ahead of Grant, sweeping over me and Quinn. Squinting against the bright light, I waited for Grant's fierce expression to dissolve to something softer, more affectionate. Instead, his jaw tightened, and his eyes when they met mine were frosty.

"I told you to wait at the jail," he said. He halted on Quinn's opposite side, one hand fisted around the seed bracelet on his wrist, his knuckles white under the pressure.

The thank-you on the tip of my tongue wilted, his reprimand a slap when I expected compassion or concern. My words came out stiff. "There were extenuating circumstances."

"Of course. There always are with you."

"What's that supposed to mean?"

"It means I can't always drop everything to rush to your rescue."

His rebuke solidified into a hard knot in the pit of my stomach, his harsh words an echo of my fears. I didn't want to rely on Grant for safety. I loathed the role of damsel in distress. But would it have hurt him to wrap me in a hug before he berated me?

"I have a job, Kylie. I can't be at your beck and call constantly. What's going to happen when you need saving and I'm busy?"

"I guess I'll save myself." His supercilious tone burned shame and indignation through my trembling body, and I spat out, "Just like I did this time."

Quinn moaned, dropping his chin to his paws. Grant scanned my bruised and bloodied body once more with exaggerated deliberation, his expression unimpressed. I curled my fingers toward my palms, hiding the cuts, and halfheartedly straightened. Sharp pain flared in my hip and down my bicep, but I clenched my teeth to keep it from showing on my face. If I could have mustered the energy, I would have stood. I settled with glaring at Grant from where I slumped.

"Was disobeying me worth it? Was it worth almost dying?" he asked, his tone so bland it bordered on apathetic. Only his choking grip on the black-and-white bracelet betrayed him. "You have people who care about you, but you insist on recklessly, *selfishly* endangering your life. That's the behavior of a child, Kylie."

Was Grant including himself in those people who cared about me? If so, it wasn't showing. "I didn't *disobey* you, Captain Monaghan, because I'm not under your command. I make my own decisions. That's the behavior of a grown woman."

"Adults think about other people when they make decisions. They can be patient. They keep their promises—"

"Like not arresting my mom?" Tears attempted to form in my eyes, and I blinked rapidly, channeling my hurt feelings into anger, not caring that my voice shook. "You said you wouldn't. You said there wasn't proof, and don't tell me that a phoenix egg hatching in her warehouse and nearly killing her is proof that Mom stole from her own company, because that's pure hogwash. So please, lecture me. I'll *patiently* wait here, thinking about the judges, lawyers, and FPD idiots who will be affected by my decision to free an innocent woman. Oh, and I'll also think about all the people who will be impacted by my decision to find the real culprit, a job that *you're* supposed to be doing."

Grant's eyebrows lifted fractionally. "Are you through?"

I crossed my arms, wincing when my injured palms scraped against my filthy shirt.

With a heavy sigh, Grant stepped around Quinn and knelt beside me. "I didn't arrest Charlotte."

"That's not what Nathan said."

"Since when do you get your information from him?"

"Since he ambushed me in front of about twenty of my peers with the information."

Grant's frown eased. "Did he? That's good."

"*Good?*" Couldn't he at least pretend to be contrite?

"I wanted him to believe it was a real arrest. If other papers report on Charlotte's arrest, all the better for her."

"How? And what do you mean 'real arrest'?"

"O'Hara isn't convinced of Charlotte's innocence, but I believe someone is targeting her. This was our compromise. We put on a show of arresting her, then transported her to a private, warded house, where she'll stay until the phoenix eggs are all recovered or hatched. So long as she remains put, she can't be accused of having anything to do with the eggs, and no one can use them to harm her."

That was . . . smart. And if Grant hadn't called me a selfish, reckless child, I might have admitted it out loud.

"So you locked my mom up somewhere, and she can't leave? That sounds like a real arrest to me." Clinging to the point was stupid and petty, but not as stupid as demanding he wrap his arms around me and apologize. Or maybe it was. The adrenaline of Zipporah's attack had bled from me, and only a miasma of anger and fatigue remained, clouding my logic.

"She's in a safe house, not jail." His tone implied I was being obtuse. "Charlotte agreed to this arrangement. She knows it's the best way to prove her innocence. She explained this all to you in a message, so you can hear her side when you get home."

Pretend or not, if the arrest looked real in the papers, Airstrong would take another massive hit. There wasn't much Dad could do to help from his offices on the East Coast, either, and after three major thefts from Airstrong's Terra Haven warehouse, and now a phoenix hatching on the premises, the company's reputation in this city was in tatters. I found it hard to believe that Mom had agreed to essentially abandon her business at such a crucial time—at least not without FPD pressure coercing her decision.

"Why do you look like you crawled through a brick kiln? Did the harpy try to incinerate you?"

I glanced down at myself. The glowball's soft light illuminated rust-colored grit coating me from head to toe, partially obscuring the soot stains I'd acquired rescuing Mom. Small burn holes pockmarked my pants, and through a rip at the knee, blood glistened on a patch of road rash. I looked away, avoiding a similar examination of my lacerated palms.

"No, but Fire Eaters did."

Tension shot through Grant. "Where? When?" He scanned the courtyard beyond the library's pillars, magic thrumming in the air around him.

"They attacked the jail. Someone hired them to free Persephone."

Grant cursed O'Hara under his breath.

"You didn't know?"

"My team and I were magic-blind inside the safe house's wards until ten minutes ago. I got the night warden's and sheriff's summons when I came out, but O'Hara countermanded both. Since I also got your message . . ."

He had come for me.

"Tell me everything," Grant ordered. "Start with where you're hurt the most."

I took an internal assessment, then lifted my hands to Grant. My palms looked as if they had been flayed with coarse sandpaper, and every finger twitch stung. Grant took my left in a gentle grip and tipped it over, cycling a cleaning spell over my palm until the last of the gravel and sand fell from my wounds. I breathed shallowly and did my best not to whimper with each torturous pass of his magic. When he switched to my right hand, I gave him a terse recounting of the Fire Eaters' attack and Quinn's heroic rescue.

"Quinn's wing was injured when he burst through the wall," I concluded. "His paws too. That's why we need to get home."

"Is there anything I can do?" Grant asked Quinn.

The gargoyle shook his head. "I need Mika."

Grant shifted to hold my wrists firmly in his callused grip. "Brace yourself. I'm going to heal your palms."

"You can't do too much magic," Quinn said.

Grant paused. "Why not?"

"The healer at Airstrong *and* at the jail said Kylie's been healed too much lately."

"They just meant I need to rest," I said.

"You haven't rested yet," Quinn said, having apparently appointed himself czar of my health.

"I'm resting now."

Quinn and Grant both gave me the look my inane comment deserved.

"I'll keep the healing to a minimum," Grant promised. Fire licked across my palm, then dove into the cuts, Grant's rudimentary healing spell knitting my flesh together with the tranquil touch of a red-hot brand.

I clenched my teeth and squeezed my eyes shut. Seconds later, the pain abated. New, pink tissue crisscrossed my palms. I flexed my fingers. Dull pain pulled at my tendons, but my hand already felt ten times better.

"I want to talk to Mom," I said, pretending I wasn't swaying as I fought my body's urge to collapse.

"Certainly." Grant's magic set fire to my opposite palm.

Clammy sweat broke across my forehead and beaded my upper lip. I swiped it away. "In person."

"Fine." Grant casually ripped the knees of my pants wide open to examine the wounds beneath.

"Tonight," I gritted out as his cleansing spell scrubbed my knee. He didn't respond, instead focusing on healing the deepest scrapes. Neither of us spoke as he ripped the torn right sleeve off my shirt, revealing a long, shallow gash from my shoulder to my bicep. Once more, a purification spell dove beneath my skin. Blackness edged my vision, then fire seared into the wound, jolting me back to full consciousness before I had a chance to faint. I braced a hand on my knee and watched through bleary eyes as Grant incinerated the scrap of fabric in his fist.

"I mean it," I mumbled. "As soon as Quinn is healed, I want to see my mom."

"If I take you to Charlotte, you have to remain with her until this investigation is through."

"What?" It took effort, but I brought Grant's face into focus.

"The whole point of pretending your mom was arrested was to keep her hidden. If you visit her even once, it could lead someone straight to her."

"I wouldn't."

"When was the last time you checked yourself for tracking spells?"

"I've been a bit busy."

Grant waited.

I ran my tongue along the inside of my teeth, holding back further argument. Someone had placed a tracking spell on me in the past, and we still didn't know who. Persephone had been at the top of my suspects, and with her locked up, I hadn't thought to check again.

Gathering the elements caused the dull pain pounding in my head to triple into a vision-blurring pulse that throbbed in time with my heartbeat. Gingerly, I built a pentagram of all five elements, then inverted it into a pentagon. Nudging the edges of the pentagon wide, I dropped it over my head and ran it down my body. The inside of the spell held passive magic tuned to my magical signature, and if it encountered another person's magic, it would create a discordant vibration. I fully expected to reach my toes without a single wiggle from the spell. Instead, it buzzed against my mental senses before it reached my shoulder blades.

I narrowed my eyes at Grant, suspecting he had already spotted the spell. He watched me impassively. Carefully capturing the tracker in a net of my own magic, I plucked it from the back of my neck and examined it. The spell itself was relatively simple, but even the most basic magic contained the creator's signature. Delicately probing the tracker, I reeled back from the familiar texture of molten embers stirring hot wind through dry foliage.

"Nathan?"

"The reporter?" Grant looked momentarily surprised, but then his expression hardened. "Do you understand the need for secrecy with Charlotte's location now?"

I crushed the tracker, snuffing out the spell. How low would that scumbag sink to get a story? Unless both people consented, the use of trackers on individuals was illegal. Nathan had stolen articles from me in the past, and he had stooped to following me around to do so, but this was an unthinkable breach of my privacy. I swept my pentagon down the rest of my body, the spell jangling only once more over Grant's badge. Of all the story-hungry reporters who had accosted me tonight, Nathan—a senior journalist at the city's most respected paper—should have been the last person to plant a tracker on me. He also should have been the last person to use his authority to malign a personal rival, but neither a sense of honor nor professional integrity had stopped him yet.

"I should press charges."

"You destroyed the evidence," Grant said.

Mentally cursing, I released the elements. "Now that we know I'm clean, there's no reason I can't go see Mom."

"I can't have you walking around the city knowing where your mom is. It's too dangerous. For her and you."

"That hardly makes any sense." I shoved to my feet, stumbling in place as my vision blackened. My thighs trembled at the exertion. I would be lucky if I didn't face-plant walking down the library steps. The healers—and Quinn—were right; I was near my body's limits.

"O'Hara is toying with the theory that you're working with Charlotte as part of some elaborate scheme." Grant rose fluidly to stand beside me, sturdy and strong. "If I take you to Charlotte, then let you leave, you'll feed into his suspicions. You'll make it harder to prove your mom's innocence."

"I thought we had to prove her guilt."

"Right now, her guilt is all but proven. It's her word against Persephone's." Grant's crossed arms pulled his uniform tight over his biceps and broad shoulders.

He made it sound as if Persephone's word, the word of a madwoman, carried the same weight as Mom's, an upstanding citizen who had never been arrested, let alone used a mental-manipulation spell. However, Grant wasn't the person I had to convince, and since I was swaying despite my best efforts and fighting back a yawn, I didn't bother to argue. All I wanted was to be held in Grant's strong embrace. Despite his harsh words, despite his domineering attitude, if Grant had opened his arms to me, I would have fallen into them.

I forced myself to take a step back.

"I need to get Quinn home."

"Can you make me air shoes again?" Quinn asked.

The thought of creating the spells made my head pound harder. "Of course. Let me—"

"What are air shoes?" Grant asked.

"Kylie cushioned my feet with little globes of air while we ran. They made it hurt less."

Grant frowned. "You ran? Across the courtyard?"

"From Stanton Street," Quinn said.

"Zipporah didn't try to stop you?"

"She showered us in rose petals and compliments," I said, shooting Grant an exasperated glare.

"Did you"—Grant looked to Quinn and made a crumpling motion with his hands—"mess with the harpy's magic?"

Quinn shook his head. "I didn't have to. Kylie deflected everything she threw at us."

Grant transferred his frown to me. I ignored him, but what I really wanted to do was shout, *See? I can save myself.* Biting my bottom lip in concentration, I reached for the elements, only to have them slide through my grasp. On my second attempt, I gathered a paper-thin thread of air and began coiling a cushion of air around Quinn's front paw.

"Stop." Grant lifted Quinn with a belt of air, floating him as if the gargoyle were made of feathers and flesh, not solid quartz. After reinforcing the carpet's levitation spell, he draped Quinn across the middle. Quinn's legs hung off either side, his paws inches from the ground. Quinn sighed and sagged into the carpet, letting his head droop and his eyes close. A fine trickle of citrine sifted from the gouge in his wing, dusting the carpet.

I let my pathetic magic dissipate and did my best to hurry to the carpet. Quinn had suffered far too long, and the sooner we got him home, the sooner Mika could relieve his pain. However, the ground undulated in my vision and pain hitched my hip, and the best I could muster was an unstable hobble.

With an indistinct grumble, Grant swept me into his arms and carried me down the stairs. The urge to cry swam through my chest again, but he propped me against Quinn at the front of the carpet before I could give in to the emotion. My legs dangled off, and after making sure I wasn't touching an injured part of Quinn's body, I clutched his neck to anchor myself in place. I considered thanking Grant, but I couldn't remember if I was still mad at him or not.

Quinn lifted his head. His eyelids drooped with weariness, but his voice was alert when he asked, "Did it change?"

I didn't understand the question until he dipped his nose toward the everlasting seed hanging from a leather thong around his neck. Twisting, I lifted the seed for a better inspection, but I could already tell by feel that it hadn't transformed. Moonlight gleamed in the mirror-bright disc. On the opposite side, copper veins snaked through the metallic-green surface, both colors muted in the dim light.

"It's the same."

Quinn let his head drop. I stroked his forehead, easing the seed back in place. The hard disc chimed against his forelegs, sounding like metal rather than something grown by a tree.

"It's still beautiful," I said.

"I'm not upset. I just wish I knew what it meant."

Grant hopped onto the back of the carpet, perching on the limited remaining space. With a prodigious funnel of air, he set the carpet in motion. We glided in silence through the streets of Terra Haven, Quinn half asleep and Grant scanning the skies, ever vigilant for the harpy's return.

"I won't let you lock me up," I said when we reached the outskirts of my neighborhood.

Grant glanced at me, his expression difficult to read in the shadows of the tall trees lining the street.

"You've seen my everlasting seed. I need to find those phoenix eggs."

"How did your conversation with Persephone go?"

His question confused me until my tired thoughts caught up with his logic. "She didn't get a chance to tell me anything before the Fire Eaters attacked."

"She was never going to tell you anything. Nathan played you."

The memory of Nathan's smug smile taunted me.

Grant continued, "He wanted to connect you and Persephone as co-conspirators, and your late-night clandestine meeting with her gave Nathan the link he needed."

My stomach sank. "But O'Hara said . . ."

"Persephone has been ranting about you since her arrest. Of course she wanted to see you again. She thinks she can still order people around with the beguiling beads, and she wanted another chance to kill you."

"And the Fire Eaters?"

"Were bad luck, and they're going to make Nathan's story even flashier."

I rubbed my queasy stomach. I should have thought through the ramifications of meeting with Persephone, but I had been so shaken by the phoenix hatching at Airstrong—at it nearly killing Mom—that I had been too eager to rush after any conceivable clue. I hadn't even considered the source.

"Promise me you'll stay out of this investigation, Kylie. It's too dangerous, and that's not counting Zipporah being on a warpath to destroy you. Stay at home. Your landlady has the right idea with those wards." He jerked his chin to indicate my home at the end of the block, the two-story Victorian sheathed in dense defensive spells. "She'll keep you safe. You just have to stay put for a few days."

"I can't—"

"Kylie, for once, just do what I ask."

There was a time when I would have told Grant what he wanted to hear, then sneaked off to carry on with my investigation anyway. But I wouldn't lie to him now. I tried one last time to make him understand. "I can't. I know you think hiding here is the best idea, but I have to do what *I* think is right."

Grant's jaw muscle flexed. He brought the carpet to a stop in front of the Victorian and gently set Quinn on the sidewalk. I slid to my feet. Miraculously, my knees didn't buckle.

We all glanced toward the porch when the front door opened. Mika stepped out in her pajamas, a satchel with the telltale bulges of quartz marbles gripped in her fist. She rushed barefoot down the steps, her gaze locked on Quinn.

I had a moment to marvel at Mika's precognition, then Oliver jumped from the second-floor balcony railing, and I realized Quinn's sibling must have spotted us and informed Mika. I checked the roof, picking out the silhouettes of Lydia and Anya, Quinn's sisters. A third gargoyle, a huge sleeping stone sea turtle balanced across the Victorian's gables, was a pleasant surprise. Yarra, formerly in residence at Persephone Kwan's estate, had come to stay with us. Or more likely, Mika had gone to retrieve her.

Quinn and I had met Yarra during the summer solstice celebration hosted by Persephone. That felt like a lifetime ago, but it had been less than a week earlier. Even before Persephone's arrest, Yarra had been lonely in Persephone's understaffed mansion. Once Persephone was imprisoned, the gargoyle had been utterly abandoned. Seeing Yarra safe among friends was the first bright spot in this miserable night.

The world tilted when I glanced down, and I took a stumbling step to catch my balance. After I assured myself Quinn wasn't waiting for me—and I was certain my knees would hold me—I turned to face Grant.

He settled cross-legged atop the carpet, lowering the levitation spell until we were eye level. Indecipherable emotions simmered in his eyes, but Grant's voice was flat when he spoke. "At least send me a message when you leave."

"I will."

I held still, hoping he would lean across the rift between us for a parting kiss. Instead, he nodded tightly and departed. I watched him until he disappeared around the corner, wondering if this investigation would ruin our fledgling relationship—or if it had always been doomed.

Grant didn't look back once.

9

"There she is!"

"Harriet!"

"Over here, Harriet."

Quinn groaned. "How did they find us so fast?" he asked, glaring at four journalists rushing to intercept us.

"Bad luck, I guess." I checked myself for trackers before leaving the house and again after we evaded the reporters camped at the end of our street. I had hoped that by taking the air bus, we would escape further harassment.

Lifting a hand to shade my eyes against the midmorning sun, I pretended to be deaf as we hustled toward the library across the same expansive courtyard Zipporah had chased us through less than twelve hours earlier. All signs of the harpy's foul departure had been eradicated, and a fresh, earthy aroma floated from the damp cobblestones. The wounds she had inflicted on me, unfortunately, remained. Increasing my pace sent a stab of pain down my hip with each step and jarred the bruised muscles in my back and shoulder. Only a healthy slathering of greenthread over my scabbed knees made my loose pants tolerable, but the same ointment dabbed across the cuts on my cheek itched and stuck to loose strands of hair.

"Ms. Grayson, where are the missing phoenix eggs?"

Tapping the elements, I cast a thick illusion around Quinn and myself, cloaking us in an opaque dome. From the outside, we would appear shrouded in a balloon of fog. From the inside, the world beyond my spell looked soft and hazy. The illusion wasn't simple, but it shouldn't have felt like a lead weight on my psyche either. I hated that the healers were right. Sleep had made me feel like I could function without collapsing, but I needed a lot more. Unfortunately, I didn't have time to laze about. I considered purchasing another Quick Boost but decided against it. Too-frequent consumption of the stimulant would lead to a hard crash I couldn't afford. Instead, I consumed enough tea this morning for three women, relying on the caffeine to keep me sharp.

"Aw, come on, Harriet," wheedled a lanky woman wearing a lapel pin with the *Full Spectrum Gazette*'s logo. "We're just the messengers. It's the public who wants these answers."

"Did you work with Persephone Kwan to steal the eggs?" the man next to her asked.

"How long do we have until the next egg hatches?"

The woman's recording sphere sank through my illusion, and I shredded it with two vindictive slashes of earth and wood. She gasped and reeled dramatically, her hand to her bony chest, but when no one paused to watch her theatrics, she scrambled to catch up. I hardened the exterior of my illusion, bouncing her next sphere aside as well as the arm she thrust out to block me. Quinn's low growl kept the others from attempting to form a united barricade. I couldn't silence them, though. Their shouted questions rang through the courtyard, and the busy foot traffic flowing toward the library and surrounding buildings slowed as people turned to stare.

"Why has no one seen Charlotte Grayson all morning? I checked: she was never admitted to the jail."

"Is your mom on the lam?"

"Was Charlotte disfigured by the phoenix's hatching? Is she ashamed to show herself in public?"

I scoffed. I hadn't bothered to stop at a newsstand this morning, but based on their absurd questions, I could guess at the outlandish tales these muckrakers had concocted for their gossip rags.

"You used to be one of us, Harriet. Or Kylie. Whatever you want to be called," a chubby man from the conspiracy-loving *Daily Elemental* whined. "Can't you give us something, for old times' sake?"

I almost dropped the illusion just so I could give the man the scathing glare his comment deserved. Instead, I took the steps to the library two at a time, ignoring my body's distress to power past the ragtag group. The library door swayed as an elderly woman attempted to exit, her arms piled high with books. I grabbed the handle, holding it open for her.

"Thank you, ah . . ." Her hazel eyes rounded as she took in my illusion-clad form, and she clutched her books tighter. A bristle of elemental splinters erupted around her frail body. "Of all the uncouth—" Her chastisement was cut short when the journalists barreled into her personal space. "Why, I never," she huffed and expanded her barbed ward another two feet. The journalists jumped back, their curses drowned out by the woman's lecture about propriety.

"Quick," I said, ushering Quinn inside. I darted into the library after him, my cheeks flaming with embarrassment.

"Wait! Ms. Grayson!"

"Harriet, what about your boyfriend? Is he—"

The closing door blissfully cut off the reporters' questions. I dropped my illusion and ran a hand through my hair. Quinn shook, fluffing his wings. My gaze snagged on the clear quartz filling the sizable gouge through the muscle of his wing and the colorless flecks sprinkled across his feathers. More clear crystal interlaced his paws where Mika had used raw quartz to heal Quinn's injuries last night. All the claws on his left foot had been completely reconstructed. Anger surged anew through me. Talking with Persephone had been a complete waste of time and caused us both so much unnecessary pain.

The library's hush penetrated my self-recriminations. I looked up to find every patron seated at the grid of tables and all the librarians gawking at us. Lifting my chin, I strode to the help desk. Quinn slunk behind me, his rock paws ringing against the tiles.

"Hey, Kylie. How are you holding up?" my favorite librarian, Dione, asked. With her curly hair braided around her head like a crown, a pencil peeking out from behind one ear and a lending stamp gripped in her hand, she looked like an archive goddess. It felt like a blessing when she evoked her powers on my behalf: glancing over my shoulder, she swept her gaze across the rest of the patrons, managing to convey in one expression that whomever her eyes fell upon was doing something wrong and she thought they could do better. Behind us, papers shuffled and chairs scraped as people resumed their activities.

"I've been better," I said.

"Well, you look good, considering. I heard about your mom's warehouse. I would never guess by looking at you that you survived a phoenix's hatching and an attack by Fire Eaters in the last twenty-four hours."

I winced, knowing her source would have been Nathan's article in the *Chronicle*. Also, having seen my pink face dappled with cuts and sticky ointment in the mirror's reflection this morning, I knew she was being too kind. "You can't believe everything you read. Those secondhand accounts rarely get all the details right." I added a wan smile, the best I could muster.

"Then I look forward to reading your next article. What are you researching today?"

I would have hugged Dione if not for the counter separating us. Despite Nathan's slanted articles and all the other bad press I had received lately, she continued to treat me the same way she always had: friendly and professional. I hadn't confessed to being suspended from the *Chronicle* yet, but I suspected that even if she knew—which was likely, considering the city's librarians lived and breathed knowledge—she wouldn't treat me any different.

"I'm looking for anything and everything about Luther Wetherill and his company, Capstone Transportation."

"Including his broken engagement to Persephone Kwan?" Curiosity gleamed in Dione's dark eyes.

"I'm more interested in his business activities." Wetherill had been on hand each time the items stolen from Airstrong had been discovered, always ready to cast blame on me. He was just as fast to undermine Mom and Airstrong in the papers, using Nathan as his mouthpiece. He was also the person who stood to gain the most from Airstrong's downfall. Capstone had been in direct competition with Airstrong for years, always coming in second. My parents repeatedly netted the biggest contracts, including those with the Federal Pentagon Defense to ship deadly items such as confiscated illegal spells, firebirds, and phoenix eggs. If Airstrong was destroyed, those lucrative contracts would go to Capstone.

And yet . . .

I forced myself to admit that I might be confounding Wetherill's terrible personality with his guilt. The full spectrum was a ruthless businessman, more than capable of capitalizing on another's misfortunes for his own gain. He could see Airstrong was sinking, and he was making the most of it.

That didn't make him the thief.

It didn't make him innocent either.

Mom and O'Hara had pursued other possible suspects —disgruntled current or ex-employees, irate customers, and competitors—and come up empty-handed. The Fire Eaters looked like potential suspects, if only the missing phoenixes were considered. But they had nothing to do with the stolen firebirds, and if they had taken the banned spells, they would have used them, not given them to Persephone.

Persephone's involvement brought me back to Wetherill. His actions, combined with his ex-fiancée's possession of the stolen spells, remained the only common thread. I needed something more substantial to link Wetherill and Airstrong's thefts. If my prayers were answered, I would find a lead tucked inside one of the library's multitudinous archives.

"We have records of all business filings over here, and while you look, I'll gather current periodicals you might find useful," Dione said, guiding me to a stand of large leather-bound journals labeled *Deeds, Permits, and Licenses*. "Quinn, do you need anything?"

Quinn perked up at being addressed. "Information about phoenixes, please."

"I know just the books. I'll be right back." Dione set off into the library, a determined swish in her long skirt.

"Good thinking, Quinn." My knowledge of phoenixes covered the basics, but maybe we could learn something that would help us pinpoint the location of the remaining eggs.

The business records went back two centuries to the founding of Terra Haven, but I skimmed only a few decades back to the inception of Capstone. Wetherill had moved to Terra Haven a few years before my birth, branching out from his mother's business on the West Coast. For several years, he focused on the sale and rental of industrial rail cars before pivoting to custom-made passenger cars for the wealthy. Shortly after Airstrong took off and began opening warehouses across the nation, he got into the shipping business, but he never could catch up with my parents' success. Not even when he began manufacturing his own line of airships and cargo wagons, started an in-house pegasus breeding program, and took on a fleet of wyvern. Along the way, he bought out smaller competitors in these side businesses until he monopolized each market in Terra Haven and the surrounding cities.

Airstrong was the only company he hadn't conquered. For now.

If I could prove he had sabotaged even one other rival outfit, I might have enough to take to O'Hara.

I began the tedious task of cross-referencing the now-defunct companies' permits and licenses, as well as the businesses' bankruptcy or sale dates. I wished I could talk with Mom—or that Dad was close enough to message. They both kept a close eye on Capstone and Wetherill, just as they did every competitor in their industry. They might even know who Wetherill had targeted with a smear campaign in the past, saving me hours of research.

"If Mom knew, she would have told O'Hara," I muttered.

"What was that?" Quinn asked, looking up from a scientific study of phoenixes Dione had dropped off while I was eyeballs deep in research.

"Nothing. Just wishing I could talk to Mom."

Quinn's eyebrows crinkled sympathetically. "That would require knowing where she is."

"I know."

We had listened to Mom's message with Mika and Oliver after Mika finished healing Quinn last night, but Mom hadn't revealed anything new: She had gone voluntarily with "your captain" to a secret location, believing it the best way to prove her innocence and keep me and her employees safe; she would remain under FPD protection and watch until the phoenix eggs were found or hatched; and I wouldn't be able to contact her, since the spell disguising her whereabouts also prevented my messages from locating her. Unlike Grant, she hadn't tried to dissuade me from pursuing the missing phoenix eggs, though her tone had been resigned when she urged me to use caution and not take any more risks. Then she had ended the message by asking if Grant had an expression other than a scowl and if I had ever seen him laugh, because laughter was an important element of intimacy.

Her relationship advice would have been easier to shrug off if Grant and I had separated on better terms. His harsh reprimands still rang in my ears. I was his girlfriend, not a child who had "disobeyed" him, I wanted to shout. Or maybe I wasn't even his girlfriend. Just a woman he had kissed—a woman who took up too much of his precious time finding stolen FPD property and getting attacked by a harpy.

Nope, I wasn't bitter. Not at all.

I slammed the record book shut and picked up a stack of newspapers Dione had collected for me. Together, Quinn and I relocated to a secluded table to continue our research. As I skimmed countless stuffy business articles about Capstone and Wetherill, I fought back repeated yawns. I had slept fitfully, waking repeatedly from nightmares of being cooked alive or eaten by harpies, and the last time, from a futile battle in which Nathan flung fireballs at me, and when I fought back, he morphed into Grant and told me I was killing Quinn with my selfishness.

Fear and guilt made terrible bedfellows and worse dreams.

"I'm not finding anything useful," Quinn said, having combed through everything Dione had collected on phoenixes. "Not unless it helps us to know that phoenixes don't mate until their third year or that they prefer to eat fish rather than mammals or that females are typically two pounds heavier than males when they're full grown."

"I'm beginning to think I'm wasting time too," I said, rubbing ink-smudged fingertips together. "If Wetherill used his underhanded tactics before, no one noticed or reported it." Such a scandal would have been an exciting diversion from the endless dry interviews and mind-numbing reports about employment opportunities and profit margins.

"So what do we do?"

"I don't know, but we're not making progress sitting here."

Frustrated, I gathered all our research materials and returned them to the help desk. People stared as I stalked past, and whispers started up behind me. I glanced around the room. A variety of newspapers lay scattered across the tables and in people's grips, and my face was splashed across nearly every single one. Most papers featured a close-up of my frazzled hair, grime-and-sweat-stained shirt, and soot-smudged glower surrounded by the blur of last night's press mob, but a few captured my bedraggled, post-jailbreak appearance through the bars of the jail gate, as if I were a prisoner, not a guest-turned-victim. Bold headlines proclaimed I was either secretly aligned with Fire Eaters or had been blackmailed into sneaking them into the jail. None of the papers used my name, instead referring to me as *the Airstrong heiress* or *the Grayson heiress* for extra dramatic flair.

The only paper that hadn't plastered the worst shot they could find of me on its front page was the *Terra Haven Chronicle*. Instead, the image of Airstrong's demolished exterior glared above the fold, the headline short and ugly: AIRSTRONG IN RUINS. I finally caved to my curiosity and snagged a copy from the sale stack, setting a coin on the counter to pay for it. Stepping out of the line of foot traffic— and out of sight of all the curious scrutiny—I crouched and spread the paper for Quinn to see too.

Mom's worried face stared back at me from the bottom of the front page, Grant beside her in profile, his large hand clamped on her forearm. Mom's wrists were bound by null cuffs.

My fingernails bit into my tender palms. Mom looked like a criminal. Any Airstrong client seeing this paper would assume she was guilty. Unless those phoenix eggs were found fast—and without causing any harm—Airstrong would never recover. My parents would be destitute.

I stared at Mom's distraught face, wishing more than ever that I could talk to her.

"Why did she do this?" I whispered. She had to have known how bad her arrest would look to her clients, how thoroughly it would shred her reputation.

"To keep people safe," Quinn said, equally softly.

I nodded, letting out a long sigh. Luck and quick magic had prevented yesterday's hatching from killing people, but four more phoenix eggs were loose in the city. Removing herself from the public meant the FPD could concentrate on finding the eggs, and it would eliminate Mom as a target. I understood Mom's logic—and Grant's—but seeing Mom treated like a felon filled me with futile outrage.

"They should never have allowed Nathan to take this picture," I growled.

"Grant said they had to make it look real."

"Humph."

"Nathan makes it sound like Charlotte had the egg hidden in the warehouse when it hatched," Quinn said.

I tore my gaze from Grant's harsh profile and read the article. My stomach churned when I reached the line Quinn pointed to. *Although Ms. Grayson claimed the entire clutch of phoenix eggs was stolen from an Airstrong shipment weeks earlier, it's obvious at least one egg remained ensconced within the warehouse walls.* "This is ludicrous." The paper ripped as I turned the page. "He's all but declared Mom's guilt. Look at this conclusion: 'Only time will tell where the remaining four eggs lurk and who will be harmed by the irresponsible handling of this volatile and deadly cargo.'"

"Look." Quinn reached across my lap to tap a claw against a photo printed on the opposite page. Quinn and I stood beneath the Fire Eaters' symbol burned into the jail wall, both our faces upturned as if we were admiring the crude graffiti.

Airstrong Heiress's Secret Meeting with Persephone Kwan Turns Violent.

My stomach turned to stone. Grant was right—Nathan had played me. I had leapt after his pathetic piece of bait, so desperate for a lead that I rushed into a trap hand-tailored by Nathan to shred my reputation. The Fire Eaters had been an unforeseeable bonus—for Nathan.

"Damn it!" I slapped the paper closed without bothering to read the article. "I'm such an idiot." The picture of my handcuffed mom staring back at me set my teeth on edge. "That's it. We're going to the warehouse. I want to see it in the daylight and get an honest assessment, not this dramatized drivel." I flicked the paper hard enough to puncture it. Wadding the entire edition into a tight roll, I stuffed it into my bag. "We should interview the minotaurs too."

Nathan's article contained only passing mention of the courageous women who saved Airstrong—the same women who worked next door to the warehouse. If anyone had seen the phoenix egg being transported into Airstrong, it would have been them.

"Didn't Grant already do that?"

"He didn't say." I tugged the strap of my satchel over my head, scraping my bruised knuckles. Hissing, I shook out my hand. Punching Persephone should have been satisfying considering she had tried to kill me twice, but it had only left me with more pain. Gritting my teeth, I tried to tamp down my fury. "I'm treating this like an assignment. It doesn't matter what Grant has done, because we interview our own sources and form our own conclusions."

I rose and stomped toward the exit, my breath catching when my body's aches flared in protest.

"Should we send a new message to Grant, letting him know where we're headed?"

"No." I slammed the door open, scowling at the world. The journalists had vanished during the hours we had been inside, but a cluster of businessmen climbing the steps flinched away from me. I took petty pleasure in striding between them, watching them skitter out of my path.

Before I left the house, as promised, I had dutifully notified Grant of my plan to visit the library—just like a child checking in with a parent. Not that Grant would see the irony.

"But Grant said—"

"I remember exactly what he said."

I have a job, Kylie. I can't be at your beck and call constantly.

The bitterness in my tone made Quinn flinch. I forced myself to take a deep breath, reminding myself I was mad at Grant—and myself—not Quinn. Stopping in the shade of a pillar, I squatted in front of my friend. Pain jabbed through my bruised hip, but I ignored it. Modulating my tone into something closer to neutral, I asked, "Are you worried about Zipporah?"

"Aren't you?" Quinn's shoulders hunched, his gaze darting between my eyes.

"She wouldn't risk attacking in front of all these people." I gestured to the busy courtyard in front of the library and the streets crowded with foot traffic, carts, and flying carpets. "We're taking the bus, which will be full, and the warehouse district is always bustling this time of day. We're as safe as if Grant himself were accompanying us. Besides, he only asked that I contact him when I left home; I don't want to distract him from his important work with unnecessary messages."

The sourness of my own words grated, but so did feeling like a burden on Grant. Quinn and I could survive a few hours in the city without Grant's supervision. And if our investigative efforts helped find the phoenix eggs—as my seed seemed to indicate—we had to try.

Quinn still looked doubtful, so I added, "If we go anywhere secluded, we'll send Grant a message. All right?"

After a long hesitation, Quinn nodded. "All right."

I straightened, quashed my anxiety under a brick of determination, and stalked toward the bus stop. With a heavy sigh, Quinn followed.

———

Fifteen minutes later, we disembarked from an air bus and stared in shock at Airstrong half a block away.

A full-building ward encased the warehouse, a conspicuous FPD logo shimmering in a cautionary red tint across its surface. The magical barrier stretched into the street and swelled in a blazing dome high above the four-story roof, warning off any incoming aerial traffic—and any potential clients. Not that it mattered. Once people got a look at the front of the building, they would assume Airstrong was closed for good.

A cavernous hole large enough to fly a pegasus team through gaped on the left. Elemental braces supported the ragged opening, preventing the walls from collapsing. Soot blackened the remaining bricks, outlining a network of thick cracks snaking across the facade to the roof. Scorches marred the cobblestones in front of the building. A crater was all that remained of the sidewalk.

I dropped a hand to Quinn's back. I had assumed fear exaggerated my memory of the warehouse's destruction, but seeing Airstrong in daylight stole the strength from my legs. If the phoenix had hatched a few feet to the right, Mom— and several of her employees—would be dead.

A team of cerberi bayed as they loped around the corner, and I jumped. Despite the attack on Airstrong, business had returned to normal along the wide boulevard. Pedestrians hustled among the horse- and oxen-drawn wagons loaded with raw materials and goods. Faster, element-driven floating carts jockeyed down the middle of the lane. Some people slowed to goggle at Airstrong; others, once they spotted Quinn, cast their censorious glares or curious stares on me.

The cerberus driver canted her air sled's spell to prevent its load of fabric rolls from tumbling to the ground, shouting for slower traffic to move aside. Curses and crude hand gestures followed in her wake, then the three-headed dogs and their owner were out of sight.

"Come on," I said. Pretending I couldn't feel the stares tracking our progress up the street, I forced my feet into motion.

I half expected journalists to be lurking in front of Airstrong, possibly even for a legitimate reason, like following up on the phoenix story, rather than on the off chance they might get to harass me. Instead, a single guard stood in front of the warehouse in Airstrong blue.

"The building doesn't look stable," Quinn said. The acrid scent of smoke wafted from the charred building, overpowering the street's ever-present odors of baked dung and sun-heated dust even from half a block away.

"I agree. And I don't think we're going to learn much from out here."

"I can fly over and check out the back."

"Good idea."

Quinn got a running start and leapt into the air, using the length of the street to gain altitude before circling over the gigantic ward. The guard shaded her eyes to watch

Quinn's flight. I did the same, monitoring him for any signs of pain. He soared out of sight without a hitch in his wing beats, and I let out a relieved breath. Mika's miraculous healing had done the trick again.

Wracking my brain for the guard's name, I waved a greeting to her, then fought back a grimace when the gesture flared pain from my shoulder to my elbow. Twin braids of silver-laced black hair framed the woman's oval face, and her brown eyes lit up in recognition, but it wasn't until I spied the tattoo of a swallow on her neck beneath her right ear that I placed her not as a company guard but as the warehouse's shipping manager.

"Melora, it's good to see you, but what are you doing out here?"

"I volunteered. I figured with no one allowed inside—and your mom told me that goes for you too, Kylie—I'm the closest thing to a warehouse manifest that we have." She tapped her head with a finger and gave me a wink, but her smile faded when she glanced at the crater left by the phoenix. "With the fair coming up, we have a full warehouse, even with all the . . . problems we've had."

Dismay sank heavily in my gut at the reminder. Terra Haven's summer fair drew crowds from across the state for its week-long extravaganza. Vendors traveled from even farther, shipping their goods ahead of them. I spent more than one teen summer working as a manager's lackey during the influx of fair-related shipments, when the warehouse was perpetually filled to capacity and the staff needed every helping hand they could get. This was Airstrong's busiest season, here and all along the shipping lanes as state fairs rolled out across the nation. The streets should have been bustling with clients picking up goods and the sky crowded with incoming airships and gryphons.

"Have many people come by today?" I asked, picturing the smoke-choked interior I had navigated last night. It had been crowded but nowhere near the typical packed-to-the-rafters fair capacity.

"A handful. I've taken down their names and where they're staying. As soon as we get someone in to check the building's integrity and give the all-clear, we'll make sure Airstrong is back up and running. Which is exactly what I told them." Melora gave me a smile that would have been more reassuring if it reached her eyes.

"And what didn't you tell them? Do you know what was destroyed?"

Melora's eyes darted up and down the street. Despite the traffic noise, she still spoke in a hush. "The damage was extensive. I haven't been allowed in, but I can tell you that we had five crates of Wise Wives' Field and Garden Saver Spell Pods stored close to the door for pickup today, and that whole section of the warehouse doesn't exist anymore. I don't need to tell you how expensive those are. We had a lot of flammable items too—fabrics, books, some paintings. Maybe they escaped the blast and the flames, but the smoke?" She lifted her hands in the air, then let them drop to her sides.

The knot in my stomach twisted tighter. "This is catastrophic."

"That's a good word for it. Between this ward and no one having the authority to sign off on the construction overhauls this place is going to need, we're at a standstill. Incoming shipments are being held—"

A flurry of doves scattered from a nearby roof, the claps of their wings echoing down the street, drowning out the rest of her sentence. Quinn soared into view, gliding on widespread wings. When he joined us, Melora greeted him, then turned back to me. "I imagine you didn't come here to listen to me complain. Unless you did. I mean, did Charlotte put you in charge while she's, ah . . . preoccupied?"

I shook my head. *Preoccupied.* If only. I wanted to assure Melora that Mom hadn't been arrested, but I couldn't. "I had to see the place for myself in the daylight. I had hoped it wasn't that bad." I tugged my gaze from the piles of crushed bricks mounded inside the FPD ward.

"It's bad. Real bad."

I nodded, and the three of us stood in silence, each contemplating our own glum thoughts. "Thanks for catching me up," I finally said, itchy to get on with my investigation.

"Give Charlotte my best and tell her we're doing all we can," Melora said. "I don't know if it'll be enough, but we're trying."

"Thank you." I started to walk away, then turned back. "Have you heard from Dad?"

I had been so caught up in trying to find the stolen goods, I hadn't checked in with Dad or even asked Mom how he was doing. The equal lack of communication from him meant Dad was likely swamped with keeping the rest of the company afloat, especially since countering bad press and appeasing leery clients had probably morphed into a full-time job. Once he heard of the phoenix hatching and Mom's narrow escape, plus her imprisonment, it would tear him up to not be able to reach us. And he would have even more work on his hands restoring this fractured warehouse remotely. What a nightmare.

Melora's face softened. "It's too soon. Even Pegasus Express couldn't get a message out to him and back overnight. But I'm sure he's going to come up with a solid plan for saving Charlotte and Airstrong."

"Yeah. All right. Have a good day." I walked away, wishing I shared Melora's confidence. Dad was brilliant and a good boss, but if he had a plan for saving Airstrong, he would have enacted it before now. As for saving Mom, he was as helpless as I was. More so because he was stuck on the East Coast, and I was here in Terra Haven, the same city where all the thefts happened. I, at least, could work toward locating the remaining phoenix eggs and ending this horrid sabotage on Airstrong.

As soon as I got home, I would send Dad a letter. Even if Mom had been given a chance to do the same before she had been sequestered away, hopefully I could share fresh information and ease his worries. I wouldn't mind receiving a reassuring word back either.

Muffled clanging and pounding emanated from the neighboring two-story warehouse, proving the minotaurs weren't wasting any time getting back to work. The building's large bay doors were locked, but a smaller door had been thrown open, allowing sunlight to spill inside. A ladder was propped against the front of the building, leading up to naked black bolts where glass letters had spelled out FEMMES OF THE FURNACE until yesterday. Sunlight glinted off green and yellow shards swept into a pile beneath the ladder. High up on the second floor, a series of window frames jutted from the building, but with the panes missing, the bars propping the frames open were redundant.

I peeked inside the warehouse, jumping back when I almost collided with a minotaur on the way out.

"Oh! Hello. My name is Kylie Grayson, and I was hoping I could ask you a few questions about yesterday's explosion."

The minotaur tipped her fawn-colored bovine head to

get a better look at me. Stacked with muscles and graced with an abundance of feminine curves her denim overalls couldn't conceal, she stood head and shoulders taller than me and nearly filled the doorway.

"Grayson? Are you related to Charlotte?" Her voice was low, the Rs softened and pronounced on the back of her tongue since her lips didn't purse the same as a human's.

"I'm her daughter. I'm trying to piece together what happened yesterday, specifically how that phoenix egg got into the lobby."

Liquid brown eyes assessed me, and her fuzzy ears flicked independently of each other. I wasn't well versed in minotaur body language, but I thought her ear movement reflected annoyance or impatience more than an attempt to pinpoint a sound.

"You're a journalist, aren't you?" she asked.

"Yes, but this is personal."

She nodded. "I don't have time to stand around talking. If you can keep up, I'll answer your questions, though I don't think I'll be much help. Call me Lianne."

"Thank you, Lianne. Would it be possible for my friend, Quinn, to ask some questions of the others? That way we can be out of your way as soon as possible."

"Your friend?" Lianne's muzzle dipped to her chest as she transferred her gaze to Quinn. "Are *you* a journalist too?"

"I haven't written anything yet, but I assist Kylie whenever possible."

"Is that so?" Amusement glinted in her eyes, and her ears rotated back. "Check with Genesis out back. She's the short one with a white triangle on her forehead. Tell her I sent you, and careful where you step."

Quinn slipped into the warehouse, and I trailed Lianne

to the glass pile.

"Here, make yourself useful." Lianne handed me a canvas bag, and I held it open while she used a soft spell to sweep the mess into it. "The FPD did a decent job cleaning the glass from the street last night, but I wanted to remove the remains of our sign myself. I didn't need them messing up the bolts. It took me a week last time to get them into the exact right shape to support the glass without adding strain, and the spell embedded in them is finicky." Hoisting the ladder under one arm, she contemplated the naked bolts a moment longer. "Now I have to add a protective layer to the spell too. Somehow." She shook her head and strode through the door. I backpedaled to avoid the end of the ladder, then rushed to follow.

Minotaurs bustled around the interior of Femmes of the Furnace, all female. None glanced our direction, busy with brooms and cleaning spells. An older minotaur with gray around her black muzzle repaired a collapsed metal stand using a bar of steel and an impressively dense elemental flame. I spotted Quinn's golden body in the sun of the loading dock behind the warehouse, a minotaur with a tan-and-black face running water through a sluice while she talked to him. Rubble flanked them, sorted roughly into dirt, brick, and glass piles. When I almost crashed into two minotaurs carrying pails of water, I apologized and jogged to catch up with Lianne.

"You can set that there." Lianne pointed to another canvas bag, this one full to the brim with glass detritus, and I set the bag I was carrying next to it. Lianne strode off with the ladder again, and I scurried after her.

"Did you notice anyone who might have dropped off the phoenix egg?" I asked, pitching my voice to carry over the bang of a metal hammer.

"We don't have time to loiter outside."

I didn't expect it to be that easy, but it didn't hurt to start with the most important question. "What about suspicious persons or conveyances?"

"Like I said, no one had a spare minute to waste out front, not with preparations for the fair. Now . . ." Lianne trailed off with a sigh. "I don't know if we're going to recover." She propped the ladder against the wall, then surveyed her shop with drooping ears.

I turned to take in the cavernous building, looking beyond the whirlwind of minotaurs, and my next question died in my throat.

A trio of cold furnaces stood along one wall, each paired with a long brick pit and surrounded by racks of metal tools, buckets of brackish water, worn benches, and drums of sand. I had never been inside a glass workshop before, but common sense told me glass remnants shouldn't coat every surface. Yet coarse, melted pools glommed the tops of the furnaces, clear fragments littered the base of the brick pits, and a rainbow of fractured panes and figurines coated wooden shelves near the loading dock. Five stocky minotaurs clustered around the front-most furnace, patching a crack with fresh mortar and stone. Against the wall closest to Airstrong hunched congealed misshapen lumps of flash-melted sand and soda ash, the wooden drums previously containing the material disintegrated or burned to ash. Beyond them, the red ward around Airstrong glinted through a hole in the building. Thick cracks bisected the front and side wall, and worrisome splits ran through several structural wooden beams.

"The phoenix did all this?" I asked.

"The explosion shattered every piece of glass outside our annealing ovens, windows and product included."

"Was anyone injured?" I didn't see any dried pools of blood, but I couldn't imagine how everyone could have escaped harm.

"My sister and two cousins are at the Blackwell-Zakrzewska Healer Clinic—one for burns, two for lacerations." Lianne crossed the floor to a pile of gritty shards and used fire-and-earth magic to begin sorting glass from dirt. "Everyone is trained on protective spells," she continued, "and we don't operate the furnaces or work glass without them. But we never thought about the building."

I followed her gaze to the ceiling. A third of the roof was missing, the network of metal frames all that remained of the skylights.

That explained the melted glass on *top* of the furnaces.

"This was going to be our big break. We've been running a small artistic studio, traveling from fair to fair every year to make ends meet. We finally saved enough to rent this space. We hired everyone in our family. We're branching out, offering specialized flat planes—windows, door inserts, cabinets, mirrors. Isla has a knack for flowers. You should have seen the rose-and-jasmine window design she created. She's not too bad with animals either. We had a dragon design that was sure to sell fast. But without any examples of our work . . . I don't know if we're even going to be able to make our lease next month."

She rubbed her hands across the wide bridge of her nose, then scrubbed the flat planes of her cheeks. "We've been putting our money and focus into the equipment and goods. I hadn't gotten around to warding the shop against anything other than trespassing. I never thought I would need to put up defenses against phoenixes."

"For what it's worth, I'm grateful you were here. Your quick actions saved many lives yesterday, including my mom's. Thank you." No one else on the street had rushed to help, and these women had plenty of reasons not to.

"It was the right thing to do. Besides, Charlotte has been a good neighbor. She's given us discounted shipping and let us store items in her warehouse when the rental agreement lagged and we had nowhere else to put them. She's a kind woman, and I'm sorry she and Airstrong have been having so many troubles." Lianne surveyed the wrecked shop with sad eyes. "Sorrier that her troubles are now ours too."

"I'm sorry too." I fiddled with the strap of my satchel. "If anyone heard or saw anything unusual, no matter how small, it might help figure out who did this."

Lianne was already shaking her head. "We've only been here six weeks—six busy weeks. I still haven't met half my neighbors."

"What about Luther Wetherill?"

"The guy with the curly gray-brown hair who was yelling at Charlotte last night?"

"That's him. Have you seen him around? Before last night, I mean."

"He came in a week after we settled, wanted to see who we were shipping with. I thought it was odd that he came himself and didn't send one of his workers."

My pulse picked up its tempo. "That *is* odd."

"Then again, Charlotte didn't send a worker either. Maybe that's just the shipping way."

I wanted to argue but settled for asking, "Have you seen Wetherill since?"

"No. Wait. Yes. He came by—" A commotion on the loading dock interrupted her.

Quinn galloped into the building, then launched into the air, flapping fast over the minotaurs' heads to reach me.

"Zipporah! She's coming!" Quinn shouted.

10

———

Quinn landed hard, his paws striking the bricks in one thunderous clap. "I'm so sorry. The harpy spotted me before I could hide. I shouldn't have been out there."

"It's not your fault," I said, dread running loose through my limbs. Zipporah couldn't find me. Not here. After all the minotaurs had suffered, I couldn't bring more misfortune to them.

"We need to leave. Come on."

A steel hand clamped around my arm, bringing me up short. "Where will you go?" Lianne asked.

"Airstrong." I blurted the answer out before the thought finished forming, but it could work. The FPD's ward would keep Zipporah out. Quinn and I just had to get inside it. Melora too. I didn't know how, but we would figure it out.

"That building is more dangerous than a harpy. You will stay." Lianne lifted her head and surveyed her family. "Circle up, on me."

All activity had stopped to watch Quinn's dramatic flight, but at Lianne's order, the minotaurs burst into action.

Lianne dragged me to the nearest wall, and in seconds, Quinn and I were encased by a herd of statuesque minotaurs, all of them facing outward.

"I appreciate this, but Zipporah isn't your problem." I tried to squeeze out of the circle, but the muscular women didn't budge.

"This harpy is coming here, and we protect our own," one of the younger minotaurs said.

Lianne ignored her, looking to the gray-muzzled matron. "I relinquish the herd to you, Vella."

Vella nodded, straightening her work-worn shoulders and dusting her hands briskly on her overalls. "Link up, ladies."

I offered my own bundle of elements to the mix, then braced a hand on Quinn to counter the dizzying current of magical signatures swirling within the link. Several of the minotaurs gasped and exclaimed in delight at Quinn's unexpected boost.

"We should ask a gargoyle to live in the shop," one of the minotaurs whispered, and multiple heads bobbed in agreement.

"Hush. The harpy's close," Vella said.

Zipporah flew into view, sweeping past the busted skylights. Her foul stench wafted in her wake, and several minotaurs covered their nostrils with their hands. Talons raked the roof, the shriek of metal setting my arm hairs on end. Vella snorted her annoyance. Folding her ears against her head, she glowered at the roof, as if she could see Zipporah through the overlapping corrugated panels.

"Harriet Kylie Grayson, I know you're here," Zipporah shouted.

"Will the roof hold her?" Lianne whispered.

"We're not going to find out." Vella spun enormous

elemental bands into a majestic ward, wielding the bounty of magic with practiced skill. The pattern was unfamiliar to me, all ice and earth and inverted air, with nominal wood- and fire-binding components, and I filed it away to try on a drastically smaller scale later. Dropping five anchors around the building—a mere two inches from the FPD's ward around Airstrong—Vella draped the two-story warehouse in protective magic as easily as she might have tossed a quilt over a bed.

Zipporah squawked. Her heavy wing beats echoed in the vast workshop, and when she flapped into view, her golden eyes zeroed in on me.

"Send out the heiress," she ordered.

"Leave us," Vella said, using a spell to amplify her words rather than shout.

"I demand the girl. She owes me." The full potency of Zipporah's putrid fumes breached Vella's ward, coiling into my nostrils and dripping down the back of my throat. I tugged my shirt up over my nose. The harpy's wings weren't designed for hovering, especially not with half her primary feathers sheared short. She pumped harder, spiraling in a circle that kept her mostly in view. It wasn't a pretty sight, with her sagging breasts slapping against her stomach and her excrement-coated undersides flaking noxious detritus. I wanted to look away, but I couldn't.

"This isn't your fight, cattle," Zipporah shouted. She stretched a talon toward the ward, jerking it back when an ice spike stabbed her foot. Baring her sharp teeth, the harpy flapped higher. "Harriet and I have a deal. She owes me, and if she told you differently, she's using you."

"We know about the child's deal," Vella said.

My shoulders hunched. Of course minotaurs I just met knew about my debt to the harpy. How could they not, since

Nathan's cursed articles had exposed my dirty secret to the entire city.

Vella continued calmly, as if addressing an unwelcome guest at a party. "Your contract with Ms. Grayson gives you no right to trespass on our property. Begone, harpy."

"If you don't send Harriet Kylie Grayson outside this minute, I will destroy you!" Zipporah screeched.

"Maybe you should let me leave," I said, feeling cowardly hiding behind these kind women. They had saved Mom's life, and I repaid them by bringing a harpy to their doorstep.

"I fear no harpy. But that harpy fears me," Vella said, speaking to me but projecting her words to Zipporah.

"You're making a huge mistake," Zipporah promised. She coasted out of sight, lashing out with elemental blades. The harpy's magic tore into the minotaurs' ward.

And rebounded.

Zipporah struck again, harder. The ward flexed and held. The harpy's strength was no match for a linked herd of minotaurs, especially not when they were gargoyle enhanced, but that didn't stop Zipporah from hurling increasingly savage attacks. I cringed, picturing crowds gathering at nearby warded windows to gape at the spectacle. Traffic had likely ground to halt up and down the street. Journalists would be arriving soon, drawn by the commotion. And I could do nothing about it.

I couldn't fight back and send Zipporah fleeing. I couldn't leave. Even if the minotaurs let me walk through their ranks and ward, I couldn't protect myself. Most importantly, I couldn't think of a way to clear my debt with Zipporah and safely end this lethal relationship.

Frustrated with my impotence, I bounced in place. When the first minotaur loosed a melodic low, I startled and stilled. Another woman repeated the bovine cry, then another. The sound came from deep in their diaphragms, guttural notes made beautiful as their voices began to overlap in waves of harmony. Zipporah circled the empty skylights. Spittle flew from her mouth as she spewed curses and demands, but the minotaurs' melody drowned her out.

Vella gathered magic, funneling it into the ward, building its power as the minotaurs' song swelled around us. The women's tempo increased, their voices rising. Elements thickened. The air grew heavy and warm, the pressure as comforting as a hug. I shared a wondrous glance with Quinn. We stood inside a primitive maelstrom of motherly energy like nothing I had ever experienced. I basked in the security, all my tension unraveling, all my worries released and whisked away into the link, feeding the swelling magic.

Zipporah flapped into view. With a twist too fast to follow, Vella altered the ward. Magic caved beneath the harpy, sucking the air from beneath her wings. Zipporah plummeted. Before she could recover, the spell reversed. A fountain of elements hit the harpy's underside and shoved her skyward. Vella tweaked the anchors, unpinning the ward. The immense might of the ward imploded, all of its energy gushing through the funnel Vella had positioned beneath Zipporah. The harpy was blasted out of sight.

Silence hummed in my ears. I gaped at the empty skylights, barely aware of Vella disbanding the link. As a group, we stepped forward, every eye trained on the rectangular opening above us. A dark speck twisted against a puffy white cloud, snapping its dark, mismatched wings open. Zipporah circled once, so high she could have been mistaken for a mangled vulture. Then she flapped south, retreating toward her nest.

Grinning, I turned to thank Vella.

"It is time for you to go, Charlotte Grayson's daughter," the elderly minotaur said. "You and your family have done enough damage."

My breath caught, my triumphant glee crumpling into bitter remorse faster than a magical backlash and twice as painful. I bowed my head. "You're right. Thank you for your protection and for all you did to assist Airstrong and my mom yesterday. I owe you all a great debt I hope to one day be able to repay."

Vella didn't acknowledge my words. The minotaurs silently parted, leaving a clear path to the door. I glanced to Lianne, wanting to remind her to contact me if she remembered anything that would help my investigation, but the words withered on my tongue.

I looked each woman in the eye, said thank you, then walked out with my chin held high but my spirit deflated.

———

Seradon stood on the street in front of Airstrong, a personal flying carpet rolled under one arm. Seradon, not Grant. He had sent her in his place. I knew it before she opened her mouth and said as much.

"I would have gotten here faster once we spotted the harpy," she added, "but I was under the impression that you were at the library."

"I had a change of plans."

"And your message got lost on the way to the captain?"

"I don't have to run everything by *your* captain," I snapped.

Seradon shared an inscrutable glance with Quinn that only ratcheted my annoyance up higher.

"As you can see, I'm fine." I flung a hand toward the sky. Zipporah had disappeared, and the minotaurs' magic had dissipated as if it had never existed. Several faces remained pressed to nearby windows, and more than one shimmering ward hung around neighboring warehouses, but most of the street's activities were already resuming. Melora detached herself from the wall of the building on the far side of Airstrong, the illusion spell that cloaked her melting away. I gave her a tight nod, shame and irritation choking the apology she deserved. But what could I say? *Sorry the harpy scared you? Sorry that my misfortunes impacted you?*

"Where are you off to now?" Seradon asked.

"Home." I spat the word like a curse. I had learned nothing, not at the library, and not here. I was hungry and discouraged and annoyingly fatigued from the day's nominal exertions. My shoulders were knots of tension. The next phoenix's disastrous hatching loomed closer with each passing minute. If I didn't find those eggs soon, someone would get hurt, and my parents would be held accountable.

And I had nothing.

"I'll walk with you."

I speared a glare toward the carpet tucked under Seradon's arm.

"You look like you could use the exercise," she said.

Gritting my teeth, I marched down the street, not waiting for Seradon or Quinn to catch up. The loss of the minotaurs' serene magic emphasized my body's aches and pains. I considered dropping by a local healer, but I already knew what they would say, and I didn't have time to rest.

"Did you learn anything new?" Seradon asked Quinn.

"Not about the phoenix eggs. I only spoke to one minotaur. She was really impressed with Charlotte's work ethic. She said she saw her often outside the warehouse, and yesterday she seemed to be in two places at once with how hard she was working."

Working to save her business, I silently added. Mom had spent every waking minute at Airstrong, trying to redeem the company's reputation and keep shipments moving. Terra Haven was a crucial hub for Airstrong, one the company couldn't survive without.

I cast a bleak look over my shoulder at the warded warehouse. I would figure out who was behind this. I had to.

Somehow.

"What about things not related to the eggs? What else did you learn?" Seradon asked.

"I've never boosted a . . . a collective before. That's what the minotaurs felt like. It wasn't like a normal group of people. Their magic all felt connected. Their signatures all had a base harmony. It was . . ." Quinn groped for the right words, and my footsteps slowed as I waited for the rest of his response. "It was a bit like how it feels when I link up with the same people my siblings are enhancing. Familiar. Familial."

"Comforting?" Seradon asked.

"Exactly. It was comforting and incredibly powerful."

"That's minotaur women for you." Soft yearning colored Seradon's words. "I worked with two early on at the FPD. I like my squad now, but I still miss those women."

"Harriet! Harriet! Did you give the harpy what she wanted?" A journalist darted out of a side street and rushed me, his recording sphere zooming to hover above my head. I recognized his face but couldn't recall his name, only that he was with the *Critical Informer*, a paper more prone to print fantasy than fact.

"Please, leave me alone."

"I will. Just give me something I can take back to my

editor." He glanced over his shoulder, then scurried into my path, forcing me to sidestep to avoid running into him. "What did you promise the harpy? What did she give you in trade? Is she helping you track down the phoenix eggs?"

Footsteps sounded behind him, and a familiar dread knotted my stomach. He wasn't alone. I gathered the elements, ready to cast an opaque illusion around myself and Quinn, only to realize we were too far apart.

"There she is! Harriet!" a new voice shouted.

"Kylie, wait!"

My head whipped around before I realized I didn't recognize the voice. Seeing my reaction, the middle-aged reporter hustling down the sidewalk shouted for me again.

"Kylie Grayson! Why did your mom try to blow up her own company?"

My nails curled into my palms, but I schooled my expression. Before I could plot my escape, three—no, five— reporters swarmed me, grinding my steps to a standstill.

"Is it true? Are there ten more phoenix eggs somewhere in the city?" someone asked.

"What's your mom's plan? Why is she trying to kill everyone?"

"Was Charlotte kidnapped? Did the harpy abduct her? Was she delivering ransom demands?"

"Wow, that's creative," Seradon said, stepping up beside me and casually swiping aside the flock of recording spheres. "You built yourself quite a story there, Annie."

The journalists scampered back several steps, giving Seradon a respectful space they hadn't afforded me. It didn't surprise me that Seradon knew the newshounds by name. I wasn't the only person who had written articles based on the FPD's actions. How many times had these reporters tracked down Grant's team to interrogate them about one of their missions? How many times had I?

I scanned the eager faces of my interrogators, fighting a snarl of disgust at their abrasive tactics. Was this how Grant had seen me when we first met?

Was this how he still saw me?

Quinn stepped into the gap between Seradon and the journalists, forcing them to give us even more space.

"Are you guarding Harriet?" Annie asked Seradon.

"Or arresting her?" the guy beside her suggested hopefully.

"On what grounds, Mitch?" Seradon asked.

"Stealing the phoenix eggs?" Mitch guessed.

"Stealing those banned spells Airstrong lost?" the journalist beside Mitch offered.

"Trying to murder her mom? Matricide!" The petite blonde jumped up and down like she had won a prize.

"Calm down, Channah." Seradon chuckled and shook her head. "You and Annie should get together and write a book. That sounds like the kind of adventure thriller I would read."

"Then tell us what's going on, Seradon," Annie demanded.

"Well," Seradon drawled, "I *was* having a lovely chat with my friends, but a bunch of busybodies with outlandish imaginations accosted me, and here we are." She smiled, and no warmth emanated from her expression.

Mitch scoffed. "You expect us to believe you're friends with Harriet?"

"Kylie," Seradon corrected. "And I like to think I'm good friends with Quinn too."

The reporters shifted their gazes to Quinn. He yawned, displaying citrine fangs longer than my fingers.

Seradon used their distraction to unfurl her carpet. It settled on a flat levitation spell a foot above the ground. The carpet was even smaller than Grant's.

"After you," she said. Looping an arm around my waist, Seradon guided me onto the carpet and stepped up behind me.

"Wait. Seradon, Har— I mean, Kylie, tell us what happened with the harpy," Channah said.

"There's not much to tell," Seradon said, tightening her grip on my waist as the carpet lifted another foot off the ground. "The harpy realized she wasn't welcome, and she left."

I widened my stance and bent my legs just in time. Seradon pulsed air into the carpet's propulsion spell, and we shot away from the journalists. Quinn galloped alongside us until he had room to open his wings and launch himself into the sky. I looked away before the sunlight reflecting off his golden body blinded me. Then he was above us, gliding over the nearest rooftop and coasting back on widespread wings. When I glanced over my shoulder, one of the reporters had a camera out, and I ducked behind Seradon's taller frame.

"Thank you," I said.

"You can owe me."

"You're going to have to get in line to collect."

Seradon chuckled, using her grip around me to give me a shake. "Buck up, little reporter."

I twisted to shoot her a withering glare, but her teasing expression had morphed into a scowl. Following her gaze, I spotted a Fire Eater's ashen tag on the corner of a vacant building. Seeing the crude phoenix mark here, on the edge of the warehouse district rather than in the blight, surprised me.

"Did O'Hara learn anything useful from the Fire Eaters arrested at the jail last night?" I asked.

"Not much."

"Did they say who hired them?"

"We're looking into it."

I stifled the urge to growl at her evasive answers. "We? Your squad or O'Hara's?"

"Does it matter?"

"I would prefer you were all focused on finding the missing phoenix eggs and clearing my mom's name."

Seradon scanned the road beyond me, steering the carpet around a slow carriage. "You'll have to trust we're doing everything we can."

"I would have a lot more faith if Grant hadn't locked Mom up last night."

Seradon's left eyebrow flicked up. "I thought he explained that to you."

"Sure. It's all for everyone's own good, because everyone should hop when he says *jump* and fly when he says *flap*." It wasn't fair, but damn it, Grant hadn't bothered to show up himself. And damn *me* for being upset for the exact reason he chastised me for last night—expecting him to drop everything and rush to my rescue.

Seradon shook her head but didn't say anything.

I waited until she navigated us through the busy downtown streets and into a quieter neighborhood before asking, "Has anyone found a link between Wetherill and the phoenix eggs?" Something I had missed? "He's been acting suspicious since the first Airstrong theft, and he hasn't made it a secret that he's trying to steal all of Airstrong's clients."

"Unfortunately, your family's problems aren't the only ones in Terra Haven."

I sucked in a sharp breath, but she continued before I decided if I wanted to apologize or get indignant.

"O'Hara's squad is heading the phoenix investigation. We've had our hands full untangling Fire Eater traps in the blight. That's where I was when we saw Zipporah, and that's where I'm headed once I drop you off."

"Fire Eater traps? Isn't that . . ." I struggled for a polite term and settled on: "Beneath you guys?" The gang was always causing trouble, especially in the neighborhoods of the blight they considered their territory. This sounded like the kind of problem usually handled by city guards.

"You were at the jailbreak. You tell me. Was that beneath Anderson? Beneath you?"

I winced. "That's not what—"

"Grant doesn't waste our time. He puts the squad where we're most needed. Today, that's traps in the blight. And, apparently, racing around the city after you."

"Seradon, I didn't mean—"

"I know what you meant, but do you? It seems to me you believe the captain is bossing you around, but you're the one expecting us to drop everything because you and your family are in danger."

"That's an oversimplification," I said, my temper flaring. "We're talking about stolen phoenix eggs on the brink of hatching. One nearly killed my mom and her staff, and four more are still out there. It's not just my family that's in danger—it's everyone."

"Which is why O'Hara is in town, devoting all his attention to finding the thief and the eggs." Seradon's tone teetered between exasperation and reassurance as she slowed the carpet in front of my house.

Quinn landed in the front yard, worry pinching his brow

as he glanced between us. I gave him a tight smile as I stepped off the carpet onto the sidewalk.

Turning, I peered up at Seradon. "Has O'Hara looked in Wetherill's direction even once?"

"Wetherill is stuffed up and self-centered, but he's also a wealthy full spectrum. He's behaved like a jerk, but he hasn't done anything wrong." Seradon dropped into a cross-legged position at the center of the carpet. "I need to get back. If you're going to leave again, send a message with your *exact* location, please. Or just stay home and have a quiet night in." Tossing a wave to Quinn, Seradon shot down the street and disappeared around the corner.

"'Just stay home,'" I mimicked in a snide tone. "Just stay home while Mom is locked up and someone's terrorizing Terra Haven with phoenix eggs about to hatch." I stomped up the walkway. "Did you hear her expert advice, Quinn? All we need to do is stay home, sit on our hands, and wait for someone else to take care of it."

Because that had worked so well in the past.

Fuming, I pounded up the porch steps and yanked open the door. A tranquil silence filled the interior of the Victorian, grating on my nerves. Grumbling under my breath, I slapped together a sandwich, taking my frustrations out in violent chops against the cutting board. Plate in hand, I flounced upstairs to my room and slammed the door shut behind me. Quinn was waiting on the balcony railing, and I crossed the room to open the door for him.

"What now?" he asked, sitting in the limited floor space between my bed and the low table in front of my love seat.

I dropped my lunch on the table, too agitated to eat. Instead, I paced the width of the room. Eight steps, turn, eight steps, turn. Frustration fueled my movements, though an underlying fatigue stole some of my coordination, and I tripped more than once over nothing. As soon as I found the phoenixes, I would rest. Until then, I had to keep moving.

"The library was a bust. You said you didn't learn anything from the minotaurs, right?"

Quinn shook his head.

"Me either."

"Did you send out rumor scouts?" Quinn asked.

"I didn't bother." Rumor scouts were a spell I had invented to capture and record sound when triggered by a particular word or phrase. The phoenix's hatching—and the remaining four missing eggs—were the talk of the town. Sending out scouts to hunt down anyone mentioning them, Airstrong, or even Persephone or Mom would only bring back a bunch of useless gossip and speculation. "If we had a lead, one small detail that only the thief would know, it might be worth it, but right now . . ." I trailed off, frustrated that none of my usual tactics were the least bit helpful.

"Then what's in the message bowl?" Quinn asked.

I glanced at the porcelain bowl sitting on a small pedestal near the window. A single elemental message waited inside. I recognized the magical signature from across the room.

Activating the spell with a flick of air, I flinched as Grant's voice spilled out, cold and clipped.

"Give me and my team the courtesy of keeping us apprised of your whereabouts. Send a message next time you change locations. It will save us time and possibly save your life."

No sign-off. No concern. He might as well have been addressing a stranger or an insubordinate FPD recruit.

I rubbed my breastbone, but it did nothing to soothe the heartache and anger seething inside my chest. Spinning away from the message bowl, I resumed pacing.

"Did Seradon say if they found anything?" Quinn asked.

"Grant's got them chasing Fire Eaters in the blight." The heat of the jail's brick walls surrounded me, the fireball devouring the air. I pushed the memory aside. Grant had taken down stronger opponents than a pack of pyromaniacs. He and his team would be fine.

"Maybe they'll discover who hired the gang to free Persephone," Quinn said.

"Maybe. But that's not necessarily going to get us closer to recovering the phoenix eggs."

"It's a lead."

"Sure, but it's not like Grant's going to share any information with us." I drummed my fingers against my thigh, then stopped when it fired off pain through my bruised knuckles. "We need a lead of our own. Since chatting with Fire Eaters is out of the question, we could try asking around at the other businesses near Airstrong. Maybe someone saw something."

I grimaced. Interviewing nearby proprietors would be an onerous endeavor. Like the minotaurs, everyone would be recovering from the hatching and working twice as hard to make up for lost time. They wouldn't likely be open to answering questions, at least not those posed by a journalist —or more specifically, by the Airstrong heiress. For a normal story, I would have accepted the tedious task as part of the job, but with the urgency of the unhatched phoenixes prodding me to action, I couldn't help but think it would be a waste of time. O'Hara had probably already gotten all their statements anyway. If he had learned anything useful, he would have already acted on it.

"Tomorrow. We can do that tomorrow," I decided. "Today, we need to act on what we have, and we have only one connection between all the thefts."

"Luther Wetherill?" Quinn asked. "Are you sure?"

The full spectrum's smug expression filled my vision, and I spun on the ball of a foot, stomping back across the room. Trying to be objective, I replayed his actions. Even if I ignored Wetherill's ongoing defamation of Mom's character as the underhanded tactics of a cutthroat businessman, he had still been suspiciously fast to beeline with O'Hara in tow to the obscure location of the stolen spells on his fiancée's forgotten property. Then, mere minutes after the phoenix hatched, he had been on hand to point fingers and cry for vengeance. His timing was simply too perfect to be coincidence.

He had to be involved.

"I'm sure."

Even if he wasn't the thief, just the mastermind, Wetherill had stolen so much more than shipments under Airstrong's protection. He had pilfered my parents' reputations, robbed them of their freedom, and was poised to destroy their futures. If he somehow convinced O'Hara that Mom was behind the thefts, she would be hanged.

Just stay home, Seradon? Not when I was the only person willing to investigate the real culprit.

I stopped pacing and focused on Quinn. "It's Wetherill, and we're going to prove it."

"Are we going back to the library?"

I shook my head. "We need to be bolder. He's too good at covering his tracks. We need to go to him."

"Question him?" Quinn canted his head skeptically. "I don't think he'll confess."

"No, he's too slippery for a direct approach. But we can't waste time either. We need to find evidence that ties Wetherill to the thefts before the next hatching. The last place O'Hara and his squad will think to look for the missing phoenix eggs is right where we'll find them: Wetherill's property."

"How can you be sure he has them?"

"The eggs need to be kept hot to prevent them from hatching, right? Maintaining such an environment takes elemental skill, something Wetherill has. But even in the right location, the eggs are eventually going to hatch. Wherever they're being stored, they'll need to be contained in a potent spell. Again, Wetherill has the power." Hearing the facts out loud convinced me I was on the right track. "Anyone who saw the spells would know straight away what they were, so that rules out public locations like his warehouse or business offices. He also needs to renew and check the spells frequently, so the eggs can't be far away. His house is the logical choice."

"He doesn't like you. He's not going to invite you into his home."

"Which is why we're not going to wait for an invitation. We're going to sneak in."

Quinn's forehead crinkled. "I don't know."

"Who better than us? The FPD can't check his property without a warrant unless they have reason to believe he has the eggs, and despite all the evidence pointing at Wetherill, O'Hara hasn't made a move." I threw my hands up in exasperation. "If he were anyone else, I would say the investigator was scared of Wetherill."

"Shouldn't we be scared of him?"

"What's the worst that blowhard can do? I already lost my job."

"You didn't lose—"

"I was suspended. That's close enough. Mom is in hiding. Airstrong is in ruins. Wetherill can't make my life much worse. And if we do nothing, he wins. Our only chance at saving Mom is by acting. We need to find those eggs before they hatch, and you heard O'Hara—it could be any minute. We need to break into Wetherill's house. Tonight." A thrill of certainty energized me.

Quinn glanced toward Mika's empty room on the other end of the connecting balcony. When he looked back, he didn't quite meet my eyes. "Isn't breaking into his house illegal?"

"So?" I crossed my arms. "Being in possession of phoenix eggs—*stolen* phoenix eggs—is worse."

"Would we get in trouble if we're caught?"

"We won't get caught." Why was Quinn arguing? We needed to find the eggs, and this was the best chance we had. "I know where Wetherill lives. We'll wait until midnight, then sneak in."

"What about wards? Defenses?"

"We'll figure out a way—"

"What if we don't?" Quinn interrupted. "What if everything doesn't go perfectly?"

"It will." My stomach tightened. Didn't he want to help me? "It's not like we're going to move the eggs by ourselves. We're just going to look. Then we'll go straight to O'Hara, he'll arrest Wetherill, and this nightmare will be over."

"What about Grant?"

"What about him?"

"Will you tell him where we're going?"

I worked my jaw back and forth. If Quinn was uneasy, snarling wouldn't help him see my logic. "He would never agree to help in this, but it needs to be done. We need to find those eggs. Mom needs me to find them. And Grant . . . Maybe it's better if we don't have his help."

Quinn lifted a paw, examined his claws, and set it back down. His silence was damning.

"You don't think I can do this without Grant, do you?" I asked, my heartbeat heavy and loud.

"It's not Grant. It's . . ." Quinn's shoulders hunched, but he maintained eye contact. "It's you."

My gut hollowed out. "Me?"

"Us. I think we're getting in the way."

"What?"

"I know you want to help your mom. I do too. But the things we've done . . . We haven't helped."

"We had no way of knowing they wouldn't. You know how it works. Not every lead pans out, but every lead has to be followed. That's why we have to check Wetherill's house."

"No."

My chest constricted, his refusal a betrayal that stole my breath. "No?"

"This isn't a story," he said.

"You're right. It's Mom's life."

"I think you've lost sight of your goal."

"What's that supposed to mean?"

The tip of Quinn's tail twitched, the scrape of quartz across wood loud in the silence. Finally, he said, "What do you want?"

I tamped down on a frustrated growl. We were talking in circles.

"I want the same thing I've always wanted," I said, exasperation making my voice louder than I intended. "I want to clear Mom's name. To find the thief. To find the phoenix eggs. While I'm at it, I want to free myself from my debt to Zipporah, get my job back, and somehow convince Grant to treat me like a partner and kiss me again!" I ran my fingers through my hair, quelling the urge to scream. Clutching the pouch around my neck, I waved it at Quinn. "And this, my everlasting seed? It backs me up. I'm supposed to find those eggs. I'm supposed to help Mom."

"I'm supposed to help you," Quinn said, tucking his chin to touch his own everlasting seed hanging from his neck. "And I . . . I think I haven't been. Not the right way." He looked up. "Breaking into Wetherill's house tonight isn't the answer."

"Are you kidding? It's the only chance we have of ending this." I couldn't believe I had to convince Quinn. *Quinn.* He had my back. *Always.* Now, when I needed him most, he balked?

"What if Wetherill finds us on his property? You wouldn't get anything you want. You would be arrested. Jailed. Nathan would write something really nasty. You might never get to work at the *Chronicle* again. You wouldn't be able to help your mom. Grant definitely wouldn't kiss you."

Each argument thrown back in my face stung more than the last. I gritted out, "I won't let that happen."

"Grant can't conduct his investigation if he—"

"You're taking *his* side?"

"You could have been killed when you ran into the burning warehouse."

"You kept me safe," I rasped.

"You insisted we go immediately to the jail, and—"

"No one could have predicted the Fire Eaters would attack."

"If we hadn't been there . . ." Quinn glanced away, leaving the last of his accusation unspoken. "Afterward, we should have waited for Grant."

"Where? At the jail with the reporters who wouldn't give us enough room to breathe? In the empty street after we escaped them? You were injured. We needed to get home." Anger laced my voice, but inside, I was crumbling. How long had Quinn thought I was making the wrong decisions?

"I know, I'm sorry."

My stomach knotted. "I'm not blaming you. You were brave."

"I should have insisted we return to the jail. I know how dangerous the harpy is. I let you get hurt."

Oh, Quinn.

"And today, I should have insisted we tell Grant where we were going when we left the library. If the minotaurs hadn't been there, Zipporah would have hurt you again. Or worse." He hunched deeper, until his wings protruded above his ears, one citrine, the other patched with clear quartz. His voice grew smaller with each sentence. "We haven't helped the investigation. We might be making things worse."

I sat heavily, my legs giving out as Quinn's words sank in. He wasn't trying to stop me; he was trying to protect me. Something I had failed to do for him. He had been healed so many times in the last weeks that his feet, wings, and sides were a patchwork of clear crystal. His body would transform those patches into his natural citrine, given enough time—less, if he didn't keep acquiring new injuries.

"Even if we didn't get caught at Wetherill's, Zipporah might find us again," Quinn said, speaking to the floor.

My chest hurt. I stared at my feet, feeling every one of my body's aches and pains. Having my failings listed so plainly had flayed my pride and shaken my confidence, but Quinn hadn't mentioned my worst flaw: I had been willing to endanger his life yet again for a plan I begrudgingly admitted was more desperation than inspiration.

I scrubbed a hand over my cheeks, dashing aside escaped tears. My actions had already cost me my job and alienated Grant. I wouldn't lose Quinn too.

"I don't know what to do, Quinn," I whispered. "Mom is in trouble. If I fail to save her—" I choked on the words and swiped more tears aside.

Quinn circled the table, squeezing close to me. "It's not up to you."

"Mom's counting on me."

Quinn snorted, and I shot him an incredulous glare.

"She tried to hide everything from you," he said. "She lied to you about the stolen firebirds. You learned about the stolen spells the same time as the rest of the city, when the FPD announced the reward. Grant was the one to tell you about the phoenix eggs. She didn't want you involved at all."

"That's because she underestimates me like everyone else." I sounded like a petulant child, but my emotions were too raw to modulate.

"I think it's the opposite. She knows you'll do anything for her, take any risk, even if she asked you not to. I think she agreed to be sequestered until the eggs are found because she thought it was the best way to keep you safe."

I nibbled the inside of my lip, replaying Mom's message in my mind. He was right, and I had missed it, determined to be the savior.

"She did it because she trusts Grant. And the investigator too," Quinn added.

I sighed. "When did you get so smart?" My doleful tone turned the teasing question into an accusation.

Quinn's ears drooped unhappily. "I don't want to make you sad."

"You didn't. I'm frustrated with myself and this situation, but not with you." I stroked his wing, then dried my face on my sleeve. "You really think we should leave the investigation to Grant and O'Hara?"

"Unless we get a lead. A real one." He glanced at me from the corner of his eye. "They know what they're doing."

"I know." Grant wouldn't rest so long as someone threatened Terra Haven, and O'Hara's sole reason for being in the city was to track down the phoenix eggs. Neither man was remotely incompetent. I had to trust that their training, experience, and dedication would be enough.

Harder still, I had to admit that despite my everlasting seed's shape, despite my connection to Airstrong, and despite having discovered the previously stolen items, I had nothing useful to contribute to the investigation. I had only desperation and fear, and neither helped me make good decisions.

It was a bitter realization to stomach.

"Is there any other way we can help your mom?" Quinn asked.

My shoulders dropped, and I sagged against Quinn. "Just one I can think of." One I swore I would never do.

I could step back into my role as the Airstrong heiress.

Before I changed my mind, I drafted a short note to Dad, informing him I would be taking over the Terra Haven branch of Airstrong until it was safe for Mom to come out of hiding—or until he told me otherwise. When I dropped the envelope into the mailbox for evening pickup, my self-appointed responsibilities settled like a mantle of lead on my shoulders. My footsteps dragged on the stairs up to my apartment.

I was doing the right thing. I had no leads on the phoenix eggs and nothing to contribute to the investigation. My parents needed me. I thought I could help by finding the culprit who had caused all their problems, but I had failed. Running the Terra Haven warehouse for a few days was the least I could do. I had to trust Grant could find the phoenix eggs without me. He knew I suspected Wetherill. He had admitted he thought the full spectrum's actions were suspicious too.

But . . .

It felt as if I was giving up on myself. So long as I was hunting for the phoenix eggs, I could pretend I was still a journalist. By returning to Airstrong, it was as if I were erasing all the tough decisions and sacrifices I had made to follow my passion along with all the credibility I had built as a reporter independent from my parents' wealth and influence.

It didn't help that I was giving up the story of a lifetime, and as selfish as it was, I grieved the loss. It had been my dream.

I tried to console myself with the faint hope of learning something from inside Airstrong that I would otherwise miss chasing the eggs, but if such a clue existed, Mom would likely have already unearthed it.

In silence, I consumed my sandwich, not tasting a single bite. Quinn slouched on the floor beside me, his chin resting dejectedly on his stacked front paws. I opened my journal, flipping to a fresh page without looking at my notes on phoenix eggs and Wetherill. Titling the page "Airstrong," I scratched out my to-do list.

"We need to get the FPD to remove the ward," I said, speaking out loud as I wrote to include Quinn in the process. "Get the building assessed by an engineer, hire a construction crew, rent a new warehouse to move undamaged product to, conduct inventory, contact anyone whose shipments were damaged, ship off delayed packages and get postponed deliveries moving through Terra Haven again, and, of course, notify staff we're back up and running." My vision blurred as I took in the impossible list.

I wished I could contact Mom. If Dad were closer, I could rely on him for direction, but I couldn't work effectively if I were waiting days between each of his responses. For now, I was on my own.

Quinn sat up to survey the list. "We have to do all that today?"

I set down my pencil and massaged my temples and the headache forming there. "Not quite all of it." Shutting off the whiny parts of my brain that wanted to accept defeat, I tried to think like Mom. "Today, we get ready for tomorrow. We can't do anything until we can get into the building."

I spent the next hour crafting and sending messages to O'Hara and key Airstrong personnel, preparing people for the warehouse to resume operations tomorrow. Melora's enthusiastic response included the name of an engineer, and I sent off a request for a building safety evaluation tomorrow morning. I hoped action would relieve the pressure sitting on my chest, but each message only emphasized how much work was in store for me.

"I really hope I don't bungle this." I contemplated the ceiling, the white paint bathed in a golden glow from the slanted sunbeam refracting off Quinn's body. "It's been so long since I worked at Airstrong, and I've never run a warehouse, only assisted. Maybe it would be better if I just sat at home and waited until everything was resolved."

"Do you really think so?" Quinn asked.

I could easily picture Mom's kind but resigned expression if I messed up, and Dad's disappointment if I failed.

"No. Airstrong won't recover if we don't turn this catastrophe around fast. We need to get back in the public's good graces. Nathan is making the company look dreadful, and no one is countering him."

"We could."

I sat up. "Are you suggesting we write a press release for Airstrong?"

"I think you should tell people Nathan is lying."

I scrunched my nose. "I love the idea, but Dahlia would never go for it." It would be too close to an advertisement, and even if the *Terra Haven Chronicle*'s editor in chief gave me the go-ahead on an op-ed piece, I was at a loss for a way to frame Airstrong's problems in a good light.

"She let Nathan basically say your mom was guilty. She shouldn't have allowed that. Someone needs to publish the truth."

"Wouldn't that be great? I wish we could. If the story had been ours, we would have done a much better job. I mean, not only did Nathan make Mom out to be a villain, but he left out so many important details."

"Like the minotaurs," Quinn said. "He didn't mention them once. They deserved a whole article all to themselves for their heroics."

His words set off a tingle in my fingertips, and I smiled for what felt like the first time in a month. "Quinn, you're brilliant."

"I am?"

"Yes! We're going to write that article." The minotaurs' bravery should be celebrated by the citizens of Terra Haven. It was the perfect way to thank them for rushing to the rescue, an apology for bringing a harpy to their doorstep today, and a means of helping them rebuild their business all wrapped up in one solution.

If we did this right.

"But you're suspended," Quinn hedged.

"Sure, but if I don't put my name on the article, who's to say who wrote it? Dahlia could publish it under 'staff,' and no one would be the wiser." My ego twinged at giving up my byline, but I let the feeling fade without pursuing it.

Quinn sat up, the forlorn expression he had been wearing for the last hour fading. "Do you think she would?"

"Dahlia publishes what's best for the paper." I leaned across the table and trapped Quinn's face in my hands, pulling him close to kiss his forehead. "And our article? It's going to be amazing."

———

I CLASPED MY HANDS BEHIND MY BACK, DOING MY BEST NOT TO fidget as Dahlia read the article Quinn and I had spent the afternoon perfecting. My gargoyle companion sat next to me, having no problem impersonating a statue.

I was proud of our piece. It had heart and drama in the descriptors about the minotaurs' brave actions, as well as details about the minotaurs' fledgling business in the aftermath of the phoenix's hatching. It mentioned Airstrong, but only to include the business and Mom among the victims of the vile individual who planted phoenix eggs in the midst of a populous city. Most important, it was stuffed with facts from beginning to end, none of them remotely slanderous.

Quinn contributed details I had been too preoccupied to notice, and I used his words verbatim. I heard his authorial voice beginning to take shape, and it made me so proud. I told him as much on our walk to the *Chronicle*—after we sent a message to Grant, informing him of our destination.

"I can't wait to see what you write about gargoyles," I said, referring to the history of Terra Haven gargoyles Quinn had been contemplating writing.

"Me either. I already picked a few gargoyles to interview. I'm trying to decide if I want to organize it chronologically or by themes."

"You've given this serious thought," I said, surprised.

"Some. I like to think about it when I'm flying. In between . . . everything."

Guilt welled inside me, self-recriminations replacing his unspoken words. *In between my impulsive actions that dragged us both into danger. In between battles. In between injuries.* An apology sat on my tongue, but I wasn't sure how to word it. Quinn had made it clear he wanted to help me any way he could. He had even used his question to the everlasting tree to ask how he could help me. If I apologized for needing his assistance, it would cheapen his actions. Worse, it would make me sound ungrateful or unappreciative, neither of which could be further from the truth. I was alive many times over thanks to Quinn.

"Once everything settles down, I'll have more time to work on it," Quinn said before I found the right words. "In the meantime, I still need to figure out *how* I'm going to write anything."

We spent the rest of the walk discussing his possible writing methods, from a pencil-holding, paw-strap invention to dictation. Neither of us brought up harpies or phoenix eggs or how long I might be buried under Airstrong's demands. But I couldn't shake the guilt of my selfishness. Quinn deserved the freedom to pursue his own passions.

"What about the harpy?" Dahlia asked, her curt voice jerking me from my ruminations. She set the minotaur article on the desk in front of her, turning her piercing gaze on me. The scabs on my face, covered in a sheen of ointment, received a cursory inspection, as did my slightly swollen knuckles. "Are you still indebted to her?"

"Yes, which is why I'm requesting this article be published under a 'staff' byline. I'm not looking for credit, but I believe the Femmes of the Furnace minotaurs deserve to be publicly praised. They are hardworking, compassionate, heroic citizens who should be rewarded for their actions, even if that reward is simply recognition in the *Chronicle*."

"Mmm," Dahlia said, the sound neither approving nor dismissive. "What are you doing about the harpy?"

"Nothing."

Finally, the editor's expression flickered, showing surprise.

"I'm focusing my attention on my parents' business. As you know, my mom was . . . arrested." I choked on the word, and I had to take a deep breath to avoid blurting out the truth. As much as I wanted to spare Mom's reputation, keeping her safe was more important. "Until she is cleared of all charges, I will be returning to Airstrong to fill in for her."

"I thought you forsook your inheritance when you became a journalist."

"That was the plan." I swallowed hard. I had promised Dahlia that my dedication to journalism was unwavering, yet here I was, going back on my word a few short days later.

"And the story of a lifetime? Are you still pursuing it?" she asked.

My stomach twisted, and my hand floated toward the pouch resting under my shirt. The moment I returned from the everlasting tree, I had told Dahlia my question. To my dismay, she hadn't been impressed. Was she interested in it now?

Clearing my throat, I said, "I've set that aside too. Making sure the company my parents built survives is more important." I let my hand fall, but the weight of my everlasting seed pressed heavily against my chest, its potential never to be realized.

Dahlia sat back in her chair. If she was disappointed the biggest story the *Chronicle* might ever print was no longer in the works, she didn't show it. Tapping the minotaur article with a blunt fingertip, she said, "This is good writing. I can fit it in tomorrow's morning edition."

"I would really appreciate that." A sliver of my anxiety dissolved. Tomorrow's responsibilities and drudgery still hung over my head, but at least I was leaving the *Chronicle* on a good note.

"Your parents are lucky to have a daughter like you. I hope you're successful in helping right Airstrong's course. And in dealing with the harpy. I'd like to see you in the bullpen again."

My chest squeezed, my yearning so strong it stole my breath.

Dahlia stood, signaling the end to our meeting. "Good luck, Kylie. You too, Quinn."

"Thank you," I choked out.

I tried not to assign unwarranted symbolism into closing Dahlia's office door behind us. I wasn't shutting the door on my dream career. I wasn't walking away from everything I ever wanted. This was temporary.

I just wished it didn't feel so final.

"Harry?"

My head snapped up at Nathan's voice, my stomach dropping. I had hoped to slip in and out of the *Chronicle* without running into the bastard.

It was late enough that half the desks were vacant, but the remaining writers and editors quieted as Nathan barreled down on me. I scanned their faces, seeing the censure I expected. My coworkers had respected me as Kylie, but when Nathan revealed I had hidden my true identity as an heiress, as *the* Harriet Kylie Grayson, they had been offended or outraged. I had lied. I had made them feel foolish in trusting me. They didn't care that I had chosen anonymity to ensure I got the job on my own merit. Or they didn't believe me and thought my parents—either their wealth or their influence—had gotten me the job, thus stealing it from someone more worthy. More like them. When I applied to the *Chronicle* as Kylie, I had never given a thought for anyone else's feelings regarding what I believed was a personal life choice, and even if I had time to make amends, I wasn't sure where to start—or how much of an apology I owed them.

Maybe it was just as well that I was leaving to work at Airstrong.

"What are you doing here?" Nathan demanded, blocking my path.

His animosity was much more clear cut: I had dared outperform him, outwrite him, and upstage him many times in the short stint I had been with the *Chronicle*. His fragile ego required he cut me down, which was the only way he knew how to make himself look better, and his initial success had only fed his demented compulsion.

In other words, he was a bona fide jerk, and he deserved nothing but my contempt.

Discreetly checking to make sure Dahlia's door was still closed, I tipped my chin up and affected an air of nonchalance. "I finished up a piece Dahlia wanted to print."

"You were fired." Nathan scowled. Having been on the receiving end of plenty of Grant's fierce looks, I almost laughed at Nathan's attempt to intimidate me.

"I was suspended." I shrugged, as if saying the words didn't make my throat hurt. "But this story was nuanced, and Dahlia felt I was the right person to handle it."

Nathan's nostrils flared, tension flexing through his shoulders. Pure hatred flashed across his face before he got control of himself.

As much pleasure as I got out of goading Nathan, I didn't

want to make an enemy of the rest of the writers listening in, so I added, "She's going to run it under 'staff.'"

"She must not have come to me because I've been so busy," Nathan said.

Behind him, several journalists rolled their eyes. A couple turned back to their work, ignoring Nathan as he continued.

"My last five articles have been picked up by national papers, and I've got a book deal in the works. I really should be thanking you. If you and your family weren't so greedy for fame, I wouldn't have had so many fascinating events to report on."

My palm itched to slap the grin off Nathan's face. I soothed it along Quinn's mane instead, drawing on the gargoyle's stillness to rein in my temper. "It's become quite trendy to report on my outings, hasn't it? I never thought I would see a senior journalist at the *Chronicle* chasing gossip with the rumor hounds. Then again, I know you have a problem with originality."

"Cute, Harry. You make it sound like I'm following you around, when it's you who keeps showing up in the most incriminating locations."

Says the man who put a tracking spell on me. I didn't voice the accusation out loud, though. Without proof, it would be my word against Nathan's, and despite the shift in the bullpen's atmosphere, I didn't think anyone was ready to take my side.

"I'm just being a good reporter," Nathan said, goading me. "But I doubt you'd understand that, having been handed the job."

"Was I handed the job because of my rich parents or was I hiding under an alias? Nathan, you're getting your stories mixed up." I tried to step around him, but he blocked me. I was tempted to ask Quinn to take the lead and watch Nathan try to halt a couple hundred pounds of stone gargoyle, but it wouldn't be fair to use Quinn like that.

"Maybe it's because you keep coming up with different versions of the events, Harry, scrambling and clawing to keep your face in the papers."

"That sounds more like what you're doing, probably because you can't find any other story to write."

Nathan gave me a pitying head shake. "My instincts are telling me your pretty castle of lies is crumbling around you. But you know what's ironic? Your blind, selfish quest for fame is going to destroy you and make me famous instead."

"Enough, Nathan," another journalist's voice piped up.

I jerked toward Audrey, who sat two desks away, arms crossed, glaring at Nathan. Audrey and I had attended the everlasting tree's blooming together, and I had enjoyed getting to know the older woman during the weeks-long special assignment. Yet ever since learning my real identity, she had been cold to me. I had resigned myself to having screwed up our friendship, but now, a flutter of hope squirmed through my midsection.

"Yeah, give it a rest. You just got a couple of good assignments," someone else said, and my heart lifted. Maybe I wasn't as hated here as I thought.

"Kylie's not interested in fame either," Audrey continued. "If she was, she would go to any paper, even someone here, and offer up her side of the story. An exclusive with the Airstrong heiress after her mother was arrested? Every paper in the city would jump at the chance."

I winced, grateful for Audrey's support but wishing she hadn't dragged Mom into it.

"Are you going to interview her?" Nathan demanded.

Audrey scoffed, flipping her gray-laced braid over her

shoulder. "That's not my kind of article. I just wanted to state a fact. I get where you're coming from, Nathan. I thought she was all about fame, too, after she asked the everlasting tree for the story of a lifetime."

My breath caught as Nathan's head whipped to me, his gaze searching my body, looking for my seed. The pouch holding it was hidden beneath my shirt, and it took all my self-control not to cover it protectively with my hand. Nathan had stolen articles from me in the past. Even if he hadn't made it his goal to ruin my life and my parents' lives, I would never have told him my question. What was Audrey thinking? That wasn't her information to share.

"But Kylie's actions say otherwise," Audrey continued. "So do her past articles, if you go back and read them. Kylie genuinely wants to write stories that help others. That's something you could learn from her. You're too fixated on front-page bylines, Nathan."

My outrage guttered. Audrey had read back through my articles? She may have been looking for confirmation to her theory about my terrible character, but my writing had changed her mind. It sounded like Audrey had forgiven me. I would have been thrilled if she hadn't also blabbed my seed's purpose to Nathan. I could tell he hadn't heard a word Audrey said after "story of a lifetime" either.

"You must be bungling the seed's clues, because you haven't written anything important since you came back from the tree," Nathan said. His eyes narrowed. "Unless it was that fluff piece about the historian."

"Actually, the first clue was about firebirds, but—" Audrey started.

"Firebirds?" Nathan's grin stretched his lips too wide, and he burst out laughing. "Are you saying the story *I* wrote about the firebirds that healed Lunacy Labyrinth was the story of a lifetime?"

"It was *a* story," I said, and immediately wished I had kept my mouth shut.

Nathan cut his laugh short. His greedy eyes pinging back and forth between mine. "Where else has your seed pointed you? Is that how you found Persephone's hidden island? No one else knew to look in the middle of Dead Man's Swamp except Luther Wetherill."

"I did research," I snapped. "I followed the facts of the story. That's how I figured out Persephone had stolen from Airstrong."

"Suuure," Nathan said, drawing out the word obnoxiously. "All of your expertise as a *junior* journalist enabled you to find spells the FPD couldn't even track. It had to be your seed."

"It might be hard for you to believe since you—"

"Funny how both times your seed pointed to Airstrong's problems," Nathan said, cutting me off. "Your parents are at the heart of the largest scandal to rock this country. Of course that's the story of a lifetime."

"No," I said, wishing my voice sounded firmer. Nathan's accuracy unnerved me almost as much as the feverish energy burning in his gaze.

"Oh, this is too good. You're not even a journalist anymore, but you've got an angle on the biggest story ever. And you've been leading me right to it, every step of the way."

"You don't know what you're talking about." My voice shook with impotent anger.

"You haven't finished evolving your seed."

"It's only a matter of time," I said, eager to wipe the grin off his face. "And when I do, *I'll* write it." It was a pretty lie.

My seed wasn't going to evolve while I was toiling at Airstrong, but Nathan didn't need to know that.

"We'll see, Harry. We'll see."

I shoved past Nathan, something I should have done before his first taunt. The other journalists in the bullpen eyed me as I passed, but it was Nathan's hungry stare that scorched my shoulder blades. Yanking open the door, I escaped into the stairwell, choking on the bitter knowledge that Nathan was going to steal the story of a lifetime from me, and there was nothing I could do about it.

13

I woke before dawn with no desire to return to my anxiety-riddled dreams. Dressing in the dim light of a minuscule glowball, I double-checked my to-do list. The daunting number of tasks reaffirmed my decision. My hunt for incriminating evidence against Wetherill might have hit a dead end, but I was still fighting. His malicious attacks weren't going to bring down Airstrong, and they weren't going to ruin my parents. I wouldn't let them.

I slipped downstairs with my boots in hand, waiting until I was on the porch to pull them on. Signaling Quinn, I trotted down the walkway, checking up and down the block for gossip hounds. The sleepy street was blessedly empty.

Quinn coasted to my side, the clack of his soft landing swallowed by the early-morning hush.

"Did you let Grant know where we're going?" he asked.

I nodded. "Right before I came downstairs." Even knowing the danger Zipporah presented, I couldn't shake my irritation at having to run my schedule by Grant.

"That makes me feel better." Quinn's gait eased, and my annoyance abated at seeing him relax.

We walked in companionable silence for a few minutes, each caught up in our own thoughts.

"I wish we had a lead," I said on a sigh.

"I'm going to keep looking."

Without me? My hair whipped into my mouth when I jerked to look at Quinn. He gave me a tentative smile, and I swallowed my jealous question, managing to choke out a half-hopeful "Really?"

"I don't know anything about shipping, but I want to help. Maybe I can learn something useful."

"That would be wonderful." I injected as much enthusiasm as I could muster into the statement.

We boarded an air bus without encountering a single reporter and without any sign of Zipporah. Quinn rode on the roof, which delighted the bus driver, and I took a window seat and stared broodingly out at the waking city. When we disembarked, Quinn flew to the nearest rooftop, eager to begin interviewing gargoyles in the warehouse district. Envy snarled in my stomach, but I decided to call it hunger. Sulking to the One-Horned Capricorn, I purchased a hot meat-and-vegetable pocket pie to go. Surprisingly, breakfast appeased my mood, and by the time I finished my last bite, I was almost eager to get started at Airstrong.

The FPD's ugly ward was still draped over the warehouse, and I grimaced at the eyesore. O'Hara better not drag his feet on removing the barrier, because I had an engineer on her way and a construction crew lined up to start repairs later this morning.

After cleaning my fingers with a quick spell and sweeping my outfit with a brush of air to remove crumbs, I squared my shoulders and marched down the block. I had chosen my outfit with care, avoiding Mom's signature khaki and cream pairings in lieu of sturdy gray pants and a tailored bright-blue top that matched my eyes. I wanted to look professional without giving the impression I was pretending to be Mom. Neither garment was especially nice, since I would be spending the day doing dirty, physical labor.

My everlasting seed remained at home, tucked safely in my jewelry box. I had made my choice; I didn't need a physical reminder of what I was sacrificing.

My simmering self-pity dissolved when Grant stepped out of the shadow of Airstrong's ward. His gray FPD uniform hugged his broad shoulders and molded itself to his biceps and chest. Delicate silver symbols glinted in a trail of defensive elemental patterns down his flat stomach and muscular thighs. The magic looked fresh. Recently renewed out of necessity or routine?

Grant stopped at the edge of the sidewalk, letting me close the remaining distance between us. Two days ago, he would have greeted me with a kiss. Instead, a faint crease ran between his brows, and his eyes squinted with suspicion. Realizing my expression mirrored his, I smoothed my face into a polite smile. Or I tried. I managed a dyspeptic grimace. Grant hadn't shown up at dawn because he missed me; he was checking up on me.

"Here I am, just like I said." I spread my arms in a mocking flourish.

Grant's jaw muscle bounced. "Where is Quinn?"

"Visiting friends."

"He left you alone? With Zipporah after you?"

I shook my head and pointed to a rooftop at the far end of the street, where Quinn's golden form glinted in the sun's first rays next to an amethyst-and-rose gargoyle.

"He's just over there. Don't worry, I've always got a

babysitter." I mentally winced, thankful Quinn was too far away to have heard me. He was much more than a babysitter. He was a friend, and he was devoted to helping me. But Grant's tone set me on edge, putting me on defense.

"What are you up to, Kylie? Why do you want the ward removed?"

"So I can get to work."

The crease between Grant's brows deepened. When he crossed his arms, I mirrored him.

"O'Hara's team and mine already went over every inch of the warehouse. If there was a clue about who planted the egg, we would have found it."

"I know."

Grant rocked back on his heels at my easy agreement. "Then what are you doing here today?"

"Taking over until my mom can resume her normal duties." A flurry of nerves skittered through my stomach. I hadn't worked at Airstrong in years. I didn't have Mom's skill, only the knowledge she had drilled into me as a teen. I didn't even know the names of all the warehouse employees. Was my plan built on false hubris?

"Not everything Mom did," I added. "Just this warehouse, getting the Terra Haven shipping routes back up and running. Dad's got everything else covered, but we need someone here who can authorize expenditures." I realized I was babbling, trying to convince Grant of my competence as much as myself, but I couldn't make myself stop. "Mostly, I'm here to give everyone else the go-ahead to do their jobs."

"You're going to stay here? All day?"

I looked away from the open skepticism on Grant's face, letting my gaze sweep over the blasted hole in the front of the warehouse. "Longer. The repairs alone will take more than a week. Sorting all the inventory too. Not to mention figuring out how to address the incoming shipments."

"What about tracking down the phoenix eggs?" Grant asked.

"Quinn is asking around. If he learns anything, we'll let you know." I tried to smile. "Otherwise, we'll leave finding the eggs to you. *I* will be here, safe inside." The bite I intended to deliver with the last statement fell flat. I rallied, managing a snide tone when I added, "No need for you to be at my beck and call today. You can focus on your important work and not worry about saving me."

"So you won't be sneaking off into trouble today?"

My temper flared. "If you don't believe me, ask the editor in chief at the *Chronicle*. I informed Dahlia yesterday that I would be taking a job here and not returning to the paper until my mom was free." And until I had cleared my debt with Zipporah, but Grant already knew the harpy was the reason behind my suspension.

"It's not that I don't trust you. This is just...unexpected." Grant rubbed the back of his neck, looking torn between being puzzled and pleased. The urge to slug him was hard to resist.

"Despite what you think of me, I *do* think about others when I make decisions," I snapped. "Mom needs me, and this is where I can do the most good for my parents."

"That's very mature of you."

My hands balled into fists.

Grant stepped forward and tapped my knuckles. The contact startled me, as did the humor sparkling in his eyes. His warm scent swirled around me, delicious and clean.

"Are you fantasizing about hitting me?" he asked.

"Of course not. It would be childish."

Grant's lips curved in a suppressed smile.

Huffing out a breath and uncrossing my arms, I added, "But it would be satisfying."

I couldn't meet his eyes. To do so would reveal how much our weak banter had lifted my spirits.

"Do you know who O'Hara is sending to demolish this ward?" I asked, jerking my chin toward the ponderous magical boundary beside us.

"I requested the task. I wanted to see you."

My stomach flipped, and I told it to calm down. Grant had volunteered because he didn't trust me, as his interrogation had proven. Still, the hint of smile shadowing his lips made my heart beat faster.

"You wanted to see if I would show, is more like it," I said.

"I wanted to see if I could modify this ward to keep out a particular harpy while you were here," he countered. "Link with me?"

"Sure." I gathered an even balance of all five elements and floated the bundle to Grant. His magic swallowed mine, plunging me into the electric heart of a thunderstorm, his magical signature simultaneously invigorating and sensual. Linking with Grant never failed to steal my breath.

I slanted a glance at him, wondering if he knew the effect his magic had on me. Probably. More importantly, had Grant requested the link because he genuinely needed the extra power or because he was flirting with me?

Appearing oblivious to my scrutiny and unaffected by our link, Grant crafted a message requesting Quinn's assistance in amplifying our magic. When the spell reached Quinn at the end of the street, he and his gargoyle friend flew closer. The magic in our link quadrupled from both their boosts. Grant sent a second message of thanks, then turned his focus to the FPD's ward. He deftly altered the bands of elements holding the spell together, removing the hardened earth and wood that prevented trespassing and reshaping the remaining elements into a standard defensive spell. Neither the original ward nor the new version were particularly complex, but the sheer scale of the elements made the spell unwieldy. Even with both gargoyles' boosts, Grant siphoned elements through me, answering my unspoken question. I quashed my disappointment, and when Grant dissolved our link, I stifled a sigh of regret.

"Thank you," I said primly.

"My pleasure." Grant winked.

My stomach performed another flip, and I reminded myself I was still upset with him. Just because he was being nice didn't mean I forgave his high-handed attitude and penchant for dictating how I should behave. If I told him I planned to continue to search for the phoenix eggs, his charm would evaporate.

The thought cast a pallor over my mood. Squaring my shoulders, I turned to face the warehouse. "Well, I better—"

"Kylie, wait." Grant caught my elbow in a light grip, releasing me almost as fast. He glanced over my shoulder, then into my eyes. "We're doing everything we can to find the person who has the phoenix eggs. The Fire Eaters have ramped up their activities fivefold in the last few days, and that's been . . . challenging."

I had to bite my lip to hold in the surge of questions on the tip of my tongue. Seradon's comments yesterday about the Fire Eaters combined with their attack on the jail had my journalist instincts on high alert. For all the good it did me. I wouldn't be writing any articles now or in the near future, no matter how intriguing they might be, so it was futile to ask for more details than Grant was willing to share.

Footsteps scuffed the sidewalk behind me. Melora strode up in work boots and Airstrong coveralls. She raised her hand in a wave, and I returned the gesture.

Grant tugged my arm, drawing my attention to him. He spoke too softly for Melora to overhear when he continued, and his eyes locked on mine with an intensity I couldn't break. "My team and I have been monitoring Wetherill as much as we can. I still suspect him of being involved in this. O'Hara is—well, he's not sharing his thoughts with me. But I'll find something. I promise, I'm going to get to the truth."

Choking on my desire to be working with him rather than stuck at Airstrong, I said, "I'm sure you'll figure it out." The words scraped like glass across my tongue, and I fought back unexpected tears. I was on the right path. This suffocating feeling would pass.

"Kylie, I—" Grant cut himself off, his expression troubled.

I gave him a sad smile. Speaking louder for Melora's benefit, I said, "Thank you, Captain Monaghan. I appreciate you taking time to get Airstrong positioned to make repairs."

Grant straightened, his professional mask falling into place. "You're welcome, Ms. Grayson."

The mantle of Airstrong heiress settled on my shoulders, heavier than ever. Taking a deep breath, I squared my shoulders and stepped across the threshold of the defensive ward.

———

MELORA AND I BARELY HAD TIME FOR A CURSORY ASSESSMENT of the warehouse, cautiously rolling aside the loading doors at the back and surveying the partially destroyed, partially waterlogged contents of the shipping floor, before the engineer arrived. Together, the woman and I tested the structural integrity of the building, wall by wall, our magic linked so I received firsthand feedback as she manipulated the elements into the foreign shapes and patterns of her profession.

By the time we finished, the construction crew had arrived along with the all the warehouse staff. I placed Melora in charge of the staff and clearing out as much inventory from the warehouse as possible, and I orchestrated the reconstruction of the building. The entire front wall of the four-story building had to be demolished, as did several interior walls, before they could be rebuilt. Essential support beams required replacements. The roof needed patching and reinforcement. All the damaged shipments had to be cataloged and disposed of, all the owners of those shipments notified.

Wagons and workers clogged the street as demolition got underway. I sent two younger members of the Airstrong staff to Mabel's Down-Home Confectionery, the city's top bakery, to purchase as many boxes of pastries as they could carry, then asked Melora to deliver them to the surrounding businesses with notes apologizing for the inconvenience and noise. I would have gone myself, but the people in the neighborhood knew Melora, and she them. Giving her a chance to make a personal overture with the owners of nearby businesses would help her—and through her, Airstrong—build better relationships over the long run.

From my workstation set atop a pallet of bricks behind the warehouse, I redirected incoming aerial shipments down the street to a cramped former granary, the only rental available on a few hours' notice, then sent the night manager to oversee the temporary facility; I coordinated with Airstrong's liaison at the Pegasus Express, staff gryphon riders, and airship captains to resume outgoing deliveries; I read shipping manifest after shipping manifest, comparing the contents with the salvaged products strewn across the loading dock; and I compiled lists of customers to be contacted about retrieving their goods currently stored in our facility for the upcoming fair. To the customers whose goods had been damaged or destroyed, I wrote personal letters of contrition and included information on how to receive compensation. A tally of losses and expenses filled a separate ledger for my parents' records, and the running figure made my head hurt.

Before noon, a stream of customers joined the chaos, steering their carts and pack animals up to the loading dock to carry away their wares. With them came journalists. Melora handled interviews while I linked with Airstrong's most elementally powerful staff and built an opaque floor-to-ceiling curtain of air, water, and earth to visually wall off my open-air office and the interior of the warehouse so I could operate without an audience. Between the augmented ward Grant left domed over the building, my curtain, and the dozens of support spells holding up half the building, the atmosphere hummed with magic, setting my teeth on edge.

At some point, Melora placed a water glass in front of me, and it kept getting refilled. Someone else dropped off a sandwich, and later, an apple and wedge of cheese. I ate methodically, thanking people without really seeing them. No matter how fast I worked, how many problems I solved, or how many decisions I made, another issue arose before I caught my breath.

By the time the sun set, exhaustion pervaded my body, but my thoughts spun in a dozen different directions. Wired and tired, I helped close the wide bay doors, locking the remaining shipments inside. The construction crew cast a second ward over the building to prevent trespassing. They grumbled about having to expend extra magic to encase the FPD's ward, but their policy of guaranteeing a building's safety during their construction had been the main reason I hired them. After a long day's labor, the crew was quick to depart, as was the Airstrong staff. I returned friendly waves and thanked each person as they left, all the while fantasizing about my bed. When the last person finally filed out, I leaned against the wall of Femmes of the Furnace and crafted a message for Quinn, letting him know I was ready to go home.

Quinn had checked in throughout the day, but never with case-breaking information. Secure in my safety, he roamed farther each time he left, widening his investigation. Early on, I envied him, but by the last time he flew away, I hadn't had the energy to do more than stare wistfully after him before refocusing my weary eyes on the paperwork in front of me.

I searched the dusky sky, not sure which direction to send my message. Quinn didn't have a magical signature I could embed as a location spell. I needed line of sight or a general idea of his whereabouts.

The neighborhood had cleared out, and a pleasant quiet settled over the street. I let my eyes drift closed, soaking in the absence of hammering or banging or anyone needing my attention. My head pounded and my feet hurt, but overall, I was satisfied. I had put in a long day of hard work, and I could see progress. I hadn't found the missing phoenix eggs, but I had helped. It felt good. Remembering Grant's smile was a bonus.

Footsteps scuffed behind me. Reluctantly, I dragged my

eyelids open. A pair of scrawny men in dark clothes sauntered out of the nearest alley, chatting softly. Something in
the way their eyes flitted to me and away set off a warning in
my brain. Were they reporters waiting to get closer to
bombard me with questions? I scanned their hands for
notepads and their shoulders for camera straps, but they
weren't carrying anything. Uneasy, I reached for the
elements.

Someone slammed into me from the opposite direction.
Shock jolted through me, and before I could react, thick
arms seized me. A foul wash of body odor and ash assaulted
my nostrils. Thrashing, I struggled to free myself, but with
my arms pinned to my side, I had no leverage. The two men
I had been watching sprinted toward us, and for a fleeting
moment, I thought they were racing to my rescue.

"This her?" one of them asked, sliding to a stop in front
of me.

"'Course it is," the other said.

I scrambled for the elements just as my captor's heavy
hand slapped a cloth over my nose and mouth. Heady
fumes as sweet as candy radiated from the drenched material, the scent reminiscent of a healer's operating room.

"Breathe deep, princess," the man growled. The rasp of
his voice sent a zing of recognition through me, but panic
overwhelmed my recall.

I held my breath and whipped a club of air at my
attackers.

"Hold her!"

Earth hacked through my weapon, shattering it. I gasped
as pain backlashed into my brain. Spearmint and honeysuckle anesthesia curled into my nose and mouth, lancing
into my esophagus. Coughing, I clawed for the elements,
but they slithered out of reach.

Hot breath fanned against my ear. "Relax. I've got you."

Revulsion crawled up my spine. I could no longer feel my limbs, no longer tell if my legs were holding me. My eyelids drooped, blinding me.

Screaming soundlessly, I fought until oblivion swallowed me whole.

14

"Where is it?" a man hissed.

"How am I supposed to know? It's too dark to see my own cock," grumbled a deeper voice.

"It would take a bonfire to find your tiny dick," a third chimed in.

"At least I could power a bonfire. You're lucky to light a torch."

My head lolled against a cloth that stank of mildew and sweat. My heartbeat pounded in my temples. Blinking took effort, and when I managed to pry my eyes open, I still couldn't see. Panic dripped through my veins, increasing with each heartbeat. I tried to recall where I was, but shadows shrouded my thoughts.

"It's not the size of the magic; it's how you wield it."

"What would you know—"

"Enough. Drop her here."

My skin chilled at the familiar raspy voice. The world tilted, and I slammed onto my side. My head cracked against the hard surface. Dizzy and disoriented, I reached for the elements. Magic surrounded me. I could feel it. I could see the protective spell I wanted to build. But no matter how hard I strained, the elements remained a hairsbreadth out of reach.

The toe of a boot shoved against my hip, and I flopped helplessly onto my back. A ping of alarm burst through the fog miring my thoughts, but it took my brain several seconds longer to process my body's reaction.

Nothing had pinched my skin as I rolled. Nothing pressed against my flesh beneath the hem on my pants.

Grant's badge was missing.

The tracking spell embedded in it wasn't going to help me.

My breaths caught in my throat, oxygen failing to reach my lungs. Revulsion chased fear, crawling like a spider down my spine. One of these men had pawed beneath my clothes while I had been unconscious. What else had they done?

A man's voice rumbled nearby, but it sounded as if he was speaking into a megaphone stuffed with linen. I fought to focus, but my awareness spiraled inward and winked out.

"Wrap it up, Eugene," Raspy Voice commanded, jolting me back to consciousness an indeterminate time later.

My eyes snapped open. A burly man stood at my feet, facing away from me, lit by a minuscule glowball hardly larger than a marble. Other figures darted in the shadows beyond him.

"Rumy, where are we—"

"Shit, she's waking."

I startled at the voice that spoke next to my head. A pimply teen stood above me, peering down at me with wide eyes. I lolled my head to the side, scanning the surroundings. Misshapen shadows loomed on either side, blocky and unnatural. The last thing I remembered was stepping out of Airstrong's warehouse, and then—

I had been kidnapped.

I yanked at the elements and willed my body to bolt. I managed a feeble wave of my hand, lassitude weighting my muscles, magic just out of reach.

"What should I do?" the teen asked, his voice cracking.

"Dose her. We're almost—"

Voices shouted in the distance. Someone shrieked. Footsteps pounded close, and a person skidded to a stop just out of sight. "A basilisk escaped! I had it tied up, hooded, you know? But I went back. It's— Ice bite my nuts, did you hear that?"

The susurrus of scaled flesh cut through the acute silence. My blood ran cold.

Basilisks possessed truncated dragon claws and alligator jaws. One bite could sever a limb, but that wasn't their most dangerous attribute. Imbued with paralyzing earth magic, their gaze petrified anyone who made eye contact. Death wasn't instantaneous either. Victims suffocated, fully aware and unable to draw a breath. Paralysis didn't last beyond a couple of hours, but it didn't need to—no one survived the first ten minutes.

The pimply teen gasped, a damp cloth dropping from his fingers to fall across my mouth and nose. I jerked aside, squirming away from the sweet fumes. Darkness swam through my vision. I tried to sit up, but my arms collapsed and my stomach muscles refused to help. My legs weren't working either, and after a moment's flailing, I realized it was because they were bound together at the ankles.

"Damn it, Hammy, you led it straight to us," the leader shouted, lunging out of sight. "Go, go, *go!*"

The men tore out, their footsteps thunderous. On their

heels, claws clacked rapid fire, closing in fast. My instincts screamed for me to run, but I couldn't even stand. Magic evaded me. Panic hammering my heart against my rib cage, I squeezed my eyelids tight and prayed.

The basilisk slowed as the last of my kidnappers' fleeing steps faded. I held my breath, ears straining to hear beyond the thunder of my own pulse. The whisper slide of the basilisk's scaled body sent goose bumps down my arms. It snuffled, then hissed, likely testing the air with its long tongue. My imagination filled in the rest of the basilisk's details—its long, thick body coated in rust-brown ridges, with paler scales down its stomach and a crest of rainbow-black rooster feathers arching like a Mohawk down its spine; its four stocky legs bent into right angles, capable of shockingly fast sprints; its claws designed to rend flesh from bones; and its lethal, beady eyes glaring above a blunt-nosed jaw fenced with interlocking teeth as it searched out its next victim. From the thump of its steps, it was at least as long as I was tall, or maybe it was only fear that made it sound so massive. It didn't matter. Basilisks were lethal at any size.

Claws gouged something metallic to my right, the squeak piercing the silence. Inside, I flinched, but self-preservation kept me immobile. The basilisk sauntered closer, the scuff of claws in hard-packed dirt audible with each step. My heart lodged in my throat, choking me. It sounded like it was inches from me. Could it hear my hammering heartbeat? Did it know I was only playing dead? One snap of its jaws and my ruse would be over.

It hissed, its tongue caressing my shoulder, drowning me in the stench of old blood and death. Stars of false light burst behind my eyelids as I squeezed them tighter. Another step. Claws caught on the fabric of my shirt. The weave tore with a soft sigh. The basilisk exhaled, its fetid breath fluttering the hairs on my forehead. Sweat broke out across my scalp. Any second, the reptile would strike. My skin hummed with dreadful anticipation, tension building in my body until my muscles felt as if they would crack under the strain.

I didn't breathe. I tried to not even think.

Pain burst through my knee as the basilisk's foot sliced through my thick pants into my flesh. Its tail flicked across my shins. My throat ached with the need to scream, my limbs an agony of abeyance when all I wanted to do was flail and flee. The basilisk's next step tore at my hair where it splayed across the ground, ripping out a hunk. Tears sprang up, unbidden. Its tail slapped my scalp, rasping through my hair, ripping out more strands. The basilisk's next step carried it past me, and I exhaled a soundless sob, wishing I had the luxury of hyperventilating.

I maintained my frozen posture as I tracked the deadly reptile's progress. A scratch. A swish. The snap of its tail against an inanimate object. Slowly, oh so painfully slowly, it ambled away.

Cold seeped into my body from the hard ground, cramping my muscles. Something tickled my neck, and I pretended it was a strand of my hair, not a bug crawling across my bare skin. Blood oozed a slow, warm path down my throbbing knee. I counted my breaths. When I reached two hundred without catching hint of a scratch or scrape, I chanced a peek through slitted eyelids. Piles of bulky objects bracketed me, half obscured by shadows, their outlines softened by large swaths of cloth draping them. *Storage,* I thought. Twisting my head, I checked the sky. No stars brightened the dark expanse. It had been a cloudless day, which meant I was inside. From the musty smell, I was either underground or in a little-used building.

Trapped in a confined space with a loose basilisk.

Cautiously, I sat up, relieved when my muscles responded, frustrated when the elements remained out of reach. Pins and needles raked my right hip where folds in my pants had cut into my leg. The pain rushed south, eating fire down my leg. I wriggled my toes in my boots, but I couldn't budge my ankles. I reached for the binding, grunting when cuffs dug into my wrists. Squinting, I examined the restraints. They were metal, but they weren't null cuffs. I recalled the cloying combination of spearmint and honeysuckle, and my memory supplied a name: Grave's Echo. My abductors had dosed me with the drug healers used to anesthetize patients for lengthy surgeries. My ability to use magic would return, thankfully, but it could take minutes or hours. I didn't have time to wait to find out.

Hissing from the pain of bending my cut knee, I traced the rope binding my ankles until I found the knot near my heels. With my hands locked together, cramping my fingers' agility, it was impossible to undo the snarl. Tugging my ankles did nothing but make noise—and make me keenly aware of my full bladder. Afraid additional struggles would attract the basilisk's attention, I patted the ground, hoping to find a convenient sharp rock I could use to cut myself free. When my hands encountered only dirt, I squirmed to my side. My head knocked against something hard. I jerked, twisting to check the object.

A man loomed over me, his fingers bent into claws, his face contorted in rage. A shriek lodged in my throat, and I lurched backward, my frantic scrambles propelling me like a knotted snake across the floor until my shoulders slammed into a jagged surface. My elbow hit a protrusion, and my arm went numb to my fingertips. Off balance, I tipped to my side.

The man remained frozen.

Panting, I shook the feeling back into my arm and cautiously sat up. Still, the man didn't move. He didn't even blink.

My stomach hollowed out. The basilisk. The man wasn't poised to attack me; he was paralyzed.

I eased myself to my hands and toes, then pushed back to my heels, concentrating all my energy into balancing as I rose to a crouch. After holding still for a count of twenty, listening for the basilisk, I hopped toward the man. Each landing jarred my full bladder, but it was the faint scuffs of my boots that made me wince. As much as I wanted to flee, I didn't know where I was or even why I had been kidnapped. The dead man might have answers.

I halted outside of his reach, unable to force myself closer. In the dim light, I could make out his features, and I was only mildly surprised it was the pimply teen who had been poised to drug me. The grimace I had interpreted as rage I could now see was terror. His eyes had gone glassy, his lips parted on his last breath. While I had been lying at his feet, playing dead as the basilisk slithered past, this poor boy had been suffocating, locked in place. I shuddered, sympathy at his horrific death warring with relief at escaping the same fate. He was my kidnapper—or one of them—but I wouldn't have wished this on him.

Tearing my gaze from his horror-struck expression, I scanned his body, looking for clues about his identity. I didn't have to search far. Tattooed on the webbing between his thumb and forefinger was a crude phoenix symbol. He was a Fire Eater.

That's where I recognized Raspy Voice—Apollo—from: he had been the leader during the prison break.

Had I been abducted because of Persephone? Had whoever hired the Fire Eaters to break her out also hired them to trap me here? Wherever *here* was. Or maybe this had nothing to do with Persephone and everything to do with Airstrong. I had made gratifying progress in restoring order at the warehouse today. Had someone—Wetherill?—hired Fire Eaters to kidnap me to prevent me from restoring Airstrong's Terra Haven facility? It seemed like a stretch, but it was the most logical theory. Without me, Airstrong would flounder again.

Only, this didn't feel like a scheme Wetherill would concoct. How would the snooty full spectrum go about hiring the city's most notorious gang? And why? Wouldn't he have better connections? People who were more reliable? People who didn't accidentally unleash a basilisk in the middle of an abduction?

I shook my head. I would figure out how all the pieces fit together *after* I was safe. Which meant getting free of my bonds, figuring out where I was, and escaping.

A short knife hung at the teen's waist. Clamping my bottom lip between my teeth, I plucked the blade from the sheath. The backs of my hand brushed against the fabric of his shirt, and a hint of heat seeped through to my cold fingers. I jerked away as if scalded. Rationally, I knew he couldn't harm me. He wasn't about to lurch into motion. Despite his wide eyes, he couldn't see me. He was dead, minutes beyond saving, even if I had the skill to counter the basilisk's paralyzing magic and the ability to use the elements to do so. But he stood upright, his skin still lifelike, his body still warm.

A shiver that had nothing to do with the chill night air wracked my body.

Crouching, I sawed through the coarse bindings on my ankles. The rope squeaked against the knife. I paused, listening for the basilisk, then resumed my frantic efforts. The tip of the blade punctured my boots more than once, poking through to nick my feet, but I didn't slow. I needed to be ready to flee if the basilisk returned.

Finally, the rope parted, and I kicked it away. Panting, I stood and rolled my ankles, willing blood to loosen my stiff joints. I flipped the knife in my grip to test the cuffs around my wrists, but the metal held fast, and I couldn't see the lock in the gloom. Reluctantly, I wrestled the sheath from the paralyzed Fire Eater's waist and clipped it to my own, safely stowing the knife.

Turning my back on the dead man, I trailed my fingers along the nearest cloth-draped mound, trying to puzzle out the shape. Light from above caught my eye. Creeping another step, I spotted a gritty square of pale gray suspended thirty feet in the air. A window. This was a building, not a cave. Which meant it had a door somewhere, and a door meant freedom.

Dense shadows in every direction made it difficult to determine the size of the building. Larger than Airstrong's warehouse, I decided. Perhaps three times as big. I closed my eyes and attempted to orient myself. The need to pee made me want to bounce on my toes, but I held still. When the men had fled, it sounded as if they had run left. If I followed—

The rustle of reptilian scales against cloth whispered from the shadows on my left. My heart leapt in my chest, and I whipped my head in the opposite direction. Tiptoeing as fast as

I dared, I hurried away from the basilisk—and likely away from the exit. Holding my hands in front of me, I navigated around another inky mound covered by a drop cloth, then another, not stopping until I slipped down a new path, hopefully out of the basilisk's line of sight. I couldn't remember how well a basilisk could see in the dark, but I didn't want to take any chances.

My bladder protested, each step eliciting a stab of pain. When no ominous footsteps chased me, I shuffled from foot to foot. Only the fear of peeing my pants made me tug them down. If I was soaked in my own urine, the basilisk would have no trouble tracking me. Bunching the nearest cloth in a pile near my feet to muffle the sound, I squatted to pee. Visions of being found paralyzed with my pants around my ankles ran through my head. If Grant discovered me like this, I would die all over again of embarrassment.

Luckily for my pride and my health, I finished urinating and pulled my pants back up without being attacked. However, the smell of urine assaulted my nostrils, and I envisioned the basilisk scurrying closer, drawn to the scent. The urge to pick a direction and run until I hit a wall nearly overwhelmed me, but I forced myself to tiptoe, feeling my way toward the next bulbous, cloth-covered pile. Judging by the size of the building and the lack of sounds or light outside, I wasn't in Terra Haven. The urgency of my bladder confirmed I had been unconscious for at least an hour or two. Long enough for the Fire Eaters to transport me far from the city, especially if they had used an aircraft.

How long would it have taken Quinn to notice I was missing? How much longer for him to locate Grant? The lack of a tracker wouldn't prevent Grant from finding me, but it would take him longer. He might not even be close. Without magic at my disposal, my survival came down to one simple task: avoiding the basilisk.

Stealth and caution. I could do this.

My toe banged against something wooden, and I nearly jumped out of my own skin. Patting the air in front of my legs, I carefully navigated around the protrusion, ears straining for sounds of the basilisk. My foot slammed into metal, and the sound rang through the cavernous building. Cursing, I spun in the opposite direction and scurried through the gloom, hands splayed in front of me. Mammoth shapes loomed out of the darkness, forcing me along a winding, confusing path, searching for a wall or a door. I waffled between straining to decipher my surroundings and being afraid of accidentally encountering the basilisk's gaze.

In a few turns, I lost all sense of direction. Panic cut through each breath, and I forced myself to stop. *Think, Kylie.* I spun in a slow circle, orienting myself on the single window. It was close, though so far above me I had to crane my head to find it. Maybe if I got higher, its faint light would help me make sense of my prison. If nothing else, getting off the ground would make it impossible for the basilisk to reach me.

Annoyed that I hadn't thought of it sooner, I circled the nearest obstacle, searching for a convenient path up. Coarse cloth shifted beneath my fingers, sliding aside to reveal lacquered wood. I brushed my fingers across the smooth surface, trying to make out the shape. The object was larger than a gryphon and twice as tall.

My fingers encountered a groove, and I shoved the cloth aside further. Rustling and rasping, the fabric slid to the ground. I froze, my fingers splayed across a metal emblem of a pegasus jumping into flight—the logo of Luther Wetherill's shipping company.

Dust plumed the air, tickling the back of my throat. I covered my nose and mouth with my elbow and tipped my head back, taking in the entire object. A dirigible, minus the balloon. I glanced around at the myriad hulking shadows, seeing them with new eyes. The high ceiling, vast width of the building, and even the grimy window that seemed to float stories above my head: I was in one of Wetherill's hangars. One of his *personal* hangars, judging by the number of covered crafts. Only an obnoxiously wealthy full spectrum like Wetherill could afford so many aircrafts and a place to store them all.

Chills swept down my arms, my improbable theory confirmed. Had Wetherill escalated the stakes because I had turned my focus to getting Airstrong back on track? Or had this become personal? Was this an act of retribution for exposing his fiancée as a thief? Was he afraid I was getting too close to exposing him too?

But why bring me here, to his estate?

Wetherill had been one step ahead of me the whole time. Maybe he had planned my death all along. From the beginning, he had attempted to frame me for his crimes, making plenty of insinuations of my guilt to O'Hara and the press. For all I knew, he could be using this time to set me up for the theft of the phoenix eggs. I could see Nathan's headline already: GRAYSON HEIRESS ATTEMPTS TO FRAME RESPECTED FULL SPECTRUM; DIES SHOCKINGLY FROM BASILISK ATTACK. Or perhaps if Nathan was feeling more poetic: AIRSTRONG HEIRESS'S TWISTED PLANS PERMANENTLY PARALYZED BY BASILISK. If Wetherill followed his pattern, the phoenix eggs would be discovered near my body, as if I had been in possession of them all along. That sounded exactly like the kind of scandal Wetherill would concoct, the final nail on my parents' coffins—figuratively—and mine, literally.

My fists clenched. He wasn't going to get away with it. I wouldn't let him.

Claws scraped dirt on my left, alarmingly close. Fear spurted through my veins. I started to turn to look but caught myself. Holding my breath, I sidled away from the approaching basilisk. A hiss rasped on my right, closer. Shock jolted like ice through me. There were two basilisks, not one. While I had been lost in thought, they had pinned me between them.

Playing dead wouldn't work for me twice. They had seen me moving. They would attack, with claws and teeth if not with their paralyzing gazes. Without magic, I couldn't defend myself, especially not with the tiny knife I had confiscated from the dead Fire Eater.

In tandem, the deadly monsters surged out of the darkness. A scream burst from my throat. *Up,* I needed to get higher. Somewhere they couldn't reach me.

I jumped blindly, bound hands grasping. My fingers crunched against the wooden railing of the dirigible's deck. I jumped again, catching the thick board with my fingertips. My body slammed against the wooden side, nearly jarring me loose. I strained to pull myself up, but I didn't have the upper-body strength. Scrambling, I flailed for a toehold. Pain lanced through my calf as a basilisk's claw gouged my flesh. I screamed again, kicking out. My foot connected with a basilisk, and claws screeched through wood beneath my dangling feet.

Yanking my knees higher, I finally snagged a boot on a slender protrusion. With a surge of adrenaline-fueled might, I pulled my dangling leg up, holding myself curled against the side of the dirigible. I couldn't have been higher than three feet off the ground, barely out of reach of the monsters below me.

A flurry of thumps shook the dirigible, and the basilisks hissed angrily. My fingers slipped, my arms trembling under the strain of holding myself at the awkward angle. Desperately, I threw my free leg higher. My heel hooked over the railing seconds before my other foot slipped off the protrusion. Panting and gasping, I hauled myself over the railing and flopped onto the dirigible's deck. My arms burned. The tops of my shoulders were twin knots of fire. My frantic pulse jabbed agony through my calf.

But I was alive.

I rolled onto my back and stared at the black ceiling, chest heaving. The dirigible vibrated under the basilisks' continued assault. The ruckus made it sound as if there were a dozen demonic lizards, and I prayed it was just the two. I had no way of checking.

Belatedly, I scanned the deck, confirming the gate was closed. Even if the basilisks circled the dirigible, they wouldn't be able to reach me. For now, I was safe.

Trembling, I sat up. From my new vantage point, I could make out more of the hangar. Cloth-shrouded airships and dirigibles studded the cavernous building, some large enough to be passenger cruisers, others too small to be anything more than personal conveyances. If a straight path existed among them, I couldn't find it. I couldn't locate the bay doors against the dark walls either. Instead, I spotted a faint orange glow at one end of the hangar. A lantern abandoned during the Fire Eaters' dash to safety?

Considering the haste in which they fled, it was likely. Which meant heading toward the light might be my best chance of finding a door out of this death trap—as long as the Fire Eaters weren't waiting outside to finish me off if I escaped.

I surveyed the window again. Unlike the glowing light,

it was a guaranteed exit. Unfortunately, it was too high for me to reach, and I couldn't climb the wall with my hands bound. I considered chucking something through the window, breaking it, and screaming until someone saved me. However, the hangar was likely located on Wetherill's country estate, which meant the only people around would be Wetherill's staff and possibly the Fire Eaters. Attracting their attention could be as dangerous as the basilisks'.

I slumped onto my tailbone. I had a third option: I could do nothing and wait for Grant's rescue. If I stayed here, the basilisks couldn't reach me. So long as I didn't look at the ground, I was safe from their gazes.

I huffed a self-derisive laugh. Even when I made a responsible, *adult* choice rather than "selfishly" pursuing the phoenix eggs, I still needed Grant to save me. At least he couldn't fault me this time.

Waiting was tempting. My knee and calf throbbed from the basilisk's cuts, and everything else hurt. And yet, I had been missing for hours. Something was delaying Grant and Quinn. Waiting might not be prudent.

I reached for the elements out of habit, and I was startled when I grasped them. Immediately, I whipped together a ward, but magic sifted through my tenuous grip, and the spell fell apart before it fully formed. I seized magic again, this time merely holding the elements. They wobbled in my grasp, but I took heart. The drug was wearing off.

Energized by renewed hope, I formed a tiny flame and examined my wounds. The cut on my knee oozed fresh blood, the rip in my pants stained crimson. My calf bled freely, soaking my sock. I hacked off the bottom of my pants leg, then tied the fabric around my calf, gritting my teeth against the pain. If basilisks could track me by the smell of blood, the makeshift tourniquet wouldn't help, but at least it would prevent me from losing too much blood.

Gingerly, I stood and tested my handiwork. Cool air caressed my bare ankle. The tie cinched painfully across my torn muscle when I flexed my leg, but it held. Satisfied, I released the flame, letting the light extinguish.

The basilisks no longer battered the dirigible, and I cocked an ear, listening for the raspy sounds of their movements. Silence ghosted through the warehouse, and straining to hear more only set a false ringing in my ears. Nevertheless, I didn't dare climb down until I was certain the basilisks weren't nearby. I needed a diversion.

Easing across the dirigible's deck, I searched for something not nailed down. A small lantern empty of oil hung on the port side. Clutching it, I stepped to the edge of the deck opposite the soft glow, careful not look at the ground where a deadly gaze might be staring back, and tossed the lantern awkwardly with both hands. At the last second, I added a meager boost of air to propel it farther. It crashed with a satisfying cacophony. Below me, the scrabble of claws indicated at least one of the basilisks had taken the bait. I hobbled to the starboard side, grabbed the lantern hanging there, and heaved it after the first. The second basilisk hurried into the darkness.

Before I lost my nerve, I grasped the railing and eased myself over the side of the dirigible. A black pit of undiluted shadows yawned beneath me, and it took all my willpower to force my fingers to release their grip. I landed heavily, stumbling when my injured leg buckled. Freezing, I squeezed my eyes shut. When no basilisk rushed out of the darkness, I eased from my crouch and forced myself to step away from the negligible safety of the dirigible.

As swiftly as I dared, I navigated the hangar, using

discreet flashes of thumbnail-size flames to illuminate lumpy objects that threatened to trip me. My shoulder blades itched with the weight of imagined eyes. My breaths came shallow and fast, whispers of inhales and exhales that rasped like sandpaper against my tuned eardrums. By the time I drew close to the mysterious orange light, my knees were nearly too tense to bend. Darkness had saved me from the basilisk's stare the first time, quick reflexes and luck the second time. If I chanced across a basilisk now, the odds of avoiding its deadly stare were nil.

A stack of waist-high crates jutted into the aisle, and I slowed. The light emanated from just beyond the low barrier. Slitting my eyes, feet tensed to run in case a basilisk lurked on the other side, I peered over the edge of the nearest crate.

A crumpled shape lay sprawled on the floor. For a split second, I didn't recognize it, then my jaw dropped.

Luther Wetherill lay curled on his side, bound hand and foot, his face slack and his eyes closed.

A blazing phoenix egg pulsed beside him.

15

I circled the crates blockading Wetherill, scanning the ground, air, and nearby piles of ropes and fabric for a trap. But mostly, I stared at the phoenix egg pulsing with fiery life just beneath its thin shell. Heat radiated from the egg, bathing me in the warmth of a campfire. It was pleasant from a distance—and I had no desire to get closer. Being within sight of the egg already had my skin crawling. If it hatched, my death would be instantaneous.

Wetherill's too.

What was he doing here?

I cobbled together all five elements, crafting a pentagram hardly larger than a coin. The simplistic spell took all my concentration, but it was more magic than I had been able to control when I had been attacked by the basilisks. I circled the test pentagram across the air above Wetherill, trying to take heart in my returning powers rather than despair that the simple magic required as much effort as blocking one of Zipporah's elemental strikes. When the pentagram failed to register any magic in the vicinity, I let it disperse.

Wetherill's body wasn't an illusion. The full spectrum was genuinely tied up. Helpless. With a phoenix melting the soles of his silver-studded boots.

My feet remained rooted in place. If this was a ruse, it was absurdly dangerous. The basilisks were risky enough, but the phoenix egg was as unpredictable as it was deadly. It didn't look as if Wetherill was faking unconsciousness either. But if he wasn't behind my abduction, then who was?

The pop of cracking wood far across the hangar unglued my feet. Squeezing between crates, I circled the phoenix egg and knelt by Wetherill's head. Sweat plastered his curly hair to his scalp and beaded his forehead and neck. I pressed my fingers to his throat. His pulse beat steadily. Grabbing his shoulders, I shook him. He groaned but didn't rouse.

I checked the phoenix egg. It looked the same as it had thirty seconds earlier and ten seconds before that. Ashes and singed tatters of cloth ringed the egg. It must have been covered at one point, which explained why I hadn't seen its light earlier. The scalding temperature of the gestating bird had burned through the fabric. Was it my imagination or was the egg radiating more heat now? How much time did we have before it hatched?

"Wake up, Wetherill," I ordered, keeping my voice low so it wouldn't carry to the basilisks. I gave him another, harder shake. His head lolled, revealing a grubby cloth beneath his cheek. I tugged it free and sniffed delicately. Honeysuckle and spearmint. Grave's Echo.

None of this made sense. Wetherill wouldn't leave himself so vulnerable just to trick me. He was too arrogant and too paranoid.

Tossing the cloth to the far side of the egg, I wiped my fingers in the dirt, then rubbed them on my pants, removing any lingering traces of the drug. Limping toward his feet, I sawed through his bindings, then did the same for the rope around his hands. Sweat soaked my shirt by the time I finished, and I silently cursed the Fire Eaters. Why couldn't they have used the metal cuffs on Wetherill and saved the rope for me?

When I glanced up, Wetherill was glaring at me. Consternation twisted his lips, and his arm lifted in a feeble wave before dropping to his side.

"You were drugged with Grave's Echo," I whispered. "You're going to be woozy for a few minutes. As soon as you can walk, we need to get out of here before the basilisks find us." I waved a hand in the direction of the petrifying lizards' last known location, inadvertently gesturing to the phoenix egg. "And because of that."

Wetherill's eyes darted from my face to the egg and back. His tongue worked inside his mouth. I turned my back on him so I could examine my cuffs in the phoenix's light. The metal bands were fashioned of crudely welded steel, secured to each other with a rigid bar. The lock on each was tiny, meant for a special key. Or magic.

Molding air into a slender pick, I prodded it into the key slot. Manipulating the delicate element strained my mental muscles, but the flex felt good. The more often I used magic, the faster my abilities appeared to be returning. On the fifth twist, the cuff snapped open and dropped from my right wrist. I caught the swinging metal before it made a sound, then freed my left wrist. Relief surged through me. I set the cuffs aside and resisted the urge to stomp on them.

Rubbing my aching shoulders, I turned back to Wetherill. Fury burned in his gaze. His voice boomed into the silence.

"You won't get away wi—"

I lunged for him, slapping my hand against his mouth. If

my palm landed harder than necessary, I didn't feel the need to apologize.

"Basilisks," I whispered.

Hoping to divert the deadly predators from our location, I shot a fistful of solidified air into the hangar, pushing it as far as my weakened state allowed. It slammed into something metal with a satisfying *clang*. Claws scrambled just beyond the crates protecting us, receding into the darkness. I closed my eyes and took a steadying breath. I hadn't heard the basilisk approaching. If we had stood up—

Wetherill batted my hand aside. The movement was clumsy, but at least he was regaining his strength. The sooner he could stand, the better.

"This is elaborate. Stupid, but elaborate," he growled softly. "Then again, so was blowing up your own warehouse with a phoenix egg."

"There's no one here but us, Wetherill. No hidden recording sphere. No zealous reporter to transcribe your words. Spare me the theatrics." I sat back on my heels, then dropped to my hip when the position set my calf on fire.

Wetherill ran blunt fingers through his sweaty hair, his eyes bouncing from the crates to the phoenix egg and finally back to my face. "Help me up."

I braced my good foot and pulled him up to a seated position. Wetherill's face went ashen, and he sucked in a sharp breath. Bending stiffly, he lifted the hem of his pants and rolled down his sock. Purple-and-black bruising engulfed an ankle swollen to twice its normal circumference. If the joint wasn't broken, it was certainly sprained.

Gritting his teeth, Wetherill asked, "What's the plan now? You 'rescue' me from my own hangar and pin the phoenix egg thefts on me? Do you really think anyone, even your boyfriend, will believe I was so stupid as to keep a phoenix egg on my own property?"

I pretended that hadn't been my prevalent theory up until two minutes ago, instead saying, "Do you really still think I'm behind this and *I'm* so stupid as to cuff and lock myself in a lightless building with loose basilisks and a volatile phoenix egg?" I shifted to expose the blood-soaked makeshift bandage on my calf. "And to injure myself?"

I caught the first glimmer of doubt in Wetherill's eyes.

"I was kidnapped from Airstrong, drugged the same as you, and woke up here."

"The same as me?" Wetherill asked suspiciously.

"Do you remember how you got here?" Now wasn't the time for a lengthy conversation, but Wetherill still looked too woozy to stand. I didn't have the strength to drag him or the magic to levitate him. With his injured ankle, he would be hopping, and I already dreaded the amount of noise he would make. Our escape wasn't going to be stealthy, so it needed to be fast. In the meantime, maybe we could figure out what was really going on.

"It was an organized strike," Wetherill said, his jaw stiff. "Professional, likely ex-military. They caught me on the street, slapped a Grave's Echo–soaked cloth over my mouth. The rest is fuzzy."

I mentally scoffed at his description of the Fire Eaters. Perhaps the gang sent its most competent members after Wetherill, but even so, labeling any of them as "ex-military" was a stretch. "Those 'professionals' were Fire Eaters."

"Rubbish."

"I don't understand it either." What did Fire Eaters gain by destroying Airstrong? I could understand the pyromani-acal gang's lust for phoenix eggs, but not how they could have pulled off such a complicated theft, let alone the thefts of the firebirds and banned spells too. Even leaving an egg here didn't make sense. Was the plan to kill Wetherill and me at once? Why?

"Gang attacks are fast, violent, and flashy. They're not"—Wetherill waved a hand at the phoenix egg—"*this*. Are you certain?"

I held up the knife I had taken from the paralyzed teen, playing the phoenix egg's glow across the crude Fire Eaters' symbol scratched into the hilt. "I took this off a boy who got caught by a basilisk's gaze. He had a matching tattoo."

"A boy." Wetherill shook his head in disgust. "Abducted by *street thugs*. And deposited in my own hangar. My *warded* hangar, which the devils bypassed by carting my unconscious body through the spell after dragging me halfway across the country. Of all the insults!"

Wetherill's quiet rant confirmed our location; we were at his country estate, miles outside of Terra Haven. That possibly explained why Grant and Quinn hadn't found me yet. At least, I hoped it did, and they weren't in trouble of their own.

The egg shifted. The movement was minuscule, but it caused us both to freeze. How long had it been sitting on the floor? Phoenix eggs required stable, hot environments to gestate. Outside of the heat, they died or hatched. At any moment, the fledgling could decide it was ready to come out, and then . . .

There would be no *and then* if we didn't get moving.

"We need to go," I said.

To be safe, I lobbed two wads of solidified air deeper into the hangar, eliciting dull thumps from shadowy objects. We both listened for footsteps, but if the basilisks were nearby, they didn't take the bait. Hopefully, they were already on the far side of the hangar.

"You know where the door is, right?" I asked, groaning as I hoisted Wetherill to his feet. He swung an arm over my shoulder and sagged against me. Pain lanced through my torn calf. I bit my lip and eased my weight to my opposite leg.

"That way." Wetherill flung out an arm, pointing to a side wall.

My stomach sank. Between us and freedom squatted a mound of ship-building material: folds of canvas cloth, lumber for baskets and airship decks, ropes, and buckets of bolts and latches. Climbing over the stacks would be slow and awkward, not to mention loud.

"What's in that direction?" I pointed into the darkness on our right, away from the basilisk's last known location.

Wetherill shook his head. "There's no way through. I keep all material warded to protect it against moisture, bugs, rodents—and sticky-fingered staff. The spell is anchored to the hangar. We can't penetrate it."

"Not even you?" I squinted at the pile, but I had stared at the phoenix egg too long to make out the subtle coating of magic in the gloom.

"Not at the moment."

I glanced left, measuring the distance we would have to traverse before we could circle around to the door, then at the much closer back wall. "I don't suppose the boards along the wall are loose or rotted, and we could break through them."

Wetherill shot me a dour look.

"Long way it is. Ready?"

I took his grunt as a yes. With one last trepidatious glance at the egg, I looped an arm around Wetherill's waist, and we crept into the shadows. Or tried to creep. With Wetherill latched to my side, half shuffling, half hopping on his uninjured foot, we weren't stealthy. I cobbled magic together and tossed another wad of air far from us, praying my diversions would keep the basilisks occupied. All too soon, the glow of the phoenix egg disappeared behind a hulking dirigible, and deep shadows impeded our progress even further. I considered attempting to form a glowball, but fear of the light attracting a basilisk—and illuminating their beady eyes—prevented me. At least the darkness provided some protection from the lizards' lethal gazes.

"Grant—Captain Monaghan—will be looking for me," I whispered, refusing to acknowledge my earlier worries. I had enough problems without letting my imagination concoct perils for others. "If we could get him a message . . ."

"That's beyond me." Bitterness etched Wetherill's hissed response.

The complexity of a message was beyond me too at the moment. But a simpler spell might work.

"What about a beacon? We could link." Between the two of us, we should be able to launch an incandescent glowball through the window. If we got it high enough into the sky, Grant would recognize it as a signal. Or someone closer would. "Do you have staff who could help us? Guards?"

"Are those wisps of air—" Wetherill's breath caught as he hopped a step. "The extent of your current strength?"

"Yes." *Incredible.* He defaulted to insults even when I was in the process of saving his life.

"Then it's pointless."

"Not linked."

"Those nitwits neutered my magic." He hopped another step. "I'm as useless as a no-spectrum imbecile." Hop. "And you don't have enough"—*hop*—"power to breach the ward."

"I thought you said the ward was down."

Wetherill stopped, jerking me to a halt. "Do you think I

keep all this under a single anti-trespassing ward? Child, this building holds aircrafts tuned with family spells. The hangar is warded to prevent anyone outside from sensing the magic in here. My family and I strengthen the spells every equinox and reinforce them every month. I doubt you *ever* had the strength to puncture the wards."

I wanted to grab him by his shoulders and shake the full-spectrum arrogance out of him, but we would be dead long before I succeeded. "Congratulations. Your fancy spells left the building weak enough to let in a gang of thugs and too strong to escape. You must be real proud of yourself."

Wetherill's jaw worked, but I didn't wait to hear his retort. Tugging him back into motion, I spun another round of air pellets into the hangar to distract the basilisks.

Magic was easier to grasp now. I wasn't able to control even half my normal level, but I was improving. Taking heart, I cycled through the elements again and again, pushing myself to hold more. Wetherill's weight dragged on me, stealing energy I didn't have to spare. Every scuff of his boot and grunt wound the tension in my body tighter. I strained my eyes, trying to make out each shape and possible routes upward, all without ever looking below knee level, where a basilisk might lurk. When we finally reached a gap between the building materials and a cloth-covered dirigible, I staggered between them to the far wall.

"One second," I panted, sagging against a sturdy beam, forcing Wetherill to brace himself against the wall and give me a breather. My calf was on fire, and the rest of my abused body trembled from the strain of supporting a man who weighed half again as much as I did. "Are we close?"

Harnesses jangled, and I jumped, shocked to find Wetherill several paces away, rifling through pegs affixed to the wall.

"What are you doing?" I hissed, swatting at his hands.

"My gold-plated gryphon harness, the matching wyvern set . . . Those rotten thieves. When I get my hands on them—"

"Hush!"

Wetherill whirled toward me, his indignant fury obvious despite the dim light. The slither and rasp of scales on canvas cut through the hangar, sounding as if it came from less than ten feet away. Wetherill's mouth closed with a click of teeth. I held my breath and tossed out a wave of air, arcing it over the nearest vehicle. It collided with something out of sight, setting off a chain reaction of sound. Snagging Wetherill, I hurried in the opposite direction, toward the door I feared we wouldn't live to see.

"Was that a basilisk?" Wetherill gouged his fingers into my shoulder, each erratic hop staggering me.

I didn't bother answering, my concentration split between staying upright and blasting globs of air into the hangar in a desperate attempt to disguise our progress. Wetherill flinched and cowered lower with each sound, dragging me down with him. Pain radiated through my entire injured leg, but I pushed us faster. I couldn't do anything about the puddle of blood squelching inside my boot with each step until we were safe.

Anytime now, Grant. I won't even mind a lecture.

"Do you see a tall dirigible with a pegasus mast?" Wetherill asked between hops.

"I'm looking for the door."

"Family chariot. In the middle," he gasped.

"Behind us?" What good would that do us? Even if the aircraft could be flown with the nominal magic I currently possessed, it would be death to backtrack. Unless . . . Was he honestly worried about which items the Fire Eaters had taken on their way out? I squinted at Wetherill. His eyes were squeezed tight. Coward. He was letting me take all the risk. No wonder it felt as if I was dragging him as much as supporting him.

"Where's the door?"

"Corner."

We were close.

I tripped, my feet tangling in heavy fabric. Wetherill toppled into me, and we both almost went down. Sheer willpower—and a strategic elbow to Wetherill's gut to get him to support his own weight—kept us upright. I slowed, stepping high through folds of canvas mounded in our path. Wetherill cursed, forced to use his injured foot to limp through the obstruction.

"Quiet." Had the canvas moved after we cleared it?

"Don't speak to me like—"

I shoved a wad of air over Wetherill's mouth. Scales rasped on fabric behind us. I squeezed my eyes shut, heart hammering against my eardrums. Wetherill stiffened, and I would have feared he had been paralyzed if his heaving side hadn't been pressed to mine. The basilisk charged.

Seizing magic, I shoved air under the crumpled cloth and blindly flung it across the stampeding lizard.

"Run!" I yelled.

I tipped my face toward the black ceiling and ran. Fabric ripped and flapped behind us as the basilisk tore through the flimsy impediment. The back wall sprang out of the darkness, and we slammed into it with twin grunts. I released Wetherill and pawed frantically for a door.

"Here," Wetherill gasped.

A rectangle of light appeared on my right, and Wetherill flung himself through the opening. I darted after him and slammed the door. Fresh air hit my cheeks, surprisingly cold and carrying the scent of churned soil and wet grass. A smattering of stars glistened in the indigo sky, the flush of false dawn hidden behind the hangar.

A basilisk hit the wall from the inside, bouncing the door in its frame. I jumped forward only to slam into Wetherill's back.

He staggered forward, grabbing blindly for my arm, his gaze locked on the sky. "Don't. Move," he commanded.

"We need to keep going. The egg—"

The screech of an enraged wyvern cut through the night. My entire body seized in primal terror.

Please let it be harnessed. Please let it be—

A wyvern swept overhead, its leathery wings eclipsing the sky. A full-grown *naked* wyvern.

I almost fled back into the hangar.

16

The wyvern crashed into a massive elemental dome arcing high overhead, though it twisted just before impact to slash the magic with talons as long as my arms. The barrier held, absorbing each strike. Back-winging, the beast screamed, shaking its head in agitation. Tucking its feet close to its sleek stomach, the wyvern used its barbed, serpentine tail as a counterbalance to flip sideways. Despite its heft, the wyvern spiraled like a falcon through the air, its leathery wings tapered for optimum speed and agility. In the indistinct light, I couldn't make out its coloring, only that it was darker on top than along its stomach. Then twin sacs inflated behind its dragon-like head, metallic-white slashes shimmering across their surfaces. The wyvern's jaws gaped, and it unleashed a torrent of white mist into the dome. The spell flared a counter element of fire, holding firm.

I wanted to wail, but I clenched my teeth and gritted out, "A Thilorier? Here?"

"I breed them," Wetherill said.

Of course he did, though I couldn't fathom why.

Thiloriers were the deadliest wyvern breed; all wyverns would devour a human unless properly bonded or harnessed, but Thiloriers were unmatched in their predatory prowess. That white cloud hadn't been a steamy exhale. It had been a spray of the Thilorier's hallmark saliva—spit so cold it froze the moisture in the air upon contact. Any creature caught in the blast would die instantly—either when their blood froze in their veins or seconds later, when the wyvern's razor-sharp teeth and piercing talons tore them apart.

"Do you breed basilisks too?" Did I have it wrong, and the Fire Eaters hadn't brought the basilisks with them? Had they been inside the hangar all along?

Wethcrill scoffed. "Only fools traffic in basilisks."

The same could be said about those who bred Thiloriers.

I scanned the elemental dome. It soared hundreds of feet into the sky, dropping in a smooth arc to enclose acres of rolling grass, a pond, topiaries, gravel and slate pathways, and a stone wyvern stable that looked half man-made, half mountain. It also enclosed the hangar. Fear squeezed my chest. We were trapped inside an enormous cage with an enraged Thilorier, hundreds of yards from the safe side of the dome.

A shriek climbed my throat when a second wyvern dove into sight, rocketing past close enough to set my hair into a cyclone around my face. Wetherill's fingers bit into my arm in a painful—and unnecessary—reminder to remain motionless. Wyvern vision was attuned to movement. As long as we stayed still, the shadow of the hangar would hide us. It was flimsy protection, but it was all we had. My heart attempted to seize when a third and fourth Thilorier blasted overhead. They struck the ward synchronously with enough force to topple a brick house. The dome flexed and held.

"Those blockheads didn't have a brain between them," Wetherill huffed under his breath. "They loosed the entire stable. Did they think they could steal *wyverns*? Imbeciles."

Fire Eaters. Basilisks. Sluggish magic. Loathsome Luther Wetherill clinging to me. Now a flock of Thilorier wyverns? If not for the throbbing pain in my leg, I would have sworn I was trapped in the longest, worst nightmare of my life.

"Can you drop the ward?" I asked. The spell was as complex as it was vast, all five elements woven tight as lace despite its gargantuan size. I didn't stand a chance of rupturing it.

"Harriet, do you know how much each wyvern is worth?"

"Less than my life." At Wetherill's dour look, I added, "Less than *your* life."

His eyes narrowed. "I won't unleash frenzied Thiloriers upon the countryside."

How telling that his concern for the lives of his neighbors came second to his greed, but now wasn't the time to chastise his ethics.

"Can you shrink the dome? Drive the wyverns into their dens?"

Wetherill snorted. "Not even if I didn't currently have the magic power of a peon. We need to get to the other side of the containment field."

Hysterical laughter bubbled up my throat, and I swallowed it down. Even uninjured, I had a better chance of outrunning an avalanche than a wyvern. With Wetherill hobbling at my side, we would be devoured before we cleared the hangar's shadow.

But if we stayed within the blast radius of the phoenix, each breath could be our last.

"How strong are you feeling?" Wetherill asked.

"Not strong enou—"

An arrow of solid earth shot across the lawn. The smallest wyvern dove for it, dousing the magic with its arctic breath. The arrow winked out of existence.

"Kylie!"

My heart soared at the sound of Grant's voice. I searched the trees beyond the dome, spotting Quinn's golden form first. They both stood on the other side of the wyvern net, safe. Grant's hand dropped to Quinn's head, restraining him. He was too far away for me to make out his expression, but his face tilted to survey the wyverns, then returned to stare at me. Releasing Quinn, Grant launched himself through the barrier.

"Stay there," he shouted.

Four wyvern heads whipped around. Four sets of furious eyes focused on Grant. Across the expansive lawn, Grant looked puny, especially as the largest wyvern flipped from the dome and dove for him. Twenty feet of deadly predator plummeted in a blur of muscle and talons. Screeching, it unleashed a freezing blast. Grant deflected the noxious attack with a ward of fire, not breaking his stride but not hurrying either.

Coming for me.

The wyvern dodged Grant's offensive fireball, gaining altitude nearly as fast as it had while diving. Flipping, it dove to attack again. A second wyvern plunged into the battle, but it was the streak of gold near the ground that caught my eye. Quinn surged across the lawn, flying fast and low, angling straight for me. A boost of magic unfurled inside me, and I grabbed every drop of Quinn's offered enhancement. Fumbling in my haste, I formed an amplification spell, then shouted into it.

"Don't get close. Phoenix about to hatch!"

Grant shouted something in return, but it was lost beneath the hunting cry of a Thilorier.

"Idiot!" Wetherill cursed. "They've spotted us."

Two wyverns orbiting the battle twisted away from Grant to wing toward us. Fear ran numb fingers through my scalp. Instinct told me to flee, to run as fast as I possibly could. Instead, I locked my knees and cobbled together even more raw magic. Adrenaline or repetitive use of the elements had finally cleared the last of the Grave's Echo from my system, and the overload of magic vibrated inside me. My skin felt as if it would burst to contain it, and my hold on the elements quivered as I jury-rigged a protective spell.

Quinn roared and turned aside. One of the wyverns bearing down on us spun to chase him. I wanted to cry out a warning, but the second wyvern hadn't altered course. It flew with shocking speed, traversing the open space between us in seconds. I readied a fire-based shield, layering it with wood to make it burn hot, but hesitated before executing the spell. The wyvern's malevolent cerulean eyes swept the side of the hangar, passing over us as it searched the shadows. My shout had drawn it to us, but unless we moved, it might not be able to pinpoint us in the murky light.

I dropped a sheet of air and fire between us and the wyvern, inversing the light of the fire to create an illusion of pure black. I layered the inside with my fire shield. Holding two spells weakened both, and I prayed it was the right decision.

Wetherill wobbled, or perhaps he trembled. My own

knees wanted to knock together in terror. Even behind the illusion, neither of us shifted more than our eyes. The wyvern had set its sights to our right, and as it pulled up to fly over the hangar's roof, it unleashed a cloudburst of ice. Thick maple planks near the roof cracked and exploded, spraying crystalized splinters into the air. A rain of ice peppered my shield, evaporating in the flames. Using a soft puff of air, I redirected the splinters rather than risk the chance of smoke attracting the wyverns' eyes.

When our attacker disappeared over the roofline, I searched the sky for Quinn. He flew high above us, zigzagging like a lion-size hummingbird with two wyverns on his tail. My heart lodged in my throat. A Thilorier's frosty assault might not be as deadly to a gargoyle as it was to a human, but if Quinn were frozen midflight, the fall would kill him. So could a well-placed blow from a wyvern's talons.

Quinn dodged and wove haphazardly, but when a wyvern blasted frigid saliva from its powerful jaws, he plummeted as fast as the stone creature he was, avoiding the deadly stream. Seconds later, Quinn caught himself and whirled toward the dome, escaping through the elemental mesh. The wyverns slammed into the ward, bellowing their frustration into the early-morning air.

The other two wyverns hadn't abated their attacks on Grant, bombarding him with a frenzy of claws, fangs, and icy blasts. Without Quinn distracting them, the thwarted wyverns turned their wrath on Grant too. Fire blazed from Grant's palm, driving one wyvern aside. A hastily erected shield protected him from the blast of another. Rather than sprint to the safe side of the dome, Grant strode into the open. The wyverns swarmed him, the downdraft of their wings whipping his uniform against his body as if he stood in the midst of a hurricane. The dragon-like predators attacked in concert, never giving Grant a breather. Blades of fire slapped aside wyvern snouts as fast as they struck, flashing like fireworks in the air, never quite incapacitating the deadly reptiles.

Grant couldn't keep this up forever. Where was the rest of his squad? Or O'Hara?

Quinn dove from above, slamming into the smallest wyvern's shoulders. The beast careened away from Grant, and Quinn launched himself in the opposite direction, flapping past the dome to safety before the wyvern recovered. Grant used the microscopic lull in the battle to amplify his next shout.

"Run, Kylie!"

I realized he was no longer progressing across the field. No longer coming for me. He had heard my warning and changed tactics, using himself as bait so I could escape.

My heart thundered in my ears. The earlier terror of playing cat and mouse with basilisks or even the last frantic rush to the door paled in comparison to the thought of abandoning the shelter of the hangar's shadow. But I trusted Grant. I wasn't going to let his and Quinn's heroics be for nothing.

"Come on." I tugged on Wetherill's waist, dropping the illusion hiding us.

"This is madness," he moaned, but he tightened his grip on my shoulder and took the first hobbling step.

Fire ignited in my calf. I gasped and clenched my teeth when the next step stung worse than the first. Wetherill groaned and cursed, pressing the barest weight to his injured foot before hopping. Curse, hop, groan. Curse, hop, groan.

"Come on, you can do it," I urged, not sure which of us I was encouraging.

The lawn stretched endlessly before us, the edge of the dome a lifetime away. My shoulders hunched, as if I could bend low enough to avoid the wyverns' detection. A phantom weight pressed against my spine, the looming threat of the phoenix pushing against my back.

"Faster," I panted.

Hidden divots in the dew-slick grass tripped me and hampered Wetherill's already glacial speed. My breath rasped in my throat and my thighs burned, my fatigued limbs running low on energy before we even began to sprint. Wetherill tugged us in the direction of a distant mansion. It meant shoving through a low, squared-off hedgerow and skidding through a gravel pathway. I mentally berated Wetherill for his greed and stupidity. Greed for having such an immense property, and stupidity for not positioning convenient trees and buildings to serve as shelter during an aerial assault. I refused to acknowledge that the open field made sense in front of an aircraft hangar and wyvern den.

Quinn dove through the dome, knocking into a wyvern's wing, sending it careening, but not before the infuriated beast jerked its head around to blast ice into the air. Quinn dove under the plume, missing being hit by inches. He landed, galloped several strides, then flapped hard and fast for the dome, a different wyvern on his tail. I hooked my fingers into Wetherill's belt loop and hoisted him against me, urgency lending me strength. Farther away, Grant deflected claws and ice with gouts of flames. Even as he fought two Thiloriers, he flicked the third in the tail with fire, yanking the predator's attention away from us. His distraction almost got him skewered, but he rolled aside at the last second.

The fourth wyvern pursued Quinn to the dome, though

it twisted to slam into the magical barrier with its legs. Flipping, it shoved itself away from the ward and speared straight for me and Wetherill. Quinn spun to give chase. His wings beat frantically, but he wasn't going to be fast enough. Wetherill cursed and fumbled for magic, forming a weak, flickering shield of fire. The wyvern's barrel sides expanded on an inhale, the sacs behind its jaws inflating. Another flap, and it was in range. Its fanged jaws opened.

I slapped a wall of fire in its face. The wyvern roared and ducked aside, talons slashing through my magic. Wetherill jerked in my grasp, nearly dislocating my shoulder when he attempted to dive aside. I propelled him forward, craning to check over my shoulder. Quinn shot past overhead, ducking and weaving as the wyvern turned its malice on him.

Movement higher up snagged my eye. The first streaks of sunlight glowed on the horizon, brightening the sky enough to make out a winged figure circling the dome. I recognized it in a split second, the half-shorn wing and off-kilter cant of its flight impossible to mistake. Zipporah had found me.

I wanted to laugh. Or maybe crying would be more appropriate. Spinning to face forward, I hoped to spot the dome's edge within reach. My curse came out on a sob. We were only halfway across the infernal field.

Maybe this *was* a nightmare, one from which I would never wake.

My boot hit ice, and my leg splayed sideways. My fingers snapped free of Wetherill's belt loop. I slammed to my back hard enough to choke on my own exhale. Helplessly, I slid across the ice patch, the frozen lawn slicing through my thin shirt and into my flesh like barbed sandpaper. I screamed when my momentum spun me in a slow, torturous circle. Then, mercifully, I fetched up against wet grass. Tucking my hands to my chest, I rolled off the Thilorier-blasted ground and lay on my side, panting. Blistering pain radiated down my back. I couldn't feel my butt. I needed to get up, but I couldn't summon the energy.

Wetherill hadn't stopped. *Coward.* Hobbling with remarkable agility, augmenting his wounded leg with a prop of solid air, he scurried toward safety. *Cowardly bastard.* Where had that magic been when I had been hauling him around?

I shoved an arm under myself, willing my body to rise. Quinn shouted, his words lost beneath a wyvern's shriek. I sought him out through tear-blurred eyes. He speared across the field, high above me, a wyvern hot on his tail.

A burst of air came out of nowhere, punching the wyvern in the jaw. Its head snapped sideways, and its body pitched to follow. Spiraling out of control, it crashed hard enough to shake the ground, sliding to a stop at the edge of the pond. Ice crackled across the water's surface on the wyvern's exhale, then exploded in jagged spikes as the entire pond froze in a lightning-fast rush. The wyvern attempted to rise, floundering due to one wing hanging broken. Its pained cry sent chills through my body.

Grant had been fighting to distract, not kill. Why had he—

"Kylie, watch out!" Quinn shouted, fighting his counter-momentum to fly toward me.

I spun, expecting another wyvern. Instead, Zipporah dove through the dome, coasting over the hangar.

With a negligent pulse of magic, she punted Quinn across the field. He tumbled through the air, struggling to right himself before he slammed into the trees on the far side. I had a second to realize it had been the harpy who had bludgeoned the wyvern—not to save Quinn, but to get the Thilorier out of her way.

Then the hangar exploded.

I reacted instinctively, throwing a shield up between Zipporah and the explosion, shoving her past the hangar. A prodigious fireball ballooned from the building, catapulting hunks of flaming wood against my shield. Slapping earth and water around solidified air, I formed a crude protective spell on the fly. Heat seared my magic, burning into my brain, but it held.

Zipporah flailed head over tail above me, wings akimbo. I had a second to relive the wyvern's horrible landing and pained cry, envisioning the same for the harpy. It would be no less than she deserved for the torment she had inflicted on me. She had freely admitted she planned to kill me. Painfully. Slowly. But a harpy was the last person I wanted to emulate. Using the last of my strength, I cushioned Zipporah's landing with a pillow of air.

My shield collapsed. The shrapnel it had blocked fell in a heap a dozen feet from me. Heat gushed over me, blowing my hair from my face. A beautiful flaming bird shot through the ruined hangar's roof, arrowing into the sky. Enviously graceful only seconds after its birth, the eagle-size newborn spiraled through the superheated air. Black bands circled its red-gold chest, and as it gained altitude, its wings cooled, until only a trail of smoke marked its passage. After a lap around the ruined hangar, the phoenix tilted its beak to the heavens. Singing a high-pitched note of pure exhilaration, it burst through the dome, looping and twisting jubilantly as it continued to climb into the night sky.

Tears leaked from my eyes, and I fell back to my elbows. My head rang from the explosion and from using too much magic. My body was spent and throbbing with alternating dull and sharp pains. But in that moment, my heart soared with the phoenix. Its birth was violent and fearsome, but its joy to be alive ignited a fierce happiness inside me.

Zipporah landed hard atop me, snapping my focus back to my own survival. The harpy's talons gouged the sod on either side of my ribs, and her fetid fumes swamped me.

Bending, she pressed her face close to mine.

"My wayward heiress," she hissed, drowning me in a carrion exhale. Golden hawk eyes glinted in the morning light, triumph gleaming in their depths. "You smell like breakfast."

17

Eyes watering, I shrank from Zipporah, wincing as rocks hidden in the wet grass gouged my tormented back.

"Grant," I croaked.

I intended his name as a warning, not a summons, but gratitude swamped me when a blast of fire-laced air tuned in Grant's magical signature knocked Zipporah aside without so much as shifting the tendrils of hair resting on my forehead. The harpy deflected the worst of the attack, flapping to an awkward landing ten feet away. Grant stalked past me, planting himself between us.

I soaked in the sight of him. From my prone position, he looked larger than life, his muscular body coiled with tension. Mud and grass stains coated his gray uniform, though the spelled material repelled any moisture that might have otherwise soaked into the garment. A rip cut across his left shoulder, another at his right thigh, but if he was wounded beneath the slashes, it didn't show. More mud spiked his dark hair, and a line of grit bisected his cheek. None of it detracted from his formidable expression. Power and anger radiated from him, and if it had been directed at me, I would have cowered in my boots. Zipporah sneered.

"She's mine," the harpy declared. "She gave her word."

"You tricked her."

Zipporah shrugged her shoulders. It was a human's gesture, one that caused her naked breasts to jiggle grotesquely and noxious fumes to waft from her oily feathers.

The ground shuddered, and Quinn skidded to a stop next to my hip. He dropped his nose to examine me, then stepped forward, straddling my stomach. His huge stone body and protectively extended wings effectively blocked my sight of Grant and Zipporah. I ran my fingers down his foreleg, surprised when my hand trembled at the effort. He appeared whole and unharmed. Relief flooded me. I wanted to curl around him and hug him to me, but we weren't out of danger yet.

I rolled to get a view of the field, searching for the wyverns. Any moment, they would swoop down—

A net of magic pinned the largest Thilorier. The spell was a simplified version of the dome, and it effectively caged the wyvern in place. A second layer of darkened elements wrapped the wyvern's head. The hood appeared to soothe the massive beast, proving that despite its fierce attacks, it was a tamed and trained wyvern—as tamed and trained as any apex predator could be.

I twisted further, rolling against Quinn's stone legs to track down the other wyverns. Two curled passively inside similar elemental cages, hooded and deceptively docile. If Grant had been able to capture the wyverns all along, why—

A team of people in FPD uniforms surrounded the fourth, injured wyvern. Ah. Backup had arrived, just in time.

Or, more likely, had been summoned by Grant. It wasn't his squad either. I recognized Anderson from O'Hara's squad first, then the rest of her team. They worked in tandem to restrain the pain-wracked wyvern as their team healer, Xinh, mended its broken wing. All five were linked, but O'Hara stood to one side, his gaze focused on the drama unfolding at this end of the field.

Wetherill was nowhere to be seen.

"I will take my payment, or I will take Harriet Kylie Grayson," Zipporah announced.

"What would you accept in payment?" Grant asked.

"After she attacked me? Retribution comes to mind." Her mouth smacked, and putrid fumes blew into the air with the sound of feathers rubbing together.

"Self-defense is not an attack."

I tapped Quinn's side to get his attention. When that didn't work, I grabbed his extended wing and used it to lift myself enough to wave a hand in front of his face. "Let me up, please," I whispered.

He shot me an anguished look. I thought he might argue, but after searching my eyes, he stepped aside. Rolling to my hands and knees, I crawled to my feet, biting the inside of my cheek to choke off a whimper. Quinn tucked his wings to his back and stepped closer, offering his body as a prop. I leaned against him in silent gratitude, then forced myself to step away.

It had been excruciatingly tempting to remain prone and allow Grant to handle Zipporah's demands. I was wounded, exhausted, and about to be bowled over by an avalanche of spent adrenaline. The shaking in my hands was likely as much due to shock as it was relief. Lying in one place until my head stopped reeling seemed like the smart decision.

But Zipporah was my problem, not Grant's. I had gotten myself into my dreadful deal with her. I would get myself out of it.

"Basilisks." I dropped the word into Zipporah and Grant's argument.

Grant whipped around, his eyes clouded with emotion I couldn't read. Zipporah squinted at me suspiciously, but the threat made her wary enough to stop speaking.

"In the hangar. There were at least two. I don't know if they survived the hatching, but there's a big hole in the side of the building . . ."

Grant formed a message, barked a warning into it, and sent it rocketing to O'Hara. Seconds after the message reached the investigator, two warriors peeled away from the wyvern. They molded mirror illusions in front of their faces and sprinted for the hangar. In minutes, the gaping hole in the side of the hangar was blockaded with a similar ward, the mirrored side pointing inward. Satisfied we were safe from accidental paralyzation, I turned my attention to the harpy.

I had to word this just right. I wasn't going to get another chance. For the first time since I had landed in Zipporah's debt, I had an idea how to save myself.

"Beldame Zipporah," I said, giving her the honorific she preferred.

Grant's hand shot out to stop me when I stepped forward. I gripped his steely forearm, my fingers brushing his everlasting seed where it wrapped his wrist like a bracelet. The black-and-white discs were smooth beneath my fingertips, shifting slightly as Grant flexed his arm. I stroked my thumb along the line of skin between his sleeve and bracelet, taking comfort in Grant's warmth and the protective aura radiating from him.

Then I gave his arm a squeeze and stepped partially in front of him, facing Zipporah. Quinn shifted to stand beside me. With Grant at my back, my bravery was largely symbolic. He could step in at any moment to defend me. But I was signaling to him that I wanted to do this on my own.

Shockingly, Grant didn't protest.

"I did not attack you," I said, looking the harpy square in her eerie avian eyes. Pain throbbed from my calf and back, but I didn't let it show on my expression. At least standing straight kept my shirt from rubbing against my ice-burned flesh. "I saved you."

Zipporah squawked in disbelief.

I took a deep breath, then announced, "My debt is served. I no longer owe you anything."

Zipporah chuffed and shook her head. "Oh, little girl, you're brave when you've got the captain at your side."

"Look." I pointed behind the harpy. A wall of jagged wood and melted metal protruded from the ground, embedded in a distinct line where my shield had spared us both from being impaled.

"That's not the payment I had in mind." Zipporah hopped forward, closing the distance between us to loom over me. Menacing magic vibrated the air around her.

I mentally braced myself for an attack—physical or elemental—but I didn't flinch, and I didn't erect a barrier between us. After the night I had been through, the harpy's attempt to intimidate me barely raised my pulse. Even though I stood within striking distance of Zipporah's deadly talons, with Grant and Quinn beside me, I was the safest I had been all night.

"It's the payment you'll have to accept," I said.

"Now you think you can dictate to me the terms of our

deal?" Zipporah cackled, revealing gore-crusted teeth. "I say what you owe me—"

"And though you kept changing the payment, the fee was always the same," I interrupted.

Zipporah's false mirth morphed to a scowl. Flexing the sharp bone-like digits at the bends of her wings, she tipped forward, leaning into my personal space. Instead of retreating, I mirrored her, pressing my face closer to hers.

"You demanded a debt equal to my life. I just repaid you by saving your life." I paused, letting her read the seriousness in my eyes and the lack of fear in my expression. "We're even."

The corners of her mouth twisted. For the space of two shallow breaths, her raptor eyes bored into mine. I had her, and she knew it. If she went back on her deal now, her word would be meaningless.

Abruptly, she rocked back, an oily smile stretching her thin lips. "I hardly think—"

"There were witnesses," I said.

Cold, predatory eyes skewered me.

"My debt is dissolved." My voice didn't quaver, though my stomach did.

"Unless, of course, you believe Kylie's life is worth more than yours," Grant said, his voice deceptively mild.

Zipporah bared her teeth. She darted a look at Grant, then returned her glare to me. I wanted to check Grant's expression too, but if I took my eyes off Zipporah, she would assume I was looking to Grant for approval. I couldn't show an ounce of weakness or uncertainty.

Irritation flashed across the harpy's gaunt face. She hid it behind a ferocious smile.

"A human? Equal to me?" Zipporah flung her wings wide in a display of her repugnant grandeur. Mercifully, the breeze shifted, carrying her stench in the opposite direction. "Not even an heiress."

"Good." The word was inadequate for the profound relief that flooded my body, weakening my knees.

"On your word," Grant said firmly.

Zipporah cast a loathsome look in his direction. "On my word, Harriet Kylie Grayson's debt is paid in full." She hunched her shoulders, pulling her wings up like a vulture's. Her back feathers lifted, then settled, and I realized I was witnessing a harpy's version of a sulk. If Grant hadn't pushed for the formal declaration, I suspected Zipporah would have tried to worm out of her agreement later.

Spitting to one side, the harpy hopped away from us. She twisted midair so she landed facing the wyverns, her back to us. Swiveling her head, her chin twisting well past her shoulder, she pinned me with her golden eyes. "If you ever need anything else, you know who to come to, Harriet."

With a cackle and a spurt of noxious excrement, Zipporah launched into flight.

Grant deflected the harpy's feces, propelling the foul matter far across the grass. I didn't take my eyes from Zipporah until she had flown out of sight.

"I'm free." The words came out a whisper, unreal and sweeter than honey. Because I could, because it was true, I repeated it louder. "I'm free. I don't owe Zipporah. She won't be hunting me anymore."

Grinning, I turned to check Grant's reaction.

His attention was on his palm, and when he glanced up, a peculiar mix of alarm and satisfaction flashed across his expression, gone before I could interpret it. Then he unleashed a heart-stopping grin, and I forgot how to breathe, let alone how to think.

Grant cupped his large palm against my cheek, his other hand bracketing my face after he dropped something into his pocket. Heat seared my chilled flesh, and my eyes tried to close of their own volition in sheer bliss, but I couldn't look away from that dazzling smile.

"You did it. You beat the harpy at her own game."

I could have floated on the pride in his voice.

Tilting my face up to his, Grant swept his lips across mine. His kiss scalded me, the gentle connection jolting me to my core. Belatedly, I reached for him, but he pulled back, catching my hands in his.

"We need to tend to your wounds," he said. "How badly are you hurt?"

I sighed, the aches of my body clamoring to answer him before I opened my mouth. "Bad enough to consider your healing."

Grant's eyebrows twitched. With a sweep of fire-heated air, he evaporated the moisture from a swath of lawn, then ordered me to sit. I complied, wincing despite my effort to appear stoic. Under the bright light of a glowball, Grant examined me. Quinn hissed when Grant lifted the back of my shirt, and he whimpered when Grant delicately removed the blood-soaked tourniquet from my leg. I appreciated the sympathy, and I was glad I couldn't see most of my injuries.

"We'll wait for Xinh," Grant decided, casting a heavenly heat spell around the three of us. "I think you'll prefer his methods to mine."

Considering Grant's method of healing felt like grinding a molten brand into my open wounds, I decided a few more minutes of discomfort was worth the wait. Grant settled next to me, resting his forearms on his drawn-up knees. Crafting a message sphere, he spoke into it.

"I have Kylie. She's safe, and O'Hara's team is here.

Thank you for all your hard work. Pass the news along, then get some sleep." Tying off the message, he keyed it to Seradon's signature. The bundle of elements and collected sound whizzed into the air and zoomed out of sight above the tree line.

I fidgeted with a rip in my shirt. "Do you want to know how I got here?"

Grant shook his head. "Not yet. There's no point in you telling your story twice."

I followed his gaze to O'Hara. The investigator was no longer paying attention to us. With two of his squad tracking down the basilisks, the injured wyvern required his full attention. Or maybe we were no longer interesting now that Zipporah had departed.

The wyvern had calmed considerably, and from this distance, it appeared its wing was almost mended. I was relieved the beast was no longer in pain and would fly again. I was even more relieved that I wouldn't be here to witness its next flight.

"Thank you for coming for me," I said. "Both of you."

"Always," Quinn said, touching his nose to my cheek.

"Always," Grant echoed. He caught my hand in his, resting it against his warm knee and covering it with both his palms.

I used my free hand to stroke Quinn's cheek. The gargoyle smiled, revealing the tips of his canines.

"I'm so grateful for you," I said. "You were amazing. I thought I couldn't be more terrified than when I realized I was trapped with basilisks, but then I saw you both battling the Thiloriers, and I . . ." Tears welled in my eyes. They had both come too close to being hurt or killed.

Grant rubbed his thumb across my knuckles. "You think

that was amazing? You should have seen Quinn before we got here. He's the reason we found you."

"Oh?" I rubbed my palms across my cheeks, drying them.

"It was my seed," Quinn said. "I didn't realize it at first, or we would have gotten here sooner. It's a map."

"A map? Wait. I don't think it's evolved."

I pulled Quinn's seed away from his chest. The copper-laced, metallic-green disc filled my palm, and in the light of Grant's glowball, it looked unchanged. Quinn ducked, and I lifted the necklace over his head so we could all examine the seed more closely.

"It's the same," Quinn confirmed.

"But this led you to me?"

"The hole represents your location here." Quinn tapped the off-center opening in the seed where the leather thong was threaded through. "Terra Haven is here." He motioned to the air off the bottom side of the disc.

I nodded, trusting Quinn knew what he was talking about. I had seen plenty of aerial maps growing up at Airstrong, but none had looked like this.

"We had a few false starts and problems—"

"Problems?" I asked, interrupting Quinn.

"Nothing we couldn't manage," Grant said.

I squinted at him. A lot could fall under that description, but since both Grant and Quinn looked unharmed, I let it go. For now. I would get the details out of Quinn later.

"After I recognized the patterns," Quinn continued, "we came as fast as we could."

"But you rescued me, so why didn't your seed evolve?"

Quinn shrugged. "I'm just glad we found you." He leaned into my touch when I slipped the necklace back over his head. "You're safe. That's all that matters." His adoring expression melted my heart, and I hugged him, ignoring the pain that flared in the scrapes across my back.

"Technically, I don't think we rescued you," Grant said. "You seemed to have that handled."

I goggled at him. "Do you not remember the crazed wyverns?"

"Do you not remember tossing Zipporah like she weighed no more than a chicken? That was an impressive display of power, Grayson."

At the reminder, I tentatively tested my connection to the elements. Rather than the pain I expected from over-exerted mental muscles—or worse, being temporarily fried and unable to touch the elements—a dull soreness was the worst I felt, even after I widened my intake, drawing on Quinn's boost.

"Maybe I'm simply euphoric from being alive, but what I did, it, well, I felt as strong as a full spectrum." I peeked at Grant through my lashes, certain he would be amused by my assessment.

His expression remained serious. "I don't think it's euphoria."

"What?"

"That was more magic than I've ever seen you use on your own. You're stronger than you used to be."

"You have been since Aurora Isle," Quinn said.

Shocked, I stared blankly at Quinn.

"It was likely the thief's key," Grant said. "Absorbing so much magic so fast—it stretched your abilities beyond your natural range. Or to your new natural range."

An involuntary shudder rattled my spine. Using the thief's key to free myself from the snare—using one spell so dangerous it had been banned to unlock another—had been terrifying. And painful. Wildly, incredibly, horrifically painful. It could have just as easily nullified me too. I never expected to gain anything from the experience.

"You should get retested to see your new range. I suspect you're close to full spectrum now," Grant said.

I blinked at him in surprise. "Why?" It wasn't as if I was still in school and might be placed in different courses to help train or advance my skills. Nor was I looking for a career change. Having the designation of full spectrum—or *almost* full spectrum—wouldn't change anything for me at the *Chronicle*.

"You need training, if not combat training, at least instruction on multiple defensive and offensive spells, since you keep—" Grant hesitated, obviously editing his words. "Since your job isn't always the safest. If you're capable of performing more complex spells, your instructor should know."

I threaded my fingers through Grant's. Suggesting I learn to protect myself was a pleasant change from being ordered to stay away from danger. "Are you offering to teach me?"

He didn't answer, his gaze shifting past me and his expression souring. I twisted to see what had caught his eye. Wetherill barreled down on us, fury blazing in his eyes.

I sighed. "Any chance you can start by teaching me how to defend myself against elitist blowhards."

"The best defense is a good offense. Allow me to demonstrate."

Wetherill had retrieved a personal flying carpet and sat atop it, his injured leg stretched out in front of him. His other leg dangled off the edge, and he braced his palms on either side of his body. He stopped the carpet almost on top of us, glaring down from his superior height.

"Captain Monaghan, what are you doing?" Wetherill demanded.

"Having a private conversation." Grant's tone was mild, but irritation burned in his eyes.

"The city doesn't pay you to sit around, holding hands with—" Wetherill's gaze dropped to mine, and I raised an eyebrow, inviting him to finish the sentence. Instead, he waved the air between us, as if he could shoo me aside. "Harriet is fine. I'll see she gets proper attention."

"I appreciate your concern," I murmured.

"In your injured state, I wouldn't want you to overexert yourself. Sir." Grant delivered the honorific flatly, after a pointed pause. Then he casually took control of Wetherill's carpet, lowering it until Wetherill's dangling foot touched the ground, dropping the irate full spectrum closer to our eye level. Ever so gently, Grant propelled the carpet backward, outside of the sphere of warmth. Wetherill sputtered at Grant's high-handedness, but Grant didn't give him a chance to speak. "Do you have a healer on staff, or will you require the FPD's field healer to look at your leg? Once Investigator O'Hara is finished saving the life of your wounded wyvern, I'm sure he or his teammates will be happy to provide healing. Or we can escort you to the nearest healer hall."

"I'm fine," Wetherill snapped. "But this is unacceptable." He slashed a hand toward the ruined hangar, then swept his arm across the field to encapsulate the captured wyverns. "Miscreants—a whole *gang* of them—*abducted* me. They planted a phoenix egg on my property, and they tried to kill me! What more do you need to hear to get off your ass and start looking for the savages?"

Quinn and I shared a wide-eyed glance. That was too far, even for a preeminent full spectrum. When Grant spoke, his tone should have frozen Wetherill as surely as a Thilorier's expectoration.

"I had a choice, Mr. Wetherill. I could chase the criminals, or I could prevent your wyverns from devouring you. I believe I made the right decision."

"Yes, yes. That was the right call *then*. But the Thiloriers are no longer a threat, and you can't let those reprobates get away with this. The more time that passes, the harder it will be to track them. You should be hunting them, not wasting time with—"

A message bubble skimmed across the lawn from the tree line, halting in front of Grant. He held a finger up to Wetherill, not waiting for the full spectrum to quiet before activating the bundle of elements. Seradon's voice floated out, drowning out Wetherill's indignant huff.

"We're coming to you. All except Velasquez, who is going to take the good news to his gargoyle healer in person. As soon as Winnigan catches up with Marciano and me, we'll be there. Give our Kylie a kiss for me." Her chuckle faded with the last of her captured words.

"Mika knew I was missing?"

"We had everyone looking for you," Quinn said. "We were worried."

"I'm sure everyone was worried about the both of us," Wetherill said, circling his hand impatiently, as if he were trying to propel the conversation along.

"Actually, no one knew you'd been abducted," Quinn said.

Wetherill scowled.

"I guess you could say you have Kylie to thank for saving your life," Grant said. "Twice, since we saw her get you out of the hangar. But if not for her, Quinn and I wouldn't have been here to distract your Thiloriers." Grant twisted until he faced me. "I was so worried about you," he said, tipping his forehead to mine, acting as if Wetherill didn't exist. Amusement twinkled in Grant's warm brown eyes. He was enjoying pissing Wetherill off.

I had never been more attracted to Grant.

"Perhaps another kiss will assure me you're all right," he murmured.

Choking back a laugh, I planted a chaste kiss on his lips.

"Captain Grant Monaghan, now is not the time for . . . for canoodling," Wetherill declared.

"I don't know. I wouldn't mind getting kissed by a pretty woman after I battled *four* wyverns," O'Hara said dryly.

My spine jerked straight. Grant choosing to ignore

Wetherill was one thing; displaying amorous behavior in front of his superior was another. Especially since the last time we spoke, O'Hara still considered me a suspect.

I attempted to pull my hand from Grant's, but he tightened his grip. He didn't rise either, maintaining his seated sprawl next to me.

"Now is hardly the time," Wetherill snapped. "Not when the hoodlums who did this are getting farther away by the second." He pulsed air into the carpet's levitation spell, elevating it so he was slightly taller than O'Hara. The abrupt motion rocked his injured ankle, and the color drained from Wetherill's flushed face.

O'Hara spoke before he recovered his voice. "If they took aircrafts from the hangar—which it appears they did, though you'll have to confirm your inventory with us— whoever did this is long gone. You have a tracker on every aircraft in your hangar, right?"

"Of course."

Yet Wetherill had felt the need to order Grant to rush after the thieves, giving no thought to Grant's well-being. I relived the pleasure of slapping magic across Wetherill's mouth, wishing I could do the same now.

"We both know those ships will be dismantled and sold for parts by noon. I don't want *pieces* of my expensive dirigibles; I want them back, whole. More important, I want the people who did this to me to pay."

"The people who did this to *both* of you," Grant corrected.

"For all we know, they did this to me *because* of Harriet."

"It's Kylie," Grant snapped, his nonchalant composure cracking.

O'Hara's eyebrows twitched. He gestured to Xinh, who

had walked up while Wetherill blustered. "Xinh, will you take down Luther's story and heal him, if he requests?"

"Certainly, Investigator. This way, Mr. Wetherill."

Wetherill's lips pinched, and he looked as if he was about to protest, but O'Hara added, "I need to have a talk with Monaghan."

"Fine." Wetherill powered his carpet after Xinh, who led them toward a distant circle of hedges surrounding a stone bench.

I had hoped Xinh would heal me first, but I decided this was preferable. Seeing Wetherill's retreating backside was already making me feel better.

"Your stable caretakers are alive and well," Xinh said, waving a hand toward the wyvern den and two people being guided across the spacious lawn by his squad mate. "Though they were a bit banged up for trying to defend the wyverns from the thieves. Also, the female wyvern will fly again, but she'll need at least a week of rest. You'll want to consult a specialist, of course."

I couldn't hear Wetherill's reply, but I doubted he expressed gratitude. Nearly dying hadn't tempered his abrasive personality. If anything, it had made the full spectrum more supercilious than before—a feat I would have said was impossible yesterday.

O'Hara knelt in front of me. "Where are you wounded?"

Since I had expected him to demand a recounting of the events or to berate Grant for his attitude, my brain was still catching up with the question when Grant answered for me.

"Lacerations on her back, scrapes on her hands, a cut on her scalp and knee, bruises on her wrists, and a slice down her calf. The calf is the worst."

"Any frost from a Thilorier?"

"No." Again, Grant answered for me.

"This is going to hurt," the investigator said, accepting a link with Grant.

My brain finally caught up: O'Hara was offering to heal me.

A gentle cleansing spell swiped across my calf, lighting a fire in its wake. O'Hara gripped my ankle, holding my leg still, and repeatedly scrubbed the wound. I gritted my teeth and squeezed Grant's hand.

"It was the Fire Eaters," I blurted out, hoping talking would distract me from the pain. "They drugged me—us. Took me from outside of Airstrong."

"I should never have left you," Quinn moaned.

"It's not—" I inhaled sharply as O'Hara's spell dug all the way to the bone. "Not your fault."

"Save your breath," O'Hara said. "I've got all the dirt out. The worst is done."

I steeled myself while the investigator spun together fire, water, and earth, but instead of Grant's molten-brand style of knitting flesh, O'Hara's healing spell warmed my leg from the inside out, as if I were standing next to a fireplace, not *in* the fire. My death grip on Grant's hand relaxed, and I shot him a pointed look. Grant was too busy studying O'Hara's technique to notice.

The investigator didn't let me speak until he had examined my back, healing the deepest of the scrapes and cleansing the rest—and cleaning my shirt too, so the wounds he didn't mend wouldn't get infected. The shallow cut across the top of my knee from the basilisk's claw also got disinfected. I kept my eyes locked on my boots, breathing deeply when the blackness lapping at the edges of my vision threatened to overtake me.

"That should tide you over until you can get to a healing hall," O'Hara said, sitting back on his heels.

"Thank you."

He nodded. "So what happened here?"

Explaining the Fire Eaters' attack made me angry all over again. Angry and embarrassed. Both emotions helped push back my fatigue. I should have reacted faster, lashed out with magic, and run before they got ahold of me. At the very least, I could have held them at bay with a ward until Quinn arrived. Reminding myself the same gang had also fooled and captured Wetherill helped, and I forced myself to take my time describing my attackers. I couldn't add many details about after I woke in the hangar, since it had been too dark and I had been too woozy, just that I was certain the gravelly voiced man, Apollo, had been among those who attacked the jail.

"They fled once they realized the basilisks were loose."

"And Luther?" O'Hara prompted.

"I found him bound and drugged next to a phoenix egg."

The sun crested the horizon, and its bright rays illuminated the grounds. Frozen-gray and charred-black grasses cut jagged swaths across the far half the field. Wisps of steam rose from the frost patches and ghosted across the frozen lake. From a distance, it looked like a serene wintery scene, but my ears still rang with the echoes of wyvern cries, and my heart pounded as I visually traced each patch and slash of ash and ice, reliving Grant's life-and-death fight. A single misstep or mistimed defense, and he could have been taken from me forever.

I drew a deep breath, refocusing on the present. Two men in FPD uniforms guided the last wyvern into its den. Fully healed, Wetherill stalked after them, barking orders and waving his arms in a way that would have gotten him attacked if the wyvern hadn't been hooded. Xinh trailed after him.

The hangar looked smaller in the light. The phoenix had taken out a third of it, and smoke wafted from charred boards hidden behind the mirror ward. Rubble scattered the ground from the hangar to the invisible wall where my shield had stood. I traced my eyes along the length of splintered boards and warped metal puncturing the lawn like a junkyard's barricade.

Grant was right. I needed to get retested.

"There's a young man, a teenager, inside the hangar. Dead, paralyzed by a basilisk," I said, pulling my gaze back to O'Hara. "His body might have survived the hatching. I think it was far enough away."

Grant's thumb, which had been rubbing soothingly across the back of my hand, froze. The muscles in his forearm flexed, then his thumb resumed its gentle caresses. I blinked moisture from my eyes.

"We found another near the entrance." O'Hara shook his head. "Stupid boys, playing with death and shocked when it finds them."

I shuddered, thankful Wetherill and I hadn't run into the paralyzed Fire Eater during our escape. This ordeal had already provided enough fuel for a month of nightmares.

"You know what this means, right?" I asked Grant.

His eyes brimmed with checked violence, and his voice when he responded came out close to a growl. "A lot of Fire Eaters are going to jail."

"Good. But also, Wetherill isn't behind the Airstrong thefts. He wasn't faking being drugged or injured, and he was too shocked and scared at finding an egg on his property. Though it fits the pattern. He's always present when the stolen items are found . . ." An inkling of a new theory squirmed through my thoughts, but before I could chase it, O'Hara spoke.

"By that logic, you're the thief. You've not only been present at each stolen item's recovery, but you've also been the person to find each item. That's quite a coincidence."

"Right. I've heard this theory before." I would have crossed my arms, but Grant still held my hand. "I gain notoriety for Airstrong, right? Which makes about as much sense as being the person who sinks a boat, then tells others about it to make the sunken wreck famous. I'm not so stupid as to lock myself in a building with at least two basilisks and a phoenix egg about to hatch all for a bit of fame. Whatever else you think of me, I'm not an idiot."

"No, not an idiot," O'Hara agreed blandly.

"And I wasn't present at *every* recovery. I had no idea about the phoenix at Airstrong until after it took out half the block, and . . ." I trailed off, and if O'Hara corrected my exaggeration, I didn't notice.

What if my theory about the thefts had been wrong all along? What if someone wasn't trying to undermine the public's confidence in Airstrong? What if violence had always been the thief's goal? Not just violence but making a big splash. The kind of spectacle tailor made for the front page of the paper.

No. Nathan wouldn't go so far.

He was a horrible coworker but a good journalist. I detested him, but that didn't make him a villain.

Yet . . .

Nathan had been at the discovery of every stolen item, there to swoop in and write the article, always poised to get his byline on the front page of the *Terra Haven Chronicle*.

I thrummed my fingers on my thigh, the tips of them tingling.

O'Hara cleared his throat. "What do you—"

"Hang on. I know that look," Grant said.

Nathan didn't like me. He made that abundantly clear. He had been furious that I repeatedly landed front-page stories as a junior journalist. How many times had he told me I was overstepping myself? He had wanted to put me in my place practically since I had been hired.

But it was more than that. Nathan believed he was the top writer for the *Chronicle*, and he didn't want *anyone* to show him up. And how better to ensure he had the top stories than to manufacture them himself? Airstrong was the perfect target. They shipped dangerous objects all the time, and any theft would net a printable story. Maybe taking me down had been a bonus.

Nathan had constructed each story on the back of the last, toeing the line of slander and building a narrative that painted me and my family as self-centered, untrustworthy, greedy, and sneaky. We had become characters in a drama of Nathan's creation. It was scandal journalism with the veneer of facts.

My parents were in danger of losing their livelihood. Grant, Quinn, and I had nearly died multiple times. Strangers had been hurt, nullified, and murdered. All so Nathan could bask in the glory of a string of front-page stories. My stomach revolted.

"It's Nathan," I said.

"Who?" O'Hara glanced around, as if expecting to see someone waltz out of the shadows.

"Nathan Aspell, senior journalist at the *Terra Haven Chronicle*." He had been standing in plain sight, pretending ignorance even as he profited on the chaos he orchestrated.

"You want me to believe a reporter would concoct all this just for a story?" O'Hara asked.

"And a book deal," Quinn added.

"That's right."

O'Hara scoffed. "That's an even flimsier motive than Wetherill had."

"And who do you suspect?" I countered. "Obviously this wasn't my mom's doing."

O'Hara's gaze skimmed my body as if he was cataloging my injuries again, and I saw the moment he mentally checked Mom off his suspects list.

Finally. I squeezed Grant's fingers in silent thanks for him having the forethought of locking Mom up. O'Hara had irrefutable proof that Charlotte Grayson wasn't involved in dispersing the stolen phoenix eggs. More importantly, she was safe. Nathan couldn't target her because he didn't know where she was.

A chill slid down my spine as I remembered the tracking spell Nathan had placed on me outside the jail, after he told me Grant had arrested Mom. If Grant hadn't denied my demands to see Mom, I would have led Nathan right to her.

"Nathan being behind everything makes sense," I said. "Even if you discount the fact that since the firebird story broke, Nathan has been handed all the prime assignments—which is the equivalent of being king of the *Chronicle*—you can't discount the power he's wielded. Nathan hasn't done this for *a* story. He's held the city in thrall for weeks now. He manipulated a full spectrum—two, if you count Persephone Kwan *and* Luther Wetherill. Now he has everyone afraid for their lives, hanging on the next edition of the *Chronicle* for news, all while you and the rest of the FPD run around chasing your own tails trying to find the remaining phoenix eggs." I returned O'Hara's glare with raised eyebrows, daring him to contradict me. "Power. Control. Fame. Those sound like strong motives to me. Plus, he hates me, and I haven't had a wonderful time lately." Hearing the facts out loud chased away the last of my doubts. And unlike with Wetherill, I didn't have that nagging feeling of forcing the facts to fit my theory.

"You're overlooking the Fire Eaters," O'Hara said. "They tried to break Kwan out of jail. They orchestrated tonight's events. They had at least one phoenix egg. Maybe they've been behind all the thefts."

"How would they have known about Airstrong's shipments?" Grant asked. "No one outside the FPD, Charlotte, and key Airstrong personnel knew the exact shipping date and route of the firebirds. Even Charlotte didn't know the contents of our disguised box of confiscated spells. We took extra precautions with the phoenix eggs. Yet the thief chose his targets with precision."

"That same logic rules out the journalist too."

"Unless he had a source inside Airstrong," I said, feeling sick at the thought.

"Or the Fire Eaters have a source," O'Hara said.

That hardly made me feel better. It also didn't feel right, but I couldn't use gut feeling in my argument. Instead, I asked, "What did the Fire Eaters gain by abducting me? They used Wetherill to break through his own ward, but me? I was an extra risk for no reward, thieverly speaking."

"Thieverly?" Quinn asked.

"Theftly speaking?" No, that didn't sound right either. "Theftily?"

O'Hara snorted softly. "You're right. Your presence here makes no sense, Kylie. I'll look into Nathan Aspell. It can't hurt. We don't have much time until the rest of the flaming birds hatch."

"The fair," I blurted out. If Nathan was looking to top his most recent articles, he would need something flashy. The fair was the biggest event to come to Terra Haven all year, and an explosive hatching amid all those people would make the front page of every paper in the nation, perhaps every paper around the world. He wasn't going to get a bigger story than that, and he wouldn't have to wait long either—the fair started tomorrow. No, make that today.

Both men nodded, having obviously already come to the same conclusion.

"We have our work cut out for us." O'Hara rose to his feet. "Get some sleep, Monaghan. I expect your team on the ground by ten."

"Yes, sir."

"I'll put a guard on you and Airstrong tomorrow, Kylie, just in case you're the target."

"Thank you." I wasn't going to turn down extra protection, not after tonight.

"Thank you," Quinn said, earning a curt nod from the investigator.

O'Hara's eyes lifted, annoyance flattening his lips. Wetherill stomped his way across the lawn toward us.

"I don't have time for this," O'Hara grumbled, striding off to intercept him.

"Can you stand?" Grant asked.

I blinked at him, my eyelids scratching like sandpaper. I was going to crash hard, soon.

"Maybe." It would be far preferable for Seradon to arrive and cart my limp body from this spot straight to my bed. "Why?"

"I was hoping to move out of sight. I don't have any more patience for Luther."

"For that, it might be worth moving."

"Wait." Quinn circled around to stand in front of us. He peeked over his shoulder, then whispered, "I spoke with the gargoyles around Airstrong."

He paused long enough for me to wrangle my weary thoughts into an insightful response. "I know."

"I didn't want to say anything in front of the investigator, especially since he finally seems like he might not suspect Charlotte, but, well, I think . . ." Quinn took another deep breath, then said in a rush, "Botan was on a rooftop three buildings down from Airstrong, and he swears he saw Charlotte go in and out of Airstrong's front doors before the explosion. He said Charlotte was carrying a bag on the way in, and not on the way out. The way she walked away, almost running, her steps loud on the wooden sidewalk, was what caught Botan's attention."

"But Mom was inside."

"Persephone insisted Charlotte gave her the spells," Grant mused, "and now we've got an unbiased gargoyle telling us she planted the phoenix egg."

"Hang on, Mom didn't—"

"No, I'm not saying she did." Grant tucked me back against his side when I would have pushed away. "There's a possibility we haven't considered."

"Well, don't leave me in suspense," I grumbled.

"Nathan has a doppelganger spell."

I gaped at Grant. Not only were doppelganger spells forbidden—impersonating another person was illegal, especially taking on their body, voice, and mannerisms—but they were also incredibly finicky. It took a minimum of five linked people to create the spell, more if everyone wasn't a full spectrum. Even then, they were notoriously difficult to embed into an object, and they had to be embedded into something. No one could maintain an unanchored doppelganger spell. All of which made them wildly expensive to make.

"Nathan doesn't have that kind of money," I said. "Splinters, does *Wetherill* even have that kind of money?"

Grant shrugged. "A doppelganger spell would explain a great deal, including how the items were stolen in the first place. I've been toying with this theory for a while, but there was no point in bringing it up until now. Quinn, your gargoyle friend has all but confirmed it."

"Yeah?" Quinn's hunched shoulders straightened, and his wings flared in excitement. "Does this mean we have proof?"

"Not quite, but we're closer. It gives us another way to look for the eggs. Doppelganger spells can be keyed to only one person, so with the real Charlotte tucked away, if anyone spots her moving around the city, we'll know we're looking at the thief."

"You mean Nathan."

"Or whoever he's working with. A Fire Eater could be using the spell. Until we find Nathan and his allies, I want you to continue to wear a tracker." Frustration darkened Grant's face, and he muttered, "Not that it did much good this time. I'm sorry, Kylie. I should have checked in more often . . ."

"If you had, you wouldn't have been able to do your job."

He winced. "I was being an ass when I said that. My job is not more important than you. It never will be."

The guilt edging Grant's eyes pained my heart.

"You can't stand guard over me."

"I should—"

I pressed a finger to Grant's lips, silencing his protest. The heat of his exhale tingled across my fingertip, and I retracted my hand with a shiver.

"I wouldn't like it. You wouldn't enjoy it." That finally got a smile out of him. "You're doing a fine job as the city's FPD captain, but even you can't make the entire world—the entire city—safe. You can't keep me in a protective ward either. It was enough that you came for me when you knew I was missing and in danger."

"I will always come for you, Kylie." Grant smoothed my hair from my face, his thumb lingering on my jaw.

My heart pounded against my rib cage. *How would the truth hex have interpreted that?* I wondered, reminded of the hex whispering Grant's *I love you* into my mind when I had rescued him from Persephone's spell. Had that been real?

"I know," I said, choking back those same three words, afraid if I blurted them out now, Grant would dismiss them as a byproduct of fatigue or gratitude.

When we were no longer in danger, and when he hadn't just saved my life, I would tell him. Until then, I hugged the knowledge like a treasure inside me.

And if some of it shone from my eyes when I leaned in to kiss Grant, so be it.

Rested, full, and sore from head to toe, I strolled to Airstrong in the early afternoon with Quinn at my side. If not for my growling stomach, I could have slept hours longer, but once I was conscious, worry kept me awake. Would Grant and O'Hara find Nathan before he hurt more people? If they found the eggs, would they be strong enough to encapsulate all three hatching blasts? What if Grant got hurt? What if Nathan had some devious plot already set in motion specifically to harm Grant? *FPD Captain Killed by Phoenix Hatching* would be a big story.

The thought nauseated me.

A dozen times—while I dressed, while I ate, while I skimmed the *Chronicle*, while I stretched my stiff muscles and applied ointment to my cuts—I stopped myself from sending Grant a message requesting an update. If Nathan were in custody or they found the eggs, he would notify me. Until then, he didn't need me interrupting him while he worked. But I loathed being so passive.

Before I had collapsed into bed, I sent Melora a message

with instructions regarding what to do in my absence. Even if she wasn't authorized to sign off on additional large-scale expenditures, the shipping manager was more than capable of keeping the warehouse repairs progressing during my absence. I didn't need to return to Airstrong today, but if I sat at home, I would drive myself crazy with worry—or envy. I yearned to chase down the phoenix eggs with Grant. One more set of eyes wouldn't hurt the investigation, especially since I knew who and what to look for. But I had made a promise to my parents.

At least at Airstrong, I would feel useful. I had to trust that Grant and the rest of the FPD could locate the phoenix eggs and Nathan without me.

Another sigh escaped me.

"I'm really pleased with the way the minotaur article turned out," Quinn said, drawing me from my morose thoughts—just as he had likely intended.

"Me too."

Dahlia had printed our article almost verbatim, trimming less than a dozen words. That said more about its quality than its location on the sixth page, half buried among advertisements. However, the goal had never been for the article to receive prominent placement, but rather to get the information out to the public. I was proud of the short piece, and I hoped it brought the Femmes of the Furnace new clients.

The sight of Airstrong gave me another burst of pride. Gone was the blackened hole and crumbling walls. In its place stood four stories of red bricks, the mortar so fresh it still glistened. Wooden frames outlined windows yet to be installed, and through these openings, I spotted brand-new support beams and freshly poured concrete.

Guards flanked the perimeter of Airstrong, standing in

the street to direct traffic past the construction and usher customers to the loading dock around the back. I recognized men and women I had hired to protect Airstrong as well as city guards, and I made a mental note to send a thank-you to the local station for lending their support.

Quinn and I wove through the crowd and down the alley between Femmes of the Furnace and Airstrong. I was pleased to see several customers lined up in front of the glass shop, half hidden in the organized chaos around Airstrong. The minotaurs' wards gleamed with power, and layers of ice insulated the furnace section of the building. No one navigating the narrow stretch between the buildings would suspect molten glass upward of two thousand degrees burned on the opposite side of the thin brick wall.

The line of customers made way for us to pass, recognizing either me or Quinn at my side. A handful attempted to air their grievances then and there, but I hustled past, casting assurances over my shoulder that everyone would be accommodated in the order in which they had arrived.

At the loading dock, Melora stood in my impromptu open-air office, deftly dealing with the client in front of her. The pallet of bricks that had served as my temporary desktop was gone—the bricks having been used to rebuild the front wall—and Melora had found a sturdy oak table, instead. Airstrong employees bustled through the spacious warehouse, organizing pallets, buckets, crates, and bins of various goods. All the rubble had been piled off to one side of the loading dock, where a handful of apprentices from local craft studios were picking through the contents for salvageable material. Good. We needed to strengthen our ties to the community, and helping supply our neighbors with free scrap was a small step in the right direction. Plus, I liked the idea of something positive and possibly artistic coming out of the destruction.

Tossing Melora a wave, I ducked into the shaded warehouse. I wanted a look around before I got sucked into the endless demands of our clients and contractors.

"It looks so much bigger," Quinn said. He reared up on his hind legs to take in the warehouse floor. Filled to less than a third of its usual capacity, the building seemed cavernous.

"All the more room for incoming shipments," I said with forced optimism.

A couple of workers glanced in Quinn's direction, traces of alarm in their expressions. My gargoyle companion cut an impressive figure on four legs. On two, he towered above me, and with his wings flared for balance, he almost looked menacing. His doleful expression, however, seemed to reassure the workers, and they resumed their tasks, releasing hastily gathered elements. I sighed. Everyone was tense after the attack. After the attack *and* all the thefts. Getting the warehouse back up to operating standards might prove simpler than assuaging the staff's anxieties.

Quinn dropped to all fours and brushed his cheek against my hip. "I think it looks better than it did before the phoenix hatched."

I smiled. "That was the plan. If we are forced to remodel, we're going to do it right."

The new brick walls were embedded with strengthening spells, which, at my request, had been left visible rather than hidden inside the mortar. The floors were clean. A protective spell hugged the building, keyed to send up an alarm if anything hotter than the body temperature of a gryphon entered the facility. Magic glistened on every surface with purity and purpose. As Mom drilled into me, appearances were important, and each prospective or existing client standing on the loading dock looking in would see a safe environment for their next shipment. Airstrong was picking itself up and dusting itself off. We weren't going to let a little thing like a phoenix egg exploding in our walls stop us from getting shipments out.

My chin lifted higher; my shoulders sat straighter. Mom would be proud of what I had accomplished—of what *everyone* at Airstrong had accomplished. I couldn't wait to show her.

Just as soon as it was safe to do so.

For the hundredth time, I considered sending a message to Grant, asking for an update. For the hundredth time, I stopped myself. My job was here, and that was where my focus needed to be. But Quinn . . .

I led him to Mom's office, intending to use the room for privacy, but the sight caught me off guard. All the furniture and paperwork had been cleared out, the ceiling and one wall had been replaced but not yet repainted, and construction dust littered the floor. It looked like a stranger's space, not Mom's.

I shook off my discombobulation. Mom would set her stamp on the place in no time. We just had to find Nathan and the missing eggs first.

We being Grant and the FPD, of course.

Stepping into the empty room, I turned to Quinn.

"I'm going to be here all day." I pointed out to the dock. "Or there. As much as I love having you around, there's nothing for you to do. If you wanted to help Grant and his team, I wouldn't mind." It was the truth. I would be jealous, but I wouldn't be upset. In fact, it would make me feel better knowing Grant had Quinn's magical boost to draw on, not to mention Quinn's clever mind and deft flying skills.

"I'm staying here."

"I promise I won't step foot beyond the dock until you're here to escort me home. I'll be safe. But Grant might need you. And the sooner we find Nathan and those eggs, the safer the whole city will be."

"Grant doesn't need me. He has his team. You don't have a team. You have me. And I wasn't here yesterday. No—" He held up a paw when I would have jumped to his defense. "I know. It wasn't my fault. Nathan was behind those horrible men kidnapping you. But that's my point. He has it out for you, and until Grant or the investigator find him, you're not out of danger."

Quinn sat, lifting his seed with his front paw so he could examine it. "Even my seed believes I need to be here. I'm not through helping you, or it would have changed." He glanced up, his heart in his eyes. "But even if it had, I still wouldn't leave you alone while Nathan is out there. It's scary, and friends don't abandon friends when they're scared."

I sat down beside Quinn and draped an arm across his back, giving him a one-armed hug. Breathing in his cool, earthy scent—one I had come to associate with safety and home—I said, "I love you so much, Quinn."

He snuggled against me, his eyes closed. "I love you too, Kylie. I don't want you to ever be hurt again."

"You and me both." I gently tugged Quinn's seed from his neck, then held it up so we were both reflected in its mirror surface on the back. Tilting my head, I rested it against Quinn's and met his eyes in the reflection. "I appreciate how well you've protected me, but I hope you know you're so much more than a bodyguard to me. You're my partner, my companion. And you're wise beyond your years. If not for you, I wouldn't have helped Mom, as much as it shames me to admit. I would still be chasing Wetherill or

Nathan, but you reminded me I have other ways of helping my parents. You're smart, and you give amazing counsel. You've had my back, even when it meant standing up to me when I was being foolish and stubborn. I value that far more than any physical protection you could offer me, and I say that knowing you've saved my life more times than I care to count. Your honesty, your loyalty, your bravery, your heart —you're one of a kind, Quinn, and I'm grateful to call you my friend."

"Always."

Quinn's eyes glowed with affection in his reflection. He shifted, pressing his cheek more firmly against mine, his chest rumbling with a deep purr on his exhale. I closed my eyes, savoring the moment.

Magic tingled against my palm. My eyes snapped open. Quinn gasped and sat up straight. Elements burst from his seed, dancing in a wild spell guided by the will and wisdom of the everlasting tree's magic. The emerald-stone-and-mirror seed transformed before our eyes, folding in half, then swelling into a sphere. The leather thong dropped free, and I let it fall to the floor, entranced by the magical evolution. When the elements settled, a pewter seed rested in my palm, roughly the size and shape of a large avocado pit, though it weighed twice as much. Silver piping ran across the surface in beautiful arcs and twists, all leading toward the tip, where a tiny green sprout protruded.

His everlasting seed was ready to plant.

"Wow," Quinn breathed. He lifted a paw, and I nestled his seed into his curled toes. "It's gorgeous."

"Stunning." I rubbed my palms together, the tickle of the seed's magic still humming against my skin.

"But . . ." Quinn tore his gaze from the seed to shoot me a puzzled look. "Why now? Why didn't it change when I fought the wyverns or when I found where you were being held? Why did it change now, here?"

I contemplated the thin green sprout, then hazarded my best guess. "You asked the tree how you can best help me, right?"

Quinn nodded.

"I can't think of a better way you could help me than by being my friend, giving me your opinions and advice."

"Always," Quinn said, echoing his earlier statement. Unexpectedly, his shoulders slumped, and a furrow appeared between his eyes. "That's nothing new, though. I've been your friend since before we went to the everlasting tree."

"We've been through a lot together since then. Our friendship has grown. You've grown. You no longer go along with every one of my plans." I bumped his shoulder with mine to show I wasn't upset. "You've taken initiative, made decisions, and become more opinionated."

"I have?"

"All in good ways. I'm proud of you, Quinn."

A huge grin split his face, and his toes tightened, his claws curling to encase the seed. "When I plant this, it will give me the final answer to my question, right?"

"Yep."

Quinn quivered with excitement, and I understood how he felt. Curiosity bubbled inside me. I couldn't wait to see what would happen when the plant grew. Just like the shapes the seed took when it evolved, the plant itself could grow into any configuration necessary to deliver its final message. Its answer.

I lifted my hand to grip the pouch holding my seed, and my excitement dimmed. I had worn the pouch today with the hope that my seed would bring me good luck, but it was depressing to realize that's all it would ever be: a talisman. I would never see my seed sprout, never receive its answer. Witnessing Airstrong bustling with activity and knowing I had helped my parents as much as possible felt good, but a part of me would always wonder where my seed might have led me, what amazing story I had given up. Nathan and his phoenix eggs were a big story, but they were just a step in evolving my seed—one I would miss.

"Let's plant it at home, tonight," Quinn said.

"You sure you want to wait?"

"Yes. I want to do it with you. After you finish what you need to do here."

"Thank you." I tucked his seed into my pouch alongside mine, closing the drawstring tight around the extra bulge and adding a protective weave of air and earth to ensure it stayed closed. "Until tonight."

Quinn grinned, radiating happiness.

———

I dropped the heavy ledger atop a stack of papers and surveyed my workstation. Melora had volunteered to maintain her post on the dock, sorting out issues with the public, which freed me up to deal with a backlog of bookkeeping. I had chosen to use Mom's office, where I could keep an eye on the entire warehouse without being underfoot. My desk was a stack of empty crates, my chair a stool with one wobbly leg. Replacement furniture wouldn't arrive until the end of the week. Until then, the staff and I would have to make do.

A stack of invoices in one hand, I tugged the ledger open with the other and froze. Mom's crisp handwriting stared back at me, precise entries dating back a full month before the handwriting changed to Melora's. A wave of fresh frustration and anger blindsided me. Mom had been trapped here in Terra Haven for weeks, under suspicion and struggling to keep her business from being demolished—by Nathan. *Nathan.* The weasel reporter who had set his petty sights on tearing apart my life, and who had dragged Mom into his maniacal schemes without a second thought. He had forced her into hiding, forced her to choose between her livelihood and her life, and I loathed him for it.

Had Grant found him yet? Would he find the phoenix eggs in time? Would he get hurt—killed—in the process?

The invoices trembled in my fist. I carefully set them down and ran a damp palm across the stack to smooth the crinkled edges. *I came here so I wouldn't obsess,* I reminded myself. Pushing thoughts of Grant from my mind, I read the top invoice—then reread it when I couldn't remember a word or number on it.

The warehouse hummed with activity, the staff wielding the elements with renewed energy despite the late afternoon hour. We all had Quinn to thank for that. He had decided the best way he could help was to claim a perch on the roof, where he could keep a lookout for anyone suspicious while simultaneously offering an elemental boost to all Airstrong employees.

I had a feeling Quinn would be missed far more than me or Mom when everything got back to normal.

My sigh disturbed the stack of invoices. I straightened them again and began entering each expenditure and profit into the ledger.

A message bubble floated into the room, butting up against the desk. I flicked it open with a twist of magic, not looking up.

"I need you."

My head jerked up at the sound of Mom's breathless voice.

"I'm on the roof," the words continued to spill from the disintegrating spell. "Quinn is here with me. Come quickly. Alone. The fate of Airstrong depends on it."

I stared at the air where the message spell had been, shocked. Mom shouldn't be here. The whole point of her going into hiding was to keep her safe and out of the way during the phoenix egg investigation. She had sworn to Grant that she would remain in his undisclosed house until he released her.

What would cause Mom to break her word? Grant would have sent word if he had caught Nathan or found the eggs, and he would have let me know if he had released Mom. Had she learned something about the phoenix eggs? How? She had no contact with the outside world.

Quinn's boost vanished, then blossomed again, like a hiccup in my gut.

I shot to my feet, toppling the stool with a crash. It wasn't just the message that had startled me. It was Mom's voice. If it had been a message from her, crafted in her magical signature, I would have recognized it instantly.

Oh crap. Grant was right.

I burst through the doorway, sprinting for the stairs even as I wove a hasty message bubble. Quinn's enhancement fluctuated again, and I fought to control the elements while I barked orders into the sphere.

"Melora, gather everyone under a ward and prepare for an attack. Then send guards after me."

My race across the warehouse floor drew everyone's attention, so I didn't bother specifying my destination. Melora was already on her feet, her wide eyes locked on me as I took the first three steps in a single leap.

"Protect the people, save what you can," I panted, then tied off the spell and shot it toward Melora. I didn't have time to key it to her personal signature, and with Quinn's boost dropping in and out, wreaking havoc with my magic, I didn't have the elemental dexterity.

Trusting Melora to catch the message and take charge, I turned all my attention to powering up the stairs.

Quinn was in trouble.

That hadn't been Mom—that had been Nathan or one of his cohorts using her voice. Somehow, he *had* gotten his hands on a doppelganger spell, as Grant had speculated.

I replayed the message in my head, listening to it in the raspy Fire Eater Apollo's voice, then Nathan's, hearing the threat disguised with Mom's stolen voice. *Quinn is here with me. Come quickly. Alone. The fate of Airstrong depends on it.*

Fear clawed up my throat, squeezing my taxed oxygen supply. Quinn's enhancement fluctuated again, warning me the only way he could.

Hang on, Quinn, I'm coming for you.

Fire burned in my thighs, my gasping breaths like sandpaper in my dry throat. By the time I reached the roof doorway, fatigue weighed my legs down as if I had sprinted up ten flights, not three, each partially healed piece of me crying out under the strain.

I paused in the shadow beside the doorway, trying to think past the panic propelling me. The door had been left cracked, but the imposter wasn't visible in the sliver of the sunbaked roof. Holding my breath, I strained to hear Quinn or his attacker. My heart thundered in my chest. Shouts and the murmur of conversations filtered up from the street. A wheeled conveyance rumbled past. Nothing. Then ... *there.* I caught the faint creak of dirigible cables sliding against a canvas envelope.

A chill of alarm shot through me. The mortar hadn't set on the front wall. Temporary braces supported yesterday's roof repairs because half the posts that normally bore the brunt of the roof's weight were still drying in new concrete slabs. The roof's structural integrity wouldn't be at full strength for another two weeks. If they had tethered a ship to our landing deck, it could pull the repairs apart and collapse half the building on the people below.

Sweat trickled down my back, stinging broken scabs. I cobbled together a message sphere tuned to Grant's magical signature and whispered into it. "The doppelganger is on Airstrong's roof."

I sent the tiny bundle of magic down through the warehouse, out of sight of anyone on the roof. If Grant was at the fairgrounds, it would take minutes to reach him, longer for Grant to return. I couldn't wait for him or the backup I hoped Melora was coordinating.

Swiping a hand across my forehead, I drew deeply on Quinn's boost, which had stabilized sometime between the second and third landing. Mentally, I formed a cage. Then, grabbing the edge of the door frame, I flung myself into the open.

The roof stretched before me, two-thirds of the flat surface covered by the thick, reinforced wooden planks of the landing deck. Evenly spaced burnished docking rings embedded in the surface glinted in the sunlight. Twin winches flanked the rear edge of the roof, each attached to tall poles and sturdy rope-and-pulley systems for lowering cargo off the back edge of the building. A mid-class cargo dirigible with a cigar-shaped canvas envelope and a suspended fifteen-foot basket scraped the planks between the winches, unanchored. The basket's bright-orange paint glistened as if still wet, as did the blue winged-A Airstrong logos painted on the basket's sides.

Mom stood in the dirigible's basket next to the open gate. Shock ran like a physical jolt across my nerve endings. Somehow, I had expected to see through the doppelganger spell, as if the strength of my love for Mom or my blood connection to her would counter the powerful magic, revealing the scumbag hiding beneath it.

Unfortunately, magic didn't work like that.

The person on the dirigible deck was Mom. They possessed Mom's blue eyes and intense stare. Mom's worry line between her pale eyebrows. Mom's tan forearms, both taut from her white-knuckled grip on the basket's railing. Mom's white-blond hair swept into a simple chignon, wind-loosened tendrils fluttering around her oval face. They wore Mom's khaki pants and cream blouse and stood with Mom's proud posture.

But they lacked the most important element: Mom's brain.

She never would have allowed a dirigible to rest unteth-ered on the loading deck, not even in an emergency—*especially* not in an emergency. One aberrant gust of wind, and the airship's delicate basket could crumple against the roof's sturdy planks. Or worse, the long cables connecting the basket and envelope could tangle in the winch lines and capsize the ship, endangering everyone below.

I didn't slow, pretending I saw nothing amiss, scanning the dirigible's deck for Quinn. My blood ran cold when I spotted him. He was hunkered down in an elemental prison near the rear of the basket, a volatile phoenix egg floating less than a foot above his wings. Heat radiated in a visible shimmer around the egg. That close to bare flesh, the egg would have inflicted third-degree burns. Quinn's quartz hide protected him, but pain still bowed his spine. Panic lent a glassy texture to his round eyes when they met mine.

The world went fuzzy around the edges. My chest expanded, but no air filled my lungs. When Quinn had been a defenseless cub, an evil person had tortured him within a hairsbreadth of his life. Mika had rescued him and healed his physical wounds, but healing the scars to his psyche had taken months longer. I wouldn't let him go through that again.

I charged, releasing the net I had intended for the imposter and swiping at the egg with a scoop of air. Earth scythes shredded my magic. Broken elements backlashed, whipping agony through my brain, but not before I recognized the magical signature behind the attack. Nathan, not a Fire Eater, hid beneath the facsimile of Mom. The confirmation of his villainy rang through my head like an echo of the backlash, but it was the strength of his counterstrike that truly stunned me. He wasn't a full spectrum. He wasn't enhanced by a gargoyle. But he had still easily overpowered me.

He had to be using boosters to amplify his magic.

A high-pitched keen pierced the air. Quinn's glazed eyes bulged with agony as the slab of air holding the phoenix egg sagged three inches closer to his back.

"One more stupid move like that, and I'll drop the egg on him." The voice was all Mom, the scathing tone and diction pure Nathan.

Revulsion churned in my stomach. My feet tripped over themselves to slow my forward momentum, and I caught myself on the dirigible's open gate. One step up into the basket, and I would be within arm's reach of Nathan. Another ten, and I would be at Quinn's side.

Nathan stepped closer, glaring down Mom's nose at me. I tipped my chin up, meeting those piercing blue eyes head on, searching for Nathan beneath the illusion.

"Let him go, Nathan."

Nathan lifted Mom's hand to Mom's mouth, feigning surprise. "Don't you recognize your own mother, Harry?"

I eyed the containment spell, calculating how fast I

could break Nathan's hold on Quinn—*if* I could break his hold. Not faster than he could drop the phoenix on Quinn's back. If the egg's molten shell touched Quinn, it would burn. If it cracked when it landed on his hard flesh, he would die. So would anyone below us. I couldn't chance it, but I couldn't let Nathan torture Quinn.

"Please." I pushed the word past numb lips. "Quinn isn't part of this. Let him go."

"So he can rush off and warn your boyfriend? I don't think so."

Sweat chilled against my skin. I heard the certainty in his voice, the conviction in his actions. He didn't plan on releasing Quinn.

He wanted us dead.

But first he wanted to toy with us.

I surged onto the dirigible, throwing a fist toward Mom's —toward *Nathan's*—midsection, suppressing my instinct to pull my punch. I wanted to close my eyes. Instead, I followed it with a rapid series of elemental punches, all of which he blocked.

"I warned you, Harry." A cruel smile twisted Mom's lips, and the phoenix egg dropped onto Quinn's folded wings.

Roaring in agony, Quinn clawed at his elemental enclosure.

"Quinn!"

Magic tore from me, atomizing Nathan's cage. Agony chased the elements, too much magic used too fast. My knees buckled, and I dropped to the deck, bracing myself with a hand to keep Quinn in sight. His haunches sagged. For a second, I feared he had lost consciousness. Then the egg slid down his canted wings to the deck, landing softly. Blackened quartz streaked Quinn's golden feathers as he leapt away.

A fist flashed across my periphery vision. I flinched aside, but the tail end of Nathan's punch snapped my chin past my shoulder. Pain exploded in my jaw, blackening my vision. Ears ringing, I toppled to my elbow.

A lion's roar split the air, fury and pain echoing off the nearby buildings. I blinked to clear my vision. Nathan swam into view, still cloaked in Mom's form, looming over me. He clutched a tiny glass spray bottle in her fist, held her slender finger poised over the nozzle. A hint of honeysuckle and spearmint floated on the air.

Terror as cold as Thilorier's ice jolted through my limbs. If he knocked me out, I was dead. Surging to my feet, I slapped Nathan's hand aside just as he depressed the nozzle. A cloudburst of anesthesia erupted between us. I jerked back, but the mist pelted my face and nostrils. Numbness crawled across my lips and cheeks, down my throat. Mom backed away from the dispersing vapors of Grave's Echo so fast she tripped.

He tripped. *Nathan*, not Mom. Fighting to keep my wits, I spat, swiping my face with the hem of my shirt.

An earthquake erupted beneath my feet, rattling the entire basket. Quinn charged, blind fury shining in his lion eyes. Nathan darted to the far railing, where the dirigible's railing extended past the edge of the roof. He made no attempt to stop Quinn, and Mom's expression radiated suppressed satisfaction.

"It's a trap," I tried to shout, but my warning emerged an incoherent mumble, mangled by a tongue too thick for my mouth. The elements fumbled beyond my reach, Quinn's boost a memory.

Nathan waited until Quinn leapt before thrusting a wave of air beneath the gargoyle's stomach. Using his momentum, Nathan tossed Quinn over the railing.

Quinn's blackened wings unfolded in slow motion, but he plummeted fast as stone. I thrust out a hand as if I could catch him and tried to sprint across the basket, but my legs moved as if through water.

My heart stuttered when Quinn hit the loading dock. I had heard him land countless times. I knew the tempo of his paws touching down when he was in a hurry or the concussion of him landing too hard or fast. This was something else. A crash, not a landing. A smashing of stone on stone, quartz on concrete.

Had he gotten his feet beneath him? Had he slowed his descent enough to avoid breaking a limb?

Had he survived?

The dirigible lurched into motion, and my legs collapsed. For a second, I teetered on my knees, then I toppled forward, helpless to brace myself. I barely felt the impact, my awareness locked on the ground far below.

Please be alive, Quinn.

Images of Quinn, shattered and lifeless on the loading dock, swarmed my thoughts. Choking back a sob, I ruthlessly shunted them aside. I had to survive before I could do anything for my friend.

Rolling over took all my strength, but I welcomed the burn in my arms and the sweat that beaded my forehead. The drug's potency would fade on its own, but exertion would degrade it faster. I sucked in a deep breath, pushed it all the way out, draining my lungs before refilling them, willing the oxygen to speed the cleansing of my system.

Nathan ignored me, tossing elements into the dirigible's spelled propellers with more urgency than skill. The basket scraped and bounced along the landing deck, jolting me. The lip of Airstrong's front wall rushed toward us, our collision imminent. I struggled to lift my head. Where was the egg? How much jostling could it take?

At the last second, Nathan engaged the series of levitation spells along the underside of the envelope. The basket bounced, clearing the roof and rattling my brain inside my skull. Cables snapped hard against the canvas envelope, the frame inside the oblong balloon shuddering as if we were caught in a thunderstorm, not sailing in a clear, windless sky. I cringed when Nathan dropped the rudder with the finesse of a flailing toddler, and a second, tortured vibration ran through the basket. The deck canted steeply, tilting my head toward the ground, lifting my feet. My stomach dropped through my spine as the dirigible spun sharply to port, gaining altitude fast. Blood rushed to my head, and I blinked black fuzz from my vision, gulping in another breath.

I stopped counting the seconds when I reached twenty-five. The guards at Airstrong hadn't been fast enough. We were beyond reach of anyone on the ground. I was on my own.

Another distressed vibration ran through the basket, shimmying the cables against the envelope with dangerous friction. A sharp hammering beyond my head made me jump. I twisted to identify the source.

The cargo ramp stretched from the inner cavity of the envelope to the basket deck. My stomach performed another weightless somersault.

Nathan had lowered the ramp. Midflight.

Was he trying to kill us?

Designed to assist with transitioning cargo to and from the envelope's interior storage hatch, the ramp should never, *ever* be employed in flight. With it lowered, the bottom of the envelope gaped open, threatening the balloon's integrity and adding drag to the delicate structure. Worse, the long wooden plank forced the basket into a perilously stiff lock-sync with the envelope. The dirigible's basket and cables weren't designed for that level of strain. One sharp counter-current and the ramp would rip the envelope, sending us plummeting to the ground.

Along with the phoenix egg.

Hysterical laughter climbed my throat. Nathan's own ineptitude might prevent him from enacting his revenge on me. Instead, he would kill us both.

. . . And whoever happened to be below us.

The thought sobered me.

Mom's voice floated across the basket, Nathan's words indistinct but agitated. Yanking a charm from a hidden pocket, Nathan funneled magic into it. When nothing happened, he tossed it aside with a sharp curse. The thumbnail-size silver clover clattered on the deck, the magic-amplification spell keyed to it spent. No wonder controlling the craft was taxing Nathan's elemental abilities. He had burned through the booster attacking me and Quinn. If only I was in a position to fight back now.

Summoning every ounce of my regained physical strength, I flopped to my stomach and braced myself up on my forearms. After a count of five, I shoved to all fours. My biceps quivered but held. In a painfully slow crawl, I angled toward the railing. If I could reach the side, I could signal people below for help. Somehow.

Nathan battered the levitation spells, and the rear of the craft lifted, the nose tipping toward the ground. Wobbling and sizzling, the phoenix egg rolled across the deck, charring a zigzagging path across the wood. Smoke curled in its wake before being whisked away in the wind. I strained for the elements, scrabbling for air to halt the egg before it hit the railing and exploded. A void stretched between me and the magic. I could sense the elements. I could see them. But I couldn't reach them.

Just when I was about to call out a warning to Nathan, the dirigible stabilized. The egg rocked in place, smoldering a divot into the planks. The basket's boards were coated with a weatherproof and fire-resistant lacquer, but they weren't designed to withstand direct flame. It was only a matter of time before the egg caught the basket on fire—or fell straight through. At its current rate, I guessed I had five, maybe ten minutes to think of a clever plan to rescue myself.

"There, that ought to do it," Nathan said, slapping Mom's hands together. "Now, Harry, we need to tal— Oh!" Nathan spotted the egg and plucked it off the basket floor with a pinch of fire-heated air. With far too little care for its delicate nature, he swung the unhatched phoenix past the ramp and deposited it in a metal cauldron. The molten egg disappeared beneath the cauldron's deep rim, and the gray metal began to glow with heat almost immediately.

"Whoops." Nathan stretched Mom's face into an exaggerated moue. "That almost got away from me. Why didn't you say anything, Harry? And what are you doing over there? You're not trying to escape, are you?" He chuckled with Mom's warm laugh, and bile swam up the back of my esophagus. "No, my dearest. You go down with the ship. That's the best way for this story to play out."

Knowing he planned to kill me had given me a sense of purpose; hearing him admit it nearly stole my strength.

Nathan dipped his hand into a pocket of his clothing. With the doppelganger spell overlaying him, it looked as if he had stuck Mom's hand into her hip, her wrist severed by her own flesh. When his hand reemerged, the familiar Grave's Echo was vial nestled against his palm.

Caught on all fours, the deck swirling in the edges of my vision, I watched helplessly as he stalked closer. The elements remained elusive. My only weapon was distraction. I worked my thick tongue in my mouth, pleased when words came out.

"You'll never—"

"Get away with this?" Nathan asked, interrupting me. "Who's going to stop me? You?" He laughed, throwing back Mom's head and sullying the beautiful sound with his derision. "I never realized how funny you are, Harry."

Nathan bent, spray bottle extended. I aimed a kick at his knee, but my arms wobbled, and my boot only grazed his shin. Cursing, Nathan swung for me. I rolled under the punch into his legs, and he crashed to the deck, flattening me under him. The glass vial glinted in the sunlight. I lunged for it, but Nathan's heavy body brought me up short. My fingers hit the bottle and sent it spinning across the basket.

Nathan surged after it, his knee crushing my thigh, his boot heel punching my stomach, knocking the air from my lungs. I clawed my way to all fours, eyes locked on the drug. It bounced along the wooden deck with a melodic tinkle, caught a groove, and rolled. In his haste, Nathan clipped the vial with his toe, sending it skittering farther. Ricocheting off the ramp, it rolled into the hole the phoenix egg had burned into the deck. Nathan stuffed his fingers in after it, then jerked his hand out, cursing and shaking his scorched fingertips. Impatiently, he plunged icy magic into the divot. Wood snapped. Nathan lunged for the vial, his arm sinking into the basket up to his bicep.

"Damn it!"

My elbows sagged, relief weakening my feeble muscles. The basket's base was less than a foot thick. Nathan had drilled a hole all the way through, and the vial and its hazardous contents were gone.

Nathan extricated himself and hammered me with a brutal blast of wind. I toppled to my side, pinned by his magic. With steady, stomping strides far heavier than Mom ever tread, he bore down on me.

"This could have been easy. Painless, Harry. But you deprived yourself of my mercy." He towered over me, staring down Mom's nose, curling her lip in disdain. Malice surfed through her blue eyes, and Nathan squatted, bringing Mom's face too close. "However, it's going to be so much sweeter to know you're awake, helpless to your fate."

Using harsh bands of elements, Nathan half dragged, half levitated me to the railing. I clutched the top rail, afraid he planned to heave me overboard, but he dropped me to my feet instead. Leaving me pinned in place with magic, he stalked to the rear of the basket.

I peered at the ground far, far below us, my plan to signal for help dying. The city sprawled across gently rolling hills, a collage of green-leafed canopies, wooden roof shingles, and snaking cobblestone roads. Air buses and wagons had shrunk to the size of my hand and people smaller than my fingers. A wave or a scream, it didn't matter; neither would be discernible from this distance.

Craning my neck, I strained to locate the distant warehouse district, hunting for Quinn's golden shape glinting in the sunlight.

A pegasus and rider surged above the city, angling for the Pegasus Express building. Another flew in the opposite direction, speeding away with the hour's most urgent deliveries. A flock of pigeons coasted between rooftops. Several hawks swooped on gentle currents. Plenty of flying carpets skimmed closer to the ground, moving squares of colors with detached shadows.

No winged quartz lion stirred the air above Terra Haven.

Despair constricted my lungs. *Please be all right, Quinn. Please be alive.*

Fresh tears blurring my vision, I peered past the bow. The fair sprawled beyond the city wall, a hodgepodge of vibrant tents and garishly painted vendor wagons forming a new town in the dry fields. The cheerful colors, the organic lines of the makeshift roads, and the dust shimmering in the air like visible excitement radiating from the people below reminded me of Seed Town.

The everlasting tree blooming and obtaining my seed felt like the events of another life. My question . . . *The story of a lifetime.* I had envisioned writing an article that would positively transform the world—not destroy mine.

Perhaps I could still complete my goal. I could save these people. I could have a positive impact, even if I didn't survive to write the story. Nathan's clumsy flying had gotten us pointed in the right direction—or rather, the *wrong* direction—but he hadn't mastered the craft's full speed. I still had time.

I grabbed for the elements, gasping out loud when I bridged the void and seized a drop of magic. I wasn't enough to light a candle, but it was a start. When Nathan returned with rope to bind my wrists to the railing, I didn't fight him, biding my time.

"What are you going to do?" I asked.

Nathan tsked. "This is why you're a terrible journalist. You ask predictable questions."

"I had more front-page stories in my first month at the *Chronicle* than you did all year." The taunt left a bitter taste on my tongue. I would trade every headline-topping story for a chance to go back and save Quinn. But Nathan was ruled by his pride, and I could think of no surer way of distracting him than by disparaging his journalistic skills.

Nathan yanked the rope, searing my skin with its coarse fibers. Blood welled in the abrasions, a whimper squeaking up my throat before I could cut it off. He smiled, his cruelty shining bright through eyes in which I had previously only seen love. Hatred for this petty man clawed at my gut with near-physical pain.

"You never were and never will be better than me, Harry," Nathan said, tying off his binding and coating it with a hard knot of earth element. "History will prove it. Now think, Harry, and if you ask me a smart question, I'll answer."

I ground my teeth. He craved the excuse to gloat. I needed the time. But it galled to give him what he wanted. "Why are you doing this?"

"There it is. Well done, Harry. I did this for you, to help you learn, because you didn't listen." Nathan tried to pull off a scolding, parental tone, but his anger overshadowed it.

Behind his back, I channeled a crosswind into the propeller attached to the side of the envelope. The elements hiccupped and sputtered in my control, slapping against the canvas. Any competent dirigible captain would have investigated the abnormal noise, but Nathan was oblivious. On my third attempt, the magic caught the propeller's spell, and it shifted, pointing crosswise to the other propellers. The deck vibrated subtly as the dirigible slowed, the sensation absorbed into the gyrations of the cargo ramp against the basket.

I kept my gaze on Nathan's, even though it meant watching Mom's lips contort into a snarl.

"I told you to go slow and respect seniority, but you were too full of yourself. You hoarded leads that should have gone to more experienced writers, people who actually *earned* their positions at the *Chronicle*."

Blindly, I batted at the rudder with magic, my clumsy elemental efforts bucking against the underside of the basket. The brass wheel affixed to the stern finally rotated. My hair fluttered around my face as the winds shifted. I waited for Nathan to notice, but rage blinded him to the altered currents. Slowly, we drifted off course.

"But a brat like you couldn't understand hard work. Your elite parents handed you the job. You didn't have to do a thing." Mom's blue eyes cut through me. "I started with nothing. *Nothing.* Orphaned. Starving. I clawed my way up from the blight. I made something of myself. Carved out a place for myself among the Fire Eaters. Oh, you didn't know that, did you? You never thought to research your competition. Another lesson you skipped over."

The puzzle pieces clicked into place. The Fire Eaters who attacked the jail *after* Nathan had sent me there, dangling a lead I couldn't resist in front of my face; the Fire Eaters whose antics plagued Grant and his team all week, thwarting their efforts to track down the phoenix eggs; the Fire Eaters who kidnapped me and Wetherill—they had been acting on the behest of a boyhood chum.

"I slogged my way through an apprenticeship in the print room before I was promoted to the writer's bullpen. I *deserve* to be called a journalist, because I did the work. I'm smart too. I kept in contact with people from my past. That's right, Harry, I have connections too. Yours might get you into good parties and drop jobs in your lap, but mine are more useful. Mine got me the most exciting stories this city has seen in a decade."

"Interesting," I said in the most bored tone I could summon. "It's bad to use connections to get a job or an interview, but it's smart to use criminal friends to fabricate stories for your own gain. I wish I had my notebook with me so I could write this down."

Nathan's fists clenched, his rage writhing across Mom's face. I braced for a punch or slap of magic, but his expression settled on a sneer.

"You're no better than me, Harriet *Kylie* Grayson. Using your middle name isn't much of an alias. You wanted someone to recognize you. Poor little rich girl exposed. You made yourself the story. It didn't turn out like you thought it would, though. I wasn't about to let you tarnish the *Chronicle* with your fame grubbing."

"*My* fame grubbing? What do you call what you've been doing?"

"Journalism. It's called journalism, Harry. Note how I haven't been the focal point of any article I've written."

I had never written an article with myself as the subject either. Everything in the papers recently had been written *about* me. If I never saw my picture in newsprint again, it would be too soon. But Nathan's attention was drifting, so rather than argue the point, I brought the conversation back to his favorite topic: him.

"What I don't get is why you had a doppelganger spell made of my mom and not me."

"You? Use your brain, Harry." Nathan hammered his finger between my eyebrows, the blunt tip pounding hard enough to bruise.

I jerked my head aside, wishing I dared to redirect my magic upside Nathan's head.

"You're a nobody, and nobody cares what you do. Charlotte Grayson, however, is practically an honorary full spectrum with a national business. Anything horrible she does, like steal illegal spells from an FPD package shipped by her own company, gets national attention, and I get national syndication."

There it was. Nathan's real reason. His need for recognition. His need for fame.

Bile churned in my stomach. I recognized the spark that drove Nathan. It lived in me too. It existed in the heart of my question to the everlasting tree. It prompted me to chase Grant up to Zipporah's nest and trapped me in her debt. It squirmed beneath my desire to rush toward danger so I could inform the public—the operative word being *I*.

If not for Quinn, Mika, Grant, Mom, even—ironically— my everlasting seed, I might have fallen down the same dark hole as Nathan, more concerned with getting a story—*the* story—than maintaining my integrity.

No. I wasn't Nathan. I would never be Nathan. We might have the same spark, but Nathan had allowed it to turn dark, to let it drive him instead of inspire him. To consume him. I wouldn't allow that to happen to me.

If I survived.

I slapped air element at a second propeller, battering the canvas with feeble handfuls of magic. My control was improving, my power returning, but far too slowly.

"Your mom's life was enjoyably easy to destroy. I mean, tracking down idiots to steal the firebirds took effort, but once I realized I didn't need to use a middleman . . ." Nathan ran a hand through his hair, forgetting the elaborate illusion. Mom's fingers passed through the knot of hair at the back of her head without mussing a strand. "It was so simple. No one questioned me going through the files in Charlotte's office. I literally walked out with banned spells and phoenix eggs tucked in a bag, and Airstrong's security waved and smiled at me."

"Our employees are a polite bunch," I said. It had to kill him that he couldn't publish any of this part of his treachery. Gloating to me was his only outlet, his only chance to revel in a bout of navel-gazing splendor in front of a captive audience. The best I could do was refuse to provide Nathan the reaction he desired. Anything to keep him angry and focused on me.

"They're a bunch of idiots," Nathan snapped.

My magic finally connected with the second propeller, flipping the spell in the opposite direction. Now only four propellers pointed in the same direction, and the other two ran counter. The envelope's wooden frame groaned, our speed decaying.

"The world is full of idiots. They only see what they expect to see. It makes them malleable." Nathan giggled, a sound that had never emerged from Mom's throat. It sent a shiver down my spine. "Full spectrums are the worst. They expect the world to revolve around them. They think everyone cares about their opinions. Look at Luther Wetherill. A nudge here, a word there, and he became the perfect lens through which I could sharpen my story. His greed and jealousy were mine to use to whip the masses into a frenzy against Airstrong. All along, I manipulated him like a marionette, and he believed he was in control."

My lip wanted to curl at his characterization of Terra Haven's citizens and the paper's subscribers as *the masses*. It wasn't just me who was beneath Nathan in his eyes; it was everyone.

Nathan stalked to the gate at the front of the dirigible, glanced down, frowned, then examined the propellers. Muttering under his breath, he adjusted the spells I had so painstakingly redirected. The ship righted itself, and a breeze pulled the sour stench of Nathan's sweat past me. With my arms tethered to the railing, I had to wrench a shoulder to see past the bow. Despite my efforts, the fair sprawled perilously close.

"I don't know what you have planned, but you don't need to do it," I said, attempting to use reason despite my doubts about Nathan's sanity. "You've proven you're a better journalist. I don't even work at the *Chronicle* anymore, and you have a book deal. You don't need to—"

"Do you think I'm a fool, Harry? I saw that minotaur article. I saw you talking with Dahlia. You're homing in on my position again. You've learned nothing. You don't even recognize an incomplete story arc."

"What?"

"Act one: Airstrong heiress recovers the missing firebirds and restores her parents' reputation. Act two: Airstrong heiress tracks down the thief of the banned spells and saves her parents from going to jail. Or did she?" Nathan winked. "Act three: Charlotte's dastardly plans to sell the phoenix eggs backfires and nearly kills her. Airstrong heiress makes off with the stolen phoenix eggs in a last-ditch effort to spare her parents from going to the executioner's block. But this time, she can't hide her parents' thieving ways. This time, her heroic efforts turn tragic as she loses control of the eggs over the fairgrounds, killing dozens." Nathan tapped his chin. "No, I think 'in the largest act of mass murder this nation has ever experienced' sounds better. More headline grabbing. It's the conclusion that will have my book flying off shelves across the nation. Around the world!"

All the moisture evaporated from my mouth, and I had to clear my throat twice to get the words out. "How many phoenix eggs are on this ship, Nathan?"

How many were on this delicate dirigible jouncing across cross currents with an open envelope hatch, lowered ramp, and saboteur hostage adding strain to every cable, board, stitch, and nail holding it together?

Nathan's gaze flicked to the cargo hold inside the envelope. "All three, of course. This is the story's finale, right? I don't want to waste this opportunity for the *story of a lifetime*."

Numbness swept my body, terror stealing what little strength I had regained. My chance of surviving a single phoenix's hatching had been negligible, but three? With the eggs in such close proximity, when one hatched, it would trigger the others. The dirigible would be annihilated—along with anyone on it. Yet Nathan didn't appear concerned. What was I missing?

"What's stopping the eggs from hatching right now?" The egg Nathan had planted at Airstrong and the one the Fire Eaters had left in Wetherill's hangar had hatched spontaneously. All the eggs were from the same clutch, maturing at roughly the same rate, meaning this ship could explode at any second.

"I timed it," Nathan said with a shrug.

"What?"

"Did you think I left an egg at Airstrong *only* for the story? It was a trial run to see how long it would take the phoenix to hatch after I removed the egg from the furnace. Last night at Luther's confirmed the time almost to the minute." He lifted a watch from a pocket hidden beneath the illusion spell and checked the time. "I have a little more than— No, let's leave that a mystery for you."

Oh, you idiot. He was basing his countdown on the speed the eggs cooled. Once the shells' outer temperatures dropped too low, the phoenixes would be forced to hatch to survive. Only, the egg at Airstrong had been tucked against a brick wall on a tile floor, both surfaces radiating the egg's heat back at it, prolonging the cooldown. In the warehouse last night, the egg had been surrounded by a small wall that reflected the egg's heat. Up here, in the chilled atmosphere hundreds of feet above the ground, with wind stealing the heat from the shells, they would cool immeasurably faster.

I scrapped my plan of distracting Nathan. Whether Nathan knew it or not, we were out of time, and I wasn't ready to give up and die.

Channeling a mixture of air, fire, and water, I shot the magic straight for the propellers. Desperation and my panicked heartbeat strengthened my magic, and though the mixture lacked my usual finesse, the propellers spun with gusto. The dirigible tilted, pivoting in place. A flick of air brought the rudder into alignment. In seconds, the ship altered course by twenty degrees and picked up speed. Another tweak to the propellers on the opposite side, and—

A cudgel of wood element swung toward my head. I blocked it with a shield of fire, and pain burst behind my eyes. I wasn't quick enough to avoid Nathan's next blow, taking a hit to my shoulder, then another to my back. Gritting my teeth, I erected a trembling ward around myself and braced for the next blow. It never came. Instead, Nathan tested the ward with a flick of magic. My spell bowed and flexed, my hold on the elements weak. Nathan's cruel smile curved Mom's lips.

"Nice try, Harry, but it's not going to work." He sauntered

closer, within arm's reach if my hands weren't bound. "I've been five steps ahead of you this entire time. You could have learned so much from me, *junior journalist*. Such a shame you won't get a chance, but at least you can die knowing you've met the best journalist ever to grace the *Chronicle*."

"Journalist? Hardly. You're a fraud. Nothing more than a muckraker and a criminal." I feigned a punch of air toward Nathan's face. He flinched, and I shot magic to the far propellers, righting the dirigible's slow turn and doubling our speed.

Nathan's magic bludgeoned my temple. Pain roared through my skull, deafening me. My legs buckled. Rope bit into my arms, yanking my shoulders hard in their sockets as I fell.

When I blinked, Nathan stood at the far end of the basket. I squinted against the needles of light stabbing my brain. The black iron cauldron holding the phoenix egg glowed orange with heat. I glanced up the ramp, searching for the other eggs. I could hear them sizzling.

Wait. The still air, the lack of worrisome gyrations in the basket, the cessation of ominous creaks and snaps—we weren't moving.

I lurched for magic, prepared to throw it into the propellers . . . and let elements dissolve. Thin scorch lines existed where the propellers had once studded the underside of the envelope. Nathan had severed the airship's means of locomotion. We were adrift.

How long had I been unconscious?

Smoke coiled in my throat, tickling a cough. Alarm thrilled through my body.

Fire.

I whipped toward the source. Dark flecks swamped my vision, clearing to reveal a glowing egg sitting directly on the foredeck. A thin red ring of embers circled the egg. Tendrils of smoke spiraled from the embers and drifted across the basket's planks. Dark amber twisted beneath the shell, the phoenix shifting restlessly within its cooling confines.

The sinuous profile of distant hills stretched beyond the egg, and it took me a second longer to realize the basket's gate was open. Nothing but air and a few inches of deck stood between the phoenix egg and the innocent people below.

With Herculean effort, I hauled myself to my feet, using my bound hands for balance. Tingles swept through my numb arms, morphing into fiery pain as blood rushed to my raw wrists. I barely noticed.

The fair sprawled directly beneath us.

I couldn't move the dirigible. Not in time. The ship weighed too much. I would have to create a wind strong enough to push the fat envelope. With it dragging the basket, its aerodynamics impeded by the lowered cargo ramp, it would take a half hour or longer to shove the dirigible beyond the fair's border. Nathan wouldn't give me the time, nor would the phoenixes.

I lashed out with a whip of air, hoping to catch Nathan unprepared, but he countered my elemental blow, shattering my magic. I attacked again. A ghost of lethargy from Grave's Echo weighted the elements, but fear, desperation, and fury lent strength to my attacks. Cursing, Nathan twisted away from a blade-sharp slice of air I jabbed at his thigh. He broke the wood spear I drove toward his back, then doused the flurry of sparks I raked across his scalp.

If any strike landed, I couldn't tell, because the doppelganger spell never wavered. I walled off the horrified part of my brain that insisted I was attacking Mom, and I didn't let up. I needed time to free myself, send a message to Grant and O'Hara, warn people below, and get the phoenix eggs to a safer, secluded place to hatch. None of which I could do until Nathan was out of the way.

I landed a hard hit to Nathan's stomach, doubling him over. Shaping air into a club, I solidified it and swung it toward his temple. I wanted him unconscious, not dead. He needed to live long enough to rot in jail.

Nathan slapped a fire ward around himself, and my magic fractured against it. So did the next blow. I cycled the elements, driving ice into his barrier. It shattered against Nathan's magic and melted into the ether.

Somehow, in the last thirty seconds, his elemental strength had doubled. Almost as if a gargoyle enhanced him, but no gargoyle would sink so low. Or he was linked, which was impossible. We were too high up for him to share magic with anyone on the ground. Flicking a glance to the side, I searched for another aircraft.

Wheezing, Nathan braced his hands on his knees and slowly straightened. Maniacal glee shone in Mom's eyes when he looked at me.

I hammered him with every offensive spell in my repertoire, but nothing penetrated his suspiciously strong ward.

"Is that the best you've got, Harry?" Cloaking himself in a layer of flames, Nathan spun a bladed saucer of fire at my midsection. I extinguished the attack with a clap of water and earth, then batted aside two additional flaming blades angled for my head and feet. Casually flinging fire daggers ahead of him, Nathan stalked across the basket, toying with me.

This was Nathan's true form, the mantle of respectable journalist burned to cinders, the sadistic Fire Eater unmasked.

"The best part about this," he said in Mom's cheerful

voice, "is the irony. You wanted the story of a lifetime, and I'm the one making that story happen."

I circled a protective shield around myself. Even so, heat from the flames dancing around Nathan battered me when he halted less than a foot away. For a heartbeat, I was transported back to the jail, caught in a brick coffin, being cooked alive. Panic edged my thoughts, and I fought it back, altering my shield into a wall of ice. Nathan chuckled and formed a fist gloved in fire. I braced myself, but his strike tore through my barrier as if it were paper. Magic backlashed hot and sharp across my brain. I flinched, but I could no more escape the pain than I could the singeing heat of Nathan's fiery ward.

The flames around Nathan's hand vanished. He snatched the pouch from my chest, severing the cord around my neck with a slice of fire that seared agony across my collarbone.

"And *I'll* be the one to write it," Nathan said, tucking the pouch into a pocket hidden beneath his illusion.

The ropes spiked pain along my arms when I instinctively lunged after the pouch. Not for *my* seed. Nathan could have that, for all I cared. But he couldn't have Quinn's.

"It won't work," I said, reduced to taunting him while I doused my smoldering pants and shirt with water element. "The seed won't evolve for you, and even if it did, this story isn't going to play out like you think it will. You've given yourself away."

"Oh, Harry, that's cute. You don't think I planned for this? It's quite simple, really. The first egg is going to fall overboard—*oops*—just to get everyone's attention. And because I need to have the explosions spaced out, not stacked on top of each other, to ensure more photographic opportunities. Any pictures printed with my article will need to hint at maimed dead bodies without being grotesque. We don't want to scare off readers, do we?"

"You're unhinged."

Nathan rolled his eyes and continued. "The second, there"—he pointed to the egg at the bow of the basket, which had burned a deep divot into the thin planks—"is on a self-guided timer. I like the randomness of it. We can't know precisely when it'll drop."

Or if it will hatch first, I wanted to add, but I was afraid pointing out the potential danger would accelerate Nathan's diabolical plans. I considered grabbing the egg and heaving it as far as I could, but the egg's volatility and Nathan's increased elemental strength stopped me, as did the view below. I couldn't guarantee I could throw the egg far enough not to kill fairgoers. Could I catch it from below before it dropped? Then what?

"I'll leave the third in the cauldron, but I doubt it'll stay there once the dirigible starts to crash. So tragic." He grinned. "And when I recover from the harrowing ordeal, Dahlia will be awed when I explain how I figured out what you were planning, and in your desperation to prevent the *Chronicle*'s preeminent journalist from writing the article, you kidnapped me. Who's going to contradict me? Not you."

"How do you expect to survive to spread your lies?"

"Terra Haven guards will rescue me, of course."

"Rescue *you*?" In what world?

On cue, a Nimblewing airship blasted into view, climbing fast off the starboard side. Marquise-shaped, with flat oblong wings protruding from its sides, it resembled a bloated dragonfly and flew with the same speed and dexterity. I whipped my head around to track its flight, my eyes locked on the prominent Terra Haven guard symbols emblazoned across the Nimblewing's green sides.

"Help!" I screamed, using the elements to amplify my voice. "He's got phoenix eggs on board. Clear the fair!"

I braced for Nathan's retaliation. When his laughter—Mom's laughter—rang through the air, I jumped.

None of the guards reacted to my warning as their ship sped closer. Three men and a woman crouched in the narrow hull, sturdy rope harnesses cinched around their torsos and taut anchor lines securing them to the ship during its steep ascent. An empty fifth harness whipped like a snake at the back. Since when did guards patrol without a full five complement?

The Nimblewing evened out with a buck that tossed the back two guards half out of the ship. They grabbed the sides, cursing as the pilot jerked them into a static hover twenty feet off the dirigible's starboard railing.

"Shut it," growled the pilot.

The voice chased a tremor of dread down my spine. I scrutinized the guards. They wore the appropriate uniforms, but the two men in the back and the woman sandwiched between them were all too young and scrawny to have completed the guards' rigorous training. The pilot was the only one who looked the part. In his early twenties and built like a boxer, he stood a head taller than his companions. His face was a stranger's—his nose crooked, his eyebrows black slashes above hard eyes—but his gravelly voice was unmistakable. I glared at Apollo, leader of the Fire Eaters, the same man who had spearheaded the attack on the jail and who had heartlessly deposited me in a pitch-black warehouse with two basilisks and a phoenix egg.

And Nathan was linked with him—with all four Fire Eaters. No wonder he had crushed my magic.

"Don't you see the beauty of this?" Nathan asked. "The public will be appalled to learn these guards were forced to rescue me, because your FPD boyfriend sabotaged the investigation. 'Captain Monaghan Embroiled in Phoenix Egg Cover-Up.' That headline is going to double the *Chronicle*'s sales for a week. Perhaps net me a second book, or at least give me plenty to talk about while on tour. And watching Monaghan squirm while he defends himself? Pure gold."

"No one will believe he's a guard," I said, jutting my chin toward Apollo. The gang leader blew me a kiss, then grinned at my reciprocal glare.

"We'll see about that," Nathan said. "Or rather, *I'll* see about it. You'll be dead. Shall we begin the show?"

Dismissing me, Nathan levitated an egg from the cargo hold inside the envelope and swung it toward the lee side of the ship but paused before thrusting it over the railing. Scowling, he gestured for the Fire Eaters to come closer. "Get the ladder ready," he shouted, then muttered "Imbeciles," soft enough that only I could hear.

I gathered magic. I would get only one chance to save the people below. Hopefully it would buy them enough time to evacuate the fair before the other eggs fell. Because if I managed to stop Nathan once, he wouldn't let me live to thwart him a second time.

A gush of elements flooded me, a gargoyle's boost surging power into my magic. Heart in my throat, I leaned over the railing. *Please, let it be—*

QUINN!

My beloved friend surged through the sky, determination etched on his expressive face. I blinked back tears, my heart bursting with joy. Scorch marks ran in ugly, painful black lines down his back and across his pumping wings, but they didn't slow him. If anything, he flew faster than ever before.

"Damn it! What did I tell you, you stupid rock beast?" Nathan shouted, swinging the phoenix egg high over the railing toward Quinn.

Panic gripped my chest in a vise. Quinn had survived the egg's touch, but if Nathan threw the phoenix at Quinn, it would tear his quartz body apart.

Quinn veered under the ship, out of sight, but not out of range. I flung a punch of air at Nathan, but he batted it aside without a glance. Quinn's boost doubled my magic, but Nathan had the power of five people within his link. In a battle of sheer strength, Nathan linked to the Fire Eaters would come out on top every time, but that wouldn't stop me from fighting.

Shattering Nathan's elemental reinforcement on the bindings holding me, I sliced frantically at the ropes with a blade of air, unheeding of the cuts and nicks I inflicted on myself. I needed to be mobile to protect Quinn. The heavy beat of his wings resounded under the basket. Nathan swung the unhatched phoenix across the basket, mirroring Quinn's progress below. Heat stirred my hair as the egg passed, then Nathan shot it toward the bow.

Fire speared from Apollo's hands, straight as an arrow and so hot the center shone blue. It seared the air, angling to strike Quinn beneath us. Nathan's grip on the egg wobbled. It plunged toward the deck, caught at the last second by Nathan's weakened magic. He hastily shoved the egg overboard, holding it suspended. Beneath us, Quinn's wing beats quieted for a heart-stopping two seconds, then resumed, fainter. He had let himself drop out of danger's range.

Apollo leaned over the bow of his ship, tracking Quinn.

"What are you thinking?" Nathan shrieked at an octave the doppelganger spell couldn't mimic with Mom's voice.

"You're wasting time," Apollo said.

"I'm holding a sharding phoenix egg, you thickwit. Give me control of the link and give me room." Nathan snapped Mom's fingers imperiously in Apollo's general direction and was too busy peering over the side of the ship to witness the venomous glower Apollo shot back. The Fire Eater's eyes flicked to the egg hovering between our ships, then to the other eggs in the dirigible's basket, cruel calculations playing across his face. Luckily, we came to the same conclusion: he wouldn't have enough time to get to safety if he set fire to Nathan.

Jaw clenched, Apollo propelled the Nimblewing away from the dirigible.

"Wise move," Nathan growled.

Quinn's wing beats grew louder. Sunlight refracted off his citrine body, setting the underside of the dirigible's beige envelope aglow. His head crested the rim of the basket. Nathan lifted the egg higher, then brought it down toward Quinn's back with the full force of his linked magic.

"Dive, Quinn!" I screamed.

23

I didn't have time for delicacy. Solidifying a plane of air, I slammed it between Quinn and the plunging egg. I channeled all of Quinn's boost into thickening the air barrier, curving it at the last minute to protect the basket too. The egg hit my magic with the force of a steam locomotive and shattered. Molten amniotic fluid exploded, immolating my fractured barrier in a flash. Magic backlash drove spikes into my brain, and my knees collapsed.

A wall of heat and sound slammed the ship. My magic lasted long enough to deflect the bulk of the explosion away from the dirigible, but the fiery forefront of superheated air clipped the edge of the envelope. The canvas dented, then flexed, sending a ripple through the entire balloon. With a snake's hiss, a cable tore from the basket and whipped skyward. The heavy rope slapped into the envelope, ripping the sturdy fabric. The basket jerked and jounced, tossing me helplessly into the air. I landed hard on my knees and clutched blindly at the railing, eyes on the envelope. If it broke, we'd plummet.

The canvas creaked and groaned but held. A cloud of

black smoke hung in the air beside the ship—all that remained of the phoenix egg.

I surged to my feet, leaning over the railing to search for Quinn.

A sea of confusion and panic swarmed beneath the ship. Fairgoers fled in all directions, the stampede shrouded in dust and magic. Somewhere among them was Grant and O'Hara. After that pyrotechnic display, I didn't need to worry about getting a message to them. All I had to do was hold on long enough for them to come to me.

An arrow of fire speared toward my face. I jerked upright, and the phoenix blasted past. Its marigold-and-black-striped wings and tail feathers streamed with the flames of a newborn, the bird appearing no worse for its violent birth. It skimmed the envelope, searing a path along the canvas before disappearing above the dirigible's curved frame. I slapped water against the smoking canvas, cooling it before flames could erupt, then leaned over the railing again.

Come on, Quinn. His boost still enhanced my magic, but that didn't mean he wasn't injured. I had a horrible vision of Quinn tumbling out of control, keeping me boosted as long as he could before he hit the ground. It was the kind of noble last act he would commit.

"Hurry, you cowards," Nathan shrieked. "Closer. Come on. We don't have much time."

That hadn't been Mom's voice; it had been Nathan's.

I spun around, only to be brought up short by the bindings I still hadn't sawed all the way through. Nathan stood near the rear of the basket in an eye-popping red shirt and teal plaid pants, his press badge shimmering spell-bright where it hung from a chain around his neck. I blinked. His ensemble was atrocious and completely out of character . . . but perfect for being spotted from a distance.

Nathan wanted the panicked people below to see him and remember him. His outfit was his alibi, or part of it. The "guards" rescuing him were the rest. Just as he had bragged, he was putting on quite the show for his audience.

The Fire Eaters sidled closer, steering the Nimblewing with more muscle than skill, squeezing it beneath the envelope on my side of the basket. I hacked at the rope bindings, praying the pyromaniacs would remain distracted long enough for me to free myself. I couldn't defend against five linked Fire Eaters and survive—or save the people below. I needed to attack, and to do that, I needed maneuverability.

The cables anchoring the dirigible's basket to the envelope proved troublesome for Apollo, spaced too closely to accommodate the Nimblewing's width and angled away from the basket. He was forced to hover ten feet off the port railing, and Nathan refused to attempt the jump. He bellowed for them to toss him a ladder, but none of his allies were paying attention.

Leaning over the edges of their hull, they flung fireballs at an unseen target. Their tactics were chaotic and unorganized, each Fire Eater unleashing their own blasts. It must have felt like a tug-of-war in their heads, linked as they were, all pulling magic through the same collective source. Nathan's cursing confirmed it.

"Focus!" he shouted. "Get me off this ship before it explodes, then we'll deal with the gargoyle."

Quinn swept past, close enough to rock the Fire Eaters' small craft. I whooped with glee. He was alive! A fireball glanced harmlessly off his hip, and he dove under the basket, out of sight.

"Ladder, Apollo. Hurry!" Nathan danced in place, waving his arms frantically to get the Fire Eaters' attention.

I cut through another layer of rope, but it wasn't enough to wiggle free. The scrawny Fire Eater at the back of the Nimblewing tossed a chain ladder over the stern railing. It rattled as it unfurled, the lightweight links shimmering in the sunlight. Thin metal bars connected the chains at regular intervals, and Nathan grabbed the bottom rung with a vise of air, tugging it into the dirigible's basket.

Quinn dropped from above, slashing a paw at the ladder as he dove past. Nathan batted him aside with a blast of wind. He must have regained control of the link, because his hit sent Quinn careening across the sky. The gargoyle's boost winked out as he tumbled out of range. Clawing the air, Quinn slowed himself, then snapped his wings open, surging back toward the ship, but it would take precious seconds for him to be close enough to help.

I sawed blindly at the bindings, finally breaking free. Blood slicked my wrists, some from self-inflicted cuts made in my haste, some from the ropes. I'd deal with it later. Nathan had the loose ladder stretched horizontally from the Nimblewing to the dirigible, the slack resting on the deck of the basket. He clung to the rung resting against the railing even as he awkwardly leveraged a leg over the top rail, the other foot planted on a rung. His arms hugged the ladder higher up. The moment he was clear of the dirigible and away from the phoenix eggs, he would have no reason not to—

"Sink it," Nathan ordered.

I jerked from the railing and sprinted for the cargo ramp's questionable safety. As I ran, I channeled fire into the base of the ladder. Quinn's enhancement unfurled inside me, and the element turned blue as I pumped heat into the metal. The bottom rung melted into the basket's deck. I cooled it with a flash of ice, fusing it in place. Swapping spells fast enough to make myself dizzy, I redirected the heat up the chains, melting them into twin rigid ropes.

Nathan jerked his foot, attempting to throw the ladder over the deck's railing. When it didn't budge, he glanced back. His eyes bulged.

"Wait!" Nathan shrieked. "I'm stuck." He slashed water through the gigantic ball of fire Apollo hurled against the dirigible's balloon and frantically followed it with a weave of ice and air to cool the canvas. I used his distraction to fuse more of the ladder to the dirigible's basket and railing. For better or worse, our two ships were locked together until Nathan climbed high enough to sever the ladder behind him.

"Damn it, take her out already," Nathan said, shooting fireballs in my general direction. The others followed suit.

I scrambled up the cargo ramp far enough to use the slope of its boards for partial protection. The angle forced the Fire Eaters to modulate their attacks or risk damaging the balloon keeping us all afloat. I extinguished their magic with counterspells, sweating from exertion as much as the barrage of heat.

Nathan swatted hot air at the phoenix egg burning its way through the bow of the basket. The shell had embedded itself halfway into the deck, so his clumsy swipe only rocked it in place. His next attempt dislodged the egg. It wobbled across the deck, searing an erratic path along the lacquered boards. Smoke chased the egg.

"What are you doing?" Apollo demanded. "Climb the frostbitten ladder already."

"The egg is seconds from hatching. What do you think

I'm doing?" Nathan spat, shoving the phoenix toward the open front of the dirigible.

Hell no. I slammed a cushion of air in front of the egg, then hacked Nathan's magic with everything else I had. It wasn't enough.

Scrambling farther up the ramp to avoid the onslaught of fireballs, I abandoned the barricade and punched Nathan with a gale of air. He shrieked, his foot slipping from a rung to fall through the chain ladder. His other foot swung free of the dirigible's railing, leaving him half dangling, half hugging the ladder. The temptation to batter Nathan with another blast, to send him plummeting to his death the way he had tried to kill Quinn—the way he planned to kill me—nearly overwhelmed me. The spell tingled on the tips of my fingers, a red haze of fury filming my vision.

Snarling, I redirected my magic, nudging the phoenix egg away from the open gate. If I survived, I wanted to do so with my morality intact. I wouldn't make the same choices as Nathan.

With the egg relatively safe, I rammed air into the Nimblewing's propulsion spells. The Fire Eaters' ship lurched. The ladder snapped taut, eliciting another scream from Nathan and causing a delicate quiver to run through the dirigible's basket. The vibration ran back up the ladder, jostling the Nimblewing. The Fire Eater in the back shouted in alarm, and everyone grabbed for the hull, their fireballs flying wide. Fear crawled across Apollo's brutish features as the boards of his small craft groaned around him.

Before they recovered their wits, I scooped up the phoenix egg in a net of hot air, matching the elemental weave Nathan had used. Careful not to jostle it, I levitated the egg toward the cauldron. Hopefully having two egg nested inside the hot cauldron would buy me precious minutes before either phoenix hatched.

Fire knifed through my net, whipping blinding pain across my vision. The egg dropped, hit the deck, and bounced. Everyone slapped wards into place.

No one breathed.

A breeze stirred the air, plastering my shirt to my sweaty back and chafing ropes against the canvas envelope. Distant screams of fairgoers stretched into the silence. I let out a breath, blinking my vision clear. The egg remained whole, the phoenix inside content to remain in its shell—for the moment.

I dropped my ward first. It wouldn't do me much good. I might be able to deflect the blast of a hatching, but I couldn't protect the dirigible, and I wouldn't be able to break my own fall if we crashed from this height.

"You're going to kill us all," Nathan screamed, and I couldn't tell if his wrath was directed at me or Apollo.

I shoved more power through the Nimblewing's propulsion spells. The first time, it had been a diversionary tactic, but now I had a plan: I would use the Nimblewing to tow the dirigible away from the fair.

The small vessel creaked, stress fractures running down the hull as it attempted to pull a ship ten times its weight. The ladder's chains squeaked under the strain. Nathan cursed and scrambled to right himself. The others attempted to block my magic, but I fluctuated my attacks, jouncing the Nimblewing. The small ship bounced and flexed, tugging the dirigible into motion at last.

One of the Fire Eaters finally thought to ward the propulsion spell, cutting off my access. The Nimblewing stalled in midair, but the dirigible didn't. At this molasses-paced drift, our collision wouldn't have been noteworthy if not for the ladder strung between the ships and Nathan hanging precariously from it. Slack caused the chain to dip, and Nathan tipped forward over empty air. His garbled scream was lost beneath the twang of the Nimblewing clipping one of the dirigible's taut cables. The small craft jolted, snapped against the ladder tethering it to the dirigible, and arced through the air to hit a cable on the opposite side. Nathan flailed on the swinging ladder, his face whiter than paper.

"Levitate me," he squeaked. "Get me on that ship already."

Bands of air reached for Nathan.

"Not going to happen," I growled.

Most aircrafts, from flying carpets to transatlantic dirigibles, possessed levitation spells designed to stabilize them in a neutral position. Nimblewings were designed for com-bat, with full 360-degree maneuverability. Any legitimate Terra Haven guard would have had the levitation gyration spell locked and warded. The Fire Eaters hadn't bothered.

With a spiral of air and earth, I flipped the Nimblewing upside down.

A chorus of screams pierced the air, drowning out the snap of four harnesses jerking against the hooks embedded in the hull, preventing the Fire Eaters from tumbling to their deaths. Arms flailed. Magic flashed. Coins and pocketknives rained from the gang members' clothing. A single scream continued long past the others until it was cut off with the dull thump of a punch. I almost couldn't make out Nathan's stream of prayers and curses as he clung to the twisted ladder, nothing but air between him and the fair below.

Quinn's steady wing beats announced his arrival before

he burst over the far side of the basket. "How can I help?" he asked as his feet touched down.

I desperately wanted to hug him, then order him far from the ship and the unpredictable phoenix eggs it carried. Instead, I gestured to the starboard railing. "We need to get the ship moving again. Fast." Before the Fire Eaters figured out what I had done and recovered. "Can you push?"

"On it."

Quinn leapt to the basket's railing, then dropped his hind feet down to brace them against the side of the basket. His front claws sank into the varnished wood, gouging divots as he pumped his stone wings. The draft stirred my hair, but it barely rocked the basket. It would take a lot more than a single gargoyle's strength to shift the dirigible.

Keeping an ear tuned to the Fire Eaters' bickering, I darted from my meager shelter to the railing several feet from Quinn. The wooden balusters rocked with each of Quinn's wing beats, and I switched my grip to one of the sturdy cables as I leaned out to get a view of the side of the envelope.

The Nimblewing had proved too small to serve as a tow craft. I needed propellers or a windstorm to get a ship this size into motion. Weaving a complex propeller spell out of the elements would take too long, and I didn't have the strength necessary to create a windstorm, not even with Quinn's enhancement. I settled for the next-best option: forming a wind funnel and twisting air, fire, and water elements to create a loop of air. I channeled everything I had into the spell, my vision blurring as the hammering in my head intensified. When I feared my synapses were going to burst, I anchored the spell to the side of the envelope and released it.

The dirigible rocked, the faintest of breezes cooling the

sweat on my neck. We were in motion. If we had hours, it would have been enough, but I was lucky if we had minutes to get the dirigible clear of the fair.

Closing my eyes, I girded myself for a second elemental push.

"Use your heads," Nathan snapped. "It's on the bottom. Here, slow*leee—*"

His words sliced into a high-pitched scream as the Nimblewing flipped itself upright. Nathan's feet slipped from the ladder's rungs, leaving him hanging from one white-knuckled fist. The Fire Eaters clutched the narrow hull, faces red with blood. The man in the back bent in half and vomited on his own shoes. Apollo locked his eyes on mine, murder in his gaze. I cobbled together a shield in front of Quinn and myself. The elements quivered and stabilized.

Nathan swung his dangling hand up and hooked an elbow over a rung. Air element whipped around him, forming a net that supported his body.

"Get me on the ship, *now,*" he ordered, his face blotchy with strain and fear.

Fire erupted from Apollo's fingers, blasting across the deck. I dove aside, trusting Quinn to do the same. Heat scorched my clothing, and I doused myself in icy elements. Jumping to my feet, I put the cargo ramp between me and Apollo. Quinn popped up farther down the deck, resuming his efforts to push the dirigible across the sky.

"What are you thinking?" Nathan shouted. "This ship is riddled with phoenix eggs. You hit one of them, and we all die. Let's go already. Lift me."

"Feds," chirped the woman, her clipped warning cutting through Nathan's rant.

Hope hit me like a punch to the gut, leaving me breathless.

Grant.

"Hurry," Nathan said. "We need to get out of here. This only works if you get me clear."

"You promised me the girl wouldn't be a problem," Apollo rasped. "You said we would be long gone before the FPD showed up."

"And you said you'd kill Harry last night. We both ran into difficulties."

I glanced around the ramp in time to see Nathan swing a foot up and hook it around the ladder. He grunted, straining to pull himself atop the flimsy ladder.

"If you don't—" Nathan's threat cut off with a gasp, and it took me a second to realize Apollo had severed their elemental link. Nathan stopped struggling, and his tone turned to pleading. "No, wait. Don't do it. I promise I'll make you rich. I'll—"

"Your promises are no good if I'm dead." With a slash of wood element, Apollo severed the ladder from the Nimblewing's hull.

Nathan dropped from view, his bloodcurdling scream chasing chills down my arms. A beat later, he thumped against the underside of the basket. Somehow, he had managed to cling to the ladder.

The Nimblewing dropped out of sight, then shot skyward, wobbling as Apollo tested the ship's gyration.

"Come back!" Nathan shrieked, his voice muffled through the hull.

A second airship spun through the air, my heart soaring with it. Black from nose to stern and coated in glossy element-enhanced armor plating, the FPD Shadow Hawk was shaped like a beetle to the Fire Eaters' dragonfly.

Bulkier through its pentagon hull, it flew on sleek, actuating wings, with multiple miniature-yet-powerful propulsion and gyrating levitation spells scattered across every surface, all warded against sabotage. Seradon sat at the helm, navigating, and Winnigan stood at the rear on an elevated platform, twin ropes hooked to the harness at her waist to keep her stable. Marciano stood in front of her, and Velasquez balanced behind Seradon, but my eyes went straight to Grant in the middle.

He stared back as they arrowed past. My heart surged faster. Fierce concentration hardened his mouth and eyes as he took me in. A message was slung from the Shadow Hawk and slammed to a halt in front of me. Grant's warm voice spilled out.

"I'm here for you, Kylie. Keep the eggs safe. We'll be back."

Relief and fear warred within me as Seradon chased the Fire Eaters into battle. A flurry of fiery blades swarmed the Shadow Hawk. Half dove for the ship's wings; the rest bombarded Grant's team. Winnigan swept the air with a sheet of water, extinguishing the blades above their heads, letting the airship's wards absorb the rest. Her spell had barely died before three elemental vises shot from the men, snatching at the Nimblewing. Apollo proved a quick study at the helm, flipping his ship nose over tail and corkscrewing in a new direction, evading capture.

Flames roared from the Nimblewing. The inferno engulfed Grant's ship, so hot it looked like a second sun suspended in the sky. I lifted a hand to protect my eyes, terror stealing my breath. The fire clung to the Shadow Hawk through a series of flips and twists before it exploded into a cloud of steam. For a second, the moisture hung in the air. Then it dropped like a miniature rainstorm.

The Shadow Hawk shot straight up, spun on its axis, and dove in the opposite direction. No one in the ship looked harmed, but they did look furious. Spells spat from the squad in perfect rhythm as the warriors masterfully cycled control of the link among themselves: traps of ice and earth, precise slices of wood and fire targeting the Nimblewing's propulsion spells, and extinguishing slaps of air knocking aside the Fire Eaters' attempts to attack. Through it all, Seradon flew with uncanny skill, wielding the ship's navigational spells as if they were an extension of her body.

The Fire Eaters didn't stand a chance, and they wouldn't have lasted this long if Grant's squad wasn't attempting to capture them alive.

Apollo dove beneath the dirigible, using it as a shield. I grabbed for his craft with a net of air, but I was too slow. The Nimblewing looped around the ship close enough for me to read Apollo's lips.

Burn it.

Fireballs pelted the envelope, then the Nimblewing tore away.

Flames licked the canvas. Cursing, I sprinted across the basket, dousing the fires I could see with water and earth element. With the envelope's frame bulging wider than the basket, I couldn't tell if flames burned higher up. I sprinted for the ramp. Before I climbed two steps, cool magic broke across the top of the envelope and poured down its oblong length, coating the massive balloon and extinguishing any remaining flames. When the magic crossed mine, I recognized Winnigan's signature atop a mix of her team's linked magic.

I scrambled the rest of the way up the ramp. Fist-size perforations weakened the canvas in a dozen places. Even as I watched, two holes ripped into gashes, the tattered edges fluttering under the pressure of air rushing through the gap. Worse, the spells lining the interior of the canvas—the spells holding the ship aloft—were deteriorating.

We were sinking.

Half running, half sliding, I tumbled down the ramp, searching the ground. I could make out individual tents now, pick out horses from cows, cerberi from hounds. The fair was coming up too fast, and we had too far to fly to reach an empty field.

"Kylie, the egg!" Quinn shouted.

The phoenix egg wobbling along the deck pulsed an ominous mottled amber, the unborn bird's churning wings and beak pressing a crimson shadow against the shell.

We had run out of time.

24

I surged toward the trembling egg, spinning fire and air together into an oven-hot cradle.

"Get ready to dive," I yelled to Quinn.

The Nimblewing darted past, and the FPD's black ship followed, skimming close to the basket. Both were a blur in my peripheral vision.

Scooping up the egg, I ran for the bow. Heat bowled into me despite the ten feet separating me from the egg. I ducked my head to the side, shielding my face with my arm.

"Everyone, *clear out!*" I bellowed. I didn't care about the Fire Eaters, but I couldn't risk harming Grant and his squad or Quinn.

Something shot toward the basket. I jerked my head around in time to see Grant soar through the air, the Shadow Hawk nowhere in sight. A levitation spell burned beneath his feet, powered by his magic alone, not a link. It was an incredible feat of strength and bravery. And if the egg hatched anywhere near him while he was so vulnerable, the concussive blast would kill him.

I flung the egg with every ounce of my gargoyle-enhanced strength, aiming for a field half a mile away.

The phoenix hatched before the egg cleared the envelope.

I had a millisecond to slap up a shield. A tsunami of scalding air laced with boiling amniotic fluid annihilated my magic, flinging me into the air like a rag doll. Flailing, I hit the deck hard, bounced, and slammed to a halt against a lacquered baluster. Something cracked, and I couldn't say for certain if it was my back or the post.

Stunned, I sprawled on my back, relearning how to breathe. Shock deadened my thoughts, blunting even the piercing knell resonating inside my skull. I floated on a world tipped upside down, the sky a blue pond atop which the dirigible's envelope bobbed and swayed. The deck vibrated beneath me, bouncing my vision, but at least the air was cool. What I wouldn't give to dive into the sky's placid waters. Or into a trough of ice. My lungs burned, and I half expected to see flames when I breathed out.

Working my jaw, I swallowed hard. My ears popped. Sound rushed into the void, a high-pitched ringing swelling to clash with the ominous dissonance of pops and cracks reverberating around the ship. A cable snapped near the bow, rebounding to slap the underside of the envelope. The basket jolted. I fumbled to sit up. I needed to check on Quinn and Grant—

The frame inside the balloon snapped. In a furor of crunching wood and ripping fabric, the tip of the envelope tore free. I dove beneath my bent arm as a squall of splinters whipped toward my face. Heavier pieces of wood slammed the deck in front of me, battering the railing as the tatters of canvas knotted around the broken hunks of frame tugged against the air currents. The basket careened sideways, and I peeked over my elbow in time to see a gust grab the fallen fabric and suck it overboard. I rolled my eyes higher, toward the balloon, and my breath caught.

Oh crap.

Wind lambasted the exposed envelope's interior, decimating the tattered spells holding the dirigible aloft. The deck dropped beneath me, and my stomach went weightless. I lunged for the railing, wrapping an arm around a post. The balloon spun in a slow circle, pulling the basket along with it. Wind caught the broken envelope again, straightening the flight path for a second, before the basket's momentum pulled the ship into another spiral. If not for the lowered ramp, the severed balloon might have been enough to keep me afloat, but the plank added too much drag on the basket. The dirigible tipped toward the bow, the ramp sawing against the basket's thin boards.

With a mighty snap, the center of the basket ruptured under the pressure and vanished. I screamed as the railing flexed under the strain, bending toward the gaping hole. The basket rotated around the broken envelope, the second time faster than the first. Metal bolts moaned under the pressure, and the ramp tore free of the envelope. It slapped flat against the deck, then slid along the tattered boards and shot out the open gate, taking half the front railing with it. In a flash, it was gone.

Slack flexed through the cables suspending the basket beneath the balloon, but it was too late. By the third rotation, the ship was helplessly caught in a corkscrew and gaining speed.

"Grant! Quinn!"

The centrifugal force plastered me to the railing, and the

wind swallowed my shouts. The horizon spun, dense green forest then pale green fields, with flashes of Terra Haven's slate wall and the foothill's golden slopes blinking in between. Beneath the deck, visible through the gaping hole, spun a kaleidoscope of crimson, teal, lavender, and brown. Claw marks gouged the railing where Quinn had clung, but my friend was no longer there.

The rest of the basket was empty. Grant hadn't made the jump.

I had been too slow.

Agony built in my chest and poured out of me in a primal scream of anguish and rage.

The cauldron holding the final, unhatched phoenix tipped, spilling the egg onto the canted deck. In a fiery rush, it slid across the boards on a collision course with the railing five feet from my head. For a fraction of a second, I considered doing nothing. Grant was gone. Quinn too, possibly. Being caught in a phoenix's hatching would be a quick death.

At the last moment, I lashed out with magic, catching the egg inches before impact.

A sob escaped me. The elements trembled in my grip as I layered more air and fire around the egg, thickening the cushion into a bowl. I couldn't feel Quinn's boost, but if he lived, he would be doing everything in his power to get back to me. To help me. To save me. He was counting on me to do my part to save myself, no matter how much my heart hurt.

I wouldn't—couldn't—disappoint him.

Heat radiated from the phoenix, baking me despite the wind whistling through the railing. Gravity had turned on its side, pressing heavily on my chest the faster the dirigible spun. Plastered to the railing, I struggled to draw a full breath, my neck muscles quivering as I craned to get a better look at the ground.

It rushed toward me, fast as a gryphon and twice as merciless. If the crash landing didn't kill me, the phoenix hatching would.

A disembodied calm washed through me, sweeping aside my grief, terror, guilt, and anger. My survival was no longer an option, but I would make sure no one else died. *I'm sorry, Quinn.*

The ship was too close to the ground to attempt to throw the egg. The horizon had become a blur. Without a distinguishable target, I might accidentally launch the egg straight into the fleeing fairgoers, killing those I hoped to protect. I didn't have the control needed to force the egg to hatch midair either. I had to keep the egg close.

Stretching for the elements, I layered cushions of heated air around the egg. Then I caged the magic inside a granite-hard spherical earthen ward. Weaving elements with desperate speed, I tied off the sphere and reinforced it with a pentagram of all five elements bent around the outside of the ward. A second pentagram followed, then a third, fourth, and fifth. My brain throbbed inside my skull. It was too much magic, too many spells built too fast, but I didn't have a second to spare.

Not much longer, the morbid voice repeated, urging me to push my limits.

Spinning a web of wood-laced air, I anchored the element-ensconced egg to the deck, the railing, the nearest cables, even the battered canvas above us and the remaining frame inside the material's thin surface. With the last of my strength, I flung a magical dome over the egg, crafting a spell of pure hope and inspiration, hardening the inside with the intention of directing any of the egg's explosion downward. When we crashed, if the rest of my spells failed, hopefully the dome would force the phoenix's blast into the earth and spare anyone nearby.

I closed my eyes and braced for impact, for all the good it would do me.

Smoke filled my nostrils, the harsh scent reminiscent of the charcoal remains of a banked fire. My magic dampened the phoenix's furnace heat, but sweat still matted my shirt to my back. Wind whistled past my ears, and beneath it, my pulse pounded against my eardrums. Tears leaked from the corners of my eyes—for Grant; for Mom, who I wouldn't get to see again; for Quinn, who would blame himself. For myself.

I didn't want to die.

The basket hit something and shook. Flinching, I curled tighter—only to open my eyes when nothing painful or crushing followed.

Quinn's golden silhouette loomed above me. His wings spanned the sky, his enormous paws clenched around the top rail. Quartz muscles strained as he curled his wings into sails, countering the basket's spiral. My stomach somersaulted. We were too close to the ground. He would be caught in the crash.

"Save yourself, Quinn," I croaked, my tears falling faster. "You need to—"

"Kylie's got the egg stabilized," Quinn yelled. He flashed me a fierce grin.

I gaped at him. Maybe I was dead. Maybe this was a hallucination.

I reached for him. My arm wavered, my muscles weak, but the ship's centrifugal force no longer had me pinned. In fact, it was almost easy to stretch up and cup my hand around Quinn's rock ankle. He felt solid.

The basket groaned and bowed. I sat up, bracing my free hand on the deck beside me, not letting go of Quinn with the other. The horizon had slowed its dizzying spin, and I chanced a glance over the side of the ship. Faces stared up at us, close enough to see expressions of awe, concentration, and excitement. Not fear. No one was running. The ground rushed toward us, but even that seemed to slow.

"Quinn, what—"

"Hold steady. You've got this." Grant's encouragement rumbled through the basket's floorboards.

I spun toward the sound, flinging myself across the deck before I realized I had moved. Crawling on hands and knees, I peered through the gap in the floorboards. Grant floated beneath the ship, his hands braced on the underside of the basket. Determination pulled his features taut, emphasizing the strong cut of his jaw and the firm line of his lips, and wind whisked sweat from his temples into his short hair. His uniform strained around his biceps and thighs, as if he held the ship aloft with pure physical strength. He looked like a god come to life.

"You're alive," I whispered. My heart swelled with joy so intense it was hard to breathe.

Magic flared from Grant in a massive spell, part air current, part elemental ship. It stretched the length of the basket and curled up the cables to support the ravaged balloon. Linked magic sung through every element strand, so many magical signatures interlaced that the individuals blurred into one chaotic, cohesive mass. Half the fairgoers must have joined their magic together to save the dirigible. To save me.

Grant glanced up, meeting my eyes through the rift in the deck. Relief shone in his gaze. His lips curved in a private smile, then he returned his attention to the complex spell keeping the ship afloat.

Strength bled from my limbs. I collapsed to my stomach, bathed in the euphoria of a second chance at life. Tears fogged my vision, but I hardly noticed. I saw only my future, and I couldn't wrest my eyes from him.

———

I slouched with my back against the dirigible's railing, my legs splayed in front of me, solid dirt beneath the battered deck boards. As soon as I had the energy, I'd stand. In the meantime, Quinn sat behind me, on the ground, since the fractured deck would no longer support his weight. He stretched his neck over the top rail so his chin pressed against my shoulder, and his breath whispered against my cheek. I wrapped my arm up around his face, holding his mane to keep him close.

O'Hara's team swarmed the basket, or what was left of it. The wooden structure more closely resembled rubble from a demolished porch than anything sky worthy. Especially with the pulverized balloon listing in the dirt beside it.

Grant had set us down as soft as a flying carpet on a feather bed in a field at the edge of the fair, and he maintained his distance while O'Hara and his team worked on dismantling my spells. His eyes skimmed our surroundings, ever vigilant, but they returned to settle on me again and again. I smiled, content to stare and half afraid if I looked away, he would disappear.

It took a surprising amount of time for O'Hara's team to unravel my magic from the phoenix, a task made more difficult by my fatigued inability to assist. Despite the hassle I caused the investigator, I took quiet pride in my handiwork.

If the dirigible *had* crashed, I was certain my spells would have held and saved lives.

When O'Hara's team finally had the phoenix swaddled in new spells, holding it in stasis, Grant seized something from the side of the basket and heaved it onto the broken deck. Nathan landed with a crash.

"Here's the culprit," he said.

"I'm a victim," Nathan protested. "Look." He held up arms crisscrossed with bruises from clinging to the metal ladder during our harrowing descent, then pointed to burns visible through holes in his pants. He'd acquired a cut across his brow at some point, and blood splashed down the left side of his face, matting his trim beard. His press badge hung down the back of his scarlet shirt, a slender burn from the chain slanting across his pale throat.

"Kylie did this to me," he said, dropping his taunting use of *Harry* now that we had an audience. "She kidnapped me to prevent me from telling you she had the phoenix eggs, then she hung me out there to die."

"Oh, really?" Grant vaulted over the railing to loom over the megalomaniac monster. Nathan cringed in his shadow. O'Hara closed in on Nathan's opposite side.

"You have to believe me," Nathan said, directing his pleas to the investigator but projecting his voice well past him.

A ring of Terra Haven city guards—real ones, not Fire Eaters in disguise—formed a semicircle around the dirigible a dozen yards away, holding onlookers at bay. A ward stretched between the guards, primed to protect them and the innocent citizens from the phoenix egg if the FPD's magic failed. However, Nathan wasn't trying to be heard by the crowd. He was performing for an audience of one: *Terra Haven Chronicle*'s own Audrey Cintrón.

The senior journalist stood inside the guards' barrier, her press badge dangling from her neck, a camera resting on a hastily erected tripod. Audrey floated a recording sphere over the basket, capturing sound from a respectful distance. Weighed down by a camera bag and multipocketed vest, her graying hair pulled back in a no-nonsense braid and coated in a layer of dust and sweat, she looked much as she had when we covered the everlasting tree's blooming together what felt like a lifetime ago. However, her usually affable expression was twisted with disgust as she glared at Nathan.

A commotion among the guards drew everyone's attention, and after a flurry of brusque words muffled behind the barrier, followed by a demand for the guards to respect the freedom of the press barked at a volume only a battle-trained warrior—or a former gryphon rider—could achieve, O'Hara gave a nod, and my boss stormed past the guards. Dahlia Bearpaw stalked to the dirigible with her linen skirt clenched in her fists, her sandals raising puffs of dust with each step. Unlike Audrey, who had obviously been working at the fair when my crash landing had usurped whatever article she had been planning to write, Dahlia looked as if she had been enjoying a rare day off.

"What in all the blue sky is going on?" she demanded, slamming to a halt at the bow of the dirigible's tattered deck. Her thunderous scowl sliced from O'Hara to the egg, then to me and Nathan.

"We were just getting to that, Ms. Bearpaw," O'Hara said.

"She tried to kill me," Nathan said, flinging a hand out to point at me. "Kylie stole the phoenix eggs, lost control of them, and nearly killed us both. I was lucky to survive clinging to the side of this death trap."

The investigator crossed his arms. "And here I thought

you got stuck on that ladder when you were attempting to crawl across ships to join the Fire Eaters masquerading as Terra Haven guards."

Nathan managed a credible sputter of astonishment. "I thought they *were* guards. Are you telling me Kylie has been working with a gang?"

Grant laughed. The cold sound sent goose bumps down my arms. Nathan flinched, freezing when Grant clamped a hand on his shoulder.

"Ah, there it is," Grant said, his voice so soft it barely carried across the deck. He dropped a delicate weave of fire and water toward Nathan's midsection. Nathan tried to swipe the elements aside, but he was too slow. The magic brushed a knotted silver belt buckle and disappeared into the spell hidden in the metal.

Nathan vanished, and Mom cowered in Grant's grip. Audrey gasped in surprise, but she was the only one. Dahlia dropped her skirt to rest her fists on her hips, her expression flinty. The investigator pulled a pair of null cuffs from his pocket.

"Nathan Aspell," O'Hara intoned, affixing a recording sphere in the air near Nathan's mouth, "you are under arrest for the use of a banned spell, for impersonating a fellow citizen, for the theft of Federal Pentagon Defense property, for the attempted murder of at least two people and a gargoyle, and for possession of phoenix eggs." O'Hara deactivated the doppelganger spell, then slapped the cuffs around Nathan's wrists, cutting off his ability to touch the elements. "Anything you say will be recorded and used in your trial."

Nathan stared at his bound wrists in stupefied silence.

Anderson and two of her squadmates collected the phoenix egg, transferring it to a nearby FPD air cruiser. The fire elemental gave my shoulder a squeeze when she strode past and shook her head.

"If anything, Monaghan downplayed your competence. Good work today."

Anderson didn't pause long enough for me to respond. Vaulting into the air cruiser, she and her squadmates powered across the field toward the empty foothills. I breathed a sigh of relief, one echoed by Quinn. When the egg hatched, it would do so far from anyone it could harm, under the watchful eye of veteran FPD warriors.

The buzz of aircrafts overhead droned louder. I shielded my eyes with my free hand. The Nimblewing descended sedately, escorted by the FPD's armored Shadow Hawk. Seradon maintained an elemental link between the ships, and it was her magic guiding both crafts simultaneously. Controlling two ships' levitation spells at once was no mean feat, but she made it look easy. Considering her astonishing flying skills during the battle, I shouldn't have been surprised.

Velasquez stood in the Nimblewing's rear passenger spot, having switched ships midflight. The Fire Eaters sulked in their harnesses in front of him, all four caught in the same null net maintained by Marciano, Winnigan, and Velasquez. Apollo looked as if he was plotting murder, but the other two males—both barely old enough to qualify as men—gazed forlornly at their shoes. The woman cast frequent glances at Velasquez, half fearful, half awed. Radiating displeasure from the tips of his combat boots to his crossed arms and clenched jaw, with soot streaking his black hair and his fierce blue eyes locked on the prisoners he towered over, Velasquez was a fearsome sight.

I wished I had my camera so I could take a picture for Mika. She would appreciate seeing her boyfriend looking triumphant and rugged after a victorious battle. Maybe I could get a print from Audrey, who had tilted the camera to capture the ships' landing.

Scorch marks etched the side of the Fire Eaters' craft, and blackened divots pockmarked its slender wings. I expected nothing less after the haphazard way the Fire Eaters had been flinging fireballs. More surprising was the dry, sun-bleached degradation of the hull and smears of rust streaking the flaking paint. Gone was the ship's iconic green coating and shimmering silver-and-gold guards' logos adorning the side. Belatedly, I realized that had all been an illusion. Somehow, the Fire Eaters had gotten their hands on a weather-beaten, decommissioned Nimblewing, then spelled it to look like the real deal. From the looks of it, they were lucky it hadn't fallen apart in the air.

Marciano and Winnigan leapt from the Shadow Hawk before Seradon finished landing, and they converged on the Fire Eaters, systematically cuffing them with null bands. In less than two minutes, the whole misfit crew was bound and seated on the dirt, each with a recording sphere anchored near their mouths. Velasquez recited their charges.

Seradon sauntered toward the dilapidated basket, her gaze skimming the growing crowd, Audrey and Dahlia, O'Hara and Xinh, and Quinn before landing on me. Sympathy softened her eyes for a moment, and when she glanced toward Grant and Nathan handcuffed at his feet, a satisfied smile tipped the corner of her mouth.

"I didn't have a choice," Nathan mumbled.

"What's that?" O'Hara asked.

"I had to take the phoenix eggs," Nathan said, louder now. Tears glittered in his eyes and his bottom lip trembled. "The Fire Eaters forced me."

Apollo's head snapped up. "You lying snitch—"

"How?" O'Hara asked Nathan.

"That one, Apollo, he said they would kill me if I didn't steal the eggs. They forced the doppelganger spell on me. I had no choice."

"Fascinating," Seradon said. She hopped the railing and strode across the broken deck, positioning herself close to the recording sphere attached to Nathan, then sidestepping to align herself under Audrey's sphere too. "Because your buddy, Apollo, claims you promised him an impressive sum of money to pick you up today."

"That's absurd. I don't have money. Kylie is the heiress. She's the one who could pay—"

"He mentioned something about a book you're writing, one you've been bragging is going to make you rich."

Nathan sputtered, his gaze darting to Dahlia. The editor's steely gaze held no sympathy.

Seradon plucked the enchanted buckle from Nathan's belt, holding it up to the light. Twisting it, she scrutinized the spell, then handed it to O'Hara.

"That's the doppelganger spell?" she asked.

"One of the most sophisticated I've seen," he confirmed.

"It's her work." Seradon jutted her chin toward the captive female Fire Eater. "She outfitted their dilapidated rig with the illusion, and the magical signature matches. She's got talent. It's too bad she chose to use it to help scum like Nathan Aspell and his band of sniveling man-boys terrorize people." Seradon's spoke the last part loud and clear, tilting her head toward Audrey's sphere.

"Thank you, Seradon. I've got it from here," O'Hara said dryly.

Seradon smiled sweetly, but I noticed she waited for Grant's discreet nod before turning away. I expected her to vault the railing, but she came to me instead and helped me to my feet. I bit my bottom lip and swallowed a moan of pain. Magic ghosted across me, assessing my wounds. Nathan received another glare, this one promising pain, but once Seradon was certain I wouldn't collapse, she gave my shoulder a gentle pat and continued on her way. She did, however, pause long enough beside Audrey to say, "If you need a quote for your article, I'll be right over there."

O'Hara cleared his throat. "All press inquiries will go through me." He shot Audrey a stern glance.

"Excuse me, Investigator," I rasped, my throat parched. I pushed away from the railing, hesitating when my thighs quivered under the strain of supporting me. Every muscle from my jaw to my heels throbbed as if I had been systematically tortured—or as if I had fought against a madman, then clung to a corkscrewing, out-of-control ship.

O'Hara pivoted toward me, arching a black eyebrow. "If you will be patient, Ms. Grayson, we'll take your statement in a moment. Or do you require healing?" He signaled to Xinh.

"No." I waved aside the offer. Healing could wait. "Nathan has something he stole from me. I would like it back before you cart him off to jail."

I took a step. Pain spiked from the half-healed wound in my calf up to my knee. Gritting my teeth, I stepped around Xinh's proffered hand.

"Don't let her near me," Nathan said. "She's going to hurt me."

"Shut it," Grant growled.

My breaths came in shallow pants by the time I crossed the dozen feet separating us. Slowly, because I was half afraid I might fall over and half afraid Nathan would attempt to strike me despite the two FPD warriors looming on either side of him, I reached into his pocket and retrieved my pouch. Unraveling the spells holding it closed, I tugged the pouch open and poured my seed and Quinn's into my palm.

The tiny green sprout on Quinn's seed remained strong and unbroken. I let out a pent-up breath. My own seed was unchanged, but I didn't care. It was Quinn's I had been worried about.

"You don't deserve that seed," Nathan spat. "You don't deserve to write this story or any story. You're not a real journalist like me. You're just a spoiled rich girl."

Cruel desperation glittered in Nathan's gaze as he slung his verbal barbs, hoping to strike one final blow. He still believed his opinion mattered to me. Pity curved my lips into a semblance of a smile, igniting fresh hatred in Nathan's eyes.

"You forfeited the right to call yourself a journalist the moment you fabricated a story, Nathan. Now you're just a sad liar." I leaned closer, as if confiding a secret. "But don't worry. The fame you crave? You're going to get it. You're going to go down in history as the biggest criminal to ever be fired from the *Terra Haven Chronicle*. Maybe someone will even write a book about it. But it won't be me. You're not worth another second of my time."

I tucked the seeds back into the pouch and slipped it into my pocket, ignoring the slew of insults Nathan spewed. On wobbly legs, I stalked to the bow of the ship and tottered to the ground. Sheer willpower kept me upright, though my knees wanted to buckle. I wouldn't give Nathan the satisfaction of seeing me stumble.

Quinn trotted to me, favoring his back-right paw. Without speaking, he sat and propped me up. Together, we watched Xinh drag Nathan to Seradon's aircraft and load him inside with the captured Fire Eaters. Apollo snarled at

Nathan. Nathan sneered, then fell over his own feet when Apollo swung his cuffed hands like a club at Nathan's face. Velasquez stepped in, forcing Apollo to the deck and wrapping him in a ward to hold him in place. The other prisoners received similar miniature holding cells.

After they were settled, Velasquez hoisted Nathan to his feet, using only one hand to lift the slender ex-journalist. He shoved Nathan next to Apollo, linking the two men's wards together. Both seemed to have forgotten the recording spells affixed to their clothing as they spat insults and accusations at each other. Xinh gave Velasquez an approving grin.

Surprise pinged through me when Velasquez met my eyes. Instead of the glare I expected, he tipped his chin and touched his hand briefly to his chest. I mirrored him, accepting his forgiveness and silently offering my own. Winking, Velasquez turned his attention back to the prisoners.

Winnigan touched my shoulder, drawing my attention. Her glass-green eyes assessed mine, her slender fingers cool on my forearms.

"Are you braced?" she whispered.

I planted a hand on Quinn's mane and nodded.

Cool magic surged into my body, assessing my injuries. Winnigan tsked over the rope burns and cuts on my arm but left them alone, concentrating her magic on my brain instead. I sighed with relief as the pounding pain in my temples subsided.

"You know what I'm going to say now."

"My energy reserves are too low to heal me further," I guessed, opening my eyes as Winnigan withdrew her magic. Exhaustion weighted my eyelids. I longed to sit, but I didn't dare. Not until I could guarantee I wouldn't need to move again for several hours—or several days.

"Use ointment on these abrasions and aloe vera on the burns. And get rest. Real rest. See a healer tomorrow for a thorough checkup. And if I see you injured in the next month, I'll let Grant heal you."

I stifled a shudder. "I promise I'll rest."

"Good." Brushing her copper hair out of her face, Winnigan gave me a fierce smile. "You made us all proud today, Kylie. Good work." Squatting, she rested a hand on Quinn's cheek. "We couldn't have done it without you either. Thank you, Quinn."

Quinn's spine straightened, but he kept his wings gingerly tented away from his spine as Winnigan strode back to the Shadow Hawk.

"I think Kylie should be the lead on this article. Do you agree, Audrey?" Dahlia asked.

"Fine by me."

I blinked in surprise, and Audrey smiled.

"You earned it," she said.

"Thank you," I said, honored that she didn't hesitate to relinquish control of such an important article to me. "But I can't. Quinn needs healing—"

"I can wait." Determination glowed in Quinn's eyes. "We should make sure the *Chronicle* gets the facts right this time."

Dahlia flinched infinitesimally. "Quinn is right. I owe you an apology, Kylie. I believed Nathan's articles were keeping the public informed—and ensuring the FPD didn't sweep this investigation out of sight, since it reflected so poorly on them too." She lifted a brow at O'Hara. The investigator's bland expression didn't change, and Dahlia turned back to me. "I can see now that I was sorely wrong about Nathan's motives, and I allowed my objective to blind me to his failings. I owe it to you to let you set the record straight. This is your story, Kylie. It might even be your story of a lifetime. And you lived it. You deserve the byline credit."

A zing of yearning shot through me. Dahlia was offering me everything I thought I wanted: a big splashy story, a boost to my career, and a touch of fame.

My gaze slid to Nathan sulking in null cuffs, his life—and very nearly my parents' lives—ruined because of his monomaniacal pursuit of fame and the next big story. He was a living, breathing cautionary tale, a monster created and fed on similar motivations and goals that existed in my heart. But we weren't the same people. I hadn't made horrific, unethical decisions in pursuit of the seed's promised story. And I vowed I never would.

"Living it was enough," I said. It wasn't unhealthy to desire to advance my career or to get excited over a story or a front-page byline, but right now, my priorities lay elsewhere. "Thank you for the offer, but I just want to see Mom's name cleared and Airstrong back in society's good graces. Audrey should write the article. She has an unbiased perspective, and I know she'll do it justice."

Dahlia studied me for a long moment, her piercing brown eyes seeming to examine my soul—and approve of what she found. "As you wish. I hope we'll see you at the *Chronicle* soon."

"I look forward to it."

Grant vaulted the basket's battered railing and landed next to me, no weakness or fatigue visible in his movements. The only sign that he had battled Fire Eaters, then prevented a dirigible's crash using raw muscle and a jaw-dropping amount magic was the sweat that slicked his hair and dampened the thick column of his throat. I let my gaze slide down his body. Splinters and ash dusted his shoulders and arms, blood crusted his knuckles, and his spelled uniform bore telltale singed holes from fiery shell shrapnel.

"If we leave now, we should reach the phoenix before it hatches," he said.

I jerked my gaze to his. He was offering more than a ride; he was giving me a chance to evolve my everlasting seed. A chance to finish my quest for the story of a lifetime.

"You'd do that for me?" I asked softly.

"The harder I try to shield you from danger, the more you seem to attract. I think it's time I try a new strategy."

A slow, unbidden smile curved my lips. Despite his wry tone, his brown eyes glowed with tenderness and a promise I yearned to hear spoken.

"But after the hatching," Grant said, his voice deepening, "I'm taking you home, and I'll get Quinn to sit on you if that's what it takes to keep you in bed until your body recovers."

A snort of a laugh escaped me, but I shook my head.

"Thank you, but as much as I appreciate the offer, I've seen enough phoenixes hatch to last me a lifetime. I just want to go home."

Grant's eyebrow arched in surprise. "Are you certain?"

A week ago, I would have leapt at a chance—my *last* chance—to evolve my everlasting seed. I would have been the one clamoring for Grant to get me close to the phoenix.

My fingers idly traced the waves of Quinn's rock mane. The seed and chasing its promised answer had nearly killed me and those I loved too many times. I was ready to set the quest for the story of a lifetime aside.

"I'm certain."

Grant smiled. Affection and something more potent glimmered in his eyes, warming me. My body was ready to be home. I wanted Mika to heal Quinn and fuss over me. I wanted to see Mom and return all Airstrong responsibilities to her and Dad. I wanted to sleep for a week. But most of all, I wanted to climb into Grant's arms and not let go.

I thought I had lost him. I never wanted to feel that anguish again.

I had so many things I wanted to say to him, but with Dahlia, Audrey, O'Hara, and the other FPD warriors watching with rapt fascination, I held my tongue.

Soon, though. Grant and I would talk soon.

25

Every muscle from my temples to my toes ached when I woke late the next morning. Quinn helped me hobble to the bathroom, assisted me in replacing the bandages on my abraded wrists, and then monitored me as I delicately stretched my abused muscles. By the time I exchanged my pajamas for lightweight gardening trousers and a blue cotton top that brushed soft as air against my scabbed back, I was moving almost normally.

Josephine knocked on my door as I finished buttoning my pants.

"Come in," I called.

"I thought I heard you up." She cracked the door open and peeked in, then stepped into my room. "I was going to leave these on your doorstep, but since you're awake . . ." My landlady clutched a platter crammed with enough peach scones for five people, a mound of butter molded into a rose bloom, a pitcher of water and a glass, and the morning edition of the *Terra Haven Chronicle*. A warming spell hugged the scones, a cooling spell protected the butter, and a third spell supported a paper-wrapped package floating at her hip. After giving me a quick once-over, Josephine set the tray on the table and guided the package to rest next to it.

"How are you feeling today?" Her hands fluttered in the air between us, waving vaguely at my battered body.

"Fine." So long as I didn't move. "Lucky, mostly," I added, eyeing the mound of scones.

After Zipporah tore apart the Victorian's roof in an attempt to abduct me, I feared my friendship with my landlady had been irreparably damaged. But fresh-baked treats —and my favorite flavor too—said louder than words that I was back in Josephine's good graces. "Thank you for being the most understanding landlady I could ask for. And for being such a talented baker."

Josephine waved my words aside, but pleasure sparkled in her green eyes. Impulsively, I hugged her, breathing in her subtle jasmine perfume. Her arms circled me gently.

"No more scares, Kylie. You hear me?" She pulled back to hold my forearms, noted the bandages, and switched her grip to my biceps. "You can't keep showing up on our doorstep looking like you let death slap you around."

I snorted, but when her fingers tightened to convey her seriousness, I said, "I promise. I'll live a tame life. No more getting caught in blood-magic labyrinths or running through thunderbird territories or pitting myself against banned spells. Or phoenix eggs." Reciting my recent adventures made me sound like a heroine in an adventure novel— or maybe the lead in an allegorical farce. I winked at Josephine and added, "At least for the next week or so."

She shook her head and chuckled. "And you, Quinn? Was Mika able to heal you?"

Quinn stretched his wings to show off an extensive clear swath down his back and across his feathers. "All better."

"So long as you rest," I reminded him.

Healing Quinn's seared body had taxed Mika and Quinn both. It was the first burn wound Mika had ever mended, and although her legendary gargoyle healer skills rose to the challenge, with Quinn's energy severely depleted, she hadn't wanted to risk delving too deep into his body's reserves. He would need to take it easy for the next week—a healer's refrain I was intimately familiar with.

"Good. While you're both recuperating, I can catch you up on the neighborhood gossip," Josephine said.

"Oh? Have we missed much?"

"Harold attempted to breed baku ..."

"The small nightmare-consuming pachyderms? How did he get his hands on those?"

"Well, they were actually dyed anteaters someone conned him into buying."

Quinn and I burst into laughter. "This is a story we need to hear. Please, join us for breakfast. You made more than enough."

"I wasn't certain if your gentleman would be joining you."

"Um." For some reason, the term *your gentleman* brought a blush to my cheeks.

"Did you know the captain came by last night and again this morning?" Josephine asked.

"No . . ." I shot Quinn an inquisitive look, and he nodded. "Did he have a message for me?" And why hadn't he come up? I peeked at the wrapped package. Was it from him?

"He was checking on you," Josephine said. "Last night, he wanted to make sure you got home all right, and I told him you were already in bed. This morning, we agreed not to wake you."

We agreed? Or did Josephine shoo Grant away? "Did he say if he's coming back?" Butterflies fluttered in my midsection, eagerness and nerves colliding at the thought of seeing Grant. "Should I send him a message?"

"I'm certain he'll be back." Josephine's eyes crinkled in a knowing smile. "But for now, I need to get the week's shopping done. We'll catch up soon. Enjoy, and don't do anything *too* strenuous today."

I gaped at Josephine. Was she referring to me and Grant…?

Laughing, my landlady patted my flaming cheek. My teeth clicked closed. She tossed Quinn a wink, then bustled out of the room, closing the door behind her. Her soft humming faded as she trotted down the stairs.

"It's nice she's no longer mad at us," Quinn said.

I pressed my cool fingertips to my cheeks. "She was never mad at you."

"It's better now, though."

"I agree." Dropping to a cross-legged seat in front of the table, I banished the spells on the food and buttered a scone. The first bite melted on my tongue, sweet peach and crumbly dough drenched in savory butter. I moaned in appreciation. This was the life.

"Who's the package from?"

"Let's find out." Brushing crumbs from my fingertips, I examined the package. It was free of magic and any identifying company logos, and my name and Quinn's were printed in unfamiliar handwriting. Gesturing to a seam in the paper, I asked, "Would you like to do the honors?"

Quinn used a sharp claw—one reshaped by Mika after our battle with Zipporah and still more clear quartz than citrine—to rip the paper. I grabbed the edges and tore it free, revealing a magnificent glass sculpture.

"It's me," Quinn said, stunned.

A miniature replica of Quinn stood on the table. The lion's body was six inches tall, his head thrown back and his tail arched. Exquisite detail curved through the claws on his feet and rippled through his mane, and the defiant expression on his face perfectly captured Quinn's protective spirit. But it was the wings that truly awed me. The artist had flared them into a high bowl above the lion's back, the arc impossible in real life but beautiful nonetheless. Each feather overlapped in hyperrealistic detail, from vanes to tips, all blunted to capture the stone nature of Quinn's form. The entire sculpture had been crafted in yellow glass liberally streaked with melted flecks of gold. When I shifted it, the lion glittered as if in motion.

I traced a finger across the smooth glass, and magic tingled against my skin. Not only was it a stunning piece of art, it was also a message bowl. I could sense the residue of the artist's magic, but the bowl was tuned to my signature.

Cradling the lion's wings, I flipped the sculpture to peer at the bottom, unsurprised to find the overlapping double-F logo of the Femmes of the Furnace pressed into the bottom of a glass paw. I levitated my old message bowl to the side, then reverently replaced it with the new one. Quinn retrieved a note from the packing paper and flipped it open with a claw.

"'Kylie and Quinn,'" he read aloud. "'Your article and your words touched our hearts, and the attention you've garnered for our business is a true blessing. Wishing you both equal joy and prosperity. With goodwill and gratitude, Vella McLeavy.'" Quinn beamed at me. "It worked. Our article helped the minotaurs' business."

I nodded, my chest tight with emotion. This was why I had gotten into journalism—to change lives for the better.

"Do you think Audrey can do the same for Airstrong?" Quinn asked.

"I hope so." We both looked at the newspaper. It was folded in half, then in half again and wedged beneath the butter tray, all but a corner of a picture obscured.

I glanced around my apartment. The sun was shining. I had fresh scones to gorge on and my good friend to talk to. Serenity drifted like a spell on the gentle breeze wafting through the open windows, and nothing hurt too badly. I couldn't remember the last time I hadn't felt driven to take action—on an article, on my seed's clues, on something time sensitive and urgent.

Closing my eyes, I savored the tranquil moment, not yet ready to let the outside world intrude.

My fingers twitched. Curiosity twanged like a physical prod in my gut.

I opened my eyes. Quinn watched me with a knowing grin. Shoving the butter aside, I grabbed the *Chronicle* and slid around the table next to Quinn. He leaned forward to read over my shoulder with palpable anticipation.

A photo of the battered dirigible filled the front page, a haze of snapped cables snaking around the broken and smoking canvas, the splintered basket seeming to deteriorate even as I scanned down the picture. Quinn clung to the opposite side of the basket, his cupped wings an elongated blur the shutter hadn't been fast enough to capture crisply.

But it was Grant below the basket that made my breath hitch. He stood suspended on empty air, legs spread wide, arms braced above his head to support the basket. The elemental platform beneath his feet and the huge flotation of magic supporting the dirigible were invisible on film, giving the impression that Grant single-handedly held the dirigible aloft. Given the flexing of his muscular arms and the tense muscles in his neck, I could almost believe his sheer physical prowess had saved us.

He was looking down and to the right of the camera, and not even the ink's bleed in the newsprint's pulp could obscure the determination burning in his eyes. My heart beat hard, heat rising through my chest. I brushed a finger over the firm lines of his face. He was too attractive. Rough and masculine. Arrogant and powerful. And a natural-born protector.

I wouldn't be the only woman lusting after Grant today.

"Look at Nathan." Quinn pointed to the dirigible.

I dragged my gaze from Grant. A shadowed figure was smashed to the side of the basket, arms and legs splayed wide as if he had been running full sprint and slammed into the wooden side. A rictus of fear contorted the visible half of Nathan's face, his eye circled in white, his mouth gaped in a scream. The ladder's thin chains looped over the railing, the rungs hidden under Nathan's body.

"How's he holding on?" His arms were too far apart to be gripping the ladder, and his feet weren't standing on a rung.

"Grant locked him in place with magic," Quinn said. "Forcefully."

A huff of a laugh shot from me. Nathan looked like he was doing an impression of a dead bug splattered against the dirigible. Fitting. I started giggling and couldn't stop. Quinn laughed too, the sound mingled with a purr of joy. It gargled his humor, which only made me laugh harder.

I had to look away from the picture to catch my breath. Wiping tears from my eyes, I read the article. Audrey had written in a fluid mix of facts and evocative descriptors that breathed life into the tale, proving why she was one of the paper's top journalists. In a few paragraphs, she laid out

Nathan's background at the paper and his personal history with the Fire Eaters, gave a similar summary of the individual gang members who attacked the dirigible, and matter-of-factly detailed Nathan's attempts to drop phoenix eggs on the fair.

Mentions of me were refreshingly positive, referring to me as "the *Chronicle*'s own Harriet Kylie Grayson," though I squirmed with embarrassment to be characterized as a civilian warrior. However, Audrey was equally effusive in praising Quinn, much to my delight. He deserved every ounce of credit and then some. Without him, I wouldn't have survived, nor would many of the fair attendees.

While being healed last night, Quinn had told his version of the events to Mika and me, which is how I knew that after Nathan tossed Quinn off Airstrong's roof, Melora had broken his fall at the last second. His landing had still been brutal—the horrid clatter of his stone body meeting the concrete loading dock would haunt my nightmares—but she had spared him from suffering more than a few broken feathers and a fractured tip of his tail. Despite his injuries, Quinn had flown directly to the fair, keeping to the shadows between buildings so Nathan wouldn't spot him. By the time he located Grant, the dirigible was already overhead, and he had raced to my aid. Not a moment too soon either.

As far as I knew, the warning I sent to Grant before racing out to confront Nathan on Airstrong's roof had never reached him. I owed my life to Quinn yet again.

The rest of Audrey's article dove deeper into Nathan's motives, his time at the *Chronicle*, and most importantly, the illegal doppelganger spell he used to impersonate Charlotte Grayson. Audrey made it clear that Mom was a victim, not a suspect, and included a quote from O'Hara promising the

FPD would continue to ship through Airstrong. I reread the paragraph twice, savoring my relief.

Mom had messaged me last night immediately after Winnigan released her from the safe house, and O'Hara had arrested Nathan in front of me, so I knew Mom was cleared of all suspicion, but seeing it in print somehow made it more real. Now the public knew too.

Though Mom had wanted to storm the Victorian to take up vigil by my bedside last night, I had convinced her Airstrong needed her more. I simply needed sleep, but I could only imagine the frenzy surrounding the company today. Press, curious citizens, and family friends would all be clamoring for insider details about the biggest scandal to rock the city in a decade. Plus, hopefully Mom would be inundated by customers returning to Airstrong, eager to show their renewed faith in the company.

After Quinn promised to watch over me all night, Mom sent back a tearful message thanking him for keeping me alive during my "ordeals" and agreed to postpone our reunion until this evening. Knowing she would worry about me until then, I swallowed my mouthful of scone and sent her a quick message letting her know Quinn and I were prepared for a day of doing nothing more strenuous than sunbathing and walking to the healer for a checkup later. Her response came back almost immediately.

"I saw the *Chronicle* this morning. You owe your captain a kiss from me, Kylie. I think half my hair went gray just looking at that picture. That dirigible . . . I've seen military ships come out of battles looking better. You could so easily have—" Her voice cracked, and she cleared her throat. "I love you. I can't wait to see you and Quinn tonight. Don't you dare go chasing any deadly birds today."

I shook my head. I had dealt with enough dangerous avian species to last me a lifetime. "Not a chance."

"Nope," Quinn agreed.

I skimmed the rest of Audrey's article, my eye snagging on the quote at the end . . . from Grant. "Nathan Aspell has been envious of Kylie Grayson's impressive instincts and journalistic skills since the day the *Chronicle* hired her. It sickens me that he took his insecurities out on the public, Airstrong's employees, and Kylie herself in such a violent and criminal fashion. I look forward to seeing Nathan convicted at trial and this threat to society permanently nullified."

The paper sank in my grasp. Grant fell just shy of calling for Nathan's execution. By placing the quote at the end of the article, Audrey gave extra weight to Grant's words. Audrey, and through her, Dahlia, was making a strong statement to the public: the *Terra Haven Chronicle* had washed its hands of Nathan and put its full support behind me.

It might be enough to counter the bad press I had received lately. Or not. Recent experience had proven that my name and image were just props for many unscrupulous journalists. They would spin lies about me and twist facts to create whatever story would sell the most copies. I had to trust the public to be smart enough to see the truth.

I flipped through the rest of the paper, smiling. Every article except Audrey's had been written under the byline "Staff."

"You might have roots in high society, Kylie, but you're one of us," Dahlia had said last night in a message, explaining that every journalist at the *Chronicle* insisted their articles in this morning's edition be published anonymously, just as my article about the minotaurs had been. It was a group apology and a statement of acceptance rolled into one.

It would take time for me to feel a kinship with my peers again—and, honestly, to fully forgive them—but at least I knew they were open to the possibility of forming friendships. And knowing I wouldn't be returning to a hostile bullpen was a huge relief.

"Look, it's a follow-up piece about your abduction," Quinn said, pointing. "Or at least about Wetherill's abduction," he amended as he read the article.

True to form, Luther Wetherill claimed to have always known something was "off" with Nathan, and that the former journalist's ties to Fire Eaters didn't surprise him. Wetherill assured the public he would press charges against Nathan for his part in "harming the person and property of a full spectrum."

I scoffed at his arrogance. Wetherill didn't bother mentioning me, for which I was grateful, but he also didn't include an apology to Mom or Airstrong for his slanderous accusations or explain why he had been so chummy with a journalist he had supposedly suspected of fabricating stories all along. I shook my head. Nearly dying hadn't changed Wetherill one bit.

Quinn and I perused a handful of articles about the fair while I polished off two more scones, but the news couldn't hold my attention. My gaze kept sliding to my dresser, where the leather pouch holding Quinn's everlasting seed rested. I caught Quinn glancing at it more than once too.

"What do you think it's going to turn into?" I asked.

He glanced at me, then back at the dresser. "I don't have a clue."

"Ready to find out?"

"Yes!" His hind end wriggled in excitement. Darting

across the room, he gently gripped the pouch in his teeth. Then his wings sank a fraction, and he turned to face me. "Unless you need more time to rest," he said around his mouthful.

"I'm burning with curiosity. Let's go." I hopped to my feet, managing to hide my wince when my back muscles spasmed from the sudden movement. Stretching as I walked, I worked the kink out of my spine. Quinn bounded ahead of me, his exuberant progress through the house rattling the walls. His racket covered my inadvertent groans as I hobbled down the stairs and through the house to the backyard.

Josephine's natural affinity for water element and patience in mastering finicky gardening spells, coupled with the benefit of living with five element-enhancing gargoyles, made the yard an oasis fit for a palace. The lawn shone emerald green; vegetables sprouted in record numbers along the back fence; lavender, gardenia, and rosemary scented the air; and bees droned happily among the bounty.

I hadn't bothered with shoes, and I crossed the flagstone patio and curled my toes into the blades of grass, seeking out the cool dirt beneath the sun-warmed surface. Quinn paused in the center of the yard, his citrine body a shimmer of sunlight almost too bright to look at.

"Will it be all right to plant it here?" he asked.

"Of course. This is the perfect garden for it."

I took the pouch from him and tugged the top open. His seed spilled into my palm along with my own. I tucked mine away before I could dwell on having lost the opportunity to evolve it and held Quinn's out for us both to admire. The seed glinted like polished metal, its sinuous silver threads dancing across the burnished surface when I rolled it in my palm. The bright-green sprout protruding from the tip had grown half an inch overnight.

Quinn's wings flexed and settled, fast and nervous. Spinning in a circle, he asked, "Where would be best?"

I led the way to the edge of a garden bed, where Josephine had recently dug up a spent patch of peas. "How about here?"

The nutrient-dense soil laced with horticultural-enhancement spells seemed like the ideal location for such a momentous planting.

Quinn gently clawed a pawful of dirt aside, and I helped him settle the seed sprout side up in the hole. Reverently, he patted the soil back in place, leaving the green shoot visible.

"Now what?" he whispered, his nose so close to the sprout that his exhale stirred the topsoil.

"Maybe give it some space," I suggested.

Together, we took a big step back.

"Should we water—" Quinn's question died when magic erupted from the seed, spurring the sprout's growth. The green stem shot toward the sky, then curved back to the lawn, squirming like a snake through the blades of grass. In a dizzying burst, dozens of shoots joined the first, arching over the low garden border and fanning outward, creaking audibly as they lengthened. Wild elements swirled around each stalk too fast to individuate, and the vines darkened from mint to moss to a deep, shimmery pewter.

Quinn and I sidled out of the way, eyes locked on the breathtaking transformation. In seconds, the stalks wove together into a rough trapezoid big enough to stand in. Broad, steely leaves blanketed the stalks, then a cluster of pewter leaves speared through the middle of the plant, unfolding into rows of perfect circles. As fast as fingers running across piano keys, a fan of rigid sprigs popped up in the middle, each just long enough to reach the thickest stem slanting across the back of the plant.

I ogled the plant, starting to recognize a familiar shape. It couldn't be ... could it?

Petite golden periwinkles blossomed out of the sides, and then earth magic rolled over the plant, hardening the stalks, deepening the burnished metallic tones, smoothing the curved edges and sleek sides, and flattening the flowers into citrine stars.

Quinn minced closer, wings flared, tail swishing. If he had been a flesh-and-blood feline, his fur would have been puffed.

"It's ... it's a typewriter," he said.

"A typewriter fit for a lion," I said, awed.

The everlasting tree's magic had grown a functional machine, complete with a rolling-pin-like platen, an extra-wide carriage return lever, and precise typebars connected to tiered rows of palm-size keys. The back was a standard typewriter width, hardly larger than a piece of paper, but it flared wide to accommodate the massive keys on the front. Instead of the usual knob, the platen could be rolled with an eye hook that looked to be the perfect size for Quinn's claw. Black ink coated the delicate letters at the tips of the type-bars, the glistening of the earth-and-water spell coating them too fine to dissect, but I predicted this typewriter would never need a ribbon or run out of ink.

Magic ebbed, chased by an arc of white fire that circled the rim of each round key. The element burned like a fuse, leaving a thin ribbon of glossy silver in its wake. With one final, theatrical pop that made us both jump, the stalks connecting the typewriter to the seed crackled to dust, and the elements disbanded.

"It's magnificent," Quinn said, circling the machine.

I fully agreed. I caressed the seamless side panel inlaid with polished citrine flowers. The typewriter looked like something made by an artisan, not grown from a seed. Then again, no iteration of Quinn's seed had resembled a plant either.

When Quinn sat in front of the keys, he looked right at home. I crouched beside him, taking in the typewriter from his perspective.

"This is amazing. You can write a history of gargoyles now—or articles for the *Chronicle*, novels, anything at all."

A furrow twisted Quinn's brow. "But I asked how I can help *you*. I don't see how this typewriter is the answer."

"Are you kidding? It's the best answer ever." I pivoted to face him, needing Quinn to see my sincerity. "You being happy and following your dreams is the best way you could ever help me. You're my friend, and I need to know you're living a life that fulfills you. And the fact that you're passionate about writing just like me?" I clutched my hands in front of my heart, feeling as if I would burst from gratitude at how lucky I was. "We can work on stories together, collaborate, and share our joy. I can't think of anything better."

Quinn cast a doubtful look toward the typewriter. "You really think I'm up for it? That I can write like you?"

"Like me? No. You're going to write like *you*, and it's going to be amazing. The world needs your perspective and your creativity."

I meant every word: the world would be better for Quinn's input and literary creations. Just as it was for my own.

Nathan had done his best to crush my desire to write. He had mocked and denigrated me, turned the city against me, and forced me to choose between journalism and my family.

I didn't regret my choice to bolster Airstrong in Mom's absence. But hearing myself, I felt my passion for journalism, for seeking out the truth and sharing my findings with the world, flaring within me.

"And I needed you to remind me why writing is so important," I said, feeling as if the everlasting tree were choosing my words. "Together, you and I are going to make the world a better place, one article and book at a time."

Quinn finally smiled, his excitement shining unchecked once more.

"Well?" I gestured to the typewriter. "Are you going to give it a try?"

I scooted to the side. Quinn pranced into place, settling and resettling his feet until he was situated. He brushed a paw across the keys. They hummed from his touch like a blade drawn from a scabbard. His toes overlapped the keys, and he played his claws across the top row, eliciting melodic chimes. When he punched down a key, the impact of his quartz paw against magic-made steel rang pure and loud through the yard. He tried a different key, creating a higher note.

As if he could no longer contain himself, he clacked through the keys at a rapid-fire tempo, sending overlapping metallic pitches singing through the yard. It was beautiful but *loud*. A flock of pigeons sprang from the neighbor's tree and flew away in a chorus of wing beats. Up and down the block, wards mushroomed around houses, as if the occupants feared the street was under attack.

The back door sprang open, slapping against the siding with an ear-splitting crack. I jumped, yanking hard on the elements. Quinn's startled leap planted him between me and the door as Grant burst through. Grant cleared the flag-stones in a single step, his second air-enhanced spring landing him next to Quinn. His gaze darted around the idyllic yard, skimmed over me and Quinn, and finally landed on the gigantic typewriter. The protective ward sizzling around us flared, then dissipated. Quinn hesitantly lowered his wings.

"You sure know how to make an impressive entrance," I said, throwing a hand over my racing heart. My thigh muscles twinged, and I uncurled my toes from the lawn.

"You didn't answer the front door. Then that clangor started up . . ." Grant glared from Quinn to the typewriter again. "Was that *you*?"

Quinn ducked his head sheepishly. "I got caught up in the moment and didn't realize I was being so loud."

"It's his everlasting seed," I said, releasing my death grip on the elements and giving Quinn a reassuring pat to let him know he hadn't done anything wrong. "When we planted it, it grew into this lion-size typewriter."

"It gave you this?" Grant's scowl faded, a slow smile dawning. It took him less than a second to grasp the meaning of Quinn's answer. "You're going to work alongside Kylie as a writer. Of course. She's going to benefit a lot from your wise perspective."

Grant's matter-of-fact acceptance of Quinn's new creative path made me want to hug him. Quinn looked up to Grant, and getting his approval made the gargoyle's chest puff with pride.

"I'm going to write a book on the history of gargoyles," Quinn said.

"I can't wait to read it." Grant studied Quinn's citrine feet. "But perhaps purchase a pair of leather writing gloves before you start."

Quinn lifted a paw, flexing his toes against the air. "Do you think they exist?"

"I'm sure a good tailor would be happy to design them for you."

Grant shifted his focus from Quinn to me, his gaze roaming lazily over my body. If he was checking to see how my injuries were healing, his focus lingered too long on my lips. When Grant reached out a hand, I stepped eagerly into his embrace. His strong arms wrapped tightly around me, dipping low to avoid the half-healed ice burns on my back and pulling me snug against his firm chest. I nuzzled up to Grant's neck, breathing in his clean, masculine scent and sighing contentedly. My fingers splayed across his back, and I stroked the soft weave of his cotton shirt, enjoying the feel of him beneath the well-worn material.

"How do you feel?" Grant's voice rumbled against my ear.

Josephine's suggestive comment about not doing anything *too strenuous* rose unbidden to the forefront of my mind. I cleared my throat and ducked my head so Grant wouldn't see me blushing.

"Really good, all things considered."

Grant shifted, holding me at arm's length. "You sure?"

I dragged my gaze from the alluring curve of his bicep half exposed by the short sleeve of his navy shirt, past his firm, kissable lips, and met his gaze squarely. Standing next to Grant never failed to make me feel petite in all the best ways. I flashed on the front-page picture of him holding the dirigible aloft. Grant's heroics, especially viewed from a distance when I wasn't terrified for his life, had been breathtakingly sexy, but I preferred him like this: relaxed, comfortable . . . and all to myself. Especially when his gaze dipped to my mouth, his eyes heating.

"I'm sure," I said, my voice husky.

Words stacked up in my throat. I needed to tell him how

my heart felt as if it had been ripped from my chest when I thought I lost him yesterday and how every cell in my body had been renewed in the euphoria of his survival. For the first time, we had nowhere to be, no one to save, no crime to stop. This was the perfect opportunity to confess my true feelings, but my emotions strangled me.

Grant spoke first.

"Do you regret your question to the everlasting tree?"

His query took me by surprise, and it took me a moment to wrangle my thoughts in the new direction. Following my seed's clues had nearly gotten me killed multiple times over, but without it, would Mom be a free woman today and Nathan behind bars? Perhaps I would still have found the firebirds, flung as I was by Zipporah into Lunacy Labyrinth, but my seed had been the only clue linking Persephone to Aurora Isle. I doubted I would have braved Dead Man's Swamp without it. And how much longer would it have taken to ferret out Nathan's vindictive plan? Because question or no question, his ire would still have locked on me, his vengeance spewing onto my family and friends. I couldn't say for certain, but the elemental strength I gained on Aurora Isle might have been the determining factor between my life and death on the dirigible when the phoenixes hatched. Every drop of my increased powers had gone into deflecting their violent births. A fraction less, and a hatching phoenix might have incinerated me, or worse, Quinn.

"I don't regret it," I finally said. "Even knowing I'll never unlock the seed's final answer, its clues helped stop Nathan before he could do more harm." Because I didn't want to spend any more time dwelling on Nathan, I added a half teasing, "And it gave me a lot of opportunities to spend time with you."

"Ah, yes," Grant said, his tone dry. "All that bonding we did keeping each other alive through thunderbird lightning and blood-magic traps."

An electric thrill zinged up my spine when I caught the twinkle of humor in his eyes. Grant's public persona was so serious, it made me feel special when he dropped his guard for me.

"Don't forget all the time we spent flying together," I said with affected seriousness.

Grant arched a questioning eyebrow.

"Don't tell me you've already forgotten the flight back from Persephone's on your tiny personal flying carpet."

"When you fell asleep and drooled on me? No, I remember that. Clearly."

"And when we flew to Aurora Isle."

"Into a thunderbird flock. Downright romantic."

I couldn't help but grin at his droll tone even as my heart pattered faster. *He thinks about romantic moments with me?* "What about the way back?"

Grant scowled and crossed his arms. "You mean when my team and I rushed you to a healer, and we weren't certain you would be able to work magic normally ever again? I could have done without that trip."

I bit my bottom lip to hold in my laughter. He was getting genuinely worked up thinking about it, and I loved it.

"Then there was yesterday." I waved a hand in the direction of the fair.

Grant grunted. "Does it count if one of us is *below* the aircraft?"

My laugh burst out at his petulant tone. A furrow plowed between his eyebrows, thunder brewing in his gaze. Impulsively, I stretched up on my tiptoes, my breasts brushing against his crossed forearms, to kiss away his frown. Warm and soft, his lips shifted under mine, curving into a smile. I darted the tip of my tongue across his bottom lip, tasting sunshine and Grant. Delicious.

Grant's arms unfolded to wrap around me again, tipping me backward. I gasped, and his tongue teased my open mouth. My fingers curled into the nape of his neck. Pleasure unfurled deep in my body, filling me with tense energy, and not even the jabs of pain throughout my bruised body distracted me from matching Grant kiss for kiss.

Quinn's delicately cleared throat, however, cut through my haze of lust. Grant straightened, relaxing his grip without letting go of me.

"I say it counts," I said, a touch breathless as I belatedly answered Grant's question. "Since without you, I wouldn't have been flying at all."

"Valid argument," Grant said, the gravelly texture of his voice proving he was equally as affected by our kisses.

"Plus, without my seed, I might not have gotten the chance to see you in your formal uniform." Grant in a head-to-toe white uniform perfectly tailored to his exquisite frame had been a magnificent sight—well worth enduring a high-society, full-spectrum event to witness.

Grant chuckled and shook his head. "What is it with that uniform?"

"Mainly you."

My honesty earned me a soft smile, but Grant's expression sobered as he studied me. Using a blunt fingertip, he traced the bruises on my cheek, then tucked a strand of hair behind my ear.

"If you had a chance to evolve your seed one more time, you would take it?" he asked.

I shrugged. "Sure, but—"

Grant released me and pulled a phoenix feather out of his pocket. The tangerine-and-black-striped feather rested flat on his palm, preserved in a thin casing of solid air. Ash dusted the outer edge of the barbs, and charcoal remnants were all that remained of the tip.

I looked at it in awe. "How?"

"It fell from the last phoenix when it hatched. It wasn't hard to grab it before it finished burning."

I reached for the feather but stopped before touching it, searching Grant's expression.

"What if with this, my seed evolves and points to something even more perilous? Each evolution has escalated the danger." And each time, Grant had attempted to convince me to sit on the sidelines while he dealt with the hazards it foretold.

"Then we'll face that danger together," Grant said.

My breath caught at the tenderness and faith in his eyes.

"And I'll be right there with you too," Quinn said, arching his neck to peer at the feather.

"Well, in that case . . ." I grinned at them both, then hurried upstairs as fast as my beleaguered legs could carry me to retrieve the firebird and thunderbird feathers. Unlike Grant's or Quinn's seeds, mine had never changed shape, instead revealing its next clue only in the presence of the feathers. In case this evolution followed the same pattern, I wanted to have all three feathers on hand before unwrapping the irreplaceable phoenix feather.

When I returned to the backyard, Grant had helped Quinn reposition his typewriter closer to the house, where the Victorian's wards would keep it safe from rain and dust. They were deep in conversation, peering at something in Grant's palm, but when the door clicked shut, Grant straightened and tucked the item into his pocket. Quinn bounded to my side with the exuberance of a cub, a dazzling grin on his face. Grant followed, scooping up my hand in his.

"Where do you want to do this?" he asked.

Distracted by our interlaced fingers, I waved vaguely toward the yard. "Here?"

"On the lawn?"

I nodded, anticipation stealing my voice. Maybe, just maybe, I would get my story of a lifetime, after all.

EPILOGUE

We formed a circle on the grass, Grant and I sitting cross-legged, Quinn lying on his stomach, his front paws curled to his chest. Grant tented us with a spell of water and air, darkening the inside of the bubble to block out the midday sun. My eyes slowly adjusted to the single light source: the firebird feather resting on my palm. I tugged the pouch from my pocket and upended it atop the lawn. My seed tumbled out.

It looked exactly as it had at the everlasting tree, like a fancy peach pit, the seam gold limned, the ridges and grooves shimmering with a firebird feather's gold-and-copper ocellus. As I had twice before, I placed the firebird feather next to the seed. The fiery glow danced across the seed's surface, transforming its markings into the stormy slate blue and navy of a thunderbird feather. If I flipped it over, I would see Airstrong's logo splayed across the back.

Unwrapping my protective spell from the thunderbird feather, I gave it a gentle shake, loosening a drop of moisture onto the seed. Amber light undulated across the grooved surface, altering it into a pulsing mimicry of a red-hot phoenix egg, though far smaller than the real thing. Even knowing what to expect, I still flinched.

"Are you certain nothing else was stolen from Airstrong?" I asked Grant, my smile tight when I met his gaze.

"Positive."

"And Nathan is locked up?"

"With a dedicated guard monitoring him at all times."

Taking a deep breath, I set aside the thunderbird feather and accepted the phoenix feather from Grant. My fingers tingled as he carefully unraveled his protective magic. None of us breathed as I brushed the phoenix feather's singed tip across the seed. Ash puffed from the tips of the vanes and settled into the seed's grooves.

Magic burst from the seed, engulfing all three feathers. I released the phoenix feather with a yelp, rubbing my stinging fingertips against my leg. Darkness swallowed us as the firebird feather disintegrated into the riotous magic. Grant dispelled the shadowed dome, and I squinted against the bright sunlight, a frisson of excitement squirming through me. Grant reached for my hand, and I gripped his hard. As one, we leaned closer to the seed.

A tempest of compressed elements pulsed and twisted across its surface, then dove inward. I gasped when the seed split with a snick, and a tiny green shoot emerged from the seam.

Without pause, magic gushed from the seed into the soil. Grass and dirt parted, swallowing the seed. Quinn's wings flared, and he scrambled back on his heels, eyes locked on the animated soil. I started to reach for him, but a green shoot burst from the disturbed dirt, spearing for my wrist. Before I could flinch, it deployed a band of climbing tendrils around my forearm, locking me in place while the vine swarmed up the back of my hand. Thicker tendrils coiled around my knuckles, splaying my fingers wide, palm up.

"Kylie?" Grant asked. He crouched on the balls of his feet, one hand poised to grab me. Magic pulsed around him, held in check but ready. Quinn had a foot raised as if he was ready to stomp the plant's base.

My heart pounded, surprise and alarm competing for dominance. Flexing my fingers, I tested the plant's hold. The tendrils stretched and creaked. Where they were wrapped around my wrist, they applied so little pressure that I couldn't feel them through my bandages. A sharp tug would free me.

"I'm fine." I tore my gaze from my hand to reassure Grant and Quinn. "The everlasting tree's magic is benign. This has to be part of my answer."

Quinn lowered his foot, and Grant dropped whatever spell he held, but his scowl remained. Magic tingled along my arm, drawing my attention back to the vine. It pulsed against the back of my hand, then curled over my palm. I stared in wonder. The base of the stalk was a vibrant green, but the tip now glowed pearlescent white shot through with veins of gold. Compelled by magic, the bright vine spun into a perfect circle atop my hand, spanning my entire palm.

Quinn pushed his nose closer. "Grant, that looks just like—"

"A firebird pearl," Grant said, interrupting Quinn.

"Only shaped like a ring." Pleased my answer in some way resembled his original everlasting seed, I grinned at Grant, but he didn't notice, too busy giving Quinn a loaded look I couldn't interpret. Before I could puzzle out their silent exchange, the seed's magic altered.

An ebony leaf unfurled from the side of the ring,

growing rapidly into a three-inch-tall harpy-shaped leaf. I gasped and would have recoiled, but the plant held me. Quinn moaned, his wings drooping to the ground. Grant cursed sharply.

Would my story of a lifetime involve a harpy? Zipporah herself? A knot of leaden dread balled in my stomach as I studied the leaf. Hickory-hued veins ran through it, defining the harpy's folded wings and clawed feet. The details weren't sharp enough to provide more than a hint of the harpy's facial features, but it looked like Zipporah.

I shook my head in denial. I had just cleared my debt to the harpy, and barely survived too. I had vowed not to make another life-and-death deal for a story—*any* story. Not even the story of a lifetime. Besides, if I contacted Zipporah again, she would kill me for sure.

The leaf curled up on itself, reshaping until a slender harpy feather protruded from the ring instead of a miniature harpy. Soundlessly, the leaf-feather folded itself around the outer edge of the ring and fused to it. The black vane and tines cupped less than a third of the ring, leaving the rest a stunning contrast of white and gold.

A new leaf sprang up beside the black feather, the fibrous material as glossy as polished gold and veined in soft copper. When it finished growing, a firebird perched on the edge of the ring.

"A firebird? Again?" Quinn asked.

Firebirds were better than harpies, but I didn't relish a second encounter with one. "I hope not," I said, then hissed when the ring sent a jolt of static electricity through my palm. The pain subsided almost instantly, reminding me of the lynxes' lie-detection magic.

"Oooh," I said, drawing out the word as a new theory swam through my thoughts, half formed.

Seeing the harpy had sparked a caution inside me that hadn't existed before the everlasting tree. The firebird inspired a different set of emotions: a twist of panic at the memory of collapsing tunnels but also the wry reminder of the importance of honesty. With a lynx monitoring our every statement, forcing candor instead of sarcasm, my relationship with Grant had evolved in Lunacy Labyrinth's terrifying depths, becoming a genuine friendship. After we rescued the firebirds, I let myself hope for the first time that Grant could be in my life in a real way—not just in a reporter-chasing-a-story way—which indelibly altered my dreams for the future.

"I think the everlasting tree and I have very different ideas about the story of a lifetime," I said, trying to explain my budding revelation.

The seed's magic whispered across my palm. The firebird leaf curled into a single feather, with the firebird's iconic ocellus, all gold and pale copper. Bending, it molded to the outer edge of the ring, overlapping the base of the harpy feather.

A new leaf sprouted, storm blue with navy veins—a thunderbird in flight.

"It's just repeating the clues it already gave you," Quinn said, miffed.

"It's reminding me." The seed was showing me what I had almost missed.

I didn't find the thunderbirds until I embraced my whole self. When I first became a journalist, I assumed I had to hide half of my life to be taken seriously. I had lied to my best friends. I had behaved as if my family and my upbringing were shameful. I had let my fear of other people's reactions dictate my decisions. But I was a stronger, better journalist when I was my true self.

Finding the thunderbirds had been pivotal in opening my eyes to another truth: I loved Grant. It took nearly losing him to hydra poison to realize he wasn't a crush or a flirtation. Grant was *it* for me, even if I had been too scared—and too wrapped up in the next crisis—to act on it.

The leaf curled into a thunderbird feather and molded itself to the ring. Before the next leaf bloomed bright orange and black like a striped, fresh-minted penny, I knew it would show a phoenix. The tiny plant rendition included fire element flickering from the tips of the bird's wings, its beak thrust toward the sky, its tail streaming magical flames that licked painlessly against my palm.

Following my seed's third clue had tested my moral fortitude, but I now possessed an unwavering conviction that I had made the correct career choice, because even if I didn't receive credit or a paycheck, I would continue to write. More importantly, I knew the safety of my family and friends outweighed my personal ambition. Nathan's rabid need to be the top journalist with nonstop front-page bylines had been uncomfortably familiar. A tiny piece of that madness existed in my heart, but I refused to feed it or allow it to grow.

The leaf folded into a shiny copper feather slashed with darker, aged-copper stripes and melted into the surface of the ring. The four feathers overlapped, but a gap remained. What else was there?

A fifth leaf unfurled from the pearlescent ring's surface, this one a striking citrine gold.

"Me?" Quinn exclaimed as the leaf flared into a tiny winged lion.

Of course.

"But the seed never showed me," Quinn protested.

"It never showed a harpy either," Grant said.

"Then why?" Quinn asked.

I smiled. "Because you were there for it all. I couldn't have done this without you."

It was Quinn in Lunacy Labyrinth who had saved me from the blood-magic snake, who had carried the firebird and her egg, who had crushed the malicious bloodstone. Quinn who had warped Zipporah's powers so she couldn't kill me. Quinn who had rushed to get help when I had been trapped in a snare and slice, and Quinn who had stood up to me, giving me advice I needed but didn't want to hear. His loyalty had buoyed me throughout this entire adventure—and saved my life many times over. The dangers we'd faced and the triumphs we'd shared had strengthened our bond. He no longer felt like a friend. He was family.

The gargoyle leaf rolled into a citrine feather and settled into the gap. Among the metallic shimmer of the other feathers, Quinn's looked like a jewel.

Magic spiraled around the band, fast and intricate. The ring contracted, snapping free of the vine. The green stalk and tendrils disintegrated. Freed, I lifted my hand as the elements chasing each other around the band imploded, the last of the everlasting seed's magic expended.

I canted my hand, examining the ring in the sunlight. In shrinking, it had lost none of its details. Reverently, I slid it onto my right ring finger, unsurprised that it fit perfectly. With a twist, I positioned Quinn's citrine feather on top.

"But . . . a ring?" Quinn asked. "How is that an answer? Where's the story?"

"We lived it. This—" I shifted my hand, letting sunlight dance across the shiny ring. "This is a souvenir. No other story we'll ever chase will affect my life as drastically as the one we just lived through. It was *my* story of a lifetime, the one that altered my life the most and set me on a new path.

It reshaped my future in ways that will have ramifications for years to come. For my lifetime." I peeked at Grant through my lashes. He had settled back on his heels, and he studied my expression intently. Quinn still looked puzzled.

"Does this mean you're no longer going to chase dangerous stories?" Grant asked, his tone unreadable.

"No, I probably will, but not so obsessively. I don't want to turn into Nathan. I want to look back on the articles I publish and have my body of work make a difference, but my life is more than my job." I turned to Quinn, cupping his cheek. "It's you. You're my family, Quinn. It's you and me, forever."

Quinn's wings flared, a multitude of expressions racing across his face—surprise, delight, affection—before he settled on joy. I held out my arms, and Quinn enveloped me in his wings.

"I love you, Kylie," he whispered, his cool stone muzzle pressed to my shoulder.

I squeezed him tight, happy tears misting my vision. When he released me, I turned to Grant, letting my heart shine in my eyes. "And you . . ."

Taking a deep breath, I spoke the words that had been on the tip of my tongue since Aurora Isle. "I love you, Grant."

Exultation shone in Grant's eyes, his smile fierce. My heart stuttered, his handsomeness stealing my breath.

"About time," he said.

My jaw dropped. *"What?"*

"I wasn't sure if you would ever realize it."

I floundered, my mouth opening and closing like a fish's. "Grant, that's not the proper response when someone says they love you!" I planted my hands on my hips, giving him my best frown, but the tenderness in his expression and the happy crinkle at the corners of his eyes made it hard to remain disgruntled. "Honestly, you're supposed to say—"

"I never told you my question for the everlasting tree," he said.

I narrowed my eyes. "And you need to tell me *now*? It can't wait?" I yearned to hear a reciprocal declaration of love, but I wouldn't beg for it. He should offer it, unprompted. Right about now would be the perfect time.

Grant's smile turned mischievous. He knew exactly how insufferable he was being. "It can't wait."

Shifting, he knelt in front of me, close enough that he could sit back on his heels and still reach me. Gently, he tugged my hands from my hips, holding them between us. I quirked an eyebrow at him, doing my best to cling to my exasperation. With his thumbs stroking gentle caresses along the backs of my hands, it was difficult.

"I asked 'Where is the most important place for me to be?' And every time my seed evolved, it was with you. Again and again."

"Only because I kept getting into dangerous situations." Was I supposed to be flattered that the everlasting tree thought I was so helpless that it sent the most powerful elemental warrior in the area to watch over me?

Grant shook his head. "A lot of people need saving, or in your case, helping," he amended when I grimaced. "My seed kept making sure you and I were together, that I was protecting *you* and keeping you in my life. Because being near you is important."

"To keep me from dying?" I guessed, fighting the urge to grind my teeth.

"At first, that's what I thought." Grant's shrug said he saw my frustration, but he wasn't going to sugarcoat it for me. "But I didn't ask the seed *who* I needed to protect. I asked about myself. I wanted to know where it was important for me to be, and the answer was with you. Not because you're a magnet for deadly creatures," he said before I could protest again, "but because you're important to me. The last form the seed took really pounded this point home." Grant released one of my hands to push back his sleeve. The seed bracelet was gone.

I jerked my eyes to his, searching back through my memory for the last time I had seen the bracelet. When he fought the wyvern? Yes. When he caught the dirigible? Maybe. I had been too preoccupied to notice. "When?"

He gently rotated our linked hands, and I didn't think he heard me.

"With it wrapped around my arm, I couldn't put it down or leave it behind. Even when it was covered by my sleeve, I could still feel it." Grant rubbed his bare wrist, as if he still felt the phantom press of the seed circling his arm. "Which meant I spent a lot of time contemplating it and my question. Those little discs of black and white always made me think of you, how you and I are locked together on this quest. How we're linked together is so many ways."

Grant searched my gaze for understanding. I nodded encouragingly, my heart pounding against my eardrums.

"I was looking for my next step in life," Grant said. "I thought it would be a job change, but it's something I hadn't let myself consider. It's you, Kylie, and me. It's us."

He shifted to reach into his pocket, keeping a tight hold on my other hand. Vulnerability skirted across his features, and my heart flipped in my chest. Beside us, Quinn began to purr, the rumble a soft undercurrent to Grant's next words.

"My seed sprouted after the wyvern battle—after you faced down Zipporah and I did nothing but back you even though I yearned to crush that miserable harpy once and for all." Violence flared in his gaze, then faded. "I realized you didn't need my interference; you needed my support. I want to give you that. I want to be your partner."

He held out his fist, then slowly uncurled his fingers. "Here is the seed's final answer to my question."

A pair of rings sat on his palm, one small enough to fit in the other, each a perfect pearl circle shot through with fiery threads of gold. Their resemblance to a firebird's pearl was unmistakable, and they perfectly matched the interior of my own seed-ring. Only these were a his and her set. Wedding bands.

"I love you, Kylie." Grant's voice vibrated with emotion. "I love you, and I need you in my life. I want you in my life— for as long as you'll have me."

My eyes felt too wide when they darted from Grant's palm to his face. "You want to get married? Now?" I squeaked.

Quinn wriggled with delight, no surprise on his face. It dawned on me that the rings were what he and Grant had been looking at when I returned from collecting the feathers. It was why Quinn had been so excited as he bounded to my side.

Light-headed, I blinked at Grant, searching for the right words. I loved him, and hearing him say he loved me made me want to dance with joy. But we had known each other only a few months. Were we ready to get married?

Grant grinned and pressed a soft kiss to my cheek. "That's about how I responded."

"What? Really?"

"The everlasting tree gave me the answer I was looking for, but we don't have to rush. I'm happy to wait until you're ready, so long as you're at my side." The vulnerability was back in Grant's eyes, tension tightening his fingers around mine. "If you'll have me."

"Yes." I sprang into his arms, knocking him backward into the grass and kissing him with unabashed abandon. "A thousand times yes," I said when I came up for air. I glanced toward Grant's closed hand. "But maybe . . ." I bit my bottom lip, feeling suddenly shy. "Maybe I should try the ring on, just to make sure it fits."

Grant roared with laughter and tugged me down for another earth-shattering kiss that promised a lifetime of happiness.

Turn the page for an exciting excerpt from

MAGIC OF THE GARGOYLES

the first in Rebecca Chastain's *USA Today*
bestselling series that introduced
readers to Terra Haven's
adorable gargoyle companions.

AVAILABLE NOW!

In a race to save the lives of baby
gargoyles, Mika must jeopardize
everything she holds dear...
including her life.

MAGIC OF THE GARGOYLES

GARGOYLE GUARDIAN CHRONICLES BOOK 1

With one last twist of a filament of earth magic, I fused together the delicate seams of the quartz tube. Slumping forward, I braced my elbows on the table and rested my cheekbones on my palms, cupping my weary eyes in darkness. Six down, six finicky tubes to go. The specifications of this project taxed my substantial skills with quartz magic, which was the point. This project would launch my business and prove that even though I was only a midlevel earth elemental, my quartz skills were equal to or better than more powerful full-spectrum elementals. These fussy tubes would fund the down payment on the lease for the shop I coveted in the Pinnacle Pentagon Center. I could finally quit my demeaning job at Jones and Sons Quarry, be my own boss, and begin a career creating one-of-a-kind quartz masterpieces I could take pride in.

My entire future rested on these fragile vials, and they were due tomorrow at four.

Dull pain pounded my back muscles. Night had crept over the city while I worked, and my jerky movements as I stood and stretched were reflected in the semicircle of bay windows in front of my worktable. Purple smears of exhaustion beneath my eyes were exaggerated in the dark windows, and my pale face floated above a dirt-smeared navy shirt. I checked the clock: almost midnight. Sixteen hours until my deadline, and eight of those would be taken up by my Jones and Sons workday. There was no time for a break. If anything, I needed to work faster.

Groaning, I redid my ponytail, tucking shorter wisps of strawberry-blond hair behind my ears before giving my hard wooden chair the stink eye. Mentally chanting, *Pinnacle Pentagon*, to motivate myself, I reached for another seed crystal.

Frantic tapping shook the glass in the balcony door. I pulled the door open, knowing it was Kylie, my best friend and the tenant who shared my second-floor apartment balcony. "I really can't talk. I need to finish—"

"Help! Help! They've got—"

Something small and hard slammed into my stomach. I staggered backward into my chair and crashed to the floor. A small boulder skipped across the wooden floor and smashed into the wall.

"You're a human!"

I shrieked. The voice came from inside my room. I twisted, scrambling onto my bed.

Against the wall, the rock moved.

Beautiful blue dumortierite quartz veined with green aventurine twisted into a winged panther no bigger than a house cat. A pissed-off, solid-stone, magical, winged house cat. A gargoyle—no, a baby gargoyle. A hatchling.

Her eyes glowed feverishly. Long polished blue claws gouged into the floor when she launched into the air. Her agile stone wings unfolded with a soft gritty sound.

I lurched backward across the bed until I was pressed

against the wall. The mattress shook when the hatchling pounced on the space I'd just vacated. Sharp claws bunched in my yellow bedspread. She raised her muzzle, mouth open, and sniffed the air.

I eased toward the foot of the bed, readying my escape into the hallway.

"It's you! Your magic smells so good. I thought—"

My magic has a smell?

The gargoyle's eyes darted to the open door, then back to me. She arched her stone back and hissed at me, the sound dying to a hair-raising growl. The tip of her stone tail slashed back and forth, gouging my wooden headboard.

"I need help."

"My help?" Gargoyles—even baby gargoyles—didn't interact with midlevel elementals like me, and they certainly didn't ask for our help. "There's a full-spectrum elemental just—" I started to point up the street but froze when she snarled at me.

"No other humans! Before it's too late." The gargoyle's words were smooth coming out of her rock throat, with just a hint of a lisp from her tongue working around enormous teeth.

I stared into her glowing blue eyes, seeing past the bared fangs and agitated movements, reading her fear for the first time. I reached for her, then pulled my hand back when she shied from me.

"Too late for what?"

"You can save him. Hurry!"

"Save him? Save who? If someone is hurt, I can send for a healer." Where were this gargoyle's parents?

"No. I need you." Large blue eyes implored me. "Please!"

A thousand reasons why I should find someone else to help the gargoyle crowded my mind, but the hatchling's urgency was contagious. Someone was injured. I didn't want to waste time arguing with her, but was I really the best choice? I could work earth, but healing usually took someone talented with all five elements.

"Are you sure you don't want me to get—" *someone stronger?* I started to ask, but she cut me off with another sharp, "Please!"

Gargoyles were creatures without guile, and this baby was obviously terrified for someone's life. If she thought I could help, I had to try. I took a deep breath. "Okay. Let's go."

The gargoyle whirled and launched for the open doorway, moving with the silent fluidity of a flesh-and-blood panther.

"I'll take the stairs," I said. I snatched up my shoes and coat and raced to the door.

My studio apartment was one of four on the upper floor of a converted Victorian house. At midnight, everyone else in the house was asleep, just the way my landlady Ms. Josephine Zuberrie liked it.

As I sprinted down the stairs as quietly as possible, shoes in hand, I reviewed everything I knew about gargoyles. It wasn't much. Gargoyles favored those strongest in magic—full-spectrum pentacle potential, or FSPP, elementals. When they chose, they could enhance a person's magic, but I'd only heard of them doing so during large-scale rituals conducted by a five linked FSPPs. Despite being creatures of earth, they were not partial to any particular elemental magic; instead, they were attracted to a person's strength of earth, wood, air, water, or fire magic.

Which is why, as a midlevel earth elemental, this was the first time I'd spoken with a gargoyle.

I eased the front door shut and dropped my shoes to the porch, wiggled my feet into them, and yanked the laces tight. When I spun around, the gargoyle dropped from the roof to the porch railing, almost clipping my head with a heavy rock wing. I swallowed a startled scream.

"Hurry," she trilled. With a squeal of protesting wood, followed by the crack of stone smashing into stone, the gargoyle leapt from the balcony to the sidewalk ten feet below. Wincing, I raced down the porch steps after her, praying to be out of sight before Ms. Zuberrie investigated the racket.

By the time I reached the sidewalk, the gargoyle had almost a block lead on me, moving unexpectedly fast for such a small creature made of stone. In wing-assisted leaps, she bounded into the darkness. I sprinted headlong down the center of the deserted street, chasing the sporadic glimpses of panther-shaped dumortierite in the puddles of lamplight. The baby gargoyle kept me in sight, but only just. My lungs and legs burned after the first five blocks. My vision tunneled to the broken asphalt and gargoyle in front of me. I didn't notice when the lamps ended, only that the dark blue gargoyle was harder to see, and by the time I did take in my surroundings, we were deep in the blight and I was lost.

———

Like what you just read? Pick up your copy of *Magic of the Gargoyles* today!

ABOUT REBECCA CHASTAIN

REBECCA CHASTAIN is a feminist, animal advocate, and nature devotee. She believes empathy is a hero's trait and love is a motive, an inside job, and a transformative energy that shapes each person's world. She is the *USA Today* bestselling author of the Gargoyle Guardian Chronicles trilogy, the Terra Haven Chronicles series that begins with DEAD-LINES & DRYADS, and the Madison Fox urban fantasy series.

If given the opportunity, Rebecca will befriend your cat.

Visit RebeccaChastain.com for updates, extras, and so much more!

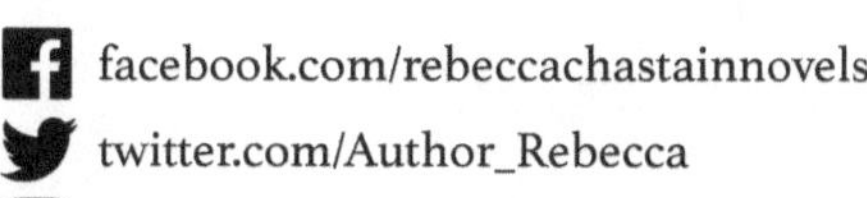

facebook.com/rebeccachastainnovels

twitter.com/Author_Rebecca

instagram.com/chastain.rebecca

FROM *USA TODAY* BESTSELLING AUTHOR

REBECCA CHASTAIN

Madison's new job would be perfect, if not for all the creatures trying to eat her soul...

PRAISE FOR THE MADISON FOX NOVELS

"a masterfully plotted urban fantasy... I highly recommend it to readers of all ilk, urban fantasy aficionados, or not."
–Open Book Society

"a great mixture of action, danger, fantasy, and humor"
–Books That Hook

RebeccaChastain.com